The Library Club
A Cozy Mystery
Representation Matters

Welcome to Stony Estancia

The Library Club
A Cozy Mystery
Representation Matters

Mr. Szilard Substitute Teacher Mystery #2

A frolicking romp! An opulent Los Angeles suburb, a high school library, and a dead body.

D.R. Oestreicher, PhD

Omega Cat Press — California

COPYRIGHT

Omega Cat Press, independent publishing since 1990

Paperback ISBN: 978-1-954225-22-0
Electronic Book ISBN: 978-1-954225-23-7
Hardcover ISBN: 978-1-954225-24-4

2 3 4 5 6 7 8 9

"Unless you are good at guessing, it is not much use being a detective."
Hercule Poirot in The Mystery of the Blue Train
by Agatha Christie

"This is a book not about superiority but about diversity."
An Immense World by Ed Yong

Dedicated to all librarians

By D. R. Oestreicher

Zarand Szilard #1: The Ecology Club: A Cozy Mystery

By J. Oestreicher and D. R. Oestreicher

Pandemic Mysteries #1: Darwin's Paradox
#2: Plague of Equals
#3: The Two Pearls

Suramarti Saga #1: Kitane, Bull Jumper
#2: The Murders, The Mosque

By Joy Oestreicher

Legends of Azureign #1: Dragon and Oracle
#2: Raka and Secrets
#3: The Pirate Queen
#4: The Compact Shatters

https://amzn.to/2SpaDMN

BLURB FOR THE LIBRARY CLUB
The Library Club
A Cozy Mystery
Representation Matters
Mr. Szilard Substitute Teacher Mystery #2

A frolicking romp! An opulent Los Angeles suburb, a high school library, and a dead body.

The Library Club is a cozy mystery that will keep you smiling. Retired detective, Zarand Szilard, expects an easy day as a substitute teacher until he hears a crash behind a door in the library. When he tries to enter the school's rare book collection, the door is stuck. That is the least of his problems.

Once inside, he finds a smashed window and the bookshelves knocked over like dominos. He frantically searches through the wreckage. Fitch, his invisible and often prescient sidekick, urges him to hurry, to find the body while there is a possibility of rescue.

Then he uncovers a gold earring...attached to an ear.

Accident or murder?

And what about the Cajon Treasure, lost for over a century?

Will Zarand, his cat Dahl, and the Stony Estancia High School Library Club be able to solve this mystery and return the suburb to its peaceful ways?

Or will Dahl be more interested in her next meal?

Or will the students be distracted by the Cajon Treasure?

Once you start reading about Zarand's zany investigations, you won't be able to put this book down.

TABLE OF CONTENTS

AUTHOR'S PREFACE
The Library Club
A Cozy Mystery
Representation Matters
Mr. Szilard Substitute Teacher Mystery #2
A frolicking romp! An opulent Los Angeles suburb, a high school library, and a dead body.

I began this book thinking about Banned Book Week—sponsored by the American Library Association to celebrate the freedom to read, and spotlight attempts to censor books. The news was full of stories about school censorship and how librarians were fighting it—serving wider communities in innovative ways. I felt this was an important issue that Zarand Szilard could support at Stony Estancia High School.

Unfortunately, the people of Stony Estancia refused. They didn't want to attack book burners. They were more interested in embracing their differences. Black Lives Matter and campaigns targeting LGBTQ+ and immigrant communities were also in the news. The people of Stony Estancia wanted to show the world how they worked together regardless of their differences.

The Library Club takes place in an imagined world where differences are expected and unremarkable—ordinary. In Stony Estancia, the more you learn about someone, the more you appreciate them. I hope that spending a few hundred pages with this mystery will move the reader closer to creating this world for themselves.

The characters in this novel are diverse. They are taller or shorter, with blue eyes or brown eyes, and a variety of hair types. The genetic lottery has awarded rare traits to some of them. They also have different skin pigmentation. Pax has a non-binary gender, and January is hard of hearing.

Some differences are not genetic. Alyce from Australia and Zola from South Africa speak different dialects of English. Pax likes to sleep on expensive sheets and Jorge has an extraordinary work ethic. Zola excels at gymnastics, Ranch at technology, and Lizzy at organization. Persey dresses in black and Pax has rainbow hair.

The question that underlies this novel is: How should these differences be treated?

The answer put forth in the following pages is: All these people represent normal variants of the human species. None of these people are more or less.

My intent was not to employ these differences as shortcuts for the reader to like or dislike the characters or as signals of the character's virtues or capabilities.

These differences are normal and representation matters.

This book is followed by historical and pop culture treasures hidden in the story, the people who inspired the names in this book, and a preview of *The Ecology Club* (book 1 in this series).

Don, living in Stony Estancia, July 14, 2023

1. NOT A TYPICAL DAY – TUESDAY AM

Wherein Zarand calls for help.

As I bounced out of the Stony Estancia High School admin building, Chuck Berry's *School Days* played in my head. With a few quick Lindy Hop steps, I headed for the library. Today had been leg day at the gym, and I could have danced fancy moves for hours, swinging the lanyard that held my substitute teacher badge. That is—until that clumsy badge clipped the principal.

"Woah there, Mr. Szilard, old gray beard. We're always glad to see you but be careful with that thing."

"*Lo siento*, Mrs. Golding of the long white braid." I ran my fingers through my brown buzz cut. "I'm here for my favorite English teacher—a library research day. What could be better?"

"*De nada*. Ms. Miller was pleased when she told me you were taking her classes. She said, 'For a retired cop, he's great—the best relief teacher ever.'"

Principal Golding disappeared into the admin building. A gentle breeze rustled the sunshine-dappled pepper trees scattered across the courtyard beneath a clear Southern California sky. Ms. Miller's students waited on the library stairs and greeted me with high-fives, "Yo, Mr. S.," and "The best sub."

'Don't let all that praise go to your head,' warned Fitch, my invisible sidekick and constant companion.

He scowled, *'I'm more than a sidekick. I'm the voice of sense in this frolicking romp and here to remind the readers to proceed with a light heart.'*

Whatever, Fitch. Whatever.

Following a ritual that began when books were scrolls in monasteries, I whispered, "Use your library voices," and let the class into the reading area surrounded by shelves of books, non-fiction to the left and fiction to the right.

Most of the class sat at round tables in groups of four or six. Some claimed a study carrel where they could work undisturbed and unobserved, and a few sat in one of the three green-and-gold rocking chairs donated by Stony Estancia parents.

Following another time-honored ritual, Lizzy, a girl with straight green hair, ripped jeans, and a GIRL POWER T-shirt, challenged the rules, testing the sub. "Can we work in groups?"

'She's a troublemaker. Don't do it. Be firm,' warned Fitch.

"No problem," I replied using my teacher's superpower to see past Lizzy's hair and clothes to her inner truth—a strong student and a natural leader.

With a smug smile, she took out her phone and showed something to the boy sitting beside her.

'I warned you,' laughed Fitch.

"Phones are not allowed during class," I reminded her.

"But, Mr. S.," she said extending the 'S' into a hiss. After checking to be sure that her friends were watching, she gathered her green hair off her shoulders and tied it back with a scrunchy that had been around her wrist. In a confident voice, she continued, "But, this is for my report."

I envisioned the strong woman she would become. "Go ahead then."

'She's walking all over you,' criticized Fitch.

He was right. I congratulated myself. This was great training for her future as a leader.

Lizzy and the rest of the class got down to work. The only sounds were the gentle clicking on laptop keyboards, and the swishing of pages as students shuffled between the back-of-the-book indexes and information to enter into their notes. I watched them work, thinking of them as my honorary grandkids and visualizing them living their best lives.

A crash interrupted this scholarly paradise. The sound came from the newly dedicated California History Annex, a research room built onto the back of the library. The teens ignored the noise, possibly thinking it was an earthquake. I ambled over to the door to investigate.

There was a muted *bang, bang*. Someone was trapped inside. I pulled on the door, but it was stuck. A WET PAINT sign explained the reason. I tapped a response to signal that help was on the way.

Jorge, a boy with a T-shirt that read, *Hecho en Mexico*, was watching me. He was going to be a journalist—nothing escaped his notice. I called to him, "*Psst*. Over here."

He jumped up and joined me.

I tugged on the door to indicate my problem.

"Someone's inside," I said like it was no big deal.

He put one foot against the wall and grabbed the doorknob. I planted my feet on the floor and placed my hands over his. I counted, "*Uno, dos, tres*." We both tugged and the door surrendered to our efforts.

"*Gracias*," I said to Jorge.

"*De nada*," he replied and returned to his seat.

I entered the annex. Once inside, I found January. Her face was pale as if she'd seen a ghost. She held out both hands—one palm up and the other down. Then she took a deep breath, shook her curly red hair, and flipped both hands over. She had signed DEAD. I didn't know a lot of ASL—American Sign Language, but I knew that one.

I was a substitute teacher at Stony Estancia High School, and this was not the day I expected when I woke up. On the other hand, as a retired Los Angeles police detective, I was the perfect first responder.

'*Slow down superhero. You couldn't even open the door,*' needled Fitch.

My eyes scanned the annex checking for a casualty, a body, someone injured, possibly dead. I recalled the countless times before I retired when the first officer on the scene confused motionless for dead. That was why I trained new recruits to call nine-one-one, always assuming the victim was alive. January had signed DEAD, but how could a teenager know that?

'*Especially a privileged one from Stony Estancia,*' added Fitch.

What had been a shiny research collection donated by the Stony Estancia parents was in shambles. The bookshelves had pitched over like so many dominoes crashing through the floor-to-ceiling windows blocking the distant narrow end of the room. A rapier of glass rose through the shelves with an impaled copy of Steinbeck's *The Red Pony* held like a flag above the wreckage—the shredded cover hanging down like blood.

The scene was a disaster, reminding me of an earthquake. January had signed DEAD. There had to be casualties, but I didn't see any signs of them.

'*Search and rescue. Quick and thorough. Don't panic,*' advised Fitch.

Right, boss, I thought in response with a touch of teenage sarcasm.

I began a systematic search.

In front of me were two rustic log chairs, still covered in protective plastic. Between the chairs, a massive stone fireplace spanned the narrow wall. The local rock, flecked with mica, sparkled like a starry night in the desert. I checked behind the chairs, in the hearth, and up the chimney. I found ashes in the hearth, but no victim.

'*What are ashes doing in a gas fireplace?*' Fitch asked, always eager to point out any details that I missed.

I brushed him off with, *I'm searching for a corpse not examining fireplaces,* and got back to my mission.

January had no interest in this part of the room. She ran past me. Each of her hands pointed with two fingers and she shook them at me. HURRY.

I was hurrying. I crawled over the collapsed bookcases and inspected between the shelves. I got down on my hands and knees to search under the wreckage. Minutes counted. My chest tightened. I didn't want to miss any victims.

January ran down the long aisle beside the wreckage until she couldn't go any farther—a dead end. She stopped where the shelves crashed through the window and kept signing HURRY and DEAD.

I followed her. To my right—the destruction varied from peaks of books and archival boxes to valleys of empty shelves—so many places someone could've been trapped. On my left—a long window wall.

I was torn between January's urgent demands and not wanting to overlook anyone.

When I reached her, there was no sign of a victim. I held up my hand and with my other hand, I pointed to the upright palm—SHOW. I pulled both hands to my chest—ME. I signed SHOW ME. Then I signed DEAD. That was my best ASL. It had to be enough. I made a little prayer. *Please let her understand.* I needed to find the victim and January was my only lead.

"Finally," she said as if she'd been waiting to be asked. She pointed to a jumble of green archival storage boxes—full of unbound papers or fragile documents like old journals. The pile of twisted metal shelves was as tall as January. She looked into my eyes—lips pursed with determination and clasped her hands behind her back. She had no more to say.

'She showed you the dead body,' Fitch explained like he was speaking to a small child.

I kicked the shelves. Nothing moved. I shouted, "Puppets. Puppies," the strongest words I used when at school.

There was no body. I looked again—books, boxes, steel shelving, broken glass—nothing else. I saw collections of London, Le Guin, Saroyan, Steinbeck, Tan, and Twain, but not January's alleged victim.

I was frustrated. January could speak. Why was she making this so hard, only using sign language?

'The girl is panicked. ASL is her comfort zone. Cut her some slack and do your job. Find the victim,' Fitch spoke in a shrill voice.

I picked up one of the archival boxes embossed with the history annex logo—a cartoon bear with a gold pan in one paw and a book in the other—something a design firm had developed for this collection.

In frustration and hoping for another clue, I showed the box to January. "What should I do with this?"

She grabbed it and tossed it out the broken window. It bounced off a triangle of glass, shattering it and scattering shards. Then she picked up another and did the same.

'*Do something,*' exclaimed Fitch, '*before the entire history collection ends up outside in the dirt.*'

That was her clue. I got it. I clambered over the twisted shelves, grabbed the boxes, and stacked them against the wall.

January jumped up and down, and didn't stop until I was running between the chaotic remains of the history collection and the orderly stacks I was building. I transferred an armload each trip, sometimes dropping a few from my sweaty hands.

January shook her fingers at me, faster and faster, bouncing her red curls. She kept signing, HURRY UP.

"I am. I am," I said, even though she couldn't hear me. I felt like the Keystone Kops, with so much frenetic activity to no effect—

Until I spied a gold stud earring—

I moved more boxes, clearing a narrow hole.

—Attached to an ear.

I'd found January's victim!

Some John Doe.

Fitch, who never concentrated on the task at hand, asked, '*He was buried under the debris. How did January know he was there?*'

Don't know. Don't care. I snapped at Fitch. I moved faster, hoping I wasn't too late, hoping John Doe was alive.

After another trip, I widened the hole and peeked through into his eyes. Clear blue eyes. Staring straight up at the ceiling.

January was wrong. Eyeballs clouded up after death. John Doe was alive.

My excavations took on an increased urgency. Each time I moved as many boxes as I could. When I dropped one, I kicked it out of the way. I was beyond worrying about the history collection. My effort was rewarded with an unobstructed view of his face.

Oops.

The victim was a woman. Jane Doe. Shaped eyebrows. Purple eyeshadow. Brown eyeliner.

I reached into the tunnel of boxes and pushed her hair away from her neck. Two desperate fingers searched for her carotid artery.

'*Please let her be alive,*' said Fitch, reading my mind.

Her neck was barely warm. She'd been dead for hours. I had no idea how many. Whoever did this was long gone. The killer had gotten away.

Fitch was upbeat, *'Look at the positive side. The school is safe. There isn't a murderer hiding in the library.'*

I ignored the evidence and refused to believe she was dead. I pressed her neck firmly, to probe for a faint pulse. My fingers scrambled to the other side in a futile quest to find a sign of life, pushing even harder this time. She was dead, but not for long since her eyes were still clear. No matter how many dead people I'd seen, they always upset me.

January signed DEAD one final time and tears ran down her cheeks.

Faced with a corpse, I examined the scene without calling for backup. I did my best work without an audience, reverting to my old habits as a solitary homicide detective—the habits that forced my early retirement—not a team player—from a department more interested in procedure than results.

Wrinkles around Jane Doe's eyes testified that she was too old to be a student. Hair of an unnatural shade—ash blonde, honey brown, a color that came from a beauty parlor—marked her as someone with disposable income.

Jane Doe wore motorcycle leathers and looked familiar. I might have met her at a parents' meeting. Whoever she was, she didn't deserve to die. I wouldn't let her killer get away. Teaching was a hobby, but being a detective was in my DNA. Instinctually, I began my investigation.

I took pictures between the green boxes and evaluated the victim. Not a student. Not a teacher. I knew all the teachers. She didn't belong in the history annex, but she wasn't some addict breaking into the school to steal electronics for a quick buck. The stakes here were higher. She was searching for rare books—to sell to a dealer or for her own collection.

'Whatever,' said Fitch discounting my analysis, *'None of that deserved a death sentence.'*

I turned to January. She looked relaxed now that I'd uncovered Jane Doe. She'd fulfilled her responsibility. However, I stood before her, face to face, and enunciated clearly, "Do you know what happened here?"

She read my lips and when she responded, "Yes," my heart raced.

I was in the flow of my investigation and wasn't going to call for help until I'd finished interrogating January.

Fitch shook his head. *This is that go-it-alone attitude that won you early retirement. Aren't you going to call Vicki?'*

Vicki. Of course, I was going to call her.

Vicki was my girlfriend, Senior Detective Victoria Yukawa of the Stony Estancia Police Force, and the reason I moved to Stony Estancia after leaving the Los Angeles Police Department.

I called her. "Hey, Vee, you might want to come to the high school. No rush."

"Really, Zee? What are your kids up to now?"

"There's a corpse in that new California History Annex."

That got her attention. "On my way. Can you secure the scene and prevent panic?"

"Done and done," I replied.

We made a good team, but I wouldn't hold up my investigation awaiting her arrival. She'd be proud of me for pushing forward and not wasting valuable time.

Wherein Zarand has a croissant.

On the previous Saturday, I arrived at Stony Estancia High School early. A group of unhappy parents was gathered outside the school gates. The crowd didn't concern me. This was Stony Estancia. I didn't expect trouble, and certainly nothing as serious as a homicide.

I could barely believe my eyes when I discovered parents protesting the ribbon-cutting for the California History Annex—a research collection and building funded by **S**tony **E**stancia for **E**ducational **E**xcellence, a parent organization that raised a lot of money.

No taxpayer expenditures. A free building housing a collection of historical documents. A research center, unlike what any other high school in the area could boast. How could it be a problem?

'Um, listen to their chants,' rebuked Fitch.

They chanted, "Fund the 3 Rs" and "Down with the elite."

The chanting paused when a neon yellow van arrived. Two larger-than-life smiling faces decorated the side of the van. The man was tagged CÉSAR and the woman, TISH, short for Leticia. STONY ESTANCIA SURFS, YOUR HYPERLOCAL NEWS SOURCE, CLICK ON US FOR THE LATEST filled the remaining space.

The crowd greeted them like celebrities. César propped his video camera on his shoulder. Tish faced him. "Good mornin', Stony Estancia. *Stony Estancia Surfs* is livestreaming from the high school where parents are protesting the new California History Annex."

She turned to the crowd. "Since none of this money came from taxes, why are you here?"

A woman stepped forward. "If those folks at the top of the hill, behind the locked gates, in Stony Estancia Haciendas, had extra money, they should have donated it to the school. We have more important needs than this research library."

Someone in the crowd contributed, "More tutors."

A woman dressed in a suit shouted, "Stony High is too elitist already."

An unmarked car with a flashing light affixed to its roof interrupted the interview.

'Here comes your girlfriend,' said Fitch.

Good. She'll clear all this up.

Principal Golding with her long white plait unlocked the gate and Vicki drove across the courtyard to park in front of the library. When the protesters followed, she produced a court order. "You may assemble but you cannot move past my vehicle."

The mob stopped advancing but continued to chant.

On the other side of the issue, cheerful people dressed in colorful leisurewear filed into the library.

The study carrels, round tables, and three green-and-gold rockers were gone, and the main reading area was set up with rows of chairs. At the back, the new door leading to the annex shone with green enamel and gold trim—Stony High colors— accompanied by a WET PAINT sign.

'Does that paint job look sloppy?' asked Fitch.

Is that all you have to do? Critique the contractors?

A green-and-gold ribbon hung in front of the door. The Stony High bear stood beside the podium with an oversized pair of scissors.

Fitch observed, *'Someone's gone to a lot of effort for this ceremony.'*

I had to agree when I saw the refreshments. I helped myself to a croissant from my favorite pâtisserie—the best in Stony Estancia.

Principal Golding stood at the podium. "Welcome parents and students. Before I introduce our main speaker, I want to thank our state assemblywoman who is also a member of the Serrano band, the original people in this area."

The crowd acknowledged her with polite applause.

"Next, we are honored by the participation of the Stony Estancia mayor and city council."

They waved.

"Now, please give a hearty Bruin welcome to Mr. Beckett, a long-time supporter of Stony High and the president of Stony Estancia for Educational Excellence, or, as we like to call it, SE-cubed."

The audience cheered, "SE-cubed. SE-cubed!"

Principal Golding smiled at Mr. Beckett in his well-tailored suit which camouflaged his middle-aged paunch.

From outside, a loud cry of "Down with the elite," interrupted her introduction. She winced. I felt sorry for her, but she carried on as if she didn't hear the demonstrators. "And the president of Stony Estancia Bank."

Mr. Beckett detached the microphone and moved in front of the podium. "Thank you all for coming here today." He stepped forward and lowered his voice as if sharing his innermost secret. "I can still remember when my oldest child didn't get into the university of his choice."

The audience responded with sighs of sympathy for this unfortunate event.

Fitch mocked them, *'So sad. So privileged. You'd think someone had died.'*

The banker continued, "I flew out to the college. The dean told me my child wasn't prepared. I could have enrolled my other children in a private school, but I believe in Thomas Jefferson's ideal of universal education. I founded Stony Estancia for Educational Excellence so no Stony High child would ever be unprepared again."

Scattered clapping interrupted him during his tale of raising money, but outside the chanting kept getting louder.

Fitch figured it out. *'They're moving closer. They've crossed Vicki's line.'*

After the Stony Estancia Bank president, Mrs. Golding introduced Mrs. Rajagopalan, a well-dressed woman wearing a green silk sari with gold embroidery. Her husband, physics teacher Dr. Chandrasekhar, escorted her to the podium. Gold bangles jingled on her wrists.

She held a green box embossed with a gold logo. "Here I have the record of a famous wagon train from Salt Lake City reminding us that Stony Estancia was settled by people from other places and that our strength is in our diversity."

'Such a Eurocentric view,' mocked Fitch. 'She's ignoring the Serrano band who lived here for millennia before the Europeans arrived.'

Good point, but for another time, I rebuked Fitch.

I brushed the crumbs off my hands and took a second croissant.

After donning white cotton gloves, she unsnapped the box and displayed two famous journals—Sister Rowley's diary and Brother Humphries' ledger. "I donate these for our children to be inspired by the Cajon Treasure buried by Sister Rowley, one of the extraordinary women who settled Stony Estancia."

'Has that treasure ever been found?' Fitch asked.

Still lost, I thought in reply. I studied this when I got my teaching credential.

Mrs. Rajagopalan continued her speech, "These documents will certainly lead to the treasure." She read from Sister Rowley's diary. THE ANIMALS ARE EXHAUSTED. THE PEOPLE AS WELL. WE ABANDONED OUR TREASURES. BURIED THEM BESIDE OUR CAMPSITE.

'Those books are valuable. Are they safe at Stony High?' Fitch worried.

The protesters got even louder. They were moving closer.

For the final act, Mrs. Golding invited the Stony High bear to cut the ribbon.

But before the ribbon was cut, the front door of the library burst open, and the protesters ran in shouting, "Down with the elite," ending Mrs. Golding's celebration.

I rushed up to Mrs. Rajagopalan's side to protect the journals.

Wherein Zarand serves snacks.

I led January out of the annex—leaving Jane Doe behind. As we left the room, I bumped the door with my hip so it would again be stuck closed, securing the scene as I'd promised Vicki.

Fitch raised an awkward point, *'You know the annex is accessible through that broken window, don't you?'*

Only if someone wants to risk all those glass shards and climb over the bookcases.

I turned my attention to Ms. Miller's class. They were safe—the killer was long gone. I didn't want them to panic. I casually announced, "The California History Annex is closed today."

Jorge gave me a questioning look, but the others took little note of my pronouncement. I had entered the annex and returned with January—end of story. The crash was forgotten like yesterday's earthquake.

January and I walked over to Ms. Blume, the librarian, who had stationed herself beside the self-checkout machines. The high-tech kiosks were arranged in a circle in the center of the room. The librarian was young and looked more like a student than a teacher. She wore jeans and a T-shirt that said, SO MANY BOOKS. SO LITTLE TIME.

"Can you keep an eye on them?" I asked—tilting my head towards Ms. Miller's students who were researching for their reports.

"No problem." In a lower voice, she added, "Did you know the annex isn't open yet? Despite the ribbon cutting, they have more work to do."

'That's news to me,' Fitch remarked.

I was more concerned about Jane Doe than any construction issues. I asked Ms. Blume, "Can January and I borrow your office for a few minutes?"

Again, she replied, "No problem."

Ms. Blume's office—no desk, just a small round table, and built-in bookshelves surrounding a large window that filled the space with cheery sunlight. There were books helter-skelter everywhere. I removed a stack from the guest chair and let January sit. I took Ms. Blume's chair and cleared the space between us.

Reaching into my backpack, I offered bottled water and cans of iced tea. January selected water infused with cherry essence. I took a pomegranate acai black tea and placed an assortment of snacks in the cleared space, along with my phone, pointing to the screen to show her that it was recording. She put her hands over her face and said, "But, my deaf accent..."

I gave her a big smile and mirrored her embarrassed gesture. "You speak much better than I sign."

"Okay," she agreed and opened a package of peanut butter on cheese crackers. I chose trail mix and ate the pieces one at a time. We enjoyed our snacks before I asked, "Can you tell me why you were in the annex?"

"My report for Ms. Miller is about John Steinbeck. *Stony Estancia Surfs* said the history collection had a good sampling of newspaper clippings," she said.

She spoke very well. I had no problem with her deaf accent. *'What about the stuck door?'* prompted Fitch.

"Did you have any difficulty opening the door?" I asked.

She shook her head. "No. It wasn't closed."

Fitch got all excited. *'It was closed when we got to it. When did that happen?'*

Fitch, you're the worst interviewer—always asking leading questions. You should know better.

I went with an open-ended question. "What happened when you entered the annex?"

She put down her water and took a bite of her crackers before leaning forward and speaking in a quiet voice. "Two guys were standing in front of the fireplace. They were shouting at each other—pushing each other." She pointed in front of her to where the two people must have been as if she was reliving that moment. She added with a sly grin, "But, of course, I couldn't hear what they were saying."

She closed her eyes and then they popped open. "I remember something," she exclaimed. "They were wearing those gloves with no fingertips. Does that help?"

I encouraged her, "Yes. They may have left fingerprints."

Fitch jumped in, *'Was one of them Jane Doe?'*

Calm down, Fitch. Don't be impatient. A good detective waits for the witness.

After a short while, January continued. "They didn't see me. I moved to the other end of the room to be out of sight."

Her breathing became shallow. I could see that these memories upset her. I slid her water bottle closer, and she took several sips.

"When I reached the windows, I saw her lying there, her feet facing me. Her boots were red. I must have gasped." She took a deep breath and closed her eyes again.

'She's talking about Jane Doe,' Fitch clarified.

I prompted her, delighted that she had a clear memory. "You're doing great. Can you describe the scene?"

She turned her head to the left. "I could see them through the bookshelves— At the other end of the room— By the fireplace— Still shoving each other."

I placed her bottle in her hand, and she drank some more.

Her head turned to the right. "The last bookcase, closest to the windows was shorter."

She stopped and wiped her eyes on her wrist.

I spied a box of tissues on a bookshelf and handed her one.

She blew her nose and spoke like she was in a trance. "The woman, all dressed in red, was lying dead on the floor." She signed DEAD.

Fitch observed, *'Careful. She's getting nervous. When she's stressed, she reverts to ASL.'*

I gave her some time, but she was stuck. I prompted her, "Did you recognize her?"

She shook her head. "I don't know anyone with a red motorcycle jacket." Then she spoke quickly. "It happened fast. They might have yelled at me, but I didn't hear them. One of them pushed me against the wall. Then the bookcases came down." She pointed down. "I had been shoved to safety, but the lady was trapped. That short bookcase crushed her, and the tall bookcases crashed through the window. Glass was everywhere. I wanted to get out of there, but the door was stuck. Those two guys were gone, and they must have slammed it shut. I sat in the corner. I don't know how long. I banged on the door, and you opened it."

January was panting and her hands shook. That was the end of the interview. I didn't think she had more to say.

"Would you like to go to the health office?"

She held up her fist and then as if it was a puppet, she nodded the head. Then her hand made a circular motion on her chest. YES, PLEASE.

I gave her a package of cheese crackers.

She ate the crackers and finished her water. "I feel better."

Since the library was next to the office, she didn't need an escort. I wrote her a note and she retrieved her backpack on the way out. Polite Stony High students didn't ask questions when girls left in the middle of class.

'You forgot to ask her what happened to those two guys,' Fitch complained.

I didn't need to ask January. I'd already figured it out. The two guys slipped from the annex into the library without being noticed and closed the door, trapping January inside.

Fitch scoffed, *'Were they invisible like me? Ms. Miller's students were on the steps by the front door. How did they get past them?'*

I stayed in Ms. Blume's office to finish my trail mix and tea while I waited for Vicki, but the Stony Estancia Police Department wasn't the first to arrive. They weren't even second.

Wherein Zarand gets down to nuts and bolts.

I sipped my tea in the tranquility of Ms. Blume's office and picked the peanuts out of my trail mix, enjoying the salt and the oil as I chewed them to a peanut buttery pulp. Jane Doe haunted me. Her clear blue eyes with brown eyeliner and purple eye shadow stared at me. "Find my killer," they implored, "I have a family and didn't deserve to die."

'If you're concerned about Jane Doe, we should be in the annex collecting evidence, not hiding in here eating snacks.'

Poor Fitch. Are you grumpy because you can't eat snacks?

Vicki was on her way. She was the detective, and I was the teacher. It wouldn't do our relationship any good if I preempted her.

'What happened to being a detective in your DNA?'

Fitch convinced me. I packed up my snacks and headed for the crime scene. Jane Doe's attackers wouldn't get away—not on my watch.

But I didn't get out of the librarian's office because Principal Golding rushed in, her white braid flicking like an angry cat's tail. "Here you are Mr. S." She pointed her phone at me. "Look at this."

Stony Estancia Surfs had posted, THE LIBRARY WAS BOMBED.

Fitch grinned, *'How can they call themselves journalists— writing headlines in passive voice?'*

Is that all you have to think about?

"Nobody is going to believe there was a bombing in Stony Estancia," I said.

Mrs. Golding dropped into Ms. Blume's chair. "Of course you're right. If they thought that was true, my phone would be going off like the Fourth of July." She placed her silent cell on the table.

I served snacks from my backpack. "I'm sure they'll call eventually. Let's get ahead of them. Something to drink?"

She helped herself to soy sauce-flavored rice crackers and matcha tea. "First, I'm going to call the police and close the library."

"The police are on their way but closing the library sounds right."

"I'm not surprised. I expected you to call your girlfriend." Mrs. Golding crunched her crackers and took a long swig of tea. She pointed to my backpack. "Anything stronger in there?"

I handed her a tequila miniature. "For emergencies."

She finished the mini bottle in one swallow. "That's better. Do you think I should close the school?"

Fitch gasped, *'That's the last thing we want. Keep everyone here until Vicki can question them.'*

"Not necessary. The killer is long gone. Closing the school will cause panic. Your phone will sound like Armageddon."

She ate a few more rice crackers before agreeing. "I can see your point. Keep calm and carry on."

"Right. Can you get someone to cover Ms. Miller's class for me?"

She stood up. "You can't have it both ways. Either we close the school for an emergency, or everything is copacetic, and we carry on."

I countered with, "What if Senior Detective Yukawa requests my assistance?"

The principal folded her arms. "You forget that I know Vicki. She's not going to do that, and you know it."

'She's got your number,' said Fitch with a guffaw.

I conceded, "We maintain the schedule."

She softened. "The best I can do is send Ms. Miller's class to the Bruin Bistro. They can wait in the cafeteria. But when the buzzer sounds for the next period, you're back on duty."

"Thank you."

Fitch gave me two thumbs up. *'She did you a favor. You can question the class—your self-styled grandkids. They'll be your confidential informants—seeing and hearing more than anyone suspects.'*

Principal Golding finished her tea and left. "You have a few minutes to play detective. Enjoy it."

'*Play detective?*' Fitch echoed. '*Let's show them how it's done.*'

I returned to the history annex to get a head start, but instead of Vicki, I found myself facing César's camera and Leticia's microphone. "This is Mr. Szilard, retired police detective and substitute teacher." Then she turned to me. "Is the bomb connected to the protest on Saturday?"

César was livestreaming, and I wasn't going to let Tish get away with that. "There wasn't a bomb. I can't believe this. You'll post anything for clicks."

Tish put on her best surprised face. "No bomb? *Stony Estancia Surfs* posts the highest quality news. Help us set our audience straight. What happened?"

'*Don't give anything away,*' advised Fitch.

"I can't say anything until the police arrive."

She flashed me a broad smile. "I can understand that. You're waiting for your girlfriend's permission, aren't you? A good relationship requires the respect of boundaries."

Tish was my friend, but that went over the line. I was my own person, and it took all my self-control to not respond to her insinuation.

'*Small town,*' said Fitch enjoying my discomfort.

César yanked the door open and poked his camera into the annex.

I pulled him away and resealed the door. "You can't go in there."

"*Dios mío.* It's a disaster. Are you sure there wasn't a bomb?" Tish exclaimed.

"Who mentioned a bomb?" I asked with more anger than necessary.

Leticia laughed. "Don't you follow your students on social media?" She faced the camera. "*Stony Estancia Surfs* is posting from the brand-new history annex which has been attacked by terrorists." After a dramatic pause, she added, "Twice." After another pause, she deepened her voice, "and leaving a fatality this time."

'*Out of control,*' said Fitch while shaking his head.

César gave her a thumbs up and said, "That will get everyone to click. It might even go viral nationally."

"You can't release that," said a stern voice.

We all turned around. I was happy to see Vicki. She was better at public relations than I was.

She had arrived with Officer Tsui. She wore her regular detective attire—unbuttoned blue blazer, fresh white shirt, bowtie, and her perfect black hair with a center part as straight as a laser beam. Tsui carried a crime scene camera and evidence kits. He reopened the annex and started taking official photos.

César tried to follow him.

Senior Detective Yukawa addressed the *Stony Estancia Surfs* team. "You can't film a crime scene until I give my approval."

"*Si, si, senorita.*" César's good-natured grin conceded they'd been through this before and he understood the ground rules.

Then Vicki peeked into the history annex. "Is there a dead woman in there?"

"Yes," I answered.

She looked at César and Tish, and back to me.

I raised both hands, palms up. "Vee don't look at me like that. They didn't hear it from me."

She smiled at me and bumped me with her hip. "I know. Stony is a small town with no secrets. Everything is online."

'*You're a digital dinosaur,*' mocked Fitch.

Who cares, I'm going to solve this the old-fashioned way. My grandkids, my confidential informants, are my secret weapon.

Detective Yukawa turned to Tsui. "Take pictures of everything. Also, call the Fire Department to help extract the body from that mess. Once that's done, we'll need the coroner. I'll call Peggy."

Tsui smiled at his boss. "I think you meant Persey. Persey Paterson is the County Coroner and Peggy Mutai is the Fire Department Lieutenant."

"Right. I was thinking Persey, but my mouth said something else. They're both old friends and I get them mixed up. Coroner Persey, short for Persephone, Greek goddess of death. Lieutenant Peggy, short for Peggoty, like the famous Kenyan chemist. I'll call Persey."

I followed Vicki and Tsui to the site of the disaster. They both put on examination gloves, and she handed me a pair.

When I heard the paramedics drive their white medical rig into the courtyard with sirens blaring and lights flashing, I ran out to meet them.

César captured a video of their approach.

Fitch found a reason to disapprove. *'Oh no. If the whole school didn't already know about Jane Doe, they do now.'*

"In here," I called to the ambulance over the siren's wailing, "We have someone trapped."

Lieutenant Peggy Mutai, with her natural hair holding her helmet high on her head, turned to her crew. "Let's go. Search and rescue equipment. Look sharp."

After the briefest interaction with Vicki, they went to work starting by the fireplace with the domino bookshelf that started the chain reaction, even though Jane Doe was buried at the other end of the room, under all the dominoes. Two women drilled holes in the cement foundation to install seismic wedge anchors to stabilize each bookshelf once it was righted. The rest moved the books and cleared a space to raise the bookcases onto.

A paramedic called to Lieutenant Mutai, "Peggy, come look at this."

Lieutenant Peggy Mutai was aghast. "Vicki, you need to see what they uncovered."

Vicki and I ran across the room to find out what the paramedics had discovered.

After the books were removed, the space where the shelves had stood was marked with rows of anchor bolts embedded in the concrete floor.

I couldn't believe my eyes. I went down on my hands and knees and touched each bolt as if my fingers might discover something my eyes had missed. "Look at this. Undamaged bolts, still in place, but not a nut or washer in sight."

'Where's the fastening hardware?' puzzled Fitch.

Officer Tsui, Lieutenant Mutai, and all the search and rescue team crawled around the wreckage, until Peggy said in a resigned voice, "Nothing. We can't find anything. No washers. No nuts."

'Did the protesters sabotage the history annex? Is that what Jane Doe and the others were doing here?' asked Fitch.

Officer Tsui came over with his camera and several bags of evidence. "I've done all I can until the victim is released from the debris."

"Let's get back to clearing the room. We need to free the corpse," Vicki said before turning to Peggy. "You've only righted two shelves. Do you have to raise each shelf starting from the top before we can get to the victim?"

"There is another way." Peggy called to her team, "Bring in the air-lifting bags."

They slid the deflated bags beneath the mountain of bookshelves. The room filled with the whir of electric pumps. Each pillow filled with air, expanding beneath the pile of steel and paper. Slowly the mound rose.

Once elevated enough to clear the body, I bent over to examine the uncovered space. "None of the missing hardware is here but look what I found." I pointed to a can of spray paint that Tsui placed in an evidence bag.

Vicki took charge. "Tsui, more pictures, and trace evidence. Lieutenant Mutai, have your team look for a cell phone or ID. No one touches the body until Persey arrives."

Everyone followed her lead.

'That lady is a natural and will be chief of detectives someday,' said Fitch with uncharacteristic optimism.

"Vicki, I found something interesting. Let me show you before I leave to teach my next class." I walked to the fireplace, and she followed.

I pointed to where the ashes were, but they were gone. "There were ashes here. I don't know what happened to them."

"Argh," she said and called Tsui, "Come here please."

Officer Tsui ran across the room.

She asked him, "Do you know anything about ashes in the fireplace? *Former* detective Szilard seems to think that ashes in a fireplace are important."

She smiled at me and squeezed my hand, even though her emphasis on the word former dripped with sarcasm.

Tsui also smiled. "I collected the ashes for evidence. This is a gas fireplace and there shouldn't have been any ashes."

"Good work. One more thing. Check the parking lots for any car that doesn't belong here. Since no one walks in this town, Jane Doe's car must be parked nearby."

"No problem, I've got a license plate scanner on my phone. I'll take care of it when we're done here.

Vicki turned to me. "Okay? Can we get back to work?"

Fitch echoed, *'Okay? Are you done distracting the real police?'*

Fitch was right. The Stony PD was doing a first-rate job.

Soon the end-of-period buzzer would sound. I was torn. Should I leave immediately and get to Ms. Miller's class before the buzzer, or should I delay to the last minute?

Vicki's phone beeped and she announced, "Persey's here."

That settled it. County Coroner Persephone Paterson had arrived. I wasn't going to leave before Persey did.

5. MOTIVES – STILL TUESDAY AM

Wherein Zarand is the last one in the pool.

I ran to the front of the library to hold the door open for County Coroner Persephone Paterson. She was a minor celebrity—a tall woman, with kohl eyes, midnight lips, and black fingernails. She'd famously appeared in her Stony High yearbook as a mortician wearing her black prom dress. She spread her arms and announced in a deep voice, "I am Persephone, Queen of the Underworld, take me to your dead." Her dog, who accompanied her everywhere, gave a soft *woof.*

'I love this lady's style,' said Fitch.

I escorted her into the annex.

Before entering, she zipped up her white protective suit, hiding away her black silk shirt. Two assistants, also sealed in white with CORONER in black letters on their backs, pushed the gurney up the ramp, across the reading room, and into the annex. They rolled out a body bag.

Persey unleashed her canine assistant. "Cerberus, search," she said in a gentle voice.

Everyone backed away while the chocolate lab with white paws circled the room. He checked the Steinbeck and Saroyan collections. When he came to the first editions, he sat down and gave two quick barks, waiting until Persey signaled him to proceed.

"That's his alert for old books," she said with a grin.

Those archival boxes I'd stacked against the wall also drew extra attention. I was afraid we'd have to open each one, but he moved on and wound his way through the broken glass. In the end, he settled beside Jane Doe.

"Good boy," Persey said to her dog patting his shoulder, and she pointed to Jane Doe. "There's just this one body."

'She sounds disappointed with only one,' observed Fitch.

Lieutenant Mutai pointed to her airlifting bags. "Jane Doe hasn't been moved. She was secured under the debris until we arrived."

Persey got down on her hands and knees to get a closer look. "Has Officer Tsui taken pictures?"

"Yes ma'am," said Tsui.

Persey addressed her assistants. "Let's take a closer look at her."

They slid an orange backboard under Jane Doe and pulled her out from the wreckage.

Everyone stepped back while Persey made her preliminary examination. She traced the reflective piping on Jane Doe's motorcycle gear with a gloved finger. "High-end leathers. Very flashy in red. I have the same suit in solid black, not cheap."

"What do you think of that mess in her hair?" I asked.

She raised Jane Doe's head revealing a patch of honey-blonde hair matted with blood. "Someone smacked her on the back of her head."

"Could that have been from the falling bookcases?" Vicki asked.

"Good thought. I'll know after the autopsy."

"Any identification?" I asked.

Persey unzipped pockets in the pants and jacket, muttering, "Empty," after each one. Finally, she opened a hidden pocket on the right forearm and withdrew a piece of paper. "Only this." She handed it to Tsui who placed it in an evidence bag.

"I would have preferred a wallet or a phone," Vicki said.

"That would have been too easy," said Persey. She addressed Jane Doe in a high-pitched, fake foreign accent. "Who are you? Not talking? Vee have ways of learning your secrets."

Fitch giggled, *'Coroner humor.'*

She directed her assistants. "The show is over. Bag her."

Lieutenant Mutai ran her fingers over the space vacated by the body and remarked, "Just blood from that head injury."

"I wouldn't expect anything else with her wrapped up in leathers," Persey commented.

"Are those bruises on her neck? Was she strangled?" Vicki asked.

Persey lifted Jane Doe's honey-ash hair from the faint marks. "Another good question. Postmortem bruising is rare, but those marks look like postmortem extravasation of blood. In plain language, someone pressed too hard looking for a carotid artery on a deceased victim."

'Caught you,' said Fitch.

Vicki looked at me. "Zee?"

That was her pet name for me. I called her Vee.

I confessed. "Sorry, Vee. Guilty as charged. I didn't want her to be dead."

She leaned close to me and whispered. "Don't worry. I love that you have an extra helping of empathy."

With Jane Doe on the gurney and rolling out the door, Persey asked, "Why don't we have a motive pool? Winner treats the rest of us to dinner."

Peggy objected. "That's gross. How can you bet on a murder case?"

Persey mocked her. "Come now, Peggy. Don't be squeamish. I do this all the time in the high desert where the population is lower, but the murder rate's higher."

"I did this in the big city," I said to support Persey. "It's just a bit of fun."

'Are you going to tell them about your witness?' asked Fitch.

I had forgotten about January. "Before we make our guesses, I should tell you what the witness said."

Vicki smacked her head with the palm of her hand. "Oh no, Zee. Did you interview a murder witness and forget to tell us? Are you having a senior moment?"

Everyone laughed.

I explained, "A student was in the research annex when Jane Doe was murdered. She was with two other people when the bookshelves were pushed over."

"And where is this witness now?" Vicki asked.

"She was shaken up. She's in the health office."

"What's her name?"

"January Shaw."

"Tsui, go to the office and secure the witness. I'll be there after I finish up here."

As Tsui left the annex, he said, "Follow the money. It's always about money. Even if it's just addicts stealing for their next fix."

Vicki said, "In this town, smart money checks the *Stony Estancia Surfs* website." She tapped her phone and showed it to us.

PROTESTERS BOMB STONY HIGH.

"Do you think it was those angry parents from last Saturday's ribbon cutting?" I asked.

"No. Wrong clickbait headline." She tapped again. "This one."

VALUABLE JOURNALS DONATED TO STONY HIGH.

"I warned Tish and César not to post that. They were asking for trouble. Rich motorcycle lady was here to steal rare books, best guess—the Cajon Treasure journals donated by Nilanjana Rajagopalan—they're not only rare, but they might lead to the lost treasure."

"Good one," said Persey. She turned to Peggy. "That's what the PD thinks. What does the Fire Department say?"

Peggy took off her helmet and finger-combed her natural hair. "The witness identified three people. Jane Doe and two others." She looked at me. "Did she mention their genders?"

I shook my head. "No. January said two guys."

"No matter. These days gender isn't important."

Persey asked again, "Three people. What does the FD say?"

Peggy smiled. "We're going to win this one. It was a love triangle, jealousy."

'That's perfect,' cheered Fitch.

Persey wasn't impressed. "Love triangle? Really? Are we in a romance instead of a murder mystery? Why break into a research library to murder a rival?" She continued, "My turn. You know I have the inside track. I attended Stony High. This has to do with college applications. Detective Yukawa will have to find the details, but at Stony High, it always comes down to grades."

Persey crossed her arms and turned to me. "Zarand?"

The end-of-period buzzer sounded, and I had just a moment before heading to my next class. I gave them the ultimate answer. "The Cajon Treasure."

6. Cajon Treasure – Also Tuesday AM

Wherein Zarand rings the bell.

I joined students crisscrossing the courtyard on the way to the next class and listened in on their conversations.

"Did you hear that a lady was murdered in the library?"

"We should be under lockdown."

"I heard it was a teacher. Remember that biology teacher?"

"Why aren't they sending us home?"

"Did you see all that yellow tape around the library?"

"Let's cut class and see if we can find clues."

Today would take all my skills as a sub to keep them from descending into chaos.

Fitch pointed to the line of teenagers waiting to get into Ms. Miller's room. *'This is not a good start. You're late.'*

While they found their desks, I faced a sub's worst nightmare. A dead body and no lesson plan. Ms. Miller had scheduled a research day, but the library was closed. The metaphorical classroom theater was open, and I was in the wings without props, costumes, or a script. The curtain was soon to rise.

"Sorry about the library," I said to stall for time.

"We walked across campus for our research day, but cops blocked the library door," complained Ranch, a short boy with glasses and a mustache.

He was supported by Alyce, a muscular girl with sun-bleached blonde hair and a simple necklace of washers on a chain. "*Crikey*, there was yellow crime scene tape everywhere."

I let them chatter while I checked the papers on Ms. Miller's desk and rifled through the drawers searching for her emergency plan.

One desk drawer had snacks—dried, unsweetened fruit, unsalted nuts, and instant ramen. Another drawer had lotion and white cotton gloves for moisturizing dry skin. In the back were a bottle of expensive perfume and a box of scented stationery. I stopped there. That was more than I wanted to know about Ms. Miller.

Did I find a lesson plan? No, nothing. I didn't panic. I'd come up with something.

"Open your laptops," I instructed them with as much confidence as I could muster. "Share with your elbow partner the 19th-century author you've selected for your report."

Fitch congratulated me, *'Good save. Never leave them with unstructured time.'*

I had bought myself a few minutes. I searched the counters. I found a *Jane Eyre* video—Charlotte Brontë's gothic classic reminded me of Persey, the goth coroner—but I discarded it. I was better than that. I wouldn't waste the class's time with a movie.

"Good call, Mr. S. A sub showed us that last week," volunteered Pax from the front row wearing a yellow-and-black hoodie printed with the name of a local engineering college.

I flashed them two thumbs up and replied, "Thanks."

I found a quiz on Greek and Latin roots. I grabbed it—just in case—and continued my quest.

"Use those, Mr. S." Pax pointed to a stack of study guides. Next to the packets was a green archival storage box embossed with the Stony High bear holding a gold pan and a book—like the ones I stacked up in the history annex.

Fitch congratulated Ms. Miller in absentia. *'She was lucky to rescue anything before someone broke into the annex and made a big mess of it.'*

I shook the box. "Pax, do you know what's in here?"

"No, Mr. S., I don't, but Ms. M. is very organized, so it must go with those study guides."

"Study guides. Right."

I divided the packets in two and gave them to Alyce and Ranch. "Please hand these out..." I checked the title and almost dropped them. "...Cajon Treasure study guides."

I had been blaming Jane Doe's murder on the Cajon Treasure, and now it was the subject of my lesson. Quite a coincidence.

'Detectives don't believe in coincidences,' Fitch declared.

While Ranch and Alyce distributed the study guides, I unsnapped the green box. I gasped when I discovered the famous journals—Sister Rowley's diary and Brother Humphries' ledger—the source documents for the Cajon Treasure—the motive for the history annex break-in and Jane Doe's murder. Double coincidence.

'Detectives don't believe in those either,' Fitch guffawed.

I wouldn't touch those valuable books with my bare hands. I remembered the white cotton gloves in Ms. Miller's desk. Properly clothed—my costume—I mounted a chair—my stage—and flashed jazz hands at the audience like a street mime. I unboxed the two books and held them up—the smaller one, colored a faded rose-pink and embossed with DIARY, and the larger one, black and embossed with LEDGER.

Waving them back and forth, I announced in a carnival barker's voice, "Today, we'll explore the legend of the Cajon Treasure—a mystery documented in these two volumes."

The room was silent. The no-lesson-plan crisis had been averted and I was in substitute teacher nirvana. All eyes were on me.

'One, two, three, eyes on me,' Fitch parroted from our student-teacher days in elementary school.

I held open Brother Humphries' ledger and showed it to the class. "You have pages copied from this journal in your handout. What can you tell me about the author?"

Ranch was first with an answer. "Look at his awful penmanship—so many cross-outs, blots, and splatters. He never received a proper education."

I added, to get them thinking, "And yet, he was in charge of the emigrants, leading them across the Great Basin and the Mojave Desert."

Before I could ask another question, Alyce raised her hand. "*Blimey*, it was like colonial Australia. The men were in charge. He was probably a criminal."

I opened Sister Rowley's diary. "What do you see here?"

"Beautiful Spencerian script. She was an expert with a dip pen. Educated, and given the era, probably a teacher," Pax replied.

"Criminal, teacher. Good guesses. Their given names are long lost, but we know he was a trapper, and she was a choir mistress. Read through your packets and answer the questions on the last page. Remember we reuse these packets, so type your responses into your laptops. Save a tree."

I walked around the room and looked over their shoulders. I didn't want to follow up with something too easy or too hard. Either case would give me classroom management problems. By checking their progress, I'd target my lesson to the sweet spot between baffling and boring.

"**Who can tell us** how the emigrants got in trouble?"

Alyce again. "Brother Humphries drove them too fast across the desert and by the time they reached the Cajon Pass—the final obstacle on their journey—the surviving people and animals were too weak to go on."

'*People died of dysentery. Like Oregon Trail,*' Fitch joked, referring to an old computer game.

"What happened next?"

Alyce was angry. "What would you expect? The stubborn man tried the force the group onward."

"But that didn't work, did it? How'd they get over the pass?" I probed.

Pax answered this time. "Choir mistress Sister Rowley and the women took over the doomed party. She sacrificed an ox to feed the survivors and buried the party's valuables to lighten the load. She recorded Brother Rowley's humiliation in her diary, along with a map to the buried treasure."

"The map and the treasure have never been found," I noted

Ranch waved his hand. "Yes, Ranch?"

He stood up and gave his response in a strong voice. "My father and I hike into the mountains every summer with a metal detector and a topo map." He proudly added, "My dad is a computer wizard. He wrote an app for searching in the San Gabriel Mountains. We'll find the treasure this summer for sure."

Alyce stared into Ranch's eyes. He didn't return her look but sat down when she laughed, "There's no treasure. You and your dad are wasting your time."

With that broadside fired, the battle lines were drawn. The treasure hunters and the doubters searched the study guides for points to support their positions. The class was engaged. The lesson was a success.

When they began to repeat themselves, I rang Ms. Miller's bell. "Where can we find the best evidence for or against the Cajon Treasure?"

I pointed to Ranch. "Primary sources—something from the period of interest—those books from the history collection."

"Your study guides have copies of the pages written when Sister Rowley hid the Cajon Treasure. You have both sides of the story from Brother Humphries and Sister Rowley. The treasure has never been found. Talk in your table groups whether the evidence supports a continued search."

Pax opened the class discussion. "Brother Humphries refused to follow when Sister Rowley took over. As the last person to leave the camp, he was in the best position to know if she buried any treasure. He says she didn't."

Alyce agreed with him. "There's no treasure." She folded her arms across her chest and pronounced, "Brother Humphries mocked Sister Rowley and told her to remember her place. That makes him a sexist patriarch, not a liar."

Ranch countered with, "He did everything he could to discredit her. I don't believe anything he wrote. The treasure is there."

Alyce came back. "Did you even read the study guide? He convinced me that the Cajon Treasure is a myth."

Ranch stood up again. "Forget the study guides. They're copies—secondary sources. Sister Rowley hid the map in her diary." He headed in my direction. "Give it to me. I'll find the map." He opened a pen knife—prohibited at Stony High—and prepared to dig for a buried treasure map in Sister Rowley's diary.

'Confiscate his knife. Take control. Don't let him walk all over you,' demanded Fitch.

I ignored him. Today, I was a teacher, not a cop. I held Sister Rowley's diary behind my back. That was enough to discourage Ranch. He put away his knife and sat down.

His outburst embarrassed my grandkids. Like children in a dysfunctional family, they denied that anything had happened, refusing to look in Ranch's direction. Some flipped through pages of the study guide, but most stared at their phones—ironically, another rule violation. A few looked up as if they expected me to do something, but the room didn't need more negative energy. I trusted the class to restore order on their own.

Pax held up his phone. It was open to the *Stony Estancia Surfs* home page. "Look at this. Why are we talking about a 19th-century treasure map when there is a dead body in the library? #BodyintheLibrary."

Alyce agreed. "This murder happened on our campus. We know the crime scene better than anyone."

That was the opening I needed. Time for my confidential informants to tell me what they knew. I rang Ms. Miller's bell. "Alyce makes a good point. This is your home turf."

"I know people who were on campus that night. Witnesses," Pax said.

"Don't give up their names. The cops will arrest them for trespassing," Ranch warned.

"Did you see the police last Saturday, the awful way they treated those protesters?" Pax agreed.

'I saw. Vicki was restrained. No one was injured or arrested,' Fitch rebutted them. Between the students and Vicki, Fitch supported Vicki.

Alyce came to my rescue. "Mr. S. isn't the po-po. He won't betray your friends."

"That's right Pax. I won't give away anything you tell me."

Pax said, "Well, that night—"

Before he could finish, the public address system crackled to life. "Attention Stony High. A police officer will visit you to gather information about the incident in the library. Please give them a cooperative Stony High reception. Go Bruins."

That was followed by a knock on the door.

Wherein Zarand is invisible.

The police couldn't have arrived at a worse time— interrupting my confidential informants.

Fitch was discouraged. *'Once the cops enter the room, you can forget your CIs.'*

The officer outside our classroom knocked again, louder this time.

You're correct. Here goes nothing.

I unlocked the door and held it open. Officer Tsui barged in, not seeing me holding the door, and marched past me to take a position in front of the class. I stood at the door behind him, with my legs spread and my hands on my hips. I was neutral, neither for nor against the guy in a uniform with pepper spray, a Taser, handcuffs, and a gun hanging off his belt.

His arrival was greeted with teenage skepticism.

"Who was murdered? Was it a hate crime?" Pax asked him.

"Was it a woman?" Alyce wanted to know.

"Did she have the Cajon Treasure map?" Ranch shouted out.

Officer Tsui's head turned from student to student as they bombarded him with questions. He spoke as if reciting a memorized speech. "There was an accident in the California History Annex. Someone was injured. We haven't identified them yet."

Fitch scoffed. *'Accident? Injured? Why wasn't he direct? Tish and César already posted about bombs, terrorists, and deaths.'*

My grandkids shouted another round of questions.

"Was another teacher killed?"

I wondered if they'd ever forget that murdered teacher.

Fitch reminded me, *'Not likely. Not with her name memorialized on the science garden.'*

"Or was it a student this time?"

"Is someone targeting our school?"

I had to admire Tsui. He held his ground. "I can't answer questions about an ongoing investigation. If you don't have anything to contribute, I'll move to the next class." He backed up in the direction of the door.

I almost took charge, but Alyce spoke first. "*Blimey*, why are you talking to us? You should be interrogating those protesters from the ribbon cutting. You do have video, don't you?" She added with teenage sarcasm, "If you don't, I'm sure *Stony Estancia Surfs* does."

Tsui stepped forward. "This is your campus. You know more than you think."

Alyce crossed her arms.

He approached her. "For instance, young lady, what can you tell me about your necklace?"

She reached for the chain around her neck holding shiny steel washers. "I didn't steal these. I found them on the football field. There were lots." She pointed to Pax and several others who also wore hardware necklaces.

Tsui took out an evidence kit. "It might be a clue. If you can drop it in here, I will give you a receipt."

Alyce held on to her necklace. "You can't have it."

Tsui took out a pair of handcuffs. "I need that necklace. If you won't give it to me, I'll have to take you into custody."

Fitch sighed. *'That isn't going to get him any cooperation.'*

His threat with the handcuffs worked, even though I was certain he had no intention of arresting anyone.

She handed her necklace over. "Make sure you give me a receipt."

While he was completing the paperwork, she took multiple pictures of her necklace and Officer Tsui.

"Leave her alone. You should be rounding up drug addicts from San Amano," Pax said.

"Young lady...er, man...student—" I could see Tsui staring at Pax's multicolor hair—shaved on one side and long on the other—and their eyebrow ring.

Pax smiled. "Student is good. My pronouns are they/them."

Tsui began again without a mention of Pax's gender. "We'll investigate the possibility of drug addicts." He added, "You students might have a rivalry with San Amano, but the police don't. There's no reason to expect addicts to be from San Amano any more than from Stony Estancia."

Ranch stood up. "Someone broke into the annex to steal the map to the Cajon Treasure."

Alyce laughed. She pointed to the green box with the history collection logo. "Too bad for them. The journals were gone. Ms. Miller must have been the first to check anything out from the California History Collection."

Pax concurred. "Not surprising. She's really organized."

Tsui approached the counter where I'd left the journals.

I got there first and grabbed the green box. I wasn't going to release it from my custody.

Tsui pulled out his Taser and pointed it at me. "Oh. Mr. Szilard. I didn't know you were here." He put his Taser away. "You're Senior Detective Yukawa's friend, aren't you? I'm so sorry."

I smiled. "No problem."

He retreated with Alyce's necklace and nothing else.

Tsui and the other officers stayed for the day to complete questioning the students. I doubt they learned much.

I repeated my lesson about Sister Rowley's rescue of the exhausted emigrants to successive classes of treasure hunters and ended my day with a forgettable dinner.

The next morning, my dreams of breakfast were interrupted by someone banging on my door. The morning dew blurred the video doorbell, revealing a low-res image of a teenager.

How did a student know where I lived?

'Small town,' said Fitch enjoying my dismay.

And what were they doing here so early, before breakfast?

8. PAX SHELLEY – WEDNESDAY AM

Wherein Zarand prepares breakfast.

The rising sun peeked over the mountains and splashed pools of light on my bed. I had opened one eye at the sound of someone hammering on my front door. I didn't want to get up. Without a substitute teaching assignment, I planned to sleep in—skip breakfast, and start the day with lunch—a big one. I closed my eyes, hoping they'd go away.

Bang. Bang. There it was again.

Dahl took the noise as a wake-up call. She meowed and pranced across my bed with her black tail high in the air. When I didn't move, she sniffed me with her white nose, mouth, and whiskers, preliminary to batting me with her pink toe beans and purring up a storm.

Thump. Thump. The pounding didn't relent.

I pulled on a robe and stumbled down the stairs. When I opened the door, I saw Pax in the same yellow-and-black hoodie they'd worn yesterday.

I rubbed my eyes and cleaned my eyeglasses with my robe. "Pax, are you okay?"

"Fine. Just fine." They brushed pieces of lava rock off their sleeves.

The rocks landed on my doormat.

"Excuse me," I said.

They looked down and noticed the fallen rocks. "Oh, sorry." Pax took off their hoodie and shook it out, returning the pieces of pumice to the landscaping. Higgs Haven's award-winning gardeners constructed an amoeba of lava rocks at the base of each palm tree.

As they put their hoodie back on, I wondered, "Have you been home?"

Before they answered, the morning silence was interrupted by an approaching vehicle. When Pax heard it, they pushed past me and scrambled up the stairs. When the police car pulled into the visitor's space in front of my unit, I stood alone, barefooted.

"Mornin' Officer Tsui. Don't you ever sleep?"

"Sleep? With all my children—five college funds, I need as much overtime as Detective Yukawa will give me."

"I see. What can I do for you?"

"Someone broke through the crime scene tape last night. Have you seen anything suspicious?"

I shook my head no.

Tsui went on. "No vehicle. They were on foot. Higgs Haven is inside our search perimeter and Senior Detective Yukawa assigned it to me."

"Do you have any suspects?"

"Just one. That strange...student."

"Do you mean Pax?"

"Yes, that's their name. The one with the rainbow hair."

Fitch cheered. *'Congrats, he remembered their pronouns.'*

Tsui pointed to a black SUV. "That's their car."

'Pax is Tsui's suspect. Turn them in,' said Fitch.

I wasn't about to snitch on Pax before I heard their side of the story. I told Tsui, "I haven't seen anything. I can't imagine that Pax broke into the annex."

He looked at me. "Really? Then why are you out here in your PJs?"

'Busted,' said Fitch with a laugh.

Dahl hissed at him. That black-and-white mischief-maker saved me.

I told Tsui, "Did you hear that? That was my cat. She woke me yowling at something in the garden. When I came down to check, a coyote high-tailed it for the hills." I turned the tables on Tsui. "Higgs Haven is a big place. Why are you at my door?"

"One of your neighbors reported someone sleeping in the gardens and Pax's car is parked here."

I laughed, hoping to distract him. "Oh, you know my nervous neighbors. They all have nine-one-one on their favorites. They call for every feral cat and lost coyote."

Tsui nodded his head. "Yes. The dispatcher told me that. If you haven't seen anything, I'll be on my way." He headed for the gym where the large windows revealed early-morning people working with the weight machines.

Pax sat on the stairs. Their hair fascinated Dahl. She batted it with her paws to make different layers of color appear.

"Do you want to tell me what's going on?" I asked.

Pax scratched Dahl's chin. She rolled over and put her legs in the air. "Not really. I've had a hard night."

"That's not going to cut it. I lied to Officer Tsui and now you're in my apartment, something that can get me into a lot of trouble."

"It's a long story."

I sat down on the step above them. "I have time."

"You asked whether I'd been home. That was the right question. I rarely sleep at home. I can't bear to watch my parents fighting."

'That's unexpected for Stony Estancia. Forget the rules. Pax needs a friend. I wish I could hug them,' Fitch said.

I had to think about what Pax had told me. Cooking cleared my mind.

"How about some breakfast."

"That would be great," said Pax.

Dahl meowed. She was always ready to eat.

I closed the front door and went into the garage. When I escaped to the suburbs, I required a car. I sentimentally chose a black-and-white one. I didn't want it to be mistaken for a cop car, so I selected a small electric model—too small for any confusion. I stepped over its thick charging cable on the way to the deep freezer to retrieve a silicone container of blueberries. I stocked up when they were in season. Dahl chirruped. She knew the freezer contained tasty packages of ground turkey, one of her favorites.

Armed with blueberries and a solid block of turkey, I climbed the stairs to my two-room apartment.

Dahl rubbed up against Pax with her black tail raised. Pax picked her up, so she didn't have to tire her delicate legs ascending the stairs.

I defrosted Dahl's turkey. With the cat satisfied, I popped a pod into my espresso machine. "How do you like it?" I asked over the hissing.

Pax took a deep breath. "Latte. Can you make a whole-milk latte? Do you have hazelnut flavoring?"

"No problem."

Fitch smiled, *'They may have slept on the ground last night, but they still drink their coffee with Stony Estancia style.'*

I pointed to my secondhand plaid sofa. "You can sit there while I get dressed."

When I returned, they were still nursing their drink. Dahl had convinced them to stroke her soft coat while I heated the waffle iron and mixed the gluten-free buckwheat batter from scratch.

After waffles with blueberries and homemade whipped cream, I questioned Pax. "Why was Tsui looking for you?"

A sullen teenager chased the few remaining blueberries around their plate.

I switched tactics. "What happened last night?"

"I didn't sleep well. Could I have another latte?"

While I brewed Pax's whole milk, hazelnut latte, Dahl finished her turkey and sat in the morning sun cleaning the pink toe beans on the bottoms of her paws.

I slid the latte across the table. Pax picked it up and told their story.

"My parents—Gunnar and Tiffany—are always fighting. I know it's my fault, but sometimes I just wish they would get divorced."

Like a good detective, I didn't react.

Fitch wasn't as controlled. He gasped, *'Divorce? In Stony Estancia?'*

You'll never be a good detective if you keep reacting like that. Fortunately, Pax can't see or hear you.

Pax moved to the sofa before continuing. "I try to make them get along, but nothing works." Pax paused as if they were considering what they'd just said. "I can't stand to see them yelling at each other. After I've tried everything, I leave the house."

I congratulated myself for not turning Pax over to Officer Tsui. Being a teen was hard. Pax had enough problems without being questioned by the police.

"Last weekend, my parents went away in two cars but returned in one. I knew better than to ask. Later, I heard Dad on the phone. He said, 'Tiff drove the car into a tree. No, not an accident.' He didn't seem angry. They fight about everything, but not that car crash." Pax sipped his coffee and scratched Dahl who had made herself comfortable in their lap. "My parents don't make sense. I'm sure there's something I can do, but I'm afraid to ask."

Pax paused again before adding, "At least no one knew about that. The cars in our garage are private and people buy new cars all the time. However, before that, he threw Mom out the front window. It's still covered with plywood. My friends can see it. It's embarrassing." He thought for a bit. "And frightening."

'Throwing his mom through the window sounds like teen hyperbole,' sneered Fitch.

Fitch might have doubted Pax, but when I looked into their sad eyes, I saw confusion and disappointment. I reminded Fitch of what Tolstoy said: *Every unhappy family is unhappy in its own way.* If Fitch doubted Pax, we could drive by the house to confirm the story.

'No one throws someone through a window. That only happens in movies. Falling bookcases are more believable.' Fitch thought for a moment before adding, *'Regardless, this has nothing to do with Jane Doe.'*

"I see," I said to Pax, remembering the lava rocks embedded in his hoodie. "Do you always sleep on the ground?"

"No. I usually bunk down in my SUV. It has plenty of room. I have 800 thread-count Pima cotton sheets and an electric blanket for cool nights. Except, last night, the cops were checking the parked cars."

"Really? How did you know?"

"There are others on the streets at night. My friends."

'What others?' asked Fitch.

After a short silence, Pax elaborated. "Most of them are young and can go home for clean clothes and a hot meal but prefer the freedom of life on the street. They call themselves the Stony Stoners."

'*So, he's hanging out with drug addicts,*' Fitch said.

That can't be right, I thought.

"That name is just ironic. Right? They're not doing anything illegal, are they?"

Pax laughed. "Depends on what you call illegal." They finished their latte. Dahl purred in Pax's lap.

I had no idea how to respond to Pax's dysfunctional home and that they were friends with the Stony Stoners. I was a substitute teacher and a homicide detective, not a social worker.

Regardless, Pax was in my apartment. I dealt with the present moment. "School starts in an hour. Would you like to take a shower?"

They retrieved a nice suitcase and matching toiletry kit from their car. "Where do you keep your towels?

I pointed to my miniscule linen closet.

Pax helped themself to two bath towels and a washcloth before disappearing into my no-tub bathroom.

'*They came prepared to shower here. Don't let them make a habit of this.*'

Don't worry. My apartment isn't going to become a flop house.

While Pax showered, I considered the Stony Stoners. I always knew there were drug users in Stony Estancia, but this put a face on them.

Pax appeared wearing a hoodie that advertised an engineering school in Massachusetts. They had camo cargo pants on—ready to blend in at Stony High even though they'd slept outside.

The shower had washed away their morose expression. I made another attempt to question them, "The Stony Stoners are your friends. Is that why you accused the addicts from San Amano of robbing the history annex?"

"Exactly. You can tell your cop friend that I'm not against San Amano, but the Stony Stoners are innocent."

As Pax drove away, Fitch noted, '*You didn't question them about breaking through the crime scene tape last night. That's why Officer Tsui was searching for them.*'

Fitch was right, but I was more concerned about Pax's home life than Tsui's suspicions.

I reviewed what I knew about #BODYINTHELIBRARY.

Jane Doe was in the morgue, unidentified, and without cause of death. There were lots of theories from rare books to treasure maps, but no evidence. Her two accomplices were still at large.

'Really?' questioned Fitch. *'Aren't you jumping to a conclusion? What you're calling accomplices, could be murderers, or innocent bystanders.'*

Oh, Fitch, you are so cautious. I believe in guessing with confidence. Self-doubt is a distraction. And don't forget someone broke into the annex last night.

'Right, and there are those missing nuts and washers from the bookshelves.' Fitch paused before he asked, *'Do you trust January? Do you believe she's uninvolved? Have you been fooled by those red curls?'*

I had no doubts about January. As I told Fitch, "Doubts are a waste of time."

I hadn't spoken to Vicki since my fingers had bruised her murder victim, and I'd interrogated her witness without police oversight. That was yesterday—a long time ago in a murder case. Had she learned more since then? I doubted it—not if Tsui was checking for people sleeping in their cars.

Now that I knew about Pax's dysfunctional home, I had something to share with Vicki, even though it had nothing to do with Jane Doe.

Dahl chirruped. *What now?*

There was a whole day ahead of me, I was dressed, had finished breakfast...and didn't have a sub assignment.

Dahl's question was answered when someone pulled into the parking spot Pax had vacated.

Wherein Zarand makes some wild guesses.

I stood on my balcony and watched Pax drive away. The fairy lights that the landscapers wrapped around the palm trees had turned off. Joggers and walkers in colorful exercise attire filled the serpentine pathways and a lone woman in a blue one-piece suit swam laps. A man nursed a large coffee with his sleepy eyes on a pair of toddlers who were playing in the kiddy playground. House finches serenaded the sun as it dried out the morning dew. Higgs Haven had come to life.

Just as I started the dishwasher, Dahl jumped up on the back of the sofa and yowled at something outside. Vicki's car was parked in front of my unit. She closed the downstairs entry door that Pax had left open and walked up the stairs. I greeted her at the top with a hug. She responded with a kiss.

After petting Dahl and giving her a treat from the jar on the kitchen counter, she turned to me. "Mornin' Zee, Tsui tells me you've been running around in your PJs with no shoes."

I laughed it off.

She gave me a box from Only Donuts—a Stony High favorite, conveniently located across from the school on Blackett Street.

I helped myself to a bear claw donut—renamed bruin claw in honor of the Stony High mascot. "Thanks, Vee. I'll make coffee."

I handed her her coffee in her favorite cup. "I had a visitor this morning."

She picked up a donut to go with her coffee and sat on the sofa. "Anything to do with Jane Doe?"

"Not really."

"Well, we can talk about it later."

"Any progress on #BODYINTHELIBRARY?" I asked.

"Gosh. Can you believe Tish and César? They'll post anything that drives traffic to *Stony Estancia Surfs*."

"What are they saying now?"

"They're running a video interview from Latino Night at the community center with a student named George. He's blaming everything on corruption."

"Corruption?" I asked.

"Yes. He claims the contractors cut corners and bribed the inspectors. Also, he predicted that when they get caught, they're going to blame it on the Latino laborers."

"George? What was he wearing?"

"A T-shirt with a red flag and a black bird-like thing."

I laughed. "His name isn't George. That's his little joke. His name is Jorge, *Hor-hay*. The shirt is a United Farm Workers flag. He'll talk about Latino civil rights whenever given an opportunity."

Like an experienced detective, Vicki considered this new information. "Some people think that after we named the city Estancia, we'd made amends for our treatment of the Hispanic settlers. Jorge is right. The city has a way to go."

She took the last bite of her donut and finished her coffee.

"Have you had breakfast?" I asked. Dahl and I had eaten, but second breakfast was always an option.

"Don't you have to go to school?"

"Not today, Vee. No substitute assignment."

"Gosh, Zee. Thanks for the offer. Your breakfasts are always special, but I've had mine. I'm not retired, my workday started hours ago." She gave me a peck on the cheek. "And I expect that both you and Dahl have also eaten." She pointed to the dishwasher chugging away.

'Busted,' said Fitch with a laugh.

I kissed her forehead. "You don't miss anything, do you?"

"If you're not working, you can join me at the library. In an hour, say?"

"I'll be there."

Officer Tsui stood in front of the yellow crime scene tape with his legs spread and his arms folded.

César captured video while Leticia approached him with her press pass held up.

Fitch mocked her. *'She makes those on her laser printer.'*

"Mornin' Officer Tsui," she said in a chirpy voice. "I'm with—"

"I know who you are. No one gets in. You've already published too much nonsense."

With a smile, Tish responded, "No such thing. Shall I quote the First Amendment for you?"

"Don't bother. You're not getting in."

I joined the discussion hoping to prevent a confrontation. "Mornin' Officer Tsui. Long time, no see."

He looked me up and down. "I'm glad you got dressed. What are you doing here?"

Tish, our omniscient reporter, said, "Welcome, Mr. Szilard. Be Careful. Officer Tsui's in a bad mood this morning. He didn't get much sleep, rousting innocent people sleeping in their cars."

"Who told you that?" Tsui snapped

I changed the subject. "Tish, you know that his boss wasn't happy with that interview you posted."

"The one with Jorge? That one?"

"Exactly."

"Give your girlfriend my apologies, but pleasing the cops is not part of the First Amendment."

I turned to Tsui. "I'm here to revisit the crime scene."

He looked left and right and nodded to the other officers protecting the library. "No, you're not—not without Detective Yukawa's permission."

"Mornin' Tsui, Leticia, César, Zarand." Vicki had arrived.

Tish spoke first. "The First Amendment—"

Vicki dismissed *Stony Estancia Surfs*. "Not this morning. Shoot some B-roll footage of the school and come back this afternoon."

They packed up their equipment and returned to their neon yellow van.

She then turned to Tsui, "Any luck scanning license plates."

Tsui frowned. "It took a bit of work, but I identified every vehicle and every driver. All are still alive. Jane Doe's car isn't here."

Fitch gave me a knowing look. *'No car? The car that isn't here is an important clue, like the dog that didn't bark.'*

Vicki took my hand and walked through the library reading room to the California History Annex.

"The silence is eerie, more like a morgue than a high school," I said. My voice echoed and I was tempted to shout, "Whoop, whoop."

When we reached the annex, we stopped in the doorway. Vicki spoke in a soft voice. "Tell me, Zee. What happened here?"

This was my chance to shine. Everything was different from yesterday. Opposite us, bright sunlight poured in. The empty bookshelves, now upright and supported by cables, cast abstract shadows over the stacks of books piled against the walls. The gray shelves showed traces of fingerprint powder in fluorescent colors—candy pink, acid yellow, lime green, and electric blue, on the uprights and the bottom shelves—making the scene look like *Holi*, the Hindu festival of colors.

I noticed some lava rocks that weren't there yesterday.

'Tsui was right. Pax was the one that broke through the yellow tape last night,' Fitch said.

I had to agree. It was an unbelievable coincidence to find lava rocks on Pax and in the California History Annex.

None of that answered Vicki's implied question. What happened to the perpetrators? How did they disappear?

I returned to the main library to confirm a theory I was developing about Jane Doe's accomplices. I reviewed my recollections of that morning when January had drawn my attention by banging on the door. Ms. Miller's students filled the reading area, sitting in groups around the tables. Solitary students worked in the carrels or relaxed in rocking chairs. In the center, Ms. Blume stationed herself with the ring of self-checkout kiosks. No one could have left the library without being seen.

To my left was the wall separating the California History Annex from the main library. To my right, I found the door I was searching for. The restrooms. For my reconstruction of the murder, regular restrooms wouldn't do.

Supporting my hypothesis, the library had a single restroom marked with one person wearing pants, another wearing a skirt, and a third in a wheelchair. That told me what

I needed. The unisex facility would be constructed with private stalls, a perfect place for the perpetrators to hide.

I answered Vee's question. "A rich Stony Estancia lady with two hired hands broke into the library to steal first editions for her personal collection. She'd promised her helpers the Cajon Treasure journals as their cut."

"Is this your instinct, gut, or whatever you're calling your wild imagination this morning? Are you making stuff up again? How did you get all of that from the evidence?"

"Percy told us that she was wearing expensive motorcycle leathers. The rest flowed logically."

She asked with doubt in her voice, "Is this something fabricated by your invisible friend, Fitch?"

'I get no respect. Go ahead, Zarand, and dig yourself a hole.' Fitch backed away to let me know that I was on my own.

"All me. And there's more."

She gave me an incredulous look, but her familiar smile told me I had her attention.

I continued, "Unfortunately for our rich thief, Ms. Miller had checked out the journals. They were no longer in the annex. There was nothing for the hired hands. They felt they'd been double-crossed and demanded cash. When she laughed at them saying, 'Don't be foolish. No one carries cash anymore,' they killed her and knocked over the bookshelves to cover their escape."

"So you think they climbed through those broken windows?"

"No. That's what they wanted us to think."

She moved close to me and bumped me with her hip. "Tell me, Zee, what really happened."

"They went the other way, sneaking into the library. First, they pushed the door shut to confine January. Then they hid in the nearby restroom."

I pointed to the sign with all the little people lined up. Vicki nodded to signal that she followed.

"Once inside, they hid behind the floor-to-ceiling stall doors until the library was empty."

Vicki poked her head inside to confirm the configuration of the stalls. "That sounds like we're in one of those mysteries you're always reading."

'Aren't we?' challenged Fitch.

"This is how I work. I take in the evidence and find an explanation that fits. Unless you're good at guessing, it is not much use being a detective, Hercule Poirot."

Vicki shook her head. "That's not a detective. That's a novelist, Agatha Christie."

"Okay, Vee. If you want evidence, I'll give you some."

"I'm listening."

"Remember when I told you I had a visitor this morning?"

"Was that the one that had nothing to do with Jane Doe?"

"Well, yes. My visitor was covered with lava rocks, and I just saw more lava rocks. They returned to the scene of the crime."

"Lava rocks? Pumice stones? Every other garden in Stony Estancia has lava rocks—they don't need to be watered and California is in the middle of a drought. That's as crazy as your story about the unisex restrooms. Let's talk some more when you have real evidence."

I hadn't figured out Pax Shelley's part in this story, so I had no more to say.

Wherein Zarand meets Gun Shell.

Vicki escorted me from the library. On the way out, she told Tsui, "We're finished. There shouldn't be anyone else entering the library today."

Tsui saluted her. "Got it, boss. No one will get past me."

Before she drove away, she told me, "I have a meeting with Persey this afternoon. Let's talk about the case at dinner."

"Great. How about Cocina de Cetto?"

"It's a date."

I picked up lunch from Four Rivers Szechuan Restaurant—dim sum, arriving home with an armful of containers—fried wontons, seafood salad, spare ribs, bao buns, and pork pot stickers for me along with plain shrimp dumplings for Dahl.

Vicki didn't buy my story about the lava rocks, but my intuition told me Pax wanted something from the annex. But what?

Pax was mixed up in this mystery. But how?

And who were their parents, Gunnar and Tiffany Shelley?

Dahl and I went to the internet. "Look at this. Pax's mother, Tiffany Shelley, runs All-Academic A-listers, a fancy tutoring service."

Fitch reminded me, *'Persey said that at Stony High, it always comes down to grades.'*

Dahl high-fived Fitch and rubbed against my laptop. I scratched her between her black ears, and she purred. "That was easy, wasn't it? Let's try Pax's dad." I typed GUNNAR SHELLEY into my browser. Dahl hit [ENTER] with her paw.

"Look at this, Dahl. Pax's father is Gun Shell, the best-selling author of humorous thrillers. I've read all his books." Dahl was not a big reader. She preferred cat videos and scrolled down by batting my mouse.

"Good move," I congratulated my black-and-white sleuth. "Here's his breakout novel, *Piece at Any Price*. I read that when it first came out. It was about a dysfunctional family of gun smugglers. You think it was autobiographical?"

Dahl licked her paws and rubbed her face. She was getting bored.

"Look at this," I said with enthusiasm to keep Dahl from falling asleep. "His most recent title is *Twelfth Knight*. I enjoyed that one." It was about a woman who disguised herself as a man and joined the First Crusade. One of his few books with a strong female character."

Dahl moved to a sunny windowsill and wrapped her tail around her feet in a classic I'm-an-Egyptian-Goddess pose.

I headed for the Shelley home. I wanted to learn more about Pax. As I got into my black-and-white car, Fitch said, *'I still think Pax made up that story about their mother getting thrown out the window.'*

The Shelleys lived in the exclusive Stony Estancia Haciendas, high in the hills, behind a locked gate.

'How can they afford to live up there?' asked Fitch. *'He's no Stephen King or Nora Roberts, but—'* Fitch giggled and muttered to himself, *'All-Academic A-listers might be a big money maker.'*

Part of the answer was their modest single-story home dwarfed by the McMansions surrounding it. As Pax had promised, the front window was boarded up with plywood.

I rang the doorbell and stepped back to allow the video camera to see me clearly.

"Who are you?" the speaker asked, not sounding happy to have a visitor.

I put on my best concerned-teacher face. "I'm from the high school. I'd like to talk to you about Pax."

I prepared for a tall, muscular Gun Shell to answer the door dressed in camo, with bandoliers across his chest, a machete hanging from his waist, and carrying an Uzi like the cover of *Piece at Any Price*.

When the door opened, I was facing a short guy with male-pattern baldness, clean-shaven, in a short-sleeve madras shirt, a matching bowtie, and khaki pants.

'He looks like a nerd from central casting,' said Fitch with a laugh.

He didn't invite me in, so I reached out my hand. "I'm Zarand Szilard, a teacher from Stony High. I was wondering about Pax. They slept in my garden last night. Are they alright?"

After a weak handshake, Pax's father explained. "Pax wants to save the world, help the underprivileged, and support social justice. Each week there's a different cause. Tiff and I trust them to make their own decisions—as long as they go to college. They're going to major in Anthropology or Archeology—both approved by their mother."

My detective instincts went wild. That was a long speech— sounding rehearsed. So suspicious.

'Forget Pax's clueless father. They hang out with druggies and are mixed up in Jane Doe's murder,' Fitch asserted.

I didn't agree with Fitch. I was sure Mr. Shelley was hiding something. He gave me a good story, but I expected as much from a writer.

When I didn't respond, he crossed his arms. "Who are you? I see an old guy. Gray beard. No badge. No uniform. What's it to you?"

Now, I was positive he was hiding something.

"As I said, I'm a teacher."

"Zarand. Do you mind if I call you Zarand?"

'Typical power move. No Mr. Szilard for you.'

Fitch was right, but I let Gun Shell get away with it.

He looked at his watch. "If you're a teacher, what are you doing here while school is in session?"

'Busted,' said Fitch with a laugh.

I looked directly into his eyes. "Just trying to help. I'm a substitute—not working today."

His face relaxed. "Something's not right here. Come on in and we can clear this up."

The humble house had a central hallway going from the front door to the backyard. I wasn't surprised to see it lined with bookcases.

Fitch agreed. *'Looks like a writer and an educator live here.'*

Mr. Shelley led me through the French doors to the left, a formal room. with a coffered ceiling and a cut-glass chandelier. Floor-to-ceiling cream-colored drapes balanced the burgundy walls. Instead of paintings, the room was decorated with antique weapons. I recognized a Civil War muzzleloader and an assortment of maces. A suit of armor stood in the corner.

We were fencers, each trying to extract as much information as we could without giving any in return.

He pointed to an upholstered chair, too big for the tiny room. "You can sit here. Would you like some tea? Why do you think Pax slept in your garden? That's not like him."

I took my seat, sank into the cushion, and deflected his question. "Thank you. I would fancy a spot of tea. Do you know where he sleeps when he doesn't come home?"

He left the room without responding but soon returned with a silver tray holding a porcelain tea set and a plate of cookies. "I discovered this Lapsang Souchong tea in an open-air market on the banks of the Li River. If I recall, that was my book tour for the Mandarin translation of *Sing Song Swords*."

I sipped the amber liquid with my pinky extended and *advanced* with a silent *en garde*. "It's best to speak to both parents together. Is your wife home?"

I dipped a cookie in my tea while he *parried*. "No. she's a tutor. She's at the city library researching a 19th-century author, Elizabeth Gaskell, a contemporary of Dickens."

I took another cookie, a chocolate-covered one this time. I pointed to the plywood patch covering the front window and *lunged*. "What happened?"

Without a pause, he *parried* again. "You won't believe this. We had a bookcase over there and it tipped over."

'*He's right. I don't believe him. No one in California puts a bookcase in front of a window.*'

"Wow! That's what happened at the school," I *feinted*.

He *engaged*. "Really? I hadn't heard about that."

I watched his face as I recounted the annex ribbon cutting and the bookshelves collapsing without mentioning Jane Doe. He tried to show surprise, but his mouth and eyes opened too wide. I didn't believe him.

I *scored my touch* when he responded, "My child had nothing to do with the death of that woman."

'Got him,' cheered Fitch.

His charade of ignorance was over. I hadn't mentioned Jane Doe, but Mr. *'I hadn't heard about that'* knew all about her. I'd learned everything I hoped for from the author Gun Shell. I declared our *bout in my favor* without letting him know that I'd seen through his act.

He picked up the silver tray. "I should get back to my writing. I haven't written my thousand words today."

I stood up and reached for one more cookie. "These are delicious."

"Yes. My U.K. publisher sends them to me from Harlesden, where the company has been baking these digestive biscuits for over a century."

"Right. Biscuits. They are a treat." I took a couple more and put them in my pocket. "For later," I explained.

I found it hard to see this short guy with male-pattern baldness tossing his wife through the window. On the other hand, a California bookcase not attached to the wall was more incredible. I believed Pax's version of the front window.

'You haven't put the pieces together,' taunted Fitch.

I made one more *advance*. "You said your wife was at the city library. How sure are you I'll find her there if I go check?"

He easily *parried* me. "Not very. If she's not there, she could be anywhere. She does a lot of tutoring at the homes of her students."

"Thank you for the biscuits."

He led me to the door.

I had a double mystery. What roles did Pax—visiting the crime scene the night after—and Gun Shell—lying about his broken window and not being forthcoming about the whereabouts of his wife—play in the death of Jane Doe? With all these questions, I was sure that the Shelleys were involved with Jane Doe's murder.

Fitch wasn't convinced. *'But how?'*

Mr. Shelley murdered Jane Doe and Mrs. Shelley was his accomplice.

'How does that explain Pax returning to the crime scene?'

Pax felt guilty. They were trying to appease their parents. That fits the pattern of a dysfunctional family, doesn't it?
Fitch thought for a minute. *'Maybe.'*

On the way to my tiny car, Vicki called. "Are we still on for dinner?"

"Absolutely, Vee. Cocina de Cetto."

"I'll have some important news," she said.

"I can't wait. Can you tell me now?"

'Sorry, Zee. You'll have to wait. I'll tell all at dinner."

Wherein Zarand has a carnitas burrito supreme.

I looked around Cocina de Cetto but didn't see Vicki. While I waited, I walked up to the window to order a couple of Carta Blanca beers and a basket of homemade tortilla chips with mild salsa verde for me and spicy salsa roja for her.

"Evenin' Zee." Vicki pointed to the second beer and the spicy salsa roja. "Are those for me?"

I pushed the mug in her direction.

"Sorry, I'm late. I was waiting for some lab results."

"No problem. Shall I order our food?" I started to stand.

She was already up and headed for the order window. "My turn. You want carnitas burrito supreme with everything except jalapeños, right?"

I shouted to her, "*Gracias.*"

While we waited for our food, I fished for her promised news. "Have you heard anything from Persey?"

She helped herself to chips and sipped her beer before answering. "Yes, she said blunt force trauma was not the cause of death. The head wound was not lethal."

"So, did she find the actual cause?"

"No. She had some theories. Jane Doe was a victim of domestic violence, but Persey couldn't connect it to the murder."

"Did she find any ID? Time of death? What about fingerprints?"

"Calm down. One thing at a time." She dipped a chip into her spicy salsa. "These are the best. Fresh out of the fryer." After a few more chips, she continued, "Jane Doe's fingerprints are not on file. Persey will pursue DNA and dental records, but for the moment, Jane Doe is a mystery."

I frowned. "January saw the bookcases fall over. I assume that matches the time of death Persey found."

"Maybe. Persey said that Jane Doe was warm enough for the death to be recent, but she wants to nail down the cause before giving us a precise time."

Vicki moved on to the other suspects. "We still need to find those two people January saw at the scene."

'Do you still think they were Mr. and Mrs. Shelley?' questioned Fitch.

I see no reason to change my mind.

Jorge brought us our food. "*Hola*, Mr. S. Any news about #BODYINTHELIBRARY?"

Vicki recognized him. "You're George from *Stony Estancia Surfs*," she said with a big smile.

"Yes. That's me," he responded. "My fifteen minutes of fame."

As Jorge walked away, Vicki whispered, "Did you notice his pendant? Is that a fad at the high school, wearing pendants from the hardware store?"

"You might say that. The boys are wearing chunky hex nuts and the girls more delicate washers."

Vicki unwrapped her tamale. "When did you start noticing this?"

"I don't know. It's been a while."

She ate a forkful of corn masa and spicy meat filling before saying, "Wild guess here. All the washers are the same size, and they match the ones Tsui collected as evidence."

"That sounds right. Why did Tsui take Alyce's necklace?"

Vicki had a smug smile. "Forensics determined that her necklace used the missing hardware from the annex."

"Can you tell one box of washers from another?"

"Certainly, Zee. Forensics has progressed since you retired. Optical Emission Spectrometry. X-Ray Fluorescence."

'That's one mystery solved.'

I took a big bite of my burrito, dripping guacamole and sour cream onto my plate. "Cocina de Cetto has the best carnitas."

"But not good for you. That exquisite taste comes from frying the pork in *manteca*—lard."

"It may be bad for the heart, but it's good for the soul." I sopped up the spilled sauces and took another bite.

'What was the missing hardware doing on the football field?' Fitch wondered.

"More beer?" Vicki asked.

I jumped up. "I'll get it."

When I returned, I said, "Let me tell you about my visitor this morning."

"The one that has nothing to do with Jane Doe?"

"That one, Vee. Except, now I think my visitor is mixed up in this mystery."

She leaned back in her chair and sipped on her beer. "I'm all ears, as long as this isn't another of your crazy guesses."

"My visitor was Pax and they were covered with pumice stone from sleeping in the Higgs Haven gardens."

Vicki favored me with a big grin. "Even if this is a guess, I have forensics to back you up."

"Really? It must be my turn to listen."

"City Attorney Blake issued search warrants for Pax's vehicle and Higgs Haven. Tsui collected pumice stones from Pax's SUV, the Higgs Haven gardens, and the annex. They are identical."

"How can you tell?"

She proudly continued. "That's why I was late. I waited for the spectrometry results. Every source of lava rocks has different levels of silicon, aluminum, iron, and trace elements—like a fingerprint. All those samples came from the same quarry. We have placed Pax in the annex."

I was impressed. The Stony PD was more sophisticated than I gave them credit for. "What is your next step?"

Before Vicki could respond, my phone sounded the opening riff of Chuck Berry's *School Days*—my ringtone for the substitute notification system. After a few quick taps, I had the assignment to cover Dr. Chandrasekhar's physics class.

This was the perfect opportunity to question my honorary grandkids. "I am going to be at the high school tomorrow. I'll question Pax and let you know what I learn."

"I don't know, Zee." She ate more of her tamale. "This is a murder. My officers politely questioned those kids and learned nothing. It's time to show them who's in charge."

'This can't be good,' said Fitch.

I told Fitch not to worry, but just to be safe, I advised Vicki, "Listen, Vee, you need the cooperation of Stony High. If I were you, I'd be looking for ways to win them to my side. Treating Pax with kid gloves will pay off later. Don't do something you'll regret."

Wherein Zarand warns Pax.

Fitch woke me in the middle of the night. *'What do you think Vicki has planned?'*

Let me sleep. I'm sure Vicki won't do anything rash.

"Good mornin', Mr. Sendak. I'm here for Chandra today."

"Yes, physics. Nice to have you back." The substitute administrator straightened out his paisley scarf before he handed me my badge and the folder with Dr. Chandrasekhar's class schedule and attendance lists.

"I love your psychedelic cravat."

He adjusted it again. "Well, thank you for noticing. It's vintage. I found it at a charity shop in Camden Town during my last trip to England."

"Nice. Any news from the police this morning?"

"Just a couple of officers guarding that fabulous yellow tape around the library."

Fitch expressed relief. *'I was afraid Vicki would show up in force.'*

"That's good news, Jared. I'm off to the science building."

"Toodles."

Vicki had taken my advice and only posted a minimal police presence on campus. As my quid pro quo, I'd observe Pax with an open mind. I was uncomfortable considering them as a suspect, but I forced myself.

On my way across the courtyard, I threaded a trail through teens intent on not going to their classes until the last moment. I passed the library to the left and the Bruin Bistro to the right. I stopped when I saw Pax sitting in the mottled shadow of a pepper tree, in camo pants and a black hoodie with a NASA logo.

"Mornin' Mr. S."

I sat down next to them. "Mornin' Pax. Would you care for some breakfast?"

"What do you have?"

I held open my backpack and he helped himself to a canned latte and a warm breakfast muffin. While he ate, I asked, "Did you sleep in your car again last night?"

"No. I slept at home. Why did you talk to Father?"

"I was concerned about you."

Fitch wondered, *'Are they acting guilty? Do they look nervous? Do they seem defensive?'*

Pax fidgeted with the straps on their backpack. They looked at me expectantly, wanting me to say something more about my meeting with Mr. Shelley. I waited them out until they asked, "Were you satisfied with Dad's answers?"

That was a strange question. I found it suspicious that Pax jumped to the conclusion that I was interrogating Mr. Shelley.

I replied simply, "We had a good chat."

Pax pursed his lips and changed the subject. "Who are you here for?"

I almost said, "I'm not here to arrest you."

Fitch cleared up my misunderstanding. *'He wants to know who you are substituting for.'*

"Dr. Chandrasekhar."

"Well, I'll see you soon. I have him for homeroom."

I watched Pax to see their reaction when I warned them, "The cops know that you were in the library annex Tuesday night."

Pax froze. They didn't move, or breathe, or blink. Finally, they crossed their arms in front of them and made tight fists. Their knuckles turned white. "So?"

'Absolutely suspicious,' said Fitch.

"What were you doing there?" I asked.

They didn't get a chance to reply because the courtyard went quiet. I looked around to find the cause. I saw a black-and-white police car at each school entrance. Officers got out.

Fitch grinned at me. *'Vicki didn't take your advice.'*

School was starting, and the courtyard was crowded. I couldn't believe she was taking this heavy-handed approach. At any other school, there would have been rioting, but at Stony Estancia, they treated this like a party. The students took selfies with the cops.

"This is crazy. What are they doing at Stony High?" Pax got nervous and spoke faster. "Do you think we have an active shooter? We've had so many drills. Do you think this is the real thing?"

I gave him my best answer. "I don't know."

The police presence united the Stony Estancia students. The diverse population of athletes, geeks and nerds, and ethnic and racial cliques, transformed into a homogeneous community. Everyone took out their phone to record whatever was going down.

A phalanx of uniformed officers moved through the crowd. They stopped at each circle of kids, comparing them to a picture on their phones—Pax's androgynous face with their rainbow hair and eyebrow piercing. The students made a game of mugging for the cops with big smiles and funny expressions.

Pax pulled their hoodie over their rainbow hair and headed for the science building.

'Follow them. Make sure they don't escape.'

I considered Fitch's advice until I heard a commotion behind me and turned around to see the trouble at the main gate.

"This is a public school," shouted Leticia from *Stony Estancia Surfs*, flashing her homemade press card.

César pointed his camera past the gate guards. "If there are police on campus, you need to let us in," he explained to the puzzled officers.

"No. You can't be here," Detective Yukawa said as she approached the reporters.

"*Sí, se puede,*" responded César. "Yes, we can."

The search for Pax stopped. The students and the cops directed their attention to the confrontation between the press and law enforcement.

The argument might have gone on for a while had Principal Golding not appeared—her low heels clacking on the pavement. Her long white braid swung left and right. "We have children to educate, and I won't have you disturbing my school. The buzzer will sound soon, and I want you all gone."

I saw a smirk on César's face.

Fitch was giggling, entertained by the conflict.

Vicki held her ground. "We are investigating a murder. A murder in *your* library. That takes precedence."

'Go girl. You tell her,' Fitch cheered.

"No, it doesn't," said Mrs. Golding.

'Looks like a stand-off,' said Fitch with a smile.

The principal handed her cell phone to Vicki. "Mr. Blake wants to speak to you."

'Trouble,' said Fitch, *'That's the city attorney. He never sides with the cops.'*

After speaking to Mr. Blake, Vicki frowned and signaled her people to retreat, the buzzer sounded, and the students headed for homeroom.

Vicki stayed and spoke with Principal Golding. After a short while, the two ladies walked together to the administration building demonstrating that Vicki could rebound from setbacks and build bridges—skills that would see her as Chief of Detectives someday.

'What are they plotting?' pondered Fitch.

I wrote MR. S. on the whiteboard. Dr. Chandrasekhar's homeroom didn't give me a chance to take attendance. They had so many questions.

"What were the police doing here?

"Why did they leave?"

"Is this about #BODYINTHELIBRARY?"

Chandra taught physics, so he had a tuning fork instead of a bell to get the class's attention. I hit the fork with a black silicone mallet. The room filled with A above middle C and some students vocalized in harmony. Like magic, an A-Major chord ended all discussion.

"If I can get roll taken before the buzzer, I'll tell you what I know."

Pax stood up and counted the students. "No need to take attendance. We have the correct number of people. Just sign the form and tell us why the police are here."

'Guilty! Guilty! Pax is guilty,' said Fitch

Following Pax's lead, they bombarded me with another round of questions about #BODYINTHELIBRARY.

'You're backed into a corner,' said Fitch with a laugh.

"The police thought that if they showed up in force, someone would panic and run. The runner would be their best suspect."

'And that worked. Pax made themselves scarce,' Fitch reminded me.

While that sank in, I waited for the buzzer to end homeroom. Instead of the buzzer, the discordant clanging of the wall phone interrupted the class. I picked up the old-fashioned handset attached to a coiled cord. "Mr. Szilard, substitute teacher."

Principal Golding said, "Senior Detective Yukawa wants to speak to Pax Shelley. Can you send them to the office?"

"No problem," I replied.

"Pax, can I speak with you?"

"Whassup, Mr. S?"

"That was Mrs. Golding. She'd like you to go to the office to meet with Senior Detective Yukawa."

"On my way," they said.

I watched Pax leave the room, uncertain about their part in #BODYINTHELIBRARY. Perhaps Vicki would have better luck when she spoke to them.

Wherein Zarand goes to lunch.

Pax had answered Mrs. Golding's summons to be interrogated by Vicki. I wanted to attend that meeting. A solitary student facing two adults wasn't fair.

Fitch pointed out, *'Except you weren't invited and you have a physics class to teach.'*

That's beside the point. Pax needs support. They should have a parent with them.

'Sorry. I checked Pax's records. They are eighteen—adult.'

Then they need a lawyer.

The buzzer sounded. Dr. Chandrasekhar's homeroom students headed out, while I wrote on the whiteboard, FINISH YOUR LAB REPORT. ALL DONE? SILENT READING. NOT ENOUGH TIME? FINISH IT AT HOME.

First-period physics students filed into Chandra's room.

"Sub today."

"Yo, Mr. S."

"Lab reports."

Soon each black table had two or three students working together. I didn't have to lecture and was free to question the students about Jane Doe.

'Perfect. Vicki will interview Pax. You have all these others. You can compare notes later,' Fitch said.

Ranch sat alone, listless, and taking shallow breaths. Jane Doe could wait. I knelt to meet him at his level. "Where's your lab partner?"

He showed me his phone. **PAX (THEY, THEM)**: NO PHYSICS TODAY. TTYL

'You're not the only one thinking about Pax,' Fitch said.

Ranch frowned, took out his book, *Alan Turing: The Enigma* by Andrew Hodges, and began reading.

"Did you finish your lab report?" I asked.

"No. I need Pax's notes."

I gave him an upbeat reply. Cheerier than I felt. "Not a problem. They're in the office meeting with Mrs. Golding. Go speak to Mr. Sendak. He'll get the notes from the principal's office for you." I saw no reason to mention Vicki.

Ranch shuffled his feet as he left on his quest.

'What a strange day. You've sent two students to the office. I hope they return,' Fitch said.

For the rest of the period, I forgot about Jane Doe and watched the clock. Where was Ranch? How was Pax getting on with Vicki and Principal Golding?

Ranch burst into the room. "Mr. S! Mr. S! Pax is missing." When everyone looked at him, he lowered his voice. "Mr. Sendak said he hadn't seen Pax and didn't want to interrupt Mrs. Golding who was meeting with someone from the police."

I inquired sotto voce, "Then, what took you so long to get back here?"

"I searched for them. I scouted out the library and the football bleachers—their favorite places to go when they want to be alone. Now, I'm worried."

I reassured the class, "I'm sure Pax is okay," but I was also anxious.

The students in the second period had already heard about Pax's disappearance and didn't want to talk about Jane Doe. The table with January, Jorge, and Lizzy discussed the upcoming senior trip while they worked on their lab reports.

January signed AIRPLANE. She waved her thumb, index finger, and pinky in the air.

"What do you want to see on the senior trip?" Jorge questioned.

Lizzy flipped her long green hair. "I want to visit the Library of Congress. They have an exhibition: Women authors since 1776." She thought for a moment. "And all the art museums."

January finger-spelled, "Helen Keller University."

"I'm going to the National Museum of the American Latino," Jorge said.

By third period, the news about Pax was posted on *Stony Estancia Surfs*. I was concerned, as were the students.

Alyce said to Zola, "Did you hear? Pax ditched school."

Zola, a refugee from South Africa, replied, "*Eish*, not possible. They would never do that. They're a good student—college bound."

Alyce countered, "No one has seen them since homeroom."

"That's not good. Did you see all those cops earlier? This reminds me of living in Joburg and *apartheid*—where people disappeared."

I had questions for them, so when the buzzer sounded, I said, "Excuse me, ladies, can I invite you to lunch?"

Zola ran her fingers through her short natural hair and asked, "You going to walk us through the line in the Bruin Bistro or are we going to get waited on in the faculty dining room?"

"I always like real plates and cutlery—and linen napkins. Good for the environment," added Alyce referring to the upscale service offered to the teachers and their guests.

"Faculty dining room it is. My treat."

Jorge came over with a napkin hanging over his arm. "Ladies, Mr. S., what can I get you?"

Alyce pointed to the menu and read with a Monty Python accent. "Organic beef burger with farm-to-table toppings on a tangy sourdough bun."

I ordered the Caesar salad with extra anchovies, saving room for dessert.

"*Ag* shame, I'll have the mac and cheese even though I'd prefer a hearty bobotie with dried apricots on top like I used to get from the street vendors in Joburg," said Zola.

"Good on you. If I was yearning for a taste of home, I'd go for a Cornish pasty from a corner shop in Adelaide," responded Alyce.

When Jorge left, Zola said, "To be fair, the Bistro mac and cheese is *lekker*."

Our food came from the steam tables in the Bruin Bistro without delay. We ate in silence, a habit that accommodated our short lunch breaks.

I put my silverware in my empty salad bowl and folded my napkin. "What have you heard about Pax?"

Alyce leaned over the table and lowered her voice. "Pax is in Ms. Miller's class with me, but they weren't there."

Zola also whispered, "I saw them in the courtyard this morning."

Alyce agreed, "*Crikey*. That's right. Pax was talking to Mr. S."

They both turned to me.

'Fess up,' admonished Fitch.

"That's right. I spoke to them in the courtyard and had Pax for homeroom, but that was the last I saw of them. Have you heard anything?"

Jorge must have overheard because he joined us. "Just between us, Mr. Mbacke told me he saw Pax drive away in their SUV."

"When was that?" I asked.

"A short while ago. He was taking the organic waste out for collection. He saw a police officer follow Pax's SUV, but he returned alone."

Alyce laughed, "Good on Pax. They lost the coppers."

I wondered, "Was Mr. Mbacke seen?"

"Of course not. Nothing like wearing a custodian's uniform and carrying trash to make someone invisible," Zola said.

'Good news. Pax got away. Vicki didn't lock them up,' cheered Fitch—now on the side of the students.

Someone cleared their throat and said, "Excuse me."

We turned to see Vicki at the entrance to the faculty dining room.

She repeated, "Excuse me," before saying, "I'm Senior Detective Yukawa looking for Pax Shelley."

The room went silent. The faculty guests, including Zola and Alyce, exited through the partition that divided the student and faculty dining areas. The faculty all asked for their checks.

Fitch chortled, *'Clearly no one wants to talk about Pax.'*

I was the one friendly face in the room. Vicki came over and sat in the chair vacated by Zola.

"Welcome Vee." I gave her a big smile to make amends for her chilly reception. "Would you like something to eat? The mac and cheese is to die for."

She watched the room empty. "I'm not making much progress here."

I was still working on the food-therapy angle. "The burgers with farm-to-table toppings are also good."

She took a long breath and leaned close to me. "Zee, I'm frustrated. I wasted my morning in Mrs. Golding's office. The old biddy went on about how wonderful the Stony High students were, but Pax Shelley never arrived."

"Vee, I don't know what happened. I got the call from Principal Golding and sent Pax to the office. The last time I saw them they were headed there."

"Well, they never showed." She paused as if she expected me to say something before adding, "Tsui pursued their SUV but lost them. Pax is gone."

"Right. I heard that from the students."

She smiled. "I remember. You're buddy-buddy with these kids." She pointed to the three settings at the table. "You had two guests for lunch today. What did you hear?"

"I don't feel comfortable repeating what they told me in confidence."

Her shoulders slumped. "Zee, I know you're overflowing with empathy, but I can't believe you cast your lot with these teens. This is a murder investigation."

"They're my grandkids."

She looked around the faculty dining room—tablecloths, a bud vase and fresh flowers on each table, and menus in leather portfolios. Jorge came over with a white linen napkin over his arm. "Good day, Senior Detective Yukawa. What can I get for you?"

'Stony High is working its charm on her,' said Fitch as her expression softened.

"Do you have lattes?" she asked in a gentle voice.

"Of course. Non-fat, whole milk, one percent, two percent, heavy cream, oat milk, or soy milk? I apologize that we're out of goat's milk today."

"Regular milk, thanks."

She turned to me and said, "Let's work together, meet halfway."

"Halfway, Vee," I repeated her word to signal agreement. "Even more than halfway. At the end of the day, you're the lead investigating officer."

"We can make that work. I'm sure we can."

"As a start..." I began, feeling close to Vicki. "I shouldn't have warned Pax that you were going to arrest them. I expect that's why they didn't show up."

"I wanted to question Pax. They are a person of interest, not a suspect."

She looked at me with her dark brown eyes. They blended in with her pupils. I found them enchanting. She blinked once and demanded, "Where are they?"

"I don't know."

Then my phone beeped.

I showed Vicki the text.

PAX (THEY, THEM): I CAN'T BE A FUGITIVE. I NEED ADVICE. DINNER AT YOUR PLACE TONIGHT?

Fitch gloated, *'A benefit of befriending the students.'*

Vicki nodded. "Do it, Zee."

I put my arm around her waist. "Will you join us?"

She bumped me with her hip. "Sounds great."

I thought: *I'm going to ask Pax, what were you doing in the history annex last night?*

'Not with a text. Wait until you're face-to-face. After dinner.'

I messaged back: **SZILARD**: KK [SMILEY FACE] [YUM YUM FACE].

'Dinner with Pax. Perfect,' said Fitch with uncharacteristic optimism.

Wherein Zarand learns about the Salem witch trials.

"What are you planning to cook for Pax?" Vicki asked while we explored the aisles of FFF—Factory and Farm Foods

I stopped at the fresh fish counter. "Can I see some of those farm-raised trout?"

The man behind the counter wearing a white coat and red toque said, "Sure, Mr. S.," as he piled several fish on a piece of shiny white paper. "Very fresh. Look at those clear eyes and the metallic sheen of the skin."

"They look good, but I need to smell them," I replied.

He wafted their odor in my direction.

I closed my eyes. "What a heavenly scent, like fishing on Big Bear Lake. I'll take them all."

While he wrapped the fish, Vicki asked, "Isn't that a lot?"

"Yes, but they're super fresh. Whatever I don't use can go into my deep freeze. Whatever I don't eat, Dahl will enjoy."

When we reached the fruits and veggies, Vicki suggested, "Maybe you should have a vegetarian option."

Fitch smirked, remembering that she wasn't fond of fish. *'I bet she had it too often growing up in Little Tokyo.'*

"Good point," I said while selecting several deep purple eggplants, which FFF had labeled as AUBERGINES, along with mozzarella and parmesan cheese.

"I love your eggplant parmesan with all its cheesy goodness, but what if Pax is vegan or lactose-intolerant?"

'Now she's pulling your leg,' said Fitch with a smile.

"Another good point. How does a…" I looked around for a vegan inspiration. "…zucchini risotto sound?"

"Yummy," she said rubbing her belly with a smile.

I placed Italian risotto rice and zucchinis, which FFF had labeled as COURGETTES, in my cart. Whatever Pax didn't eat, I'd have for another day. Nothing would be wasted

I whispered, "I enjoy meal planning with you," and gave her a quick peck on the cheek. When she returned my gesture, I ventured, "Why don't I move in with you? Your house has lots of spare bedrooms."

She pushed our cart to the checkout line and challenged me. "How long have we been together?"

I wasn't sure of the number. I went with, "Too many years to count."

'Nice save,' applauded Fitch.

She let me get away with that. "Right, and what's our secret?"

"Two cops? My cooking? True love?"

"Not close," she said with a wink.

"Come on, Zarand. You've had this discussion many times,' chided Fitch.

"I know. We never get married."

"Close. The secret is separate houses."

"After all these years..." I let my voice trail off before starting again. "Do you think we'll ever get married?"

She gave me an air kiss. "Never say never."

I parked my tiny car in the garage and plugged it in. Vicki left hers in the visitor's space and helped me carry the groceries upstairs.

"Hey, Dahl. I'm home." I set my reusable shopping bags on the floor.

My tuxedo cat stood up, stretched, and greeted me with a yawn. She strutted to her dish to let me know that it was dinner time. I opened a can of cat food, but by then she had discovered the trout and was rubbing against the package.

"That's for my dinner guests. You have your food."

She gave me a doleful meow and continued to love against the fish in between visits to her bowl of canned dinner.

I sliced the eggplant, grated the cheese, and layered it all into a baking dish with San Marzano tomatoes, extra virgin olive oil, and my recipe of spices. My secret ingredient was white wine vinegar adding enough acidity to cut through the heavy richness. I set it to bake in the oven. I prepared the risotto and let it simmer on the stovetop, while I pan-fried the trout.

I checked the time. "Pax should be here soon."

My phone sounded. I tapped ACCEPT, expecting something from Pax, but it was the substitute notification system. After a few more taps, I was assigned to cover Dr. Chandrasekhar's class again.

"The eggplant and the risotto smell great. I'm getting hungry. Where's Pax?" Vicki said.

I sent Pax a text, **SZILARD**: WHAT'S YOUR ETA? [YUM YUM FACE].

Bing. Bing. The timer went off. Dinner was ready.

I took the eggplant from the oven and placed the glass baking dish on a redwood trivet. I scooped the risotto into a serving bowl and left the trout to stay warm in my cast iron skillet. "Let's eat. I bet they'll be here before the food gets cold."

Vicki set the table, including a place for Pax.

"This risotto is excellent. What's your secret?"

"Chopped scallions and the best olive oil. Wouldn't you like dinners like this every night?"

Vicki ignored my question. "The eggplant is also good. I don't know which one is my favorite."

Fitch giggled. *'I called it. No fish for her.'*

I checked the fridge. "I have apple pie and vanilla ice cream for dessert."

She laughed. "Apple pie is my favorite."

My phone beeped. "That must be Pax."

I showed Vicki a red NOT DELIVERED. It wasn't Pax because he hadn't received my text.

"Not surprised," she said. "They ghosted you. What's their phone number? Even if it's turned off, I can find the last cell tower it connected with."

I gave her the number and she called it in.

'Pauli Falls,' whispered Fitch.

"Pauli Falls trailhead," said Vicki.

'Called it,' chuckled Fitch.

I wasn't surprised. "That's where my smart grandkids go," I said with pride. "The San Gabriel Mountains provide them sanctuary—beyond cell coverage, electronic tracking, and parental supervision."

"I hope you're right. If Pax is in the mountains, they'll get hungry or cold and return soon. Stony High kids aren't survivalists."

We had our apple pie without seeing Pax.

Vicki asked, "Can I help you clean up?"

"No need. Dahl and I can handle it. I'm still expecting Pax. They slept on the ground once this week and won't do it again. They prefer high-thread-count sheets to rocks."

"I hope you're right. Call me when they arrive. No matter the time."

"Will do. I'm a substitute teacher tomorrow. I'll get my grandkids to tell me what they know."

She headed down the stairs. "Let's debrief over dinner again tomorrow. You have plenty of leftovers, so you won't need to cook."

"I don't like to eat the same thing two days in a row. How about Szechuan?"

"Great. Four Rivers," Vicki said as she left.

I left the food on the table for Pax, still expecting them.

My phone chimed. The video doorbell app. Pax. They'd arrived. Food always worked with teenagers.

'Guess again,' said Fitch with a laugh.

I opened the app and it showed me Persey, the county coroner, dressed in her customary black. I unlocked the door with the app and shouted down the stairs, "Welcome. Let me guess. You worked late and forgot to take something out for dinner."

She laughed, "You got it in one," and came up the stairs with Cerberus, her chocolate lab.

Dahl issued a questioning meow as if to ask, "What are they doing here so late?"

Cerberus stretched his front legs forward bringing him down to Dahl's level. Dahl arched her back and hissed.

Persey stroked Dahl's fuzzy body. "He wants to play with you."

Dahl looked at me wondering what we were doing with visitors when it was time for sleep. She turned around and retired to the bedroom.

"It's been a long day. That eggplant parmesan smells tasty. Can I get some of that?"

I sat her at Pax's place and served the eggplant. While she ate, Cerberus curled up under the table waiting for something to drop.

"I've got a body in my morgue. Do you and Vicki have a suspect?"

"Have you identified your guest?" I countered.

"No. There is no record of her fingerprints or DNA—whoever she is, she hasn't crossed paths with the law or needed a professional license. I released a morgue photo of Jane Doe to *Stony Estancia Surfs* to see if someone in the community will recognize her."

"That's a good idea. I suspect she's a resident. Vicki said you didn't have a cause of death either."

In between bites of eggplant, Persey explained. "My preliminary cause of death was traumatic asphyxia."

"What's that?"

"It's not common. You might have heard of the Salem witch trials."

"Seriously? Centuries ago?"

"Yes. In 1692, Giles Corey was executed by piling rocks on his chest until he couldn't breathe. Traumatic asphyxia."

"Ah. That makes sense. Jane Doe was trapped under all those bookcases."

"Not the answer. Not enough weight. I'm still researching other causes. I mention it because of the historical curiosity."

"I'm at school tomorrow. The students will know who she is."

'You place too much faith in those kids,' rebuked Fitch.

"Good. Cause of death might take some time. I need Jane Doe's identity. Her medical history will help me determine what killed her," said Persey.

'Persey's not telling us everything. Coroners never do.'

I encouraged her to share her thoughts. "You've seen a lot of cases—you must have suspicions."

Persey looked around as if checking that we were alone. Dahl took the hint and shut the bedroom door with a farewell hiss. I closed the curtains.

Persey leaned close to me and whispered. "Jane Doe led a violent life. She had a surprising number of fractured bones."

"Are they the cause of death?"

"No. Absolutely not, but—" She looked around again. "Cases like hers are my highest priority. Jane Doe was a victim of domestic abuse. I don't have all the evidence, but I will find it."

Fitch rubbed his hands together and hunched his shoulders. *'Mysteries within mysteries. Do you still suspect the Shelleys?'*

Yes. Domestic abuse is just a red herring.

'Clever,' said Fitch with an evil grin.

15. Finger Spelling – Friday AM

Wherein Zarand directs a movie.

My sleep was disturbed by nightmares of Jane Doe's fractured bones. I had seen too many cases of domestic abuse during my years in the big city.

'And the perpetrators weren't always men,' Fitch reminded me.

Two double-shot lattes woke me up and I was soon in Dr. Chandrasekhar's room.

I picked up a physics textbook from the stack on January's table, held it at eye level, and let go. *Thud.*

I said, "Today we're going to collect data for a conservation of energy experiment." I picked up the book and dropped it again. *Thud.*

All the chitchat stopped. I silently thanked Chandra for this lesson plan.

Fitch concurred. *'Aren't you glad you don't have to watch the same movie over and over until you've memorized it and can't stay awake?'*

When I picked up the book for the third time, I had everyone's attention. "What kind of energy does this book have when I hold it up?"

Lizzy, her hair blue today, wore a T-shirt with a black-and-white image of Helen Reddy. She said, "Potential energy. It has the promise of energy but nothing yet."

"What's going to happen when I let go?"

This time Jorge answered, "That promise—" He smiled at Lizzy. "—will be realized, fast as a speeding textbook. Kinetic energy."

I dropped the book again. *Thud.* "For today's experiment, you'll take slow-motion videos with your phones. When Mr. C. returns, you'll use the logging app to analyze those videos."

I didn't know how slow-motion worked and Mr. C. hadn't left any instructions. With a silent prayer, I checked with the class, "Do you know how to do this?"

"*D'oh,*" "Doesn't everyone?" and "Easy peasy," were the responses.

Fitch laughed, *'You're a digital dinosaur.'*

January raised her hand, "What should we drop?"

I checked the lesson plan, but it wasn't any help.

I improvised. "Anything you like."

Fitch laughed, *'Now you did it.'*

I quickly added, "Nothing breakable— Or explosive— Or dangerous."

They happily dropped stuff while taking videos. Objects as small as keys and pens and as large as backpacks and shoes.

When they finished capturing video, I announced, "We're close to the buzzer. Please clean up the room."

While they put everything away, I asked Jorge, "Did you see the picture of Jane Doe on *Stony Estancia Surfs*?"

He said, "*Si*. Yes," without looking up.

"Did you recognize it?"

'He won't talk to you,' predicted Fitch.

I waited for him to say more but he concentrated on dropping a few more coins while his lab partner captured the video.

Fitch gave me an I-told-you-so look.

I pressed Jorge for an answer. "Why won't you help?"

He looked me straight in the eye. "I don't cooperate with *La Migra*, I have nothing to say."

He was one of the few at Stony High that had experience with law enforcement, and it wasn't good. I left him to his physics experiment and moved to Lizzy. "Did you see the murdered woman posted on *Stony Estancia Surfs*?"

"Yeah. I saw her."

"Did you recognize the lady?"

"Of course. Everyone knows her," she said in a sarcastic voice.

'Everyone? Is that possible? All the teens and no one in law enforcement?' Fitch answered his questions with a disbelieving tone. *'Teenage hyperbole.'*

I disregarded Lizzy's attitude. "That's great. Who is she?"

"We're not helping the po-po."

Another refusal. I couldn't find Jane Doe's killer until I had some identification.

I hit Dr. C's tuning fork. "Someone was murdered in your library this week. The police need help identifying the victim. Who was she?"

The class looked at each other. Several students shook their heads no. Others pursed their lips to signal that they had nothing to say.

I tried again. "No one is safe until we apprehend the killer."

Lizzy snapped back, "Those scare tactics won't work with us."

I took a wild guess. "That lady was your friend. Help me find her attacker."

Several students looked uncomfortable.

'Good one, Szilard. They know Jane Doe and like her.'

Jorge stood up. "Forget it. We don't work with *La Migra*."

Fitch sneered, *'These privileged Stony Estancia kids have never heard of La Migra—Mexican slang for U.S. Immigration and Border Patrol.'*

Right.

The class got the message to shut up and I faced a room full of sullen faces.

I took another tack. "This happened at your school. You want that trespasser to be punished. I won't share anything you tell me with the Stony PD."

Lizzy stood up again. "Your girlfriend is the po-po. We don't trust you."

'Small town,' Fitch laughed.

Before I could make another plea, the buzzer sounded, and the class rushed for the door.

The last person to leave was January.

On her way out, she finger-spelled, Pax. Then she touched her thumb to her chin and waggled her fingers. She signed, MOTHER. Pax's mother. Jane Doe was Tiffany Shelley, proprietor of All-Academic A-listers.

Mrs. Shelley didn't murder Jane Doe because Jane Doe was Mrs. Shelley. But why would anyone kill a tutor?

Fitch reminded me, *'Persey said that at Stony High, it always comes down to grades.'*

My head swirled with questions. What was Ms. Shelley doing in the California History Annex? What was her cause of death? How much did Pax know? Who were her accomplices? How is this connected to grades and college admissions?

Fitch reminded me, *'Persey said Jane Doe, now Tiffany Shelley, was a victim of domestic abuse. Pax said that their dad threw her out the window.'* Fitch added, *'And now she's dead.'*

I knew the Shelleys were involved. With this new evidence that Mrs. Shelley was the victim of domestic abuse, it was obvious. Pax's dad murdered Pax's mom. Case solved.

16. DINNER FOR TWO – FRIDAY DINNER

Wherein Zarand orders too much food.

Now that I'd solved the case of Tiffany Shelley, I looked forward to my dinner date with Vicki. I opened the heavy circular doorway of carved wood into the Four Rivers Restaurant. Gold Chinese characters...

四川

...spelled out Szechuan on a red enamel background and told me I was in the right place—a conclusion confirmed by the pungent aroma of Szechuan chilies. Circular family-sized tables with Lazy Susans filled the cavernous dining area. Brush and ink landscapes of Li River karst formations—Chinese, but not Szechuan—covered the walls. I found Vicki sitting in a corner booth.

She greeted me without standing. "Evenin' Zarand. How was your day?"

'Don't forget you told Chandra's class you wouldn't say anything about Tiffany Shelley.'

Right, Fitch. Trust me. I'll find a way to let Vicki know without breaking that promise to my grandkids.

"I had a great day. Dr. Chandrasekhar left me an experiment. The class enjoyed dropping stuff in the name of science."

Vicki dropped her head to the table. "I'm glad they had a good time." One look at her—still in her work clothes, her jacket unbuttoned, the part in her hair no longer straight, and her bottle of Tsingtao beer already empty—told me that her day had been hard, but I asked anyway. "How was yours?"

"Some good, some not," she said with a sigh while waving her empty bottle at the waiter.

"I love good news," I said with a smile.

"The forensic techs retrieved DNA samples from Pax's SUV, so we'll have a reference DNA profile for them."

"That's good. Where'd you find their car?"

"Like you said—parked at the Pauli Falls trailhead."

The server brought us plates, chopsticks, hot tea, and menus. Vicki ordered without needing to refer to the menu. "Sizzling rice soup, General Tso chicken, eggplant with garlic sauce, and rice."

I added, "Plus Mongolian beef and moo shu pork."

"Do you want fried rice?" queried the waiter.

"No. Plain steamed rice, thank you," she said. She winked at me before adding, "All dishes mild, please."

"Not spicy," the server confirmed and wrote in Chinese on the order:

不辣

When he left, Vicki continued her report. "On the other hand, I still don't have an identity for that Jane Doe you found dead in the school library."

I wanted to shout out, "She's Pax's mother. Tiffany Shelley. Owner of All-Academic A-listers, a fancy tutoring service."

Fitch cautioned, *'Don't say anything. You promised your grandkids. Vicki has DNA from Pax's SUV. She'll match it to Jane Doe's and discover the truth soon enough. No problem.'*

Yes problem. Vicki is my friend. I'm wasting her time. Withholding evidence is against the law.

While I pondered this dilemma, I found a safer topic and asked, "Do you know anything about the Cajon Treasure?"

"Unfortunately, yes." She pointed north. "It's rumored to be somewhere in the San Gabriel Mountains, a sprawling area with rugged terrain, the size of Yosemite National Park. The police department gets called with annoying regularity to rescue hikers who got lost searching for it." She looked at me. "Do you think it has something to do with our case?"

"Could be. Why else would Jane Doe have been in the local history annex? *Stony Estancia Surfs* announced that the Cajon Treasure journals were the centerpiece of the collection."

At that point, our food started to arrive, one plate at a time. Soon the small table was covered, and we were engulfed in a cloud of garlic and toasted sesame oil. We served ourselves without denting the feast set out before us.

Vicki said, "The last people we rescued from the mountains were the Frank twins—Tafari and Wiha, but they go by Frank and Frankie. They graduated from Stony High a few years ago. And they're always in some minor trouble, I'm sure we have their fingerprints, but I doubt we've ever arrested them. I should question them."

'And here they are,' announced Fitch.

I looked around and didn't see any twins, but then the red doors opened, and two young people strode in like they owned the place—tall, gangly, dreadlocks, and fingerless leather gloves. They both wore tight jeans. I turned to Vicki. "Is that them?"

She stood up and shouted across the dining room. "Frank. Frankie. Come join us."

They looked at each other and then at the door as if they were considering leaving. They didn't appear happy, but they walked over to our booth.

Frank greeted Vicki. "Evenin', Senior Detective Yukawa," as if they were friends.

His sister Frankie said, "What a pleasant surprise," while her face said the opposite.

Vicki stood and shook their hands. "Please join us."

The twins accepted our hospitality as if it were expected. Vicki signaled to the server to move our feast to a circular table, and said in a cheery voice, "Plates, chopsticks, and Tsingtaos for our friends."

The twins acted like visiting royalty as they sat down and helped themselves to food.

We ate in silence, spinning the Lazy Susan and drinking our beers. In consideration of our guests, I ordered more food— spring rolls, fried wontons, pot stickers, and more steamed rice.

When everyone was sedated with full stomachs, I gave the server my credit card in exchange for a bag of takeout containers and distributed the fortune cookies.

I read mine first. "Too many secrets, too few friends."

Fitch laughed. *'When are you going to tell Vicki that Jane Doe is Tiffany Shelley?'*

Soon, Fitch, soon.

Vicki read, "Seek and you shall find."

Frankie remarked, "Obvious. You're a detective, aren't you? I'll read next." She cracked open her cookie. "What lazy fortune cookies. I got the same one as Detective Yukawa."

'Take notes. Watch how Vicki uses this to question her suspect,' Fitch said.

"I'm looking for a murderer. What are you looking for?" said Vicki.

Frankie clicked her chopsticks before answering. "You know. You rescued us. We're going to find the Cajon Treasure."

An awkward look passed between the women, so I said, "Frank, what did you get?"

"Your fortune will arrive when you stop seeking it." He crumpled up the small piece of paper and threw it into an empty serving dish. "Stupid cookie."

Frankie got up and grabbed her brother's hand. "We'll be right back."

"Keep an eye on the restrooms, and I'll watch the door. I want to know if they leave," said Vicki.

"Do you think they have something to do with #BODYINTHELIBRARY?"

"I hate how *Stony Estancia Surfs* attaches hashtags to everything, but yes. Your witness said there were two others in the annex, so I have two unidentified perps. The twins are after the Cajon Treasure and those journals were in the annex."

"Lots of people are searching for that treasure. A boy in my class hikes into the mountains every summer with his father. Are they suspects?"

"The twins have been in trouble before and they hang out with the Stony Stoners. They are certainly people of interest."

I spotted the twins returning. "Here they come."

'Now,' said Fitch, *'Trick them into a confession.'*

I leaned in close to Vicki and said, "Let me talk to them."

She hissed, "Go for it," as the twins sat down.

'Show them how the master does it,' Fitch encouraged me.

I pointed a chopstick at Frank's fingerless gloves. "Your fingerprints were found in the California History Annex." I pointed to Frankie. "Both of you."

'Really? Did Tsui find their fingerprints?' Fitch asked.

Call it a good guess.

No one in our little group said anything. We all ate our crisp vanilla cookies. The multi-lingual chatter of the surrounding tables washed over us like a rising tide. The twins squinted their eyes and pushed out their chins—arrogant disdain.

I shook my chopsticks at them and repeated, "Both of you."

"We're not saying anything without our lawyers," Frankie said.

Fitch cheered. *'Gratz buddy. That was a good guess. They were there.'*

I folded my arms and said, "That's your right." Then I waited.

Frank broke. "We didn't have anything to do with the murder of Ms. Shelley. We noticed the broken window when we cut across the schoolyard to go to Only Donuts. She was dead when we arrived. We weren't there when she was attacked, and we didn't take anything."

'He let the cat out of the bag. You should have told Vicki about Ms. Shelley before,' Fitch said.

Frankie ran out of the restaurant and her brother followed.

I got up to chase them, but Vicki grabbed my wrist. She made a call. "Officer Tsui. The Frank twins just left. Keep a tail on them and make sure they don't leave town."

Again, I was impressed by the Stony PD. Vicki had been prepared for the arrival of the twins. I was also proud of myself. "Were you taking notes? Did you see how I tricked them into confessing?"

Vicki lectured. "You didn't read them their rights. Nothing they said is admissible."

"No problem," I replied, "Solve the case first. Legalities later. That's how we old-time detectives do it. I placed those two at the scene. That's something."

"More important is that they identified Jane Doe," Vicki conceded.

"That's right," I said, trying to look surprised.

Vicki examined my face. I held my eyebrows raised and my mouth wide open. After what seemed like forever, she said, "You knew, didn't you? You knew it was Ms. Shelley. Your quote-unquote grandkids told you."

'She caught you,' said Fitch with a laugh.

When I didn't respond, she continued, "And you weren't going to tell me, were you?

"I was going to tell you. I was waiting for the right time."

She looked at me with hard eyes. "You make everything complicated. You're your own worst enemy. Fortunately, I have this investigation in hand. Tsui has the Frank twins under surveillance. I'll get a search warrant for their apartment and close this case with no more funny business."

I took her reprimand to heart and didn't mention that I didn't think the Frank twins were guilty.

'Coward,' was Fitch's commentary.

Wherein Zarand tells a story.

The Four Rivers' circular door closed, completing the hand-off of the Frank twins to the omnipresent Officer Tsui.

I asked Vicki, "Would you like some dessert?"

She patted her belly. "Not me, I'll just have some tea. Get whatever you want. I swear you have the metabolism of a teenager."

I ordered egg-custard tarts and sesame balls with red bean paste. "Do you really think the Frank twins murdered Ms. Shelley?"

"I suspect it was an accident, involuntary manslaughter, but they had a motive, the Cajon Treasure."

She interrupted herself to make a call. "Tell me, Tsui, did you find fingerprints for the Frank twins?"

"Thank you."

"They had opportunity. Tsui placed them at the scene with none of your trickery. I'll have means as soon as Persey gives me the cause of death. Means, motive, opportunity—the murder trifecta."

"I see it differently."

She smiled at me and took a spoonful of my custard. "Of course you do. You're going to tell me one of your stories, aren't you?"

I drank some tea. "I start with Persey's autopsy. Ms. Shelley was an abused spouse. She cajoled her husband to break into the California History Annex, but something went wrong, and he lost his temper." I paused to let that sink in. "From there, I agree with your analysis, involuntary manslaughter."

She smiled and kissed my cheek. "Great story. You should be a writer, but I don't see the evidence to support your piece of fiction."

Vicki's phone sounded a siren—her ringtone for PD headquarters. She answered on speaker.

"Pauli Falls Open Space is closing for the day. Should we impound Pax Shelley's SUV? It's the only car left in the parking lot."

"Don't bother. I expect him to return when it gets cold. Just attach a tracker to it."

'Is that even legal?' asked Fitch.

Since when do you care about what's legal? You're not legal, or even real, yourself.

I started on a sesame ball. "Do you think Pax is still in the mountains?"

"What's the other choice? We have their SUV. I wouldn't expect a Stony Estancia kid to abandon their car and walk home."

I didn't want to argue with Vicki. We couldn't determine if Ms. Shelley was killed by the Frank twins searching for the Cajon Treasure or Mr. Shelley, the abusive spouse, without more evidence, especially the cause of death. "I'm worried about Pax. Stony Estancia kids are more prepared for the mall than the mountains."

Vicki agreed and called county air support. "Senior Detective Yukawa here. Stony Estancia PD. I have a teenager lost in the mountains. Can I get a flyover before it gets too dark?"

"Pax Shelley. Rainbow hair. Pauli Falls trail. Is that the one?" they replied.

"Yes."

"Officer Tsui alerted us. We just completed low-altitude surveillance. We didn't see your target."

"Thank you." She ended the call. "I don't want anything to happen to Pax. That would be terrible—first, the mother is murdered and then the child is lost. But it's too late to do anything tonight."

"Good point. If we went out tonight, we'd have more people lost. Regardless, we should take this seriously."

Vicki called Tsui. "Activate search and rescue. Notify the fire department that we need a mobile command post. If we're lucky, extending cell coverage into the hills will flush out our lost teen."

Fitch enjoyed the chaos. *'If you're really lucky, they'll return to their car tonight when it gets cold.'*

Next, she called Leticia. "We have a Stony High student lost in the mountains."

"*Stony Estancia Surfs* is here to help. What can we do?" replied Tish.

"Pax Shelley's car is in the Pauli Falls parking lot, but they are nowhere to be found."

"Have you tried county air support?"

"Yes. No help. I'm organizing a search and rescue operation for tomorrow morning."

"Got it. That's why *Stony Estancia Surfs* is here. We'll mobilize the community. Volunteers. Food trucks. Horse patrol. Rapper Amar. The works."

"Thank you."

Before Vicki hung up, Tish asked, "Did you hear about the embezzlement of SE-cubed funds? You know they raise millions with their fundraisers, don't you?"

The ever-cynical Fitch remarked, *'They had a gala last month, a raffle this month, and a silent auction next month. What do they do with all that money?'*

Vicki ignored this. Her laser beam was focused on Pax Shelley. She'd find Pax and they'd be the deciding vote in the Frank twins versus Mr. Shelley as the killers.

PLAN A – SATURDAY AM

Wherein a teenager ignores their cell phone.

I headed for the Pauli Falls Open Space at dawn. The best-case scenario was that we'd locate Pax Shelley, and their testimony would decide between the Frank twins and Gun Shell, wrapping up Tiffany Shelley's murder before lunch. The worst case was that Pax was out there alone and exposed, too afraid to come home.

I drove my electric car out of Higgs Haven to Blackett Street where I turned right. My visor was already down to block the rising sun. I continued past the high school to the T-intersection with Bohr Boulevard and turned left going uphill to the Pauli Falls trailhead.

The unpaved parking area was full. I had mixed feelings when I spied Pax's SUV. It would have been nice if Pax had returned on their own. I could imagine how cold and scared they must be after spending the night in the wild.

As soon as Lieutenant Mutai activated the mobile command post, the mountains would have a strong cell signal. Pax's phone would notify him of his missed calls and messages. The hungry teen would contact someone for help. Within minutes, we'd know where to send the rescue team.

Fitch chuckled, *'When will you learn that any plan that requires a long sequence of steps is an assured failure? KISS. Keep it simple, stupid.*

Stony Estancia Surfs delivered as promised. Pauli Falls Open Space was like a music festival. Food trucks. Police vehicles. Cars parked haphazardly. People everywhere—in brightly colored clothing. There was no place to park and no room to turn around. I had to shift into reverse.

My tiny car silently backed down Bohr Boulevard until it found a space. I opened my door with care not to ding the pickup truck and horse trailer beside me, put on my backpack heavy with drinks and snacks, grabbed my climbing gloves and trekking poles, and walked back uphill to the assembly point.

The scene appeared chaotic but wasn't. Stony Estancia knew how to search for lost hikers. When the red and gold fire truck arrived, Vicki greeted Lieutenant Mutai with a smile. "Mornin' Peggy, can you find a place to set up?"

"No problem." Peggy jumped down and unlocked the gate to the fire access road. "Right this way," she called to her crew. Within minutes, they'd raised a portable cell phone tower, aligned their satellite dish, and deployed a small farm of solar panels. The crowd cheered when their devices jumped from no bars to a strong signal.

Fitch admired the technology and mused, *'If they're lucky the emergency base station is enough.'* Now that all the shiny tech was up and running, he supported Plan A. *'The lost hiker will phone in as soon as their phone jumps from no bars to all the bars.'*

Tish and César, our ever-present internet news team, were the first to connect. The search for Pax would be livestreamed online.

Vicki called nine-one-one. She identified herself and gave her badge number. "I'm calling from the mobile command post." She asked with hope in her voice, "Have you heard from our lost child?"

Vicki listened to her phone and frowned. "Too bad. Let us know if you hear anything. On to plan B."

Wherein a rattlesnake takes a nap.

When Pax didn't respond to the strong signal broadcast by the Fire Department's portable cell tower, I resigned myself to tramping into the San Gabriel Mountains. The search would cover difficult terrain and require serious organization.

While the community volunteers connected to the internet, Vicki and I met with Mr. Amar. He wore a bright blue robe with a high collar and a matching belt fastened with a copper buckle—a traditional Mongolian deel—and was accompanied by a similarly dressed teen.

I said, "That's a beautiful white pony you have there." I've found that complimenting someone's animal was always a good way to open a discussion.

Mr. Amar sat tall in his Western saddle and tipped his American cowboy hat. "She may be small, but she is a full-sized, full-blooded Mongolian horse. Direct descendent of the ones Genghis Khan rode when he conquered Asia."

"Are they hard to ride?"

He smiled. "I wouldn't know. Back in Ulaanbaatar, where I learned, they started us young. I learned to ride bareback until my legs were long enough to sit in a saddle."

The teen, wearing a purple deel and mounted on a bay, said, "You tell them, Dad. I recall that you taught me to ride when I was in kindergarten. Mom wouldn't let you start any earlier."

Vicki climbed atop the fire truck and addressed the volunteers. "On that magnificent white Mongolian horse is Mr. Rinchen Amar. He will explain the GPS app we're using."

Mr. Amar waved his cowboy hat and introduced himself in a rich baritone. "You can forget that *Mr. Amar* stuff. My friends call me Rapper. I'm the owner of Rinchen Amar Phone Repair." He paused before softly adding, "and Sammich Shoppe." He raised his voice again and sang, "That's R. A. P. R.—Rapper."

In response, the fans chanted, "Rapper, the phone wizard," from his ads on *Stony Estancia Surfs*.

Fitch mocked the crowd. *'When will the real bands arrive?'*

Rapper clapped his hands over his head and the crowd did the same. "Thanks to Peggy and the Stony FD, we have WiFi." There were sporadic cheers for WiFi. "If this is your first time, you'll need to download my GPS app. Old-timers might need to get the latest update. My son Richie—"

"Pa!" shouted the indignant teenager.

"Sorry. My son Ranch will assist you."

Fitch recognized the teen before I did. *'That's Ranch from the high school.'*

While the newbies downloaded the app, I visited the food trucks. I bought a large latte and a bruin claw from Only Donuts and a breakfast burrito from Cocina de Cetto. I sat on the ground to adjust my trekking poles and eat breakfast.

Father and son circulated through the crowd getting people set up. I was surprised by how popular Rapper was and how many women went to him for assistance.

My goal was to find Pax and if Rapper attracted more volunteers, that worked for me.

'What if Pax doesn't want to be found? If they're intent on hiding, you won't find them in these mountains,' a pessimistic Fitch declared.

He was right to be concerned, but we had to look. I had a plan to make my participation serve double duty.

Rapper lined us up along the fire access road. "Organize yourself in small groups."

Vicki added, "We don't want to lose anyone. Make sure you have a buddy and stay hydrated." She pointed to water bottles provided by the fire department. "It'll be hot today."

Peggy reminded everyone. "The bottles are reusable. Don't forget to return them."

The crowd milled around finding partners and picking up water. Some people paired up right away, but others looked awkward, reminding me of middle school dances.

I spotted my target. A short man wearing a wide-brimmed hat with a neck flap—the kind that got high marks for protection and none for style. The hat, and the rest of his outfit, down to his boots, looked just-out-of-the-box new. He was Pax's father, best-selling author Gun Shell, and my number one murder suspect. "Hey, can I partner with you? None of these kids want me in their group."

He nodded in agreement but gave me a suspicious look.

I pointed to my backpack. "I've got snacks."

He looked around. We were the only old guys. "Snacks? Great. You can call me Gunnar." He reached out his hand.

'He doesn't remember you,' chortled Fitch.

I shook his hand. "Nice to meet you, Gunnar. I'm Zee."

We claimed a position on the search line. Rapper and Ranch trotted their horses along the fire road to check our spacing. Our apps flashed us a heading and we set off toward the ridge.

We were in chaparral—primarily sagebrush—tough desert dwellers, waist high and prepared to defend their territory. Snakes, lizards, mice, and rabbits hid from the people stomping through their neighborhoods. The rising sun had sent the coyotes into their cool dens. A lone red-tail hawk circled overhead on the lookout for careless prey.

Gun Shell didn't look comfortable bushwacking through the chaparral. He was nothing like the macho characters in his novels.

Fitch scoffed, *'I know the type. Strong in his imagination and with his wife, but nowhere else. Classic abuser.'*

I thought about the broken bones Persey's autopsy had revealed. I wouldn't let Mr. Shelley's mild manners fool me. He was the murderer.

Gun Shell jumped each time Rapper's app beeped at us for diverging from our assigned track—something unavoidable to get around sagebrush and deep ravines.

I doubted we'd find Pax—the area was too vast and the terrain too rough.

Fitch, always ready with a worst-case scenario, predicted, *'We won't find him alive.'*

Regardless, I took the opportunity to interrogate Gunnar Shelley—multitasking search and rescue with the murder investigation.

"What do you do?" I asked as an icebreaker.

"I'm a writer," he said smugly.

I softened him up before asking my hard questions. "What's your next book about?"

"The working title is *Perish the Thane*—about an assassin who used a knife that had a jewel-encrusted hilt to kill enemies of Prince George IV." He went on and on about the weapons, manners, and customs of the Regency period.

I could see why his books sold so well, he enjoyed the research and loved his characters. Once he was talking about his writing, he stopped jumping each time the app complained about our path weaving back and forth.

I pointed to a combat knife he had strapped to his thigh. "Did he use a knife like that?"

Fitch laughed. Gun Shell laughed. "You know nothing about knives." He paused to smile. "And I didn't say the assassin was a man."

He took it out of the sheath and began a dissertation on the history of melee weapons sounding like some gamer, which is where I think he did his research.

Fitch noticed, *'That knife isn't new like the rest of his stuff.'*
Brilliant. That's the murder weapon.

'Slow down cowboy. Persey didn't find any knife wounds.'

Gunnar and I did our best to appease Rapper's app, keeping the off-track beeping to a minimum. With each hour that passed, I feared that this massive community effort was futile.

When the sun reached its peak in the sky, Rapper and Ranch rode down the line to exchange empty water bottles for full ones and distribute lunches from Cocina de Cetto. We had a choice of burritos or tacos, beef or vegetarian. Gunnar chose a vegetarian burrito, and I selected one of each. After a short break, the apps signaled for us to RESUME SEARCH.

Gunnar and I marched uphill until we were faced with a large sage blocking our way. Gunnar turned right, and I went left hoping that the app would give us credit for following our assigned path on average.

There was no pleasing Rapper's app. We were chastised with beeps, and I was subjected to Fitch's gleeful laughter. I used my trekking pole to maintain my balance on the rough terrain and soon I was back on track.

I glanced at the app and saw that our blue dot was no longer in line with the red ones. "Hurry up Gunnar. We're falling behind."

He didn't move.

He didn't say anything.

He stood there.

I walked over to his side of the sagebrush. Across his path was a rattlesnake, as thick as Gunnar's arm and much longer. "She's no threat, Gunnar—all stretched out like that, basking in the sun. Do you see that rat-sized lump in her middle?"

He nodded, not moving.

"That's her full belly. She's recently eaten. She's not interested in you. Back away and come around the other side."

He took several small steps back before he ran to catch up with me.

"That's scary. I'm putting that snake in my next book. A Western. *The Forest be with You*."

As we continued up the mountain, I looked for an opening to question him. We noted lots of lizards and Gunnar kept saying. "Ooh, look at that," each time we saw coyote or bear scat. We even found a regurgitated pellet from a red hawk. We were thorough but were not rewarded with any signs of human activity or a reason for me to introduce his wife's murder.

By mid-afternoon, we approached Pauli Falls—visible from afar, having the only trees for miles around, supported by the oasis that surrounded the falls. The search and rescue team had covered an enormous territory and still no sign of Pax. I was tired...and hot. My water bottle was empty again. I wanted a place to rest and enjoy my snacks.

Then something caught my eye.

"Look at this." I pointed to a crude rock shelter—a sign of human activity but not recent. Gunnar was breathing hard, and his brand-new duds were streaked with sweat. I suggested, "Shade. Let's stop here."

He jumped at the chance and crawled into the man-made cave.

I had granola bars, trail mix, and beef jerky. I offered him his choice. While he chewed on the jerky, I thought, *now or never*. "Do you think Pax murdered their mother?" I queried.

Watch the pro, I thought to Fitch. *I'm going to get him to confess. If nothing else, he's going to confess to protect his child.*

'*I doubt it. These cases are never as straightforward as you imagine,*' replied Fitch.

"Wait a minute," shouted Mr. Shelley. "You're that busybody teacher. Mr. Silly-something."

"Szilard," I said.

"You're pretending to help find Pax, but you just want to accuse them of murdering their mother."

'*Let's see you save this one,*' Fitch challenged.

"I apologize for not introducing myself. I thought you recognized me."

"Pretty presumptuous of you. You aren't important enough to remember."

I looked down and backed away. "That's harsh," I said under my breath.

He gave me a half-smile, satisfied with his comeback.

'*Lucky you. That insult was retaliation for his hurt feelings. You're even now.*'

I started again. "I'm just trying to solve your wife's murder. Do you think Pax did it?"

"Pax a murderer? What are you thinking? Never. The child picks up spiders and carries them outside. They wouldn't harm any living thing." Gunnar helped himself to a root beer from my backpack and took another bite of beef jerky. "Murder their mother? They love her."

He stopped. His shoulders slumped, his voice weakened, and his breathing became shallow. I was afraid he was going to start sobbing. "Pax *loved* her. She supported their lifestyle. They were a mommy's child for life."

I sensed best-selling author Gun Shell's disdain for them both. The way he said *mommy's child* further convinced me that Mr. Shelley was the murderer.

While he was in a talkative mood, I asked, "Do you think Pax spent last night in the mountains?"

Gunnar thought that was the funniest idea. "My Pax? Sleeping in the open? I once took Mommy and her *delicate child* camping. Not some wilderness trek, but a luxury, guided adventure—glamping. We had cooks and porters. Tiffany is rough and tumble. She didn't need that support. She could be dropped in the middle of the wilderness and be home in time for dinner."

He continued, "On the other hand, Pax lasted one night. They hated tents, food cooked over a fire, sleeping bags—even on cots, all of it." Mr. Shelley moved closer and lowered his voice as if sharing some important secret. "When Pax stays out all night, they are sleeping in their SUV. Not in a sleeping bag, but on Pima cotton sheets with an electric blanket. Their mother never taught them her hardness and strength, quite the opposite."

Even though Mr. Shelley was a central-casting nerd, he wanted Pax to be like the characters in his books, not a *mommy's child*. He resented Mrs. Shelley's support for Pax's choices. That convinced me. Gunnar Shelley was my man. He murdered his wife.

I turned on my phone flashlight and searched our shelter. Something yellow caught my attention. "What is this?"

Gunnar looked. "That's Pax's hoodie."

Fitch was elated. *'We found Pax. I knew we would.'* His good cheer lasted a moment before he reverted to his pessimistic self. *'Their dead body must be around here. Shine your light in the corners.'*

There's no body here. I'd smell it.

Gunnar stared at the hoodie and seemed to be in a trance. "I remember visiting that campus. Pax loved the upscale dormitories and cleaning service. Their mother loved Pax returning home for the weekends."

He snapped out of the trance. "I wanted Pax to cut the apron strings from his mommy. That university was too close. She'd visit to check his homework and do his laundry. He was too old to still be *mommy's baby*."

There was that word *mommy* again, and again. He resented her.

Rapper's app beeped again. We weren't off track. I looked at the screen. RETURN TO BASE.

"I was afraid they planned for us to spend the night," Gunnar said with relief.

'He's more concerned about himself than finding Pax. Not a good sign,' Fitch remarked.

I tapped the SAVE LOCATION button on the app.

Gunnar grabbed the yellow shirt. "I'll carry that. It belongs to my child."

I didn't object. That sweatshirt wasn't going to lead to Pax or their mother's murderer.

A yellow hoodie was little to show for a whole day trekking through the chaparral. I had one last question for Mr. Shelley. "The police learned Ms. Shelley has a red SUV, but haven't located it. Does it have any decals or bumper stickers?"

"I've been looking too. No decals or bumpers stickers, but there's a large car magnet on each side advertising *Tiff the Tutor*."

"Thanks, that's a help."

When I met Vicki in the parking lot, she said, "Zee, this is a mess. We didn't find Pax. We need to get out of the office for some lateral thinking, new ideas, and a change of direction. I've called a meeting at my house tomorrow to shake things up."

That was the kind of creative leadership that would get her promoted to Chief of Detectives.

THE BRAIN TRUST – SUNDAY

Wherein Zarand trips down memory lane.

I started the dishwasher after breakfast. Dahl was napping on the back of the sofa. The clock approached lunchtime and Vicki's strategy meeting—she'd have pizza. I drove down Blackett Street past the high school. At the T-intersection with Bohr Boulevard, the uphill turn to Pauli Falls tempted me—one final trek into the mountains to locate Pax. Resisting that adventure, two quick rights took me into Vicki's quiet neighborhood with modest ranch homes of pastel stucco and tile roofs. I parked in her driveway and walked past the bees buzzing in the rosemary.

Cerberus greeted me at the door. I let the chocolate lab smell my hands. "Good boy. Where's everyone?"

With a friendly bark and his tail wagging, he escorted me through the combined kitchen, dining room, and living room and out to the pool. Another bark announced my presence before he took his place beside Coroner Persey. She was dressed for swimming in a black maillot and a matching cover-up with a spider web pattern. She patted Cerberus and said, "Welcome Zarand."

I greeted her and Vicki. "Afternoon, ladies."

Cerberus looked at the children splashing in the pool and wagged his tail. He looked at Persey, back to the kids, and then at Persey again.

She said, "Go ahead boy," and he took a flying leap into the pool accompanied by the laughter of the children.

"Afternoon, Officer Tsui. Are those all yours?"

"Yes sir, Mr. Szilard. My five college funds. Sunday is my day to take care of them, so here we are."

The doorbell app on Vicki's phone announced the pizza delivery. She headed to the front door accompanied by a very wet dog.

Persey shouted, "Stay," before the dripping Cerberus entered the house.

I went to the kitchen for plates, napkins, a pitcher of lemonade for the kids, and a six-pack of Tecate *cervezas* for the adults. I shouted to Vicki. "What happened to the paper plates?"

"No more paper plates. Reusable bamboo ones are in the cabinet next to the refrigerator along with cloth napkins."

After Tsui fed his children, Vicki opened the meeting. "Since the city is paying for our lunch, we should get to work. "Tsui, have you located Ms. Shelley's red SUV?"

"No luck so far."

I jumped in. "I learned something from Mr. Shelley. The car has a large *Tiff the Tutor* car magnet on each side."

Vicki gave me a side hug, "Good work, Zee."

She turned back to Tsui, "Anything else?"

"Do you have a laptop? It's going to be hard to see on my phone."

Vicki handed him a tablet. "This'll have to do."

He brought up a picture of black pieces of paper fit together like a jigsaw puzzle.

"Are those the ashes from the gas fireplace in the annex?" I asked.

"You got it in one," he said with a big smile. "This is from the murder scene. The folks in the lab performed a miracle to enhance the ink. Let me read it to you."

I was impressed. Once again, the Stony PD proved themselves to have state-of-the-art forensics.

Vicki and I leaned in to examine the reconstruction.

Tsui read aloud,

HEY BLUE EYES,
BIG PERFORMANCE TONIGHT.
LOVE, SAMMY.

He continued, "Blue Eyes is Jane Doe. I mean Ms. Shelley." He paused for a moment, and as if we didn't remember, he added, "She had blue eyes."

Everyone nodded in agreement.

"But who is Sammy?" he asked.

'The murderer,' chimed in Fitch.

Gun Shell, I said to myself.

"These aren't their real names. Ol' Blue Eyes is Frank Sinatra. Sammy is Sammy Davis, Jr. They performed together in Vegas," Persey said.

I didn't think that bit of popular culture was very helpful, but it was better than Vicki's contribution. She said, "Frank Sinatra. Chairman of the Board. Frankie. This is a sly hint that the Frank twins are involved."

'And you thought you'd gotten her off them, didn't you,' Fitch teased me.

Vicki turned to Tsui. "Do you still have them under surveillance?"

He looked at his phone. "Yes boss. Right now, they're at the city library. Do you want to know what they're reading?"

"No, that's okay,"

Tsui continued, "We served them with a search warrant. You should have seen their apartment. They're obsessed. We found boxes and boxes of documents related to the Cajon Treasure, piled to the ceiling. One wall had a large topo map of the San Gabriel Mountains, covered with map pins and red yarn connecting them." He took out his phone and showed everyone a picture of the map crisscrossed with red yarn. "The only suspicious thing we found was a tube with a rolled-up document written in an old-fashioned script, like the Declaration of Independence. I'll text you a photo."

"Did you tell them not to leave town?"

"I sure did. As soon as I saw their half-packed suitcases and first-class tickets to the Cayman Islands, I collected their passports."

"Good job," she said, sounding a bit like Persey saying, "Good dog."

"Thank you. They protested that this trip had been planned for ages, and threatened to call their lawyers, but I insisted," he added with a sly smile. "I looked through their passports. They had the extra thick ones and they do travel a lot."

I was glad to hear that the PD hadn't lost track of the Frank twins, but I still believed they were innocent.

Fitch didn't see it as that clear cut. *'Someone burnt that note. It must be important. What does it mean?'*

I served myself another slice of pizza.

Persey grabbed a *cerveza*. "Cerberus and I hiked up to that rock shelter where you found Pax's yellow hoodie."

"Did he pick up Pax's trail?" Vicki asked.

The chocolate lab stood tall and turned his head slowly, looking at each of us, as if to say, "Did you doubt me?"

Persey hugged her dog. "You did great, didn't you?" She explained, "He tracked Pax from the rock shelter to Pauli Falls and into the deepest part of the pool."

I looked at Cerberus. "Was that the end of the trail?"

He barked.

"Of course not," Persey interpreted. "That's a myth—fooling a dog by crossing a stream. Cerberus tracked them into the pool and out the other side."

"Where is Pax? Which way did they go?" I asked.

"Unfortunately, he went every way. Cerberus followed a trail out of the pool until Pax turned around and returned to the water. After we followed a half-dozen similar U-turns, we were late and headed back here."

I put my best positive spin on her attempt to track Pax. "Well, now we know he's not lost. He purposely disguised his trail. He didn't want us to follow him."

Vicki didn't get discouraged, "How about Tiffany Shelley's cause of death?"

Persey replied with admiration. "That woman should have lived forever. I couldn't find anything. She was in great shape. Good muscle tone. Healthy organs. Took great care of herself. I sent samples to the FBI for comprehensive toxicology testing. I can't figure out what killed her."

She wasn't telling the full story. I prompted her. "Any signs of trauma?"

She gave me a look that said she didn't appreciate my interfering, before saying. "Ms. Shelley had a surprising number of bone fractures. But nothing recent."

Vicki wasn't concerned. "So, nothing to do with her cause of death."

'Don't let them sweep domestic abuse under the rug.'

I tried again. "I had an interesting discussion with Mr. Shelley while we were hiking through the chaparral."

Vicki helped herself to a glass of lemonade.

Tsui checked on his kids.

Persey cleared away the empty pizza boxes.

I waited until everyone returned.

"Mr. Shelley called Pax, *mommy's baby*. He resented his wife. He wanted Pax to be like the rough-and-tumble characters in his books. His wife had other ideas."

No one responded.

'Drop it. You'll need more evidence before you can get them interested,' Fitch said.

I changed subjects. "What do you think of the embezzlement rumors posted on *Stony Estancia Surfs*?"

Vicki hugged me. "Look Zee, if you're intent on following futile leads, run down those rumors with your computer-hacker friend."

I smiled at her and kissed her forehead. "Okay Vee, I'll talk to Vinnie Purcell, the smartest guy in the room—the one those three-letter agencies in Washington call when they get stuck."

"Yes, Zee, that one. Doesn't he owe you a favor?"

'You found the granddaughter he didn't know he had. He owes you, like, forever.'

I had my marching orders, Purcell and Associates—computer security experts.

"In addition to Vinnie Purcell, I'll track down the Stony Stoners. My intuition tells me they're key to solving this mystery."

All those plans were delayed when I received a call from Jared Sendak, the Stony High substitute coordinator. "Ms. Miller called in with a personal emergency. She asked for you."

When I was specifically requested, I always accepted. Besides, Ms. Miller had a great schedule, AP Literature, all classes the same. After school, she coached track and field—a special treat for the runners because she'd competed in 100 meters and 400 meters at the Olympics. The detective gods were smiling at me. I looked forward to interrogating my confidential informants. They had identified Tiffany Shelley and my intuition told me they had more secrets to reveal.

21. MOVIE DAY – MONDAY

Wherein everyone gets popcorn.

I stationed myself at Ms. Miller's door with a box from Only Donuts. I welcomed the homeroom students with high-fives and handshakes. They helped themselves from the box.

Ranch was the celebrity of the day after his role in the search and rescue operation.

Lizzy, now with purple hair, said, "I love your horse. What kind is it?"

His chest puffed out. "She's Mongolian, like the horses Genghis Khan rode."

"Beauty."

"Would you like to go riding with me?"

She had eyes for his horse, not him. She gave him a half-smile and said, "Not really."

After I took attendance, I looked for the lesson plan. It wasn't on top of her desk, so I looked through the papers. Marked essays. Graded quizzes. Jane Austen worksheets. Permission slips for the senior trip to Washington DC. A folder labeled SE-CUBED. Another labeled LESSON PLAN. I found it in the last place I looked.

I finished reading the teaching instructions as the buzzer sounded and the homeroom students filed out.

While the first-period class entered the room, I put up the MOVIE DAY sign. January and Lizzy jumped up and ran to Ms. Miller's collection of microwaves and started making popcorn.

"We're the popcorn squad," Lizzy said.

Jorge announced, "Sparkling water. *Agua con gas.* Bring me your water bottles." He stood by the carbonation machine turning water into soda.

Ms. Miller had left me a selection of *Pride and Prejudice* DVDs, so I didn't have to watch the same one over and over. I went through the stack and chose *Bride and Prejudice*, a Bollywood version of Jane Austen's classic.

I introduced the film. "Ms. Miller wants you to notice how prejudice hurts people's relationships and write an essay on its relevance to today's society."

On seeing a room full of glowing computers prepared to accept the assigned essays, I started the DVD. They were okay writing about prejudice, but when the movie began, they objected.

'What now?' said Fitch, entertained by their fickle behavior.

"Not yet."

"Wait for the popcorn."

"I don't have my drink."

I stopped the DVD and checked the lesson plan. Sure enough, she'd told me not to start the video until everyone had their popcorn.

'While they're waiting for popcorn, this is a good time to interrogate them.'

"I want to thank everyone who joined us on Saturday. I'm sorry we didn't find Pax. Can someone tell me where they are?"

January emptied a steaming bag of popcorn into bowls before holding her palm down. Then she took her fist and put it under that hand. She signed HIDDEN.

Lizzy put another bag of popcorn into her microwave. "*D'oh.* No. They used an encrypted message service and warned us not to snitch to the po-po." She made a pair of scissors with two fingers and closed the blades in front of her lips. She signed SHUT UP giving a hard look to January and the others.

Fitch for once took the optimistic view. *'At least we know that they're alive.'*

I concurred and resigned myself to convincing Vicki to arrest Gun Shell without Pax's testimony.

'That's better for the family. No need to foster resentments.'

While my grandkids watched the colorful version of Pride and Prejudice with all its songs and dances, I checked out the SE-CUBED folder. The first thing I noticed, on top of the stack, was a handwritten note: FAITH, DECLAN'S GONE TOO FAR. WE MUST STOP HIM. TIFF.

'Wow. That's to Faith Miller from Tiffany Shelley, may she rest in peace, about Declan Beckett, president of SE-cubed.'

That note was the motive for Mr. Beckett to murder Ms. Shelley—adding him to my list of suspects, but not higher than her abusive husband. The note also raised the priority of my embezzlement investigation. I found an envelope and slipped the note into it using the eraser end of a pencil.

The next page in the folder was another handwritten note reminding board members to pick up their monthly cash disbursements. I slid it in with the first one.

'I wonder how much money we're talking about here,' Fitch mused. *'Dispensing cash is a big red flag.'*

A quick internet search confirmed that SE-cubed board members included Tiffany and Faith, tying the two women and Mr. Beckett together in a scheme to profit from SE-cubed fundraising.

Between classes, I stashed the notes in my car.

For the next class period, I knew the routine. Ranch microwaved popcorn and Alyce made sparkling water.

Fitch prodded me. *'Question this group. Lizzy isn't in this class to enforce silence.'*

"The police are investigating Ms. Shelley's killing. She was murdered at night, in the dark, before school opened. Have you heard anything? Were you a witness, or one of your friends?"

Fitch interrupted, *'Why do you make this stuff up? Just because Persey can't pin down the time of death, doesn't mean it happened at night. Your witness, January, said it was during school hours.'*

I ignored Fitch. My half-truth was close enough. "We need witnesses. Who's on campus at night? This is a murder case. No one will be arrested for trespassing."

Ranch stopped making popcorn and said, "The Frank twins, maybe. They hang out with the Stony Stoners."

The class broke out in nervous chatter at the mention of the Stony Stoners.

Fitch laughed. *'Everyone, except you, believes the Frank twins are involved. They keep showing up.'*

Alyce held up a bottle of sparkling water. "Last one. *Blimey*, we're out of carbon dioxide. We should have had enough."

I didn't care about carbon dioxide, except in the context of climate change, or the Frank twins. I asked, "Where can I find the Stony Stoners?" I had a hunch they were important.

Now the room went silent except for those who were already chomping on their popcorn.

"No worries, mate. The Stoners aren't a big secret. They've been avoiding the school since the murder. I expect they're hanging out at Heisenberg Park," Alyce said.

'Once again, your grandkids know more about this case than law enforcement. Human sources beat forensic science every time.'

I entered STONY STONERS, HEISENBERG PARK into my calendar app. When the app asked, WHAT TIME? I tapped in 8:00.

Fitch reminded me, *'You don't want that many witnesses.'*

You're right. Fitch loved to trip me up on the details.

The community center was tucked in a corner of the park. Clubs and special events were held there every night. This was where *Stony Estancia Surfs* interviewed Jorge. I edited the calendar to MIDNIGHT to avoid running into Leticia and César.

I selected *Pride and Prejudice and Zombies* for the next class. When the title sequence came up, they all cheered. While they watched I went back to the SE-CUBED folder.

I found a stack of emails with the subject: ANNEX CONSTRUCTION, APPARENT LACK OF PROGRESS. Mr. Beckett was insistent that the ribbon cutting happened on schedule. On one memo, he scrawled in the margin, FORGET THE INSPECTORS.

'That may be a motive to silence Ms. Shelley,' opined Fitch, *'but it doesn't explain how the nuts and washers ended up strewn across the football field instead of holding the shelves in place.'*

For the rest of the day, I showed more traditional versions of *Pride and Prejudice.*

When I opened the pizza app to order dinner, Fitch objected. *'Did you forget you're going to Heisenberg Park to track down the Stony Stoners tonight?'*

"Puppets," I exclaimed before switching from tryptophan-laden pizza to a chicken mole with caffeine-rich dark chocolate. I drank a double-shot latte while I waited for delivery.

I'd be alert for my visit to Heisenberg Park.

Wherein Zarand meets Kurt Vonnegut.

Despite my caffeine-laden dinner, I fell asleep on the sofa. My calendar woke me at midnight. I brushed my teeth and got dressed while Dahl swished her black tail. Before I braved the night, I fortified myself with a second dinner of eggplant and zucchini—*aubergines* and *courgettes.*

Dahl batted her empty food dish across the kitchen floor.

'She wants her second dinner,' Fitch said.

She yowled her confirmation.

I appeased her with lickable cat treats, which she loved.

I jogged down Higgs Road in my tracksuit—the one with reflective piping. At the Pacific Electric Trail, I turned left. Vicki and I often jogged this trail, named for the defunct Pacific Electric Railway—a missed public transit opportunity. The trail ran through Heisenberg Park and miles beyond.

I slowed to a walk on the barely illuminated path. The well-lit parking lot surrounding the community center glowed in the distance. I was in the undeveloped part of the park, where I expected to find the Stony Stoners.

I stopped between puddles of light to stare out into the darkness. A clump of sagebrush attracted my attention. Did I see some movement? Were the Stoners hiding there? I saw a flash. Was it a cell phone or a lit joint? It was nothing. I walked forward to the next dark spot and repeated the process.

'Nothing. Waste of time. You should be home in bed,' was Fitch's assessment.

When I reached the place where a second trail diverged uphill, I considered where to go next. Turn? Straight? I listened. In the distance, cars drove on Higgs Road behind me and Millikan Road ahead. In between those cars, silence.

Then someone, several someones, were charging towards me. Feet kicked up lava rocks from the trail. I dove into the sagebrush, preferring to get scratched by the brittle foliage than run down by my attackers.

Fitch laughed when my *attackers* turned out to be a doe and her fawn.

With the silence restored, my hand reached into my backpack for a granola bar. The crinkling wrapper sounded like thunder. I did my best to open it without disturbing the peace.

A finger tapped on my shoulder and a voice hissed, "Evenin', Mr. Szilard."

I jumped. When I turned around, there they were. After I caught my breath, I said, "Stony Stoners, I presume."

A tall young man with a bushy red beard and a welcoming smile said, "We've been expecting you to make the scene."

A woman in a peasant blouse and a long homespun skirt offered me a lit joint. "Here. Get your kicks on Route Sixty-Six."

I waved her off and she passed it to the guy with a short afro standing next to her.

"You know who I am. Who are you?"

The woman said, "Joan Didion."

The guy with the afro said, "Kurt Vonnegut."

And the big smile laughed, "Allen Ginsberg."

Fitch also laughed. *'And you can call me Jack Kerouac.'*

I didn't mind that they were having some fun at my expense, but I was getting cold standing still. "Is there someplace warmer we can sit?"

Kurt pointed to the uphill trail. "Follow me on the road less traveled."

We'd gone a short way before he turned and pushed through a narrow gap in a thicket of sagebrush. I held my arms in front of me to fend off the intertwined branches. As we penetrated the foliage, the faint light of the trail faded. The arms in front of my face disappeared and I followed Kurt by sound. Soon we broke through to a clearing. There I saw a circle of boulders illuminated by a fire ring containing smoldering coals.

"Welcome to our pad. Can you dig it?" Joan said.

I took off my backpack and displayed my collection of chips and chocolate. "Help yourself."

Fitch approved. *'Munchies, a peace offering for stoners.'*

Kurt said, "Way out," and they all started eating.

Joan said, "You're no square," and stuffed some chocolate bars into her pockets for later.

While they ate, I asked, "Were you at the high school on the night of Ms. Shelley's murder?"

Everyone looked to Allen Ginsberg with his bushy red beard. He said, "She was a cool chick. Thanks to her I got it together and graduated from **S**tony **E**stancia **C**ommunity **C**ollege. Now I have a way-out job in aircraft maintenance."

"She was outta sight. I also attended SECC. Now, I'm a paramedic," Joan said.

"Of course," I exclaimed, "I didn't recognize you out of uniform. You are on Peggy Mutai's team."

She didn't seem happy that I identified her. I reassured her. "Don't worry, Joan Didion. This meeting never happened. I'm an old guy and my memory can't be trusted. I'll forget you before I get home."

'Nice save,' Fitch congratulated me, but couldn't resist adding, *'It would have been better if you never admitted that you knew her.'*

"We made the scene that night. We saw them ride up on a groovy chopper," Kurt said.

Joan continued, "I thought they wanted a quiet place to get their kicks, but then they broke that window—a downer—and disappeared into the annex."

Everyone reached into my backpack for more snacks.

"What happened next?"

"We did our own thing until he bugged out on his bike," Kurt said.

Allen added, "That scene was nowhere, so we split."

"Did you see who the guy was?"

Joan shook her head. "He wore a motorcycle helmet." After a short pause, she said, "It could have been a chick."

"How about the motorcycle? Can you identify it?"

"It might have been black, but it was night," Allen said.

Kurt spoke slowly. "And we were stoned."

I didn't press them any further. I'd decided that it wasn't a woman—it was Tiffany's husband.

"Would you like the rest of these snacks?" I dumped out my backpack in response to their Cheshire Cat smiles. "One other thing. What does everyone have against the Frank twins?"

Joan laughed, "How did you get mixed up with those space cadets?"

"Well, a witness saw two guys at the scene and the police thought of the twins."

Joan said, "I can see that. They think they are Stony Estancia royalty—trust-fund darlings. Like that time when the fire department rescued them from the mountains. We brought in a helicopter and everything. Did they thank us? No. They complained that we took too long, and they were missing their dinner reservations."

"I see."

"I'm sure your friend Senior Detective Yukawa has similar stories."

"Thank you again. Enjoy your snacks. If I see you, I won't know who you are."

We all high-fived and I jogged home.

The sun would rise in a few hours, but my visit with the Stony Stoners had made the loss of sleep worthwhile. Tiffany had arrived at the annex on the back of Gun Shell's motorcycle and the twins were harmless rich kids. Vicki's prime suspects—the Frank twins—were innocent and mine—Mr. Shelley—was guilty.

I congratulated myself and looked forward to sleeping late.

'Not so fast. You promised Vicki you'd speak to Vinnie.'

"Puppies." I set my phone to wake me and rehearsed my meeting with Purcell and Associates.

Vinnie, my friend, Vicki suspects corruption at SE-cubed.

Yes, Declan Beckett himself.

Can you hack him?

What can you find?

I fell asleep before I finished the scenario.

Wherein Zarand admires a cute grandchild.

A few hours of sleep and a quick breakfast barely prepared me for the Stony Estancia warehouse district. My fearless electric car, with a full charge, used its high torque and low mass to zip around the eighteen-wheelers that clogged Appleton Way. When it reached Purcell and Associates, it braved a sudden right, slipping between two competing trucks—an internet retailer and a national chain of brick-and-mortar stores.

The little car grabbed the last space in a lot that was as much dirt as asphalt, driving over the weeds—shepherd's purse and buckhorn plantain. I had no doubt those hardy plants would survive to provide oxygen to the unappreciative humans another day. Before I left my car, I admired Purcell and Associates' new steel door, compliments of Stony Estancia after SWAT broke down the previous one. The new door had an unwelcoming keypad lock and a sign that read PURCELL AND ASSOCIATES. TEXT FOR ENTRY with no phone number provided.

I turned to the right, recalling the custom swimwear shop with mannequins modeling bikinis in their window. On the other side sat a mixed martial arts studio. Vinnie could have been on Zeeman Way near the Civic Center and the Stony Estancia Bank. He had government clients in Stony Estancia and the three-letter agencies surrounding Washington DC, but he liked his privacy.

Farther to the right was an out-of-place shining star—a window display of sleek new phones and colorful accessories, a glass door, and a flashing digital sign scrolling, WELCOME TO RINCHEN AMAR PHONE REPAIR AND SAMMICH SHOPPE, HOME OF RAPPER, THE PHONE WIZARD.

Fitch scoffed, *'Stony Estancia's high-tech hub, the silicon strip mall.'*

Before I could text Vinnie for entrance, the surveillance cameras panned to the far left directing my attention to a flatbed tow truck, a black and white, and an unmarked car converging on a red SUV.

'That's it,' Fitch cheered. *'How could anyone miss those* Tiff the Tutor *car magnets?'*

Officer Tsui got out of the patrol car carrying his crime scene camera and evidence kits. Detective Yukawa emerged from the unmarked vehicle.

The tow truck lady loaded the red SUV onto her flatbed while Tsui went to work taking photos, filling evidence bags, and dusting for fingerprints. Vicki walked over to me.

I kissed her cheek. "Hey, Vee. Whassup?"

"You're here to speak to your buddy Vinnie, right?"

"Yes, you assigned me to check out the SE-cubed corruption story. Can you tell me what's happening here?"

She might have answered, except the *Stony Estancia Surfs* van arrived.

She muttered, "Who told them?"

The arrival of Tish and César tickled Fitch. *'We live in a small town with omniscient reporters.'*

Vicki returned to me. "That's Tiffany Shelley's car."

"Do you know what it's doing here, miles from her body?"

"That's what I'm going to find out."

I moved closer to her so *Stony Estancia Surfs* couldn't hear us, "I'm not surprised."

"Gosh, do you have something to tell me?"

"I spoke to the Stony Stoners last night."

She smiled. "What did Stony's favorite anachronistic potheads have to say?"

"Tiffany arrived at the annex on the back of a motorcycle."

"Motorcycle? Did they identify the driver? The type of bike? The color?"

I shook my head. "It was dark and they're the Stoners."

"Right, thanks. Have a good meeting with Vinnie."

As befitting a new grandfather, Vinnie's office was decorated with pictures of granddaughter Alex—so many photos. Big studio pictures on the walls and digital photo frames on his desk. I pointed to one with little Alex sitting next to a stuffed panda. "She has grown much bigger since the wedding." Then I stood up and walked over to a big wedding portrait with Annie's natural box braids finished with crystal beads, his stepson Jackson with his white hair and pale blue eyes, and little Alex between them. "It was a beautiful ceremony."

Vinnie smiled. "She's the best, already rolling over and sleeping through the night. She loves jazz music and tummy time."

He might have gone on longer and I always loved to hear about happy babies, but the door opened, and a young man with blond tips, a scruff and stubble beard, and dazzling white teeth appeared—looking more like a maître d' or a hair stylist than a technocrat.

"Chad is here to offer us refreshments," Vinnie said.

Chad asked, "Can I get you some juice or water? We have *mille feuilles* today We get all our snacks from that wonderful pâtisserie around the corner."

When we didn't reply, he suggested, "If you want something more substantial, I can run over to the Sammich Shoppe next door."

Vinnie turned down the sandwich offer and ordered juice— fresh-squeezed orange. I said, "Same for me," confident the assistant would bring a tray of the flaky French pastries unasked.

When Chad left, Vinnie said, "Don't let Dr. Wilde's appearance fool you. In addition to fetching delicacies from the pâtisserie, Chad manages our deep neural network for threat identification."

A hidden speaker responded, "I heard that," at which point Vinnie laughed and said, "And automated surveillance."

"I suppose you're wondering why I'm here," I said.

Vinnie laughed again, "Not wondering. You're here about the rumors of SE-cubed corruption."

"Yes, can you use your super-power computer skills to find out what's going on?"

He turned to his laptop, typing faster than anyone I'd ever seen. "Most nonprofits post everything on their website, but not SE-cubed."

"Puppies," I exclaimed, "Isn't that a big red flag?"

"If it's not too personal, why do you say puppies all the time?"

I hadn't even realized I'd used that expletive. "Oh, nothing personal. I don't want to use stronger words when teaching, so I've trained myself to say puppies."

"Good idea. Now that little Alex is older and repeating everything she hears, I might do the same. Can I use your word?"

"Sure, no charge. If you don't like puppies, puppets work as well."

"In answer to your question, their lack of transparency is a red flag." He returned to his laptop and lost himself in a cyberspace trance.

While he performed his computer magic, I enjoyed the light-as-air puff pastry, vanilla cream, and chocolate icing while watching little Alex frolic on the digital photo frames. I was in no rush, which was good because I had time to finish several *mille feuilles* before Vinnie returned to the present. "Puppets," he said, laughing at the word. "Tish and *Stony Estancia Surfs* were right. I don't know where to begin. There are too many cash withdrawals. Most suspicious is a large one to Ms. Shelley before her murder."

'Do you think she was extorting Declan?' suggested Fitch.

I didn't ask for details. Nothing he'd discovered by hacking SE-cubed could be used as evidence. I didn't want to contaminate Vicki's case any more than necessary.

With that and the note I found on Ms. Miller's desk, handwritten by Tiffany Shelley, Declan Beckett moved to the top of my suspect list.

"Thanks," I said to Vinnie. "One more favor please."

"Sure, no problem."

"What can you tell me about your neighbor?"

"Do you want to buy a swimsuit for Vicki?"

I smiled. "No. On the other side."

"Puppets." He laughed at this again. "You're a bit old for martial arts."

I could tell he was pulling my leg, but I played along. "Rapper. What do you know about Rapper? You're two computer geeks, aren't you?"

"Not really. He's a phone guy. He puts apps together from toolkits. I doubt he can tell a protocol stack from an OS kernel."

"Do you guys talk at all?"

"Just to order sandwiches. My fav is the eggless breakfast croissant with bacon and Swiss. The Sammich Shoppe uses the finest ingredients—all the breads come from that wonderful pâtisserie around the corner." Vinnie took a forkful of *mille feuilles* before adding. "He's a client. I manage his network, like I do for the city, the school district, and many others."

"Do you think he could be mixed up with the SE-cubed crowd?"

"No, that's a big money crowd, he's small-time. However, his store attracts as many of Stony Estancia's good-looking women as that swimwear shop. Sometimes I see them in the surveillance videos walking from one place to the other."

I finished my last *mille feuilles* and thanked Vinnie again. I sent a text to Vicki- **SZILARD**: DECLAN BECKETT IS DIRTY.

Vinnie blocked all signals within his offices so that text wasn't sent until I exited Purcell and Associates.

By the time I reached my black-and-white car, Chuck Berry's *School Days* riff announced a sub assignment. After a few quick taps, I booked a job standing in for Ms. Blume, the librarian. That implied that Vicki had removed the crime scene tape.

I looked forward to library duty—easy and uneventful. I checked the Stony High website to prevent any surprises. In addition to research periods and study halls, there was a meeting of the Library Club—a perfect place to interrogate my grandkids, my confidential informants.

24

APOLLO AND ARTEMIS

Wherein the OG Gods intervene.

Far from Stony Estancia, on Mount Olympus, the Greek gods observed the mortals as they had for many millennia.

"Can I offer you some more tea?

Artemis held up her cup.

Apollo filled it, put down the teapot, and collapsed into his favorite throne with a sigh.

She looked at her brother. "Aren't we lucky?"

"Yes, still around many years since our temples have been deserted."

She laughed. "Not all of them. They still visit my temple at Ephesus."

He loved her laugh. "And my temple at Delphi draws larger crowds than ever."

They sat in silence while a couple of hummingbirds performed an aerial battle around a bougainvillea vine. One retreated while the other visited the multitude of new flowers that bloomed every moment. When the victor left, the vanquished also drank its fill.

Artemis watched over the tiniest of eggs that hatched into the tiniest of baby birds. She wondered aloud. "Brother, do you have any regrets?"

"Maybe one."

She reached her hand, wrinkled and soft with age, across the space between them, across the Aegean from Ephesus to Delphi. "Tell me."

"The lady who was murdered was a good person. Helped so many with her tutoring, like my half-sister Athena."

"Yes," she agreed. "I've heard many positive things about her, and now she's dead."

Artemis took her hand back and replaced it in her lap. She didn't have the strength to hold it out for long.

He dunked his biscuit in his tea to soften it before taking a small bite. After he swallowed, he said, "And, I worry about the child lost in the mountains."

She added a splash of milk to her tea. "And now I hear they're going to investigate those generous people who built that beautiful annex at the high school, a modern temple to Athena."

He added, "And the police are harassing those young people who stay up late at night. Do you think all of this is because of that treasure?"

"I do. I do," she said.

He looked at her with love, admiration, and a sly grin. "But you know where the treasure is hidden, don't you?"

She smiled, but not too much. She didn't like to show her dimples. "Yes, brother. I figured it out. After all these years, someone had to, and it was me."

It was his turn to reach across the sea. He caressed the back of her hand with his thin fingers. "How clever of you. What are you going to do?"

"Well, I'll make a game of it," she chuckled.

He loved how the mortals entertained her.

"I'll send clues to those nice people at that website. I'll be like your Oracles."

"How will you do that?"

"The regular way. Dreams and talking animals."

He dunked another biscuit in his tea. "I look forward to your clues posted on *Stony Estancia Surfs*."

Her eyes sparkled. "I will make them exceedingly clever."

He ate his biscuit before it became too soggy. "Will you use classical references? Homer? Aristophanes?"

She finished her cuppa. "Oh no. That would be unfair. My clues will be high tech, 21st century."

"Jolly good. I will enjoy seeing them struggle when the answer is just in front of them."

25

THE LIBRARY CLUB - WEDNESDAY

Wherein the OG Gods deliver the first clue.

I arrived at the Library Club meeting hoping to slip in some questions about Tiff the Tutor's murder. But the library reading room was full, standing room only—too many for a subtle interrogation. I ordered a Pizza Napoli with extra anchovies from the Bruin Bistro and stood by the entrance to await delivery.

Lizzy stood at the front of the room, near the history annex. She rapped her gavel on a round table. "New book requests are the first agenda item."

'No one is making eye contact with her,' observed Fitch. *'They don't care.'*

She displayed the request list onto a huge 8K monitor that dropped down from the ceiling, a gift from SE-cubed.

Fitch was right. The indifferent audience became restless.

Then Lizzy said something rarely heard in Stony Estancia, 'We need to make cuts."

'That woke them up,' Fitch said with a smile.

Lizzy pushed on. "For example, why do we need more Rust programming manuals?"

Ranch ate his lunch in one of the study carrels. I glimpsed the wrapper. Not surprisingly, it came from Rapper's Sammich Shoppe. When Lizzy mentioned Rust, he jumped up. "The ones we have are out-of-date. We need the latest versions."

January, who sat at Lizzy's table with Alyce and Zola, rubbed her fingers together making the sign for CASH. "How much money do we need? I'm sure we can raise it. This is Stony Estancia."

Alyce agreed. "We can have a barbecue. That's always a popular fundraiser. Put some shrimp on the barbie."

"A *lekker* idea. Everyone loves a *braai*. My gymnastics team in Joburg held one every month," Zola said.

Lizzy lost control of her meeting.

Ranch stood up and stepped from behind his carrel to address the full room. "Let's get serious. Forget the budget. Forget barbecues. Even forget my Rust manuals. Our friend, Tiff the Tutor, was murdered here. Let's do something about that."

The large crowd had doomed my murder investigation, but Ranch saved my agenda by derailing Lizzy's.

Lizzy took a deep breath and forced it out through her pursed lips.

'She hates it when someone disrupts her meeting,' Fitch observed.

In an astute move, she took back control by unwrapping her lunch—a can of tea and a Caprese sandwich with a thick slice of mozzarella and dripping with olive oil.

The others followed her lead. The Library Club ate in silence, all waiting to see what Lizzy would do next.

Zola ventured. "*Eish.* Like my gymnastics coach always says, 'Keep your eyes on the prize.' We're on a quest to track down Ms. Shelley's killer."

Lizzy didn't respond and the group went back to eating their lunches.

'No one is here to review book requests,' Fitch noted.

Obviously, I thought.

Lizzy, eating her lunch in silence, was in charge. *What would she do?*

Jorge delivered my pizza. "Here you go, Mr. S." He looked at the quiet room, and asked, "Whassup?"

"They're going to find Ms. Shelley's murderer," I optimistically replied.

"I loved Tiff the Tutor." His phone beeped. "George here." After a pause, he said, "I was delivering Mr. S's pizza, but now I'm going to stay in the library and find Ms. Shelley's killer."

I gave him a couple of slices of pizza. He picked off the anchovies and returned them to me. I piled them on top of my remaining slices.

After eating, Lizzy rapped her gavel on the table again. "Thank you all for coming today. I can see you want to solve Ms. Shelley's murder."

I was encouraged when the group murmured agreement.

'Clever Lizzy sure can read a crowd. And just like that the book list is ancient history.'

"Here's what we're going to do. And all of you can help. We're going to check out everything from the California History Collection," Lizzy said.

"*Qué*?" exclaimed Jorge, standing up from his comfortable green-and-gold rocking chair.

"*Crikey*. Why would we do that?" asked Alyce.

'Brilliant,' said Fitch.

I understood the plan. "Come on everyone. Let's go." I pulled on the California History Annex door, but I couldn't open it. "Ugh. Sloppy painters. A little help, please."

Zola did a forward flip, stuck the landing right next to me, and opened the sticky door.

Lizzy smiled. "You go, girl."

"You're strong," I said.

"I'm going to be a superhero someday," Zola replied.

I loved this about my adopted grandkids. For all their differences, when something needed to be done, they rolled up their expensive sleeves and worked together.

With the annex wide open, Lizzy folded her arms and waited, like a kindergarten teacher.

"One, two, three, eyes on Lizzy," I said in support.

They got the message and gave Lizzy their attention.

"The cops know someone broke into the annex, but they don't know if anything was taken," she said.

I supported her. "That's right. There are so many books and documents. How could they know what's missing?"

"We're going to sign out everything in the room," Lizzy said.

Alyce clarified, "*Bonzer*. I get it. Anything not checked out must have been stolen."

"*Vamos*." Jorge headed for the annex.

Soon a bucket brigade was moving archival boxes and books from the annex to the team at the self-checkout stations.

Alyce opened an archival box to check out the contents. "*Blimey*. This doesn't belong here."

I shouted, "That may be evidence. Don't touch it."

She'd found a wallet. I ran back to the annex and returned wearing cotton gloves. After examining Alyce's discovery, I called Vicki. "We found Tiff the Tutor's wallet."

"Gosh," she exclaimed. "I'm sending Tsui with an evidence kit. Did you also find her phone?"

"No. No phone. Can't you track it?"

"We did. The last time it registered was Wednesday morning, the day after the murder. Someone turned it off."

"Well, at least we have her wallet."

I told the Library Club, "Stony PD says thank you."

Lizzy got them back on task. "Good work, but like Zola's coach says, 'Keep your eyes on the prize.' We need to scan everything."

The bucket brigade resumed their work. The stacks of books and boxes in the annex were rapidly disappearing.

Everyone cheered. The annex was empty, and the end-of-lunch buzzer hadn't sounded.

"Mr. S., can you log in as the librarian and tell us what's not checked out?"

I entered the library circulation system from Ms. Blume's computer and was happy to find just a single California History Collection document not checked out. I sent the entry to the printer: *Un tratado de paz, amistad, limites y arreglo definitive (original at National Archive)*.

I handed the page to Jorge. "*¿Qué es esto?*"

He thought for a moment. "That's the Treaty of Guadalupe Hidalgo, the Mexican Cession. Someone is interested in Mexican land grants."

"Why?" I asked.

"They're looking for the Cajon Treasure," he laughed.

I showed Jorge the photo of the document found in the Franks' apartment. "Is this it?"

"Go to the last page," said Jorge.

I scrolled down to the signatures, easily recognizable by red wax seals.

"That's it. There's Nicholas Trist's signature at the top. Where did you find this?"

Before I could answer, the end-of-lunch buzzer sounded. Everyone cleaned up their trash, pushed their chairs under the tables, and prepared to head for their next class, but they were interrupted.

Ranch blocked the door. "Go to *Stony Estancia Surfs*. Tish is reporting that she received a clue to the Cajon Treasure in a dream with a promise of more clues to follow."

'Isn't that just like Stony Estancia Surfs, *printing clues from a dream?'* scoffed Fitch.

Ranch read, "Star-crossed triangles origin nexus you travel twelve miles."

'Is that a clue?' wondered Fitch.

"I hope the next clue is better. That one seems more like a nightmare to me," Zola said with full teenage sarcasm.

On Mount Olympus, *Apollo turned to Artemis, "Is that the best you could do?"*

Artemis laughed, "My clues are perfect. Just wait and see."

Apollo loved it when his twin sister laughed.

With the promise of more clues, the Cajon Treasure seemed close. Gun Shell was still at the top of my list given his wife's unfortunate assortment of broken bones. However, evidence was mounting against Declan Beckett, the corrupt banker. Vicki was interested in the Frank twins, who looked guilty because they stole the Treaty of Guadalupe Hidalgo.

As everyone exited the library, Lizzy said, "Good work. We found something the cops missed. Let's do that again. Meet me at the gym after school. We're going to search outside."

My intuition told me Lizzy had the right idea.

Lizzy stood on the hill leading up to the football field. "Jorge will lead a group to search the bleachers. January will take the construction area outside the annex. Alyce will go walkabout around the field. Meet back here before we lose daylight."

I joined January's group. We took pictures of footprints and tire tracks outside the shattered window. There were a surprising number of them. The construction area was ideal to preserve impressions in the dirt.

Fitch was discouraged, *'I'm sure Detective Yukawa's forensic team has checked here.'*

January came to the same conclusion. When she reported back to the group, she touched the tips of her index finger and thumb. ZERO. She made a sad face and said, "Nothing."

Alyce's groups came back with a collection of washers and nuts. Again, I was confident this was not new evidence.

Jorge stood behind the bleachers. "Come look at this." He pointed to a small circle of washers, some standing on edge, half embedded in the dirt.

Alyce pulled one of them out of the ground. "This is the same as the others we found. I wonder how it got stuck like that?"

Fitch joked, *'Must be an important clue.'*

I had a feeling that Dr. Chandrasekhar's science experiment—the one I supervised when I subbed for him—would shed light on this clue.

My phone beeped. I received an invitation from my friend and frequent dinner guest County Coroner Persephone Paterson to attend her inquest into the cause of death for Tiffany Shelley. The washers strangely buried in the dirt would have to wait. I wasn't going to miss Persey's inquest. She presided with flair and panache.

Wherein Tsui plays the bad cop.

I woke. Without checking my phone I could tell it was still night. Dahl touched my cheek with her pink toe beans and purred, time for second dinner. I agreed and put on my robe. A couple of slices of sourdough went into the toaster. A hamburger patty sizzled on my Korean BBQ grill pan. The savory aroma of seared beef filled the room. I found a ripe tomato in the fridge and sliced it. In a few minutes, the table was set with two plates—one with a cheeseburger and all the trimmings, and another with just beef. Dahl's purring made for relaxing dinner conversation.

I was clearing the dishes and Dahl was asking for another second dinner when Vicki called. I answered with, "Evenin' Vee. Whassup?"

"Have you cleaned up after your midnight snack?" she asked with a cheerful voice.

'She's got your number,' said Fitch with a sly smile.

"Just loading the dishwasher."

"Do you want to join an after-dark operation?"

She didn't offer any details, and I didn't ask. "Sure."

"Meet at the community center. In an hour. Lights out. Stealth."

"I'll be there."

What could be stealthier than jogging? I wore black with a reflector belt and a headlamp for safety. When I reached the Pacific Electric Trail, it was darker than my last visit. The few lights installed on the trail were off tonight.

'Lovers or vandals?' Fitch theorized.

I hadn't brought my trekking poles and wasn't going to risk jogging on the dark path. I continued down Higgs Road for a short way before turning left on Bridgman Road, which still had traffic. When I reached the community center, I removed my reflector belt and turned off my headlamp to honor Vicki's request for stealth. I entered the parking lot where I rendezvoused with Vicki's team, all dressed in black. She wore night-vision goggles.

She handed me a black balaclava to cover my head. I was happy to see they were not carrying weapons—no rifles, no shotguns, no grenades, not even sidearms.

'Not vandals or lovers. The PD turned off the lights.' Fitch realized.

My shuffling gait stirred up the lava rocks, making a small racket in the quiet park. I studied Vee, who moved soundlessly, placing each foot with firmness and purpose like a dancer. I did my best to copy her walk, again regretting that I hadn't brought my trekking poles.

Fitch mocked me, *'Are you admitting that you're getting too old for this?'*

I responded by standing up straighter and walking stronger. I had plenty of good years left. I concentrated on my footsteps while Vicki's head turned right and left, scanning the open space with her night-vision goggles.

She made a fist and held it at eye level.

Everyone froze.

She pointed to a clump of sagebrush.

At first, I didn't see anything, but my eyes adjusted, and I saw their dying campfire. A short while later, I could see the joint they were passing around the circle.

Vicki raised her fist again and thrust it in the direction of the embers.

I didn't want them to see me, so I stayed in the shadows.

The team circled the sagebrush and charged in, shouting. "Police. Freeze. Show us your hands."

No one followed the instructions. The police rushed through the sage towards the inner clearing. The Stony Stoners barreled through the same sage in the opposite direction. In a moment, it was all over. Most of the Stoners had disappeared into the darkness and the cops were standing around the fire. Only two stoners remained, looking dazed and confused.

Tsui was holding Frank and Vicki had Frankie.

She read them their rights. They were cuffed and marched back to the community center parking lot.

After we returned to PD headquarters, Tsui placed the Frank twins in a single interrogation room.

He stood over them. "We know you didn't work alone, but you're the ones we have. Do you want to go down for a murder rap?"

Frank and Frankie looked at each other but didn't say anything.

Tsui slammed his palm on the table. "It's late. You are keeping me from my children. You better start talking soon."

"We have nothing to say without a lawyer," Frankie said.

'So much for the bad cop,' said Fitch who was enjoying the show through the two-way mirror.

Vicki entered the small room carrying a tray of coffees. "Would you like something to drink? She pointed to the different cups. "Black, sugar, cream and sugar. Only the best for our VIP guests."

Frank reached for a coffee, but Frankie slapped his hand. They both sat with their arms crossed and defiant stares.

"You don't need to say anything. We already have enough to book you," Vicki said with a smile.

She held up her index finger. "You admitted you were at the murder scene. Now we know you didn't tell us the full story."

The twins maintained their contempt.

Now she added her middle finger. "We found a can of spray paint next to Ms. Shelley's dead body."

Frank flinched when she said, *dead body.*

Vicki continued with her best imitation of a friendly aunt. "Whose fingerprints did we find on that can? Nice clear prints. Tiff the Tutor? No. We found Tafari's, aka Frank's, prints. Do you want to say something now?"

Before Frank could respond, Frankie shouted, "No," and she jabbed her elbow into her brother's side.

Vicki kept up her friendly approach. "I understand your position, Frankie. After all, those weren't your fingerprints."

'Go Senior Detective. Drive a wedge between them.'

She popped out her thumb. "Last time you said you were on your way to Only Donuts."

Frankie was firm, but Frank looked nervous.

Vicki smiled. "Do you know what the Library Club uncovered this afternoon?"

Frankie closed her mouth so tightly that her lips disappeared. Frank mouthed, "What?"

"They discovered the Treaty of Guadalupe Hidalgo was missing. We found a copy in your apartment."

Frankie responded, "It's a *copy*. Doesn't mean anything."

"Maybe. Maybe not," replied Vee. She scratched her chin as if she was thinking. "They also found Tiff the Tutor's wallet. It had a piece of paper with your contact information on it. Names. Address. Cell phones." She paused before adding the clincher. "The note said, *Tuesday, first period*. You were set up."

Frank moved away from his sister. "I'll tell you."

'Good cop for the win.'

He spoke rapidly. "She paid us. Cash. Crisp Benjamins. Sequential serial numbers." He opened his wallet and fanned out the new hundred-dollar bills. "See. She planned to steal the Cajon Treasure journals and find the treasure."

"I don't know where you got those, but they don't prove anything," Vicki said.

Frankie smashed her palm on her forehead and her resistance faded. "We were all going to share the treasure."

Frank continued, "I was told to spray paint, *down with the patriarchy*. She made me learn how to spell *patriarchy*."

"Tiff the Tutor to the end," Frankie said with disdain in her voice.

"That was meant to divert the police to the protestors," added Frank.

Vicki addressed the twins. "If you don't have a better story, I'm going to charge you both with the murder of Ms. Shelley."

Frankie lost her cool. "That's unfair. You can't do that."

Vicki turned to Tsui. "Book 'em and give Miss Tough Gal her phone call."

Wherein Zarand goes to court.

I crossed an ocean of light-gray California granite before entering the Stony Estancia Civic Center. I admired the façade of columns and acres of steps, but the interior, rather than harking back to a monumental public building, reminded me of an airport. I checked the electronic directory, reminiscent of an arrivals/departures board.

'Oh look,' exclaimed Fitch. *'The coroner's inquest is on the third floor and you're late.'* With a sadistic chortle, he added, *'And look at that crowd in front of the elevators.'*

I took the stairs, using my arms, pulling myself up by the handrails.

Fitch glided beside me, *'I'm impressed. For an old guy, you're making good time.'*

County Coroner Persephone Paterson addressed César and Leticia. "This inquest is open to the public, but you cannot record the proceedings." She pointed to a young man wearing a white shirt and a black tie. "We have a court reporter who will file the official record." He waved and graced us with a shy smile. "Hi," he said before murmuring to himself. "I'm not supposed to talk unless addressed by the presiding official."

Persey waited while I walked down the aisle between the wooden benches—not unlike church pews. Everyone stared at me as if I'd arrived late to a wedding. Mr. Shelley waved until his lawyer stopped him.

I took a seat next to Vicki and slid close to her on the bench. She squeezed my knee and placed her finger across her lips. *Shush.* There was one person I didn't recognize. He wore an expensive suit, pinstripes, a white shirt with gold cuff links, and a blue and red power tie. I whispered to Vicki. "Who's that?"

"That's the Franks' attorney from a big Los Angeles firm, someone they keep on retainer for occasions like this."

Persey wore a black velvet robe. "I conduct my inquests with a certain degree of informality. I notice we have lawyers here today. I assume you'll want to ask questions to justify your billable hours. Raise your hands and I will recognize you."

'She runs this like a kindergarten,' Fitch remarked with some glee.

"I call my first witness, January Shaw." She turned to her clerk. "Please bring in Miss Gallaudet."

The clerk returned with a thin woman wearing a white blouse, a purple poodle skirt, and a matching neck scarf. She looked old enough to have worn that skirt to her high-school hop. She smiled at January. The court was quiet while January and Miss Gallaudet conversed in sign language.

With Miss Gallaudet's assistance, Persey swore in January and requested, "Please tell us, in your own words, what happened the morning you discovered Ms. Shelley in the California History Annex."

Miss Gallaudet responded. "She prefers to testify in ASL. I'll interpret."

'She must be nervous,' remarked Fitch.

January recounted her interaction with the Frank twins. How they argued. How Tafari Frank saved her from the falling bookshelves before the twins disappeared.

Persey asked if anyone had further questions for January. No one spoke.

Persey released her. "Thank you. You are free to return to school."

January took a seat in the front pew and signed something.

Persey turned to Miss Gallaudet. "Can you tell us what she said?"

The ASL interpreter laughed to herself. "I'm not going back to school and miss this."

January had a broad smile and shook her head in agreement.

Persey said, "You go, girl."

The Franks' lawyer raised his hand, stood up, and said, "Pardon me, Ms. Paterson, Your Honor, —"

Persey interrupted him. "Don't let my informality fool you, Mr. Kafka. You may address me as Persey, but not until I recognize you. If you persist in disrupting my inquest, I will cite you for contempt and have you removed."

He looked around at the court officers who had serious faces and their arms folded across their chests. "My apologies, Persey, Your Honor." He sat down.

That showed him. His big-city swagger doesn't mean anything in Stony Estancia.

Persey began again. "First, we report on the cause of death." She paused to give a hard look at Mr. Kafka. He returned her look but didn't speak.

"The autopsy findings were unremarkable. Cause of death is still undetermined."

Mr. Kafka raised his hand.

Fitch was enjoying this. *That's a good boy. You're not in your home court. You must behave.*

Persey pointed to the Franks' lawyer. "Do you have a question?"

He stood. "Have you considered drugs?" When Persey didn't respond, he added, "Your Honor?"

Sounding like a sarcastic teen, Persey lectured him. "Your Honor is not necessary. Persey is fine. Yes, even though we're out here in the burbs, we sent samples, blood, urine, stool, stomach, more on that later, to the FBI for comprehensive testing. Nothing."

Mr. Kafka raised his hand again.

Persey continued, "And before you ask, we checked for diseases. I prepared tissue samples from all internal organs, brain, heart, liver, etcetera, and sent them to the pathologist at Stony Estancia Regional Hospital. Would you like those slides to be examined by your pathologist? Something else to bill to your client?"

"Not necessary. Persey. But what about the head trauma?"

"Good question, Mr. Kafka. It was caused by a fall against a steel bookshelf. We matched the paint. It might have caused loss of consciousness, but it wasn't fatal."

"Thank you. Persey."

"The other question before us is the time of death."

Mr. Kafka crossed his arms and leaned back in his pew.

"The time of death was near to the discovery of the body by Ms. January Shaw."

January smiled and signed ME poking her index finger to her chest.

Persey prefaced her report with, "I understand the exact time is important. After considering the standard tests, body temp, rigor mortis, and lividity, the time of death was still uncertain. A difference of a few hours is critical in this case."

Mr. Shelley's lawyer raised her hand.

"Yes, Ms. Brautigan?"

"Persey, didn't the witness, Ms. Shaw, see the murder and didn't that establish the time of death?"

"Her testimony did not determine either the time or cause of death. Those bookcases that piled on top of Ms. Shelley were postmortem. She was dead before the shelves tipped over."

Persey digressed to tell her audience about traumatic asphyxia and the witch trials in Salem Massachusetts where Giles Corey was killed by a heavy weight on his chest.

'She likes to tell that story, doesn't she?' chuckled Fitch.

I don't think that is something to make light of, I chastised him.

"Thank you for that clarification, Persey." Ms. Brautigan turned to her client, Mr. Shelley. They both looked concerned.

Fitch questioned, *'Since the Frank twins are under arrest, why did Mr. Shelley show up with a lawyer?'*

I didn't know why Fitch was confused. The Frank twins were innocent, and Gun Shell was guilty. He was preparing for his inevitable arrest.

Ms. Brautigan was right to be concerned. Persey hadn't announced anything yet, but my gut told me it wouldn't be good for my prime suspect, Gunnar Shelley.

César could also see the writing on the wall. He sketched the serious Ms. Brautigan and nervous Mr. Shelley with dark storm clouds in the background.

'Gun Shell is going down,' snickered Fitch.

With Persey getting ready to proclaim the time of death, Mr. Kafka relaxed and spread out in his pew, arms stretched out like he was the man in charge.

Here, César's sketch was more optimistic. He put rainbows behind Mr. Kafka.

My instincts agreed. This inquest was good for the Franks. Vicki might have to release her favorite suspects.

Persey didn't reveal the time of death right away. She told us a little story. "We were fortunate in this case. Thanks to the Stony PD's excellent detective work."

'I knew this. It was Officer Tsui,' said Fitch.

Persey continued in a confidential voice like she was sharing with a few good friends. "At midnight, the victim ordered a couple of pork rib dinners to-go from the Firehouse Barbecue."

'You love that place,' interjected Fitch.

"The server observed her sitting on the back of a motorcycle eating her food before discarding the bones and packaging in the Firehouse trash receptacles."

'I knew that, too. It was Jorge,' said Fitch.

I turned to Vicki. "I'm getting hungry."

She shushed me. "You're always hungry."

"When we performed the autopsy, we found pork, traces of cornbread, and none of the barbecue sauce in her stomach. The sauce, mostly sugar, was digested before the starches and proteins."

She looked at her audience like an experienced raconteur. "I told you I'd get back to her stomach, didn't I?"

January nodded yes, enjoying the performance. Everyone else waited for Persey to continue.

"Evidence shows—"

The room was silent except for the sound of César's charcoal capturing Persey draped in her velvet robes and sitting above us at her bench. He put sunbeams from a rising sun in the background.

"We know when she ate those ribs—it was just after midnight. Her digestion stopped no more than four hours later. Ms. Tiffany Shelley's death occurred, and her digestion stopped, no later than five a.m."

Mr. Kafka jumped to his feet and shouted, "My clients are innocent. Everyone agrees they didn't arrive at the school until hours later."

Persey whispered, "I've already spoken to you. Kindly, sit down."

He obeyed with a self-satisfied expression. He was done with the inquest.

'I'd say that he's won this round,' Fitch said.

The good news was that without the Frank twins, we had narrowed our suspect pool.

'But without getting any nearer to closing the case,' Fitch added in his pessimistic way.

When I left the courthouse, *Stony Estancia Surfs* had already posted a story with the headline: YOU WON'T BELIEVE WHAT TIFF THE TUTOR ATE FOR HER LAST MEAL. While I read a recap of the inquest, another post appeared: THE SECOND CLUE TO THE CAJON TREASURE REVEALED TO CÉSAR BY A TALKING CAT.

That clue was as cryptic as the first one: THE WAYS NO ONE READS TREASURE HOW UNCOVERS.

'Talking cat,' laughed Fitch. *'César and Tish will do anything for clicks. I think they're making up these gobbledygook clues.*

On Mount Olympus, *Artemis turned to Apollo, "How did you like the talking cat?"*

Apollo laughed, "I would have preferred a griffin or centaur."

Artemis replied, "This is the 21st century and my choices were dog or cat, and the internet prefers cats.

Wherein Zarand's intuition gets him in trouble.

I didn't have an assignment on Friday, so Dahl and I enjoyed brunch. I had time to make coconut flour waffles accompanied by a fried egg and applewood smoked bacon on the side. I served Dahl a plain omelet.

After Dahl licked her plate clean, she swiped a strip of bacon and carried it to the sofa where she enjoyed her plunder and recharged her batteries in the morning sun.

"What do you think?" I asked. "Was it Gun Shell the abusive husband? Or perhaps Tiff the Tutor was extorting Mr. Beckett, the corrupt banker?"

Dahl washed her whiskers.

"So, you don't think it was either of them?" I asked her to clarify her response.

That got a definite meow.

'I'm with Dahl,' chimed in Fitch.

My intuition told me that my grandkids had the answers. I packed a lunch of Chinese food from the takeout containers in my fridge and headed for the Library Club meeting. When I arrived, the meeting was in progress, so I sat in a green-and-gold rocking chair at the back of the room and ate my General Tso chicken with chopsticks.

Lizzy was in the front, near the history annex, reading hotel room assignments for the senior trip. "Jorge and Ranch are sharing a double, as are Alyce and Zola. I'm with January, and as usual, Pax has a single."

I was eager for any news of Pax. I put down my lunch and stood up. "Are you sure that they're coming back? They have been camping out in the mountains for a long time."

"Did you say camping, Mr. S.? We are talking about Pax—high-thread-count sheets and electric blankets. They are not going walkabout," contributed Alyce.

That was news to me. I probed for more information. "Not camping? So where is Pax? The police haven't seen a signal from their cell phone."

"I told Pax to keep their phone off and use secure messaging over VPN," Ranch said.

"Pax has gone to a lot of effort to disappear and we're not telling," January said while tracing out a question mark shape with a flat hand and shaking her head. NEVER.

"My parents will room together," Lizzy said.

"Are your parents coming?" asked Jorge.

With her best teenage sarcasm, Lizzy said, "Dr. Chandrasekhar, the physics teacher? He goes every year."

Jorge laughed. "I keep forgetting that he's your father."

She gave him a playful punch on his arm. "Try to keep up. That's why we have the same last name."

"But your mother is Nilanjana Rajagopalan," Jorge retorted.

"I'm rooming with Jared. I mean Mr. Sendak," I contributed. "Will you put Mrs. Golding with Ms. Miller?"

"No. Ms. Miller gets a single room because her CPAP makes too much noise," Lizzy explained.

"*Eish*, what kind of American tech is a CPAP?" exclaimed Zola.

Alyce looked at her phone. "*Blimey*, I had to look it up. Continuous Positive Airway Pressure, whatever that means."

Lizzy ignored the interruption, "Mrs. Golding was going to double with Ms. Shelley, so she'll be in a single also."

January also checked her phone. "A CPAP is for sleep apnea. Do you think Ms. Miller has been having trouble sleeping? She's been acting strangely."

"Has she been behaving suspiciously?" I asked, wondering if Ms. Miller might be my replacement suspect since Fitch and Dahl had downvoted Gun Shell and the corrupt banker.

"Yes, she's been showing movies. My father says she used to rant against them as bad teaching"

Alyce smiled. "I know why. She has a new boyfriend."

Zola said, "I agree. New boyfriend. She had her hair braided. Way cute. She used to wear it like mine." Zola ran her fingers through her natural hair.

"I can slip a tracker into her purse and see what that uncovers," Ranch said.

"Do it. I'm curious about her boyfriend." Lizzy banged her gavel. "That's the room assignments. Meeting adjourned."

I asked Ranch for the tracker information.

He replied, "Use my dad's GPS app," and texted me the details.

Before the library emptied, every phone sounded with an assortment of whistles, beeps, and bells.

Stony Estancia Surfs.

"*Blimey*, Tish got this clue from a talking coyote."

Ranch read from his phone, BIG CLUE AS JAR OPENS NIRVANAS AND ECSTASYS.

"That's the best clue yet," said Alyce. "Jar. Nirvana. Funerary jar. The Cajon Treasure is buried in a cemetery."

On Mount Olympus, Apollo and Artemis joined hands and danced in a circle. With every step, the ground burst to life with petunias, pansies, and primroses.

Apollo cheered, "The Aussie girl figured it out, didn't she?"

Artemis had a smug smile, "Not even close. She missed both the real clue and the decoy clue."

While everyone talked about the Cajon Treasure clues, I set up my phone to track Ms. Miller.

'*Vicki's not going to like that tracker plan,*' warned Fitch.

Don't be so sure. She was willing to put a tracker on Pax's SUV.

'*A lot of good that did. The car didn't move, and Mr. Shelley had to get it towed,*' countered Fitch.

I just won't tell her. As the Jesuits say, Forgiveness is easier than permission. I'll stake out Ms. Miller before Vicki finds out anything. Tonight.

Wherein Zarand eats in his car.

After I finished lunch, I turned on notifications for Rapper's GPS app and settled into a library rocking chair to read *The Ecology Club* on my phone. That turned into a nap until the app woke me.

Ranch had activated the tracker and dropped it into Ms. Miller's purse. SIGNAL ACQUIRED. FAITH MILLER 0.1 MILES. With the time remaining until school ended, I went to Factory and Farm Foods to stock up. Without a stakeout partner, I had no idea when I'd have a break.

'It's going to be difficult to find something to eat,' Fitch predicted. *'No microwave. No refrigerator.'*

No problem. Just watch me.

FFF had a wide selection I could store in my car for the evening—sushi, fried chicken, sourdough rolls, sliced cheese and salami, with chocolate chip cookies and fresh berries for dessert. I also picked up a couple of bottles of Bass Pale Ale which I'd drink warm, like the Brits.

I hid my little car between a couple of pickup trucks in the faculty parking lot and waited. Soon Faith appeared. She drove a teal sedan which was easy to follow as most Stony Estancia cars were neutral colors. My car blended right in.

I followed her down Blackett Street to the T-intersection with Bohr Boulevard. I pulled into the left-turn lane and drove a short way up the hill toward the Pauli Falls Open Space, keeping my eye on her in my rear-view mirror. I didn't worry about losing her because I had Rapper's GPS program tracking her.

To my surprise, her teal car made two quick right turns into Vicki's quiet neighborhood.

'Oops,' Fitch said. *'Now you need to avoid being seen by both Faith and Vicki.'*

I made a quick U-turn and raced downhill in time to see the teal car pulling into the garage of Vicki's next-door neighbor.

I didn't slow down until the road took a lazy curve and I could observe without being seen.

I finished the sushi, chicken, and one beer. I regretted not having any caffeine. It was getting dark, and this was the time that someone would have arrived to take the next shift, but I was on my own.

Fitch joked, *'You can take a nap and I'll keep watch.'*

I broke open the raspberries and ate them with the cookies, hoping for a jolt of sugar to keep me awake.

That wasn't necessary. The garage door opened, and the teal car took off.

I silently followed her taillights onto the Desert Freeway. After a few exits, she got off in San Amano and worked her way to the San Amano High School. There she parked. I drove past her, hid my little car, and took out my night-vision binocs.

With the sushi and chicken gone, I prepared cheese and salami sandwiches on sourdough rolls, regretting that I hadn't bought any dark mustard.

I didn't have to wait long.

A young girl, high school age, went up to Faith. They talked. I zoomed in to see what was happening. They exchanged envelopes.

'Drugs for money,' Fitch surmised.

Ms. Miller was a drug dealer. No problem sleeping. No boyfriend. Just drugs.

She was too far away for me to take pictures with my phone. I had an infrared camera with a long zoom lens, but I hadn't unpacked it.

And the drug deal was over.

Faith returned to her car.

'Productive night,' Fitch congratulated me. *'It's a shame you didn't get any photos.'*

I ate my sandwich and waited to make sure she was leaving.

A group of boys showed up. I dropped my food and grabbed my binocs. It was like the first time. Brief discussions and the exchange of envelopes.

'She's a drug dealer.' An excited Fitch jumped up and down.

I opened my glove compartment and took out my infrared camera. By the time I'd focused it on Faith, the local pusher, her customer was gone.

'You've got to be faster, old man,' Fitch taunted me.

I picked up my sandwich, again regretting the lack of mustard.

Finally, another group approached. Girls and boys. Again, they exchanged envelopes, but I got pictures this time.

Fitch got bored of drug deals and reverted to his negativity. *'What does this have to do with Ms. Shelley's murder?'*

I went back to basics and reviewed the facts. Mr. Declan Beckett, bank president, was distributing a lot of cash from SE-cubed funds. SE-cubed board member Ms. Faith Miller was dealing drugs in San Amano. Ms. Tiffany Shelley, another board member, knew all of this and was going to blow the whistle on them.

Putting all this together, I deduced that they killed Tiff the Tutor. I was sure of it. Mr. Beckett replaced Mr. Shelley as my number one suspect.

***

I returned to Higgs Haven in time for second dinner and Vicki's midnight call. "Evenin' Zarand. Anything new?"

I couldn't wait to tell her my discoveries. "I solved the case. You won't believe this, but your next-door neighbor is a drug dealer."

"Do you mean Faith?" she laughed.

"That's the one."

"I find that hard to believe. Do you have evidence? Or is this another of your guesses?"

"I have photos. And not only that, but Mr. Beckett is skimming money from SE-cubed."

"This sounds like a long story. Can you join Lieutenant Mutai and Coroner Persephone with me at the Firehouse Barbecue for lunch? "

"Perfect. I'll bring my evidence."

Dahl and I went to sleep, confident we'd close the case in the morning.

Wherein Zarand doesn't get any cookies.

"Mornin' Zee," Vicki called while Dahl and I were eating breakfast. "Change of plans."

"Whassup?"

"I want to search Tiffany's car before our meeting. I don't have a search warrant. Can you get Mr. Shelley's consent?"

"No problem. Gun Shell and I bonded while hiking in the Pauli Falls Open Space and fighting off a mean rattlesnake."

"Perfect. I'll pick you up."

I scratched Dahl's black ears. She stuck her tail in the air and purred. "You're on your own. I left you some kibbles and lots of food in your puzzle feeders."

Dahl jumped on her favorite catnip mouse and eviscerated it with her hind claws to remind me that she'd rather live on a farm where she could stalk and pounce on rodents. Once the cat toy was done in, she retreated into the bedroom and was sound asleep before I descended the steps, reminding me that she wouldn't miss me.

Vicki showed her badge to get through the gate into Stony Estancia Haciendas. As we drove by the homes on large lots, she wondered. "Let me get this straight. He's a writer, but not a Dean Koontz or a Sue Grafton. Right?"

"That's correct, Vee, and she's a tutor."

"Then, how do they afford to live up here?"

"Some tutors make a lot of money."

Vee was incredulous. "That's possible, but not enough for the Haciendas. I might ask Tsui to investigate their finances."

Approaching the Shelley's home, I was reminded of part of the answer. Their modest single-story home was dwarfed by the McMansions surrounding it.

Vicki parked in their driveway and pointed to the plywood window. "Are they replacing their front window? I've heard that bay windows are popular."

I shook my head, "I think Mr. Shelley has been busy with his wife's death and Pax's disappearance."

"Gosh, then what happened?"

"Pax said their dad threw their mom out that window."

"I find that hard to believe. Did you question Mr. Shelley?"

"Sure did, Vee. He blamed a falling bookcase."

"Really, Zee? Just like the California History Annex?"

Vee got out of the car, and we walked to the door.

"Do you know what Persey says?" I asked to change the subject.

"What?"

"She says that Tiffany was an abused spouse. Mr. Shelley killed his wife. Maybe by accident."

'Didn't you recently decide the murderer was Declan Beckett, the embezzler?' Fitch reminded me.

Vicki hugged me. "I love how your mind bounces around. Last night you said it was my nice neighbor Faith. This abusive husband theory is your worst yet. Persey can't find the cause of death. Everyone knows that wife beaters leave lots of evidence, nothing that can be hidden on the coroner's autopsy table. Something else killed Ms. Shelley."

I rang the doorbell and stepped back so the video could see us.

The door opened and a cheerful Gunnar Shelley greeted us. "Welcome Zarand, and Senior Detective Yukawa. I remember you both from that futile search and rescue mission in the mountains." He looked at me. "And I already put that rattlesnake in my next book." He turned back to Vicki. "If you've come about Pax, I haven't heard from them."

Vicki took the lead. "We're here about your wife."

When she mentioned Ms. Shelley, all that good cheer drained from him. He slumped over and backed away from the door.

We let ourselves in.

Vicki sniffed, "This place smells like the California History Annex—sweet vanilla." She looked down the long hall lined with bookcases. "Are those books from researching your novels?"

He rubbed a few tears from his cheek with the back of his hand and moaned, "Not my books. Those are Tiff's. She collected old books."

We followed him into his formal sitting room decorated with antique weapons.

He took a deep breath and pulled himself together. "Would you like some tea?"

I was hoping for more of those delicious cookies from his U.K. publisher, but Vicki turned down his offer.

I went directly to the purpose of our visit—permission to search his wife's car. "We found Tiffany's vehicle."

"That's good news. Where is it?"

"If you have a spare set of keys, I can drive you to it and you can take it home," Vicki said.

"I'll get them." He rushed out of the room.

When he returned, I said, "We'd like to search it for evidence to find your wife's killer." I watched for signs that he was guilty. "If that's okay with you?"

"Righto. I don't see how that could be a problem."

Gunnar was more despondent than nervous, strengthening his position in second place behind Declan Beckett, the corrupt banker, and his drug dealing accomplice, Faith Miller.

Vicki parked next to a red SUV in the county impound lot. "Is that your wife's car?"

"Sure is. Those are her Tiff the Tutor car magnets."

"Would you unlock it for us?"

"Righto." He clicked the key fob and the car beeped in acknowledgment.

Tsui pulled up in his black and white.

"Let's check for damage while Tsui dusts for fingerprints."

Tsui used a trace evidence vacuum cleaner on the floor mats and seats.

'Didn't they do all this when they collected the car from the strip mall?'

Fitch was partially correct. They'd checked for damage, but this was the first time Tsui had access to the interior.

Gunnar remarked, "Wow. Officer Tsui is thorough."

I replied, "Yes. We're doing everything possible to find your wife's *killer*," emphasizing the word killer, but he was unflappable.

He was calm while asking. "Do you think her murderer might have been in that car?"

'He's a great actor. I bet he already knows the answer to that question,' Fitch said.

"It's possible," Vicki said.

"I see she has a gun safe in the back of her SUV. Do you have the combination?" Tsui interrupted.

"Sure, but it's empty. All our weapons are in the gun safe at home. I checked."

'Um, in addition to the weapons displayed in his front room, he also has more weapons in a safe. If you ask why he needs an arsenal, I bet he'll say, research. He's our murderer. Check the cold cases. Maybe a serial killer.'

"Gosh, let's open it," Vicki said.

He walked to the back of the vehicle. I didn't buy his innocent act. I imagined he was hoping for an excuse not to open it."

He spun the combination wheels but stopped at the last one.

'Here it comes. His excuse,' predicted Fitch.

"Should I have a lawyer here?"

'I told you.'

Vicki was cool. "If you like. We can wait for your lawyer. Do you have one?"

"Just the guy who reviews my publishing contracts."

I jumped on that. "Not the right kind of guy, but he could recommend someone."

Gunnar said, "Whatever," and unlocked the chest.

Everyone looked inside. All that it contained was a paper bag from the Firehouse Barbecue.

Tsui responded first. "I'm wearing gloves. I'll get it."

After everyone backed away, he took pictures and collected trace evidence before extracting the bag.

He peeked inside. "Oh my. Look at this." He held the bag open.

We all looked inside at several banded packets of C-notes.

I wondered if this money explained how they afforded to live in the Haciendas.

Gun Shell was silent before gasping with surprise. "That's a lot of cash. I don't know where it came from."

For the first time, he looked nervous.

'We're getting close.' Fitch vibrated with glee.

I knew where it came from. Those were hundred-dollar bills from the SE-cubed slush fund and some of them were given to the Frank twins to stage a diversion. Once again Declan Beckett and his corrupt operation claimed the distinction of being the top suspect.

'I'm not giving Mr. Gunnar Shelley a clean slate. Not yet. His performance today was good but I'm still suspicious,' Fitch weighed in.

"I'm going to have to hold that for evidence," Vicki said.

Mr. Shelley paused as if he was thinking of his best response. Then he replied, "I've no objection. I've never seen that money."

After he thought for a minute, he added, "Can I get a receipt?"

'Got him. He recognizes the cash. He's guilty,' Fitch concluded.

Tsui took pictures, put the money in an evidence kit, and handed Mr. Shelley a receipt.

Gunnar looked a bit shocked. "Er. Thank you. Can I take my wife's car home?"

Vicki turned to Tsui. "Are you done?"

"Yes, Senior Detective."

"Mr. Shelley, the car is released."

When he pulled out of the impound lot, she said, "He was too nervous to be innocent. I'll see you at the Firehouse Barbecue and we can discuss this further."

She whispered to me, "Don't forget to bring your evidence that my nice neighbor is a drug dealer."

Wherein Zarand upgrades his lunch order.

I pulled my small black-and-white car into the parking lot in front of the Firehouse Barbecue, but it was full. The restaurant was next to the fire station and the two buildings were doppelgängers, red brick cubes with enormous garage doors. Because of the real fire trucks behind the real garage doors, street parking was prohibited and strictly enforced. I drove across Higgs Road to the Stony Community Church lot. The megachurch was a repurposed supermarket, so it had plenty of parking space.

The Firehouse Barbecue dining room was a large open space, like the fire station next door, and saturated with the aromas of different sauces—garlic and onion with notes of chili, cumin, and mustard. I claimed the largest table. Like everything else, it was painted with red enamel. The décor consisted of old-time firefighting tools—red pumps with red handles, red buckets, red axes, and red ladders. I exercised the privilege of being first and ordered for the group. The menu was laminated and folded in half. I raised it to signal that I was ready. The server came over with a tray of water glasses and a basket of small hushpuppies with mild and spicy sauces.

"*Hola*, Mr. S."

I had to check twice before convincing myself that the server was indeed Jorge. "*Hola*, do you work here also?"

"Oh yes, Mr. S. I'm saving my money for when I graduate from Stony High."

"You're bright. Can't you get a scholarship?"

He gave me that teenage smile meaning he didn't expect me to understand. "Scholarship? Easy peasy, if I wanted to go straight on to college. I'm planning a gap year. For that, I need my own money."

"Gap year? That's when you take time off between high school and college, right? What are you going to do?"

"Promise not to laugh?"

"Cross my heart."

"I'm going to visit every Spanish-speaking country in the Western Hemisphere before going to journalism school. There are about two dozen of them."

I had never heard of such a thing, but it was a great idea. I said, "I'm not laughing. I'm jealous."

"*Gracias*," he said, "Do you still want to order?"

"Yes, thank you. In addition to me, Detective Yukawa and Officer Tsui from the police, Lieutenant Mutai from the fire department, and County Coroner Persephone Paterson will be here."

"I know Lieutenant Mutai, Peggy. Her fire station is right next door. We're named for them, and she comes here often. She likes rice with beans and chicken. She always says, 'Make the sauce firehouse hot.'"

"Thanks for the intel. I'll include those in my order. Give me a medium family feast—there's not enough of us for the large—with baby back ribs, beef ribs, and a whole barbecue chicken. Use Peggy's favorite sauce on the chicken."

"What sides would you like with that?"

"Cornbread, corn on the cob, mild chili, red beans with rice, and more hushpuppies, the big ones. Aren't you going to write this down?"

Jorge smiled. "No need. I've never gotten an order wrong."

That memory is going to be important when he becomes a journalist,' Fitch said.

Jorge repeated my order before asking. "Any salads? We have locally grown salads. This time of the year the greens come from Ventura in the west. After Christmas, we switch to Imperial Valley to the east. What kind of salad would you like? Caesar? Spinach? Taco?"

Fitch was impressed. *'That's a pretty hard sell for salads at a barbecue place.'*

I wasn't buying his salads. "This group has a rule at the Firehouse. Nothing green."

"Whatever works for you. Anything else?"

"Yes, some Ice-Age-style ribs. One order of back ribs and one of short ribs, both beef."

"Ice-Age-style is only beef. You know those are raw, don't you? Ice Age means like before barbecue sauce—before fire."

"Sure do. The back ribs with the large bones are for Cerberus, a very special chocolate lab. He'll be here. The short ribs are for my tuxedo cat, Dahl. Hers'll be to-go."

Persey arrived first, as did the Ice Age ribs. While Cerberus enjoyed his treat, I asked her. "Any luck on the cause of death?"

Persey exhaled between her teeth making a gentle hissing sound. "I was out of all the ordinary causes and dove deep into espionage—ricin, sarin, polonium 210, carbon monoxide. None of those were right."

At that point, Jorge brought out the family feast, in time for the arrival of Officer Tsui and his five children. The kids each grabbed a hushpuppy and chomped into them like they were apples. I could have watched their smiles for hours.

'He's taking care of the kids again. Good father.'

I signaled Jorge. "*Hola, amigo.* Please upgrade our medium feast to a large and add the barbecue brisket, chicken wings, and French fries, a double order of French fries."

"You got it, Mr. S."

I looked at Tsui. "Fruit juice?"

"Apple," he replied.

"And apple juice for the kids. You might as well make that a pitcher."

Jorge said, "No problem," and brought activity placemats with crayons for the children.

Peggy walked over from the firehouse when Vicki arrived.

While eating, we each shared our meal with a borrowed kid. I had Tsui's youngest. She sat on my lap, and we discussed whether ribs or wings were best.

She argued, "Wings are the best size. They fit in my hands and my tummy." After some thought, she added, "French fries are also a good size, but my dad won't let me eat them for breakfast."

"That's unfair," I commiserated.

Vicki had the oldest child. Despite that he was in elementary school, she was recruiting him to the PD. "You get your own police car, a cool badge, and a fancy radio." She let him play with her radio and he seemed ready to sign up right away. She was great with children.

Occasions like this always made me wonder why she didn't want to get married, or even live together. We could be great foster parents.

After lunch, Jorge cleared the table and packed up the leftovers.

The kids retreated to a big open space on the floor with the older ones managing the younger ones.

"Let's start with Tsui. Can you tell us what you found in Ms. Shelley's car?" Vicki said.

"We found the red SUV parked in a strip mall in the warehouse district. It was Ms. Shelley's. With Mr. Shelley's consent, we searched it and discovered a paper bag—"

He interrupted himself. "It was from the Firehouse Barbecue and contained a large amount of uncirculated currency packaged in hundred-note straps. All the straps were complete except for one."

"Can we tie this money to her death? Is any missing?" Vicki asked.

I went first. "Vinnie found a large cash disbursement from the SE-cubed account. The bands on the cash matched this transaction—SE-cubed money ended up in the back of Tiffany's car."

Tsui continued, "When we arrested the Frank twins, they had C-notes that they claimed came from Tiffany. Those bills matched the missing ones from Tiffany's cache."

Fitch giggled. *'Cache of cash.'*

"I didn't believe the Frank twins' alibi, but this corroborates it. They were all over our crime scene, but it turns out they're innocent. I'm going to release them," Vicki said.

"Foolish kids. Bad judgment. Wrong place, wrong time. But not our murderers," Tsui added.

'If the Franks are cleared, things don't look good for Declan Beckett,' declared Fitch.

"Or Mr. Shelley," I replied under my breath.

Everyone looked at me. I said, "Here's how I see it. Declan gave Ms. Shelley thirty thousand dollars in cash, three straps.

She handed five hundred to the Frank twins to create a diversion to cover up her break-in of the California History Annex. Her objective was to steal the Cajon Treasure journals and locate the treasure for herself."

Vicki continued, "But the plan was a mess. She didn't get the journals as Ms. Miller had checked them out for a lesson on 19th-century literature, and Ms. Shelley was murdered before the Frank twins could execute their diversion."

Fitch loved this. *'Amateurs, more like a cozy mystery than a thriller.'*

I agreed with Fitch. *We have a cat and recipes.*

Persey, who often restricted her comments to dead bodies, added, "Since the murderer left all that money, we can forget robbery as a motive."

"Look at this. Look at this," shouted Tsui's family. Everyone turned to see a long row of menus balancing on end.

"That's what has kept them quiet. They were working on an engineering project. I encourage hands-on activities—IRL physics—instead of computer games," he said.

The youngest child, my friend who wanted fries for breakfast, spread her arms out and said, "Ta-dah," before kicking the first menu. The row fell over one at a time, like so many dominoes.

Tsui repeated, "IRL physics."

The children cheered and shouted, "Again. Again."

They set to work building—this time stacking the laminated menus like a house of cards.

Cerberus, the chocolate lab, looked at Persey. He sat next to her chair, but his rump kept rising. "Sorry boy." She petted him. "I know you want to play with the children, but this isn't a dog-friendly activity." She gave Cerberus a beef rib. When he settled down, she said, "That reminds me of the bookcases in the California History Annex. SE-cube's extra money came from cutting corners on the construction." She gave Cerberus another bone before adding, "That shoddy construction could have killed someone. We're lucky I didn't receive more victims into my morgue."

Peggy jumped in. "Before you get ahead of yourselves, let me warn you not to blame anything on the inspectors. I spoke to the fire inspector and the building inspector, and neither of them approved the annex. They weren't even called. Officially, as far as they're concerned, the project is still in progress."

Fitch was shocked, *'That's a surprise. That dedication ceremony made it look like everything was complete.'*

I gave SE-cubed the benefit of the doubt. The door was painted shut as a safety measure. Not sloppy construction.

Fitch was ready to be judge and jury. *'Declan and SE-cubed again. I see a pattern here. I never expected big-time criminals in Stony Estancia, but here they are.'*

"So Declan embezzled from the building fund by cutting corners on the annex construction to finance Tiffany's quest to recover the Cajon Treasure. How valuable is that treasure?" Vicki inquired.

Fitch, who was ready to convict Declan moments ago, was skeptical. *'That's a pretty crazy chain of events.'*

Vicki declared, "I'm ready to arrest him on a corruption charge and get him to confess to the murder during interrogation."

Fitch pumped his fist in the air. *'Go get 'em, girl.'*

While that sunk in, Jorge came by. "Anything else?"

"Yes, could we have a couple of your famous pecan pies?"

"Slices or whole pies?"

"Whole pies, of course. And lots of plates and forks. And milk for the growing kids."

"Whipped cream or ice cream?" offered Jorge.

"Both," I replied.

"And another Ice Age rib for Cerberus," Persey said.

Vicki looked at me. "Thanks for ordering dessert, though after that meal, it might just be for you and the kids. Did you have something to contribute to the investigation?"

'That's your cue. Tell them about Ms. Miller dealing drugs.'

"Yes, I have the final nail in Mr. Beckett's coffin."

"Do tell."

"Last night I followed Ms. Faith Miller to San Amano High School. I parked out of sight and watched her dealing drugs. This went on for a while. Her customers came in singles, couples, and larger groups. She exchanged envelopes of cash for envelopes of drugs."

"Gosh, you're saying that Declan is at the head of a wide-ranging criminal enterprise. We can bring racketeering charges under the federal RICO statutes," Vicki said.

"Exactly. SE-cubed is a front for Declan's criminal activities. Tiffany and Faith are also involved. They're on the SE-cubed board."

"Well, Ms. Shelley's not involved anymore," Persey said.

Once more, Tsui's kids interrupted us. This time with notes from the older ones and drawings from the younger ones. My small sweetheart handed me a page of scribbles. "This is me. That's you. We're flying on the unicorn."

I hugged her. "Thank you. I will hang it on my refrigerator."

Fitch interrupted child playtime to ask, *'What about those notes you stashed in your car?'*

I smashed my palm on my forehead. "I forgot them."

"Forgot what?" Vicki asked.

"The notes. I forgot the notes."

"What notes?"

"Wait a minute."

I ran out to my car and returned with the notes I'd found in Ms. Miller's SE-CUBED folder that day I was showing *Pride and Prejudice* videos.

I slid them onto the table.

Vicki studied them.

FAITH, DECLAN'S GONE TOO FAR. WE MUST STOP HIM. TIFF.

BOARD MEMBERS: PICK UP YOUR MONTHLY CASH PACKETS.

"Tell me, Zee. Where did you get these?"

"They were on Ms. Miller's desk. I forgot about them."

She looked at Tsui. "Can you secure this evidence?"

He reached into the bag that accompanied his children. "I never go anywhere without diapers, wipes, snacks, and evidence kits."

"Tiffany was going to blow the whistle on Declan. That's his motive for murder," I said.

Vicki agreed, "That cinches it. I'll arrest him tomorrow. Tsui, can you organize the paperwork and put together a team? Zarand, you're welcome to join us."

Jorge arrived with pies, plates, forks, milk, and the check.

"Isn't he great?" I bragged, "Never forgets anything."

The children cheered for pie and milk.

After a brief tussle over the bill, I emerged victorious. "I arrived on time, so it's my privilege to order and pay."

I dropped my credit card on a little tray advertising a different card and Jorge took it away.

"However, you can contribute," I said to all those disappointed that they couldn't pick up the bill.

I took an empty pie plate and put it in the middle of the table and told everyone Jorge's gap year goals. "I'm sure generous tips will be appreciated."

The adults piled on dollar bills and the children donated pictures and well wishes. My small sweetheart drew him a picture of a sloth. "Green grows on dem. Slou live in da jungle." She thought hard before saying. "Sou A-may-ica."

Vicki admired the drawing. "We've been like a sloth, but we can speed things up now." She touched my shoulder. "Vee, meet me at the Civic Center tomorrow morning. We'll drive to the Stony Estancia Bank together. I'll be happy to have Declan Beckett arrested and this case closed."

SECOND ARREST - SUNDAY

Wherein Zarand brings donuts to the bank.

We arrived at Stony Estancia Bank prepared for any eventuality. Vicki parked in the front on Zeeman Way. I held two bags, one from Only Donuts and the other from FFF, on my lap. Vicki's black satchel embossed with the Stony Estancia seal sat on the floor at my feet. Tsui and the backup team waited in the rear parking lot out of sight.

A few cars with well-dressed families drove west in the direction of Higgs Road and the Stony Community Megachurch. The eastbound traffic consisted of a man walking a pair of dachshunds and a woman jogger in spandex.

We waited until the man and the woman passed before we got out of Vicki's unmarked car. A stern Declan Beckett spotted us standing in front of his bank. He slowly approached the door, giving the uniformed guard time to join him. "It's Sunday. The bank is closed."

The guard opened his navy blazer displaying his Taser and crossed his arms in front of his chest.

'That guy would be more impressive if his arms weren't resting on his substantial paunch,' was Fitch's commentary.

Vicki displayed her badge.

The guard backed away nervously, buttoned his jacket, and clasped his hands behind his back, standing at parade rest.

Mr. Beckett didn't move. "You didn't need to show your badge. I know who you are. Why are you here?"

I said, "We'd like to talk to you. Can we come in?"

He repeated, "It's Sunday. The bank is closed."

Vicki said, "We can come back with a warrant and *Stony Estancia Surfs.*"

Mr. Beckett reluctantly unlocked the door and showed us to a conference room. "I apologize for not offering you coffee, but I wasn't expecting visitors."

I replied, "No problem. I brought a light breakfast."

His eyes opened wide when he noticed my bags.

I put out coffee, fresh milk, sugar, bagels, flavored cream cheeses, an assortment of donuts, some fresh fruit, and a tray of sliced meats and cheeses.

"Well, that was thoughtful of you." He gave us an uneasy smile, poured himself a cup of coffee, and made a thick sandwich of Emmentaler and prosciutto with mayo and dark mustard.

'Nothing works like food to relax a witness,' Fitch observed before adding, *'It's a good thing you didn't forget the mustard again.'*

I helped myself to a bruin claw with black coffee.

Vicki picked up a clementine orange, peeled it, and popped a segment into her mouth. I expected her to arrest him, but she took a more cautious approach.

Declan hadn't finished his sandwich when Vicki launched into her interrogation. "We were wondering about the dedication ceremony."

He was chewing his ham and cheese, so she continued, "Did you know that the building and fire inspectors never signed off on the California History Annex?"

He leaned back in his chair and his grip on the sandwich relaxed leaving deep indentations in the bread. "Is that what this is about?" he asked, giving us his first real smile.

She ate several clementine segments while waiting for him. He continued to chew.

'I love watching two pros face off like a pair of mating peacocks. They could stare at each other all morning.'

Vicki outwaited him. He said, "The annex was a big project, and I was in charge. Of course, I knew. There were no inspections because the work wasn't complete."

After a shorter delay, he explained, "The ribbon cutting was scheduled in advance to get it on the calendars of some very busy people. The ceremony couldn't be delayed. That's why we held it in the main library. I instructed the painters to seal the door. That was my low-key way to keep people out of the unfinished California History Annex."

Vicki's face expressed surprise. "It was a nice ceremony, despite the protests."

Mr. Beckett went on. "And I know that the bookshelf installers scattered the unused nuts and washers over the football field to express their disapproval of raising the shelves without time to attach them to the anchor bolts." He gave a small grin while shaking his head. "That was childish of them, but those small pieces of hardware are easy to replace, and I didn't see any reason to raise a fuss."

Vicki dug out a plastic evidence bag from her black satchel. She slid the note onto the conference table. "This is a note where Ms. Shelley accuses you of going too far and saying you need to be stopped."

Declan studied it for a moment before he started laughing. "What is that? Why are you carrying it around in a plastic baggie? Wait here a minute."

He went to his office and returned with a thick folder. "Tiffany was the board secretary for SE-cubed. She got the job because of her exquisite penmanship. Here are pages and pages of her notes." He kissed his fingertips like an Italian chef. "Things of beauty we'll never see again as the current generation doesn't learn cursive."

I looked over Vicki's shoulder and agreed. The penmanship was a work of art. It reminded me of Sister Rowley's 19th-century Spencerian script.

'Well, that note wasn't written by Ms. Shelley, so it's not evidence of anything except a bad forgery.' Fitch said with a chortle, always pleased to see me fooled.

Vicki tried another tack. "Ms. Shelley had thirty thousand dollars in her car. Do you know anything about that?"

'Like, was it hush money so she wouldn't reveal your criminal operation?'

Declan placed his hands on the conference table, palms up. "You got me. Misallocation of funds. Do you want to cuff me?"

"Not yet. First, tell us about the money."

"SE-cubed raised lots of money. Millions. More than we needed. Rather than kill our momentum, the board agreed to disburse the excess to worthy causes. That wasn't according to our charter, but most of our major donors were on the board and they agreed. The money you found was going to Stony Estancia Family Shelter."

We gave him the silent treatment until he explained. "If Tiffany still had the cash, then the shelter hadn't received it before she was murdered. However, you can check with them, and they'll confirm similar donations in the past."

Vicki said, "I doubt we need to do that. Thank you for your time."

Vicki and I silently retreated. I didn't even bother to collect the leftovers. The only smile belonged to Fitch.

As she drove us to Four Rivers for lunch, she summarized, "That was a total bust. The bookcases weren't criminal negligence, but simply a way to accommodate some politicians' schedules. Not proper, but not something City Attorney *'I don't waste taxpayers' money on cases I might lose'* Blake would prosecute. And diverting funds to the family shelter? Also, nothing to prosecute. Tish and César wouldn't even be interested in that story. Money donated to a family shelter is hardly a clickbait headline."

By the time she stopped talking, I slouched down in my seat, feeling bad to have embarrassed her. I apologized. "I should have been more careful. I'm sorry I didn't do a better investigation."

She reached over and touched my knee. "Don't beat yourself up. You'll do better next time."

I wasn't ready to give up. "But what about drug dealing? Selling drugs to high school students? I have plenty of photos of Ms. Miller's sales, and on school grounds too."

"I'd like to see those surveillance photos first, and if they look legit, we can confront Ms. Miller."

'After that embarrassing meeting, she doesn't trust you. I don't blame her. You gave her that bogus note and the money was legit.'

I wondered why someone had forged a note from Ms. Shelley. This arrest attempt made us look like amateurs. We'd redeem ourselves when we arrested Ms. Miller for drug dealing.

Wherein Zarand spends a day off the grid.

Dahl woke me for second dinner by placing her fuzzy paw in my mouth. *Ptooey. Ptooey.* I spit out her fur. "Dahl. Don't do that." She meowed and ran into the kitchen where she headbutted her food dish making an awful sound as it scraped across the floor.

"Okay. I'm getting up."

Dahl did a gargoyle imitation from the top of the fridge, a position that afforded her an overview of my two-room apartment. I dressed and brushed my teeth under her constant surveillance. After receiving cat treats and kibbles in her puzzle feeders, she returned to ignoring me. For my second dinner, I checked the refrigerator, but nothing inspired me. I wanted dolmades and moussaka.

I wanted them now.

Fortunately, Stony Estancia boasted a 24-hour Greek restaurant, Epicurean Eats. I got dressed and drove down Higgs Road.

Fitch took the opportunity for some constructive criticism. *'So many suspects. So few arrests. The Frank twins. Declan Beckett. What makes you think your evidence is any better for Faith Miller or Gunnar Shelley?'*

I was tired and hungry, ideal conditions for self-doubt.

Had I been too complacent?

Fitch pounced on my vulnerability. *'Too lazy.'*

Lazy seemed a bit strong. There was only one witness I hadn't interviewed.

Fitch read my mind. *'Pax.'*

How could I interrogate them if I couldn't find them? Their mother was dead. Their father was clueless. My grandkids at Stony High weren't talking.

'What about the Stony Stoners?'

Pax was friends with the Stoners, and they were awake in the middle of the night. I ditched my moussaka plans and took a hard left onto the Pacific Electric Trail. The path was marked with a blue and white sign, PEDESTRIANS, EQUESTRIANS, AND BICYCLES ONLY. I was on a mission, so I didn't let that stop me. My small electric car fit between the stanchions erected to block vehicular traffic. It didn't take me long to locate the Stoners' ever-moving pad.

I jumped out of the car and crashed through the sagebrush. "I must speak to Pax. Take me to them."

They just blew off my request.

"You're a square. Why are you driving your car on our turf?" Allen Ginsberg said.

"You're going to attract the fuzz," added Joan Didion.

I tried to connect them to the case. "Did you know that the police arrested your friends, the Frank twins?"

"What a ripoff," Kurt Vonnegut said.

Allen added, "The twins may be space cadets, but they're not murderers."

I needed to make friends with them. "Right on. The twins are not murderers, and the cops are going to release them." I shared chips and chocolates from my backpack, while I pondered about my next move.

"Thanks for the snacks. See you later, alligator," Joan said.

'You have to make it personal,' advised Fitch.

"The cops are frantic. You're friends with Pax. I expect they're going to arrest you next."

Fitch congratulated me. *'Perfect. Look at their worried faces.'*

"Lieutenant Mutai won't be cool with me getting arrested," Joan said.

"Neither will the airport. Security is very strict. I can't keep my way-out job in aircraft maintenance if I get arrested," Allen agreed.

"How can we help?" Kurt said.

Threatening their jobs did the trick.

"Pax. I need to see Pax."

Allen took the lead. "Split. Take your groovy wheels home and we'll pick you up."

I returned to my little car. "Will your wheels have room for all of us?"

They just laughed.

"And leave your phone," Kurt Vonnegut said.

"And you'll be blindfolded," Joan Didion added.

They drove up to my apartment in a 1960s land yacht, sleek, two-tone white and turquoise, tailfins, whitewall tires, and so much chrome. After Joan searched me to make sure I didn't have my phone, she placed a black cloth bag over my head and sat me in the back. The Stony Stoners fit comfortably on the bench seat in the front.

The gentle rolling of the soft suspension quickly put me to sleep.

When the car left the paved road, I was bounced off the seat onto the bump in the middle of the floor. "Whoa. Slow down," I shouted.

Kurt said, "Welcome to Kerouac Kanyon," and slammed on the brakes, jostling me further.

When Joan removed the black sack, I shielded my eyes from the morning sun. In front of me was a cabin nestled among pine trees and granite boulders. It had a door in the center and a window on each side. The roof was green sheet metal and pale gray smoke rose from a chimney on the left.

'Look at that,' said Fitch gleefully. 'No wires. No electricity. Miles from the closest cell tower. No internet. Off the grid.'

I couldn't believe my luck. If Pax was camping out in these primitive conditions, they'd be ready to return to civilization, even if that meant giving testimony to the police. This was the breakthrough I needed.

I picked up my backpack and threw the car door open.

The air was filled with the unmistakable aroma of an outhouse. No indoor plumbing. Even better.

Joan covered her face with a handkerchief and said, "This is Pax's pad. You'll find them inside."

Kurt started the car, "Close the door. We'll get you after dark." And the Stony Stoners were gone.

Pax couldn't be happy here. I'd easily convince them to return to electricity, high-speed internet, and hot showers.

Even Fitch was optimistic. *'I told you Pax was the key witness.'*

I held my breath and looked around to get my bearings. The mountain ridge was now to the south. Kurt had driven through Cajon Pass. We were in the area where Sister Rowley and Brother Humphries had camped.

Fitch could hardly contain his excitement. *'Not only will we return with Pax, but the Cajon Treasure is nearby.'*

The cabin door opened. "Hello, Mr. S. I was wondering how long it would take you to get here."

'So was I,' echoed Fitch.

I opened my backpack. "I brought you ribs from Firehouse Barbecue, General Tso chicken from Four Rivers, and chili rellenos from Cocina de Cetto."

'That's putting all those leftovers in your freezer to good use.'

Pax took the food from me. "Thanks. I don't get into town often."

"What town is that?"

Pax laughed, "Nice try, Mr. Detective."

The exact town wasn't important because Pax was leaving. "Do you have a way to keep this stuff? To heat it up?"

Fitch was enjoying Pax's predicament. *'Rub it in. I'm sure they're tired of roughing it.'*

I expected a sad face, but Pax smiled and led me around back. I politely didn't mention the outhouse.

"Over here is the compost. I turn it by hand." Pax picked up a pitchfork and demonstrated mixing the compost like a big, tossed salad. It smelled different from the outhouse, but not any better.

Fitch held his nose, though I was sure he couldn't smell.

After the compost, we hiked into the woods where Pax revealed a surprise. "And here, I have my energy source. A woodpile. You know what they say, chop your own wood and it will warm you twice." I tried to imagine them wielding an axe, but I couldn't.

Then Pax gave me a wink. "Behind the woodpile are my batteries and solar panels."

Pax had electricity. Their life wasn't as primitive as I assumed.

"Let me show you where I live."

We entered the cabin.

"To the right are my bedroom and office. All the comforts of home—electric blanket and satellite internet."

That was the death of my plan. *All the comforts of home.* The bed was made with satin sheets, and the office had a tower computer with two large monitors.

Pax pointed to the left, to a stone fireplace and a kitchenette. "There are my refrigerator and microwave. I can store and heat your welcome gifts."

The kitchen was basic. The sink had a hand pump. Their open pantry shelves stored a bag of sugar, a few spices, baking soda, baking powder, and a big bottle of vanilla, along with a variety of pasta—fettuccine, fusilli, linguini, and macaroni. Pax pointed to a row of stoneware crocks. "There I have my staples, flour, rice, and beans."

I couldn't hide my surprise. "Do you cook?"

"You're here until dusk. Can I offer you coffee and a warm slice of a homemade sourdough loaf? I just took it out of my wood-burning oven," Pax replied.

'That answers your question,' Fitch grinned.

I enjoyed a thick slice of fresh bread with butter and jam. "These are the best preserves ever."

"I came here in June to pick wild blackberries and brought them to a lady in town who made jam for me."

'Like home,' said Fitch noticing that this place was the same size as my apartment at Higgs Haven. *'Except they have a fireplace, and you have optical fiber internet.'*

We hiked into the hills after a lunch of chili rellenos from Cocina de Cetto.

"Can you tell me what happened that morning when you broke through the crime scene tape and entered the annex? If I know the truth, I can get the cops to quit harassing you."

Fitch scoffed. *'After that debacle at the bank, Vicki isn't doing anything you suggest.'*

I scowled at Fitch. *Never underestimate true love.*

We climbed up a slope covered with scree. The loose rocks didn't offer a good footing. I regretted not bringing my trekking poles. "Please slow down."

Pax watched me struggle to maintain my balance. "Here, take my walking stick. You need it more than I do."

That helped a lot. I had a third support point, and they didn't. They had to slow down. "Why did you return to the annex?"

Pax and I sat on a large boulder. I handed them a package of trail mix and took one for myself. After wiping the sweat off my brow, I ate my trail mix one piece at a time.

Finally, Pax got around to my question. "When I came home on Tuesday, my dad was working on his latest novel. He hadn't seen my mom all day. After dinner, still no mom. I went out searching for her red SUV—down Higgs Road past the fire station and the mega church, across Bridgman Road and the community center. I even drove up Bohr Boulevard to the Pauli Falls Open Space."

"You didn't find it, did you? It was abandoned in the warehouse district."

Pax took a drink of water. "Thanks. That explains what happened. I'd never look that far south. Why was she in the warehouse district, anyway?"

I had finished the chocolate candies in my trail mix and started on the nuts. "What did you do next?"

"I went to the Stoners and told them my mom was missing. She tutored them and they love her."

The nuts made me thirsty, so I drank some water.

"People laugh at the Stoners, but they knew what to do. They asked me if I could track my mother's phone. I could and I located it."

"Where was it?"

"It was in the annex. I knew the murdered lady had been removed, so tracking Mom to the annex was good news. That meant she wasn't the murdered lady."

"But..."

"Right. I didn't find her there. I didn't find anything. In desperation, I beeped her phone."

Pax got very quiet, and a few tears rolled down their cheeks.

I whispered, "Did you find it?"

They blew their nose before saying, "It was in one of those green boxes. I grabbed it and ran."

"You turned it off, didn't you?"

"Yes, and when I went into the hills, I turned mine off also."

"I know. What I don't know is how you got here."

"It should be obvious. Everyone thinks that because I like to be comfortable—nice sheets, warm bed—that I am some weak incompetent. I just walked over the mountain. It's not that far."

'D'oh,' Fitch said and smacked his face.

When people asked about my grandkids, I struggled for words to describe how wonderful they were. My heart filled with admiration for Pax. They exceeded everyone's expectations.

We returned to the cabin in time for dinner.

While we were enjoying the Firehouse Barbecue ribs, Pax's computer went crazy, flashing, playing loud music, and shouting. "Another clue. Another one."

We both ran to their office to check out the next Cajon Treasure clue published on *Stony Estancia Surfs*. It read: SKYWATCHING CHIPMUNKS REJECT EVERY ECO KANYON AROUND CAMPS.

"That one makes even less sense than the others," I muttered in frustration.

Pax danced around the room. "Got you. Got you."

"Did you figure it out?"

Pax was all smiles. "Yes, after the second clue. The next two confirmed it."

On Mount Olympus, *Apollo turned to Artemis, "Do you think the one with rainbow hair decoded your clues?"*

Artemis got serious, "Oh yes. Pax is the unlikely hero of this story. Everyone underestimates them."

Apollo scratched his head, "Now that you mention that, it all makes sense."

"I'm good at word puzzles. Can you give me a hint?" I begged Pax.

"Hint? Sure. I'm dyslexic and never learned to read very well. I suck at word puzzles."

Fitch laughed, *'Speed readers need not apply. You might as well give up.'*

I agreed with Fitch, *Like* Revenge of the Dyslexics. *I loved that film.*

"I give up. Can you just tell me?"

"Maybe after I dig up the treasure," they replied with a smug smile.

As discouraging as that was, I didn't give up.

I wanted to ask Pax about their father. To ask if they thought their dad murdered their mom. But I was out of time. That turquoise and white, long sleek rocket ship pulled in front of the cabin. I was again blindfolded and tucked into the back seat, while the Stoners shared the front bench.

I had learned what happened to Tiffany's phone, but not Pax's location. I knew that Pax had solved the Cajon Treasure clues, but I was still lost.

'And you aren't any closer to Ms. Shelley's killer.'

Wherein Zarand doesn't figure out anything.

Dahl pushed her food dish across the kitchen floor, making that annoying scraping noise.

Fitch was beside himself with glee. *'She knows it's breakfast time and you're staring at* Stony Estancia Surfs *while you should be preparing her food.'*

I dumped a few kibbles in her bowl to appease her. "Dahl, give me a moment."

She swatted the bowl, scattering the kibbles to let me know she'd prefer something freshly made, served at the table, like an omelet or a burger.

I ignored her.

"Look at this, Fitch." I pointed to the daily release of Cajon Treasure clues, along with a summary. I noted that they attributed the latest clue to César's dream.

Fitch felt that dreams were more credible than talking animals.

NANOSECONDS DISAPPEAR BEFORE WOMEN EAT SILVER TRENCH PEARS.

SKYWATCHING CHIPMUNKS REJECT EVERY ECO KANYON AROUND CAMPS.

BIG CLUE AS JAR OPENS NIRVANAS AND ECSTASYS.

THE WAYS NO ONE READS TREASURE HOW UNCOVERS.

STAR-CROSSED TRIANGLES ORIGIN NEXUS YOU TRAVEL TWELVE MILES.

Fitch muttered, *'What is a trench pear? These are getting worse and worse.'*

Pax's words were etched into my memory. "I figured it out after the second clue. The next two confirmed it." If Pax could figure it out, so could I. I closed my browser. Maybe one more clue tomorrow would do it.

'Maybe this is the last one,' Fitch suggested in his diabolical way.

On Mount Olympus, Artemis purred like a cat.

Apollo cawed like a Raven, "Is Fitch correct? Was that the last clue?"

Artemis hissed, "I am not that cruel. I will give them a few more chances to figure it out."

Dahl ate her breakfast of defrosted trout served on a proper plate with a catnip garnish. I had fried eggs, over easy, with cheese and chives, and my sourdough bread, toasted. My store-bought bread tasted stale compared to that fresh slice from Pax's oven.

After breakfast, I again checked the clues, but they didn't make any more sense on a full stomach.

'Eating never helps. You're the only one who imagines another meal, maybe third lunch—' Fitch chortled at his joke. *'—will help them think.'*

Vicki called, discouraged. "This hasn't been a good week. I've arrested and released two suspects."

Fitch corrected her, *'The Frank twins already are two suspects, so the total is three.'*

"Even worse, everyone is distracted by the Cajon Treasure. I have no time for a treasure hunt. My job is to find killers."

I encouraged her. "Look how much we've figured out. We know why the shelves weren't bolted down, where the money in the Firehouse Barbecue sack came from, and why there was a spray paint can at the scene."

Fitch added, *'And we know Declan Beckett is not a crook.'*

I quipped, "We're looking for someone on a motorcycle who isn't a Frank twin."

I looked for a smile from Vicki, but she refused to be cheered up.

In a gloomy voice, she said, "Persey doesn't have a cause of death, and I don't have a suspect."

"You're forgetting Mr. Shelley. I've read his books and he doesn't shy away from violence against women," I reminded her.

"Right. That's great evidence. Do you want to arrest Kathy Reichs and David Baldacci too?" she replied with the sarcasm of a teen.

I softened my voice. "You need a break. Come to the Library Club meeting today."

"I told you. I'm not interested in treasure hunts."

"It'll be a diversion. Clear your mind." After a pause, I gave her my best smile and added, "They need another chaperone for the senior trip to the Capital. Maybe you'd like to join me?"

"I have a murder to solve, and I'm not interested in watching over your grandkids."

I was still flashing my smile, so she added, "Or any kids."

I kissed her on the nose. "Come to the meeting. They'll grow on you."

That kiss always worked. She wiped her nose as if I'd slobbered on her. "Okay, but I'm not signing up to be a chaperone."

Lizzy called the Library Club to order. "Mr. S. has something to report."

I told them about my visit to Pax without mentioning the Stony Stoners. "They said, 'I figured it out after the second clue. The next two confirmed it.'"

January put her two fists together in front of her and then raised them, spread her fingers, and puffed out her cheeks. She signed EXPLOSION. She said, "Genius. Pax is a genius. They make my head explode."

Ranch agreed. "They see patterns where the rest of us see random noise."

"Random noise? More like gibberish. Bad grammar. Bad spelling. Nonsense," said Alyce.

"Pardon me," said Vicki. She'd entered the library a few minutes ago. "Zarand—I mean Mr. Szilard—invited me."

The Library Club went silent.

"The police are trying to find Tiff the Tutor's killer, but we're stuck."

Everyone in the room suddenly looked down and became interested in their phones.

I jumped in to introduce Vicki. "This is Senior Detective Yukawa. I'm sure she'd be grateful for any ideas you have. At this point, no idea is too crazy."

Alyce started. "I'm Alyce Fox. I suggest you keep an eye on Ms. Miller. She's been absent a lot."

"Nice to see you again, Detective Yukawa. I dropped a tracker into Ms. Miller's purse. I can tell you that she drives around a lot at night," Ranch said.

Vicki gritted her teeth. I could see she didn't approve of his extra-legal surveillance, but she didn't say anything.

Zola towered over everyone. "I'm Zola Butler. She just got her hair braided. So maybe a new boyfriend explains the driving." Zola paused for a moment before adding with a sly grin. "And those absences too."

Everyone giggled at the idea of a teacher taking off time to be with her boyfriend.

They're not making much of a case. Are you going to mention the drug dealing?' prompted Fitch.

The buzzer sounded. Lunch was over. Everyone left for their next class.

"I apologize. That wasn't very helpful. More teen gossip about boyfriends than anything else."

Vicki gave me a little smile. "I am intrigued by them calling the clues gibberish. That might be the key to the treasure and the murder."

'Smart lady,' said Fitch, *'Nothing is what it appears to be.'*

Wherein Zarand misses movie night.

We stood together in the Stony High parking lot after the Library Club meeting. I said, "Vee, let me make amends for wasting your time with teen gossip. How about dinner at Cocina de Cetto?"

She kissed me on the nose. "Great idea. This Tiff-the-tutor case has kept me so busy that I haven't been eating. I have a craving for enchiladas. I'll meet you there."

I wanted to arrest Ms. Miller, the drug dealer. A righteous collar would be good for everyone's morale. On the other hand, I knew Vicki would consider it a distraction, so I let it go.

While we waited for Jorge to bring our food, Vicki had an *aguas frescas*.

Between sips of my *horchata*, I asked, "Do you feel like a movie tonight?"

"Sure, but no murder mysteries."

"How about *Cutthroat Island*? It has a treasure hunt, and the good guys win. You have the DVD."

"Oh Zee, I love movies with strong female leads."

"Plus the star went on to create an institute to research and promote gender equality in the media."

"I've heard of that. It is based in our neighborhood."

If we weren't going to arrest someone, a relaxing movie would be second best.

I looked out Vicki's front window while she searched for the DVD. Then, something happened that changed everything. I shouted, "Vee, forget the movie. Your next-door neighbor just opened her garage door."

"You mean Faith Miller? That neighbor?"

"Yes. You don't have to review my surveillance photos. You can see her dealing drugs with your own eyes."

"Zee, are you sure you wouldn't prefer to sit on my couch and watch Geena Davis swashbuckling?"

"No, Vee. Your neighbor is selling drugs to high school students. That comes first."

"Once a cop, always a cop. You're never going to retire."

"Thanks, Vee. We need to hurry. Her car is backing out of her driveway."

"You drive. My car is in the garage."

We hid behind the curtains until Ms. Miller's teal sedan drove by. Then we ran to my car and zipped after her.

A short while later, I was parked in the same place as last time and Ms. Miller was standing outside San Amano High School.

"Now watch. Do you see all those envelopes in her backpack? Those are the drugs. She's going to exchange them for envelopes of cash."

While we watched, Ms. Miller completed several drug deals.

Then Vicki said, "Well Zee, it's my turn to apologize. This looks like a righteous bust."

"Do we have to get the San Amano police involved?"

"No. Since we followed her from Stony Estancia, we're covered under the hot pursuit doctrine."

"Should we call for backup?"

"Not necessary. We'll wait until there's just one juvenile. We should be able to handle that. I'm not interested in attracting a lot of attention or arresting a bunch of kids."

"Good point. The cash and drugs in her bag will be sufficient evidence."

I turned on my car. It was ready to go at a moment's notice and silent. I loved my EV for stakeouts.

One child wearing a hoodie approached Ms. Miller.

"Wait," Vicki said.

When they exchanged envelopes, she said, "Go. Go."

Before our targets knew what was happening, I stopped my car in front of them. Vicki had identified herself, and two people were standing with their hands raised.

The girl had tears running down her cheeks and she was shaking. "Don't shoot. Please don't shoot."

Across the field, another group approached, but one of them saw us and said, "Po-po. Run."

I grabbed the cash and the drugs before Ms. Miller could get rid of them. The envelopes were too flat. They felt like they were empty. That was the first indication that something was wrong.

The next indication was Ms. Miller shouting at us. "What are you doing? Do you know how long it took me to gain their trust?"

While we were watching, she grabbed the envelopes from me, gave the girl her drug envelope, and said, "No one's going to shoot you. Go home." She gave us a hard look, daring us to stop her.

Ms. Miller walked across the street.

Vicki pointed her gun at Ms. Miller. "Don't try to escape."

"I'm not going anywhere. Hurry up. I don't want us to be seen by any more than already has."

We followed her to her car. She lectured us like misbehaving students. "I don't want to hear your excuses." She handed Vicki the envelope she got from the girl and passed me one from her bag.

"Okay. Mr. S. Open your envelope. What was I handing out?"

The almost-empty envelope contained a single C-note. One hundred dollars. "You were giving these kids money?" I asked, not able to hide my surprise.

"Yes. They don't have as much as the Stony Estancia kids. That girl was Louisa. She uses the money to buy her family a Sunday roast to break up the monotony of rice and beans. The rest goes to pay the rent. The boy before her was Kenny Hesse. He pays for his siblings' clothes and laundry and his older sister's college textbooks. The group that you frightened away included a pair of twins, Jamie and James White. They pay for their dad's cancer treatments. One hundred dollars is not that much, is it?"

'You can't argue with that,' said Fitch.

These weren't *my* grandkids. They attended San Amano High, not Stony High. Still, they were just as wonderful and just as underappreciated. I put my arm around Vivki's waist and whispered in her ear, "Vee, aren't these children terrific?"

Ms. Miller ignored me and turned to Vicki. "What's in Louisa's envelope?"

Vicki shined her cell phone light inside the envelope and extracted a single piece of paper. "It's a grade report. Louisa Henley." She examined it for a minute. "It's pretty good. All As and Bs."

"No surprise. They need no Ds and no Fs to get paid, but Louisa is one of the better students," Ms. Miller said.

Vicki holstered her weapon. "What's going on here?"

Ms. Miller continued to address us like children, speaking slowly, enunciating each syllable. "I expect Declan told you how good we are at raising money. The board never refuses or refunds donations. When our funds exceed our budget, we find good causes to support. Each board member has a pet project. Ms. Shelley contributed to the Stony Estancia Family Shelter. This is my project."

"What exactly is this?" Vicki asked.

"A bit of social engineering. These students don't have the advantages of those at Stony High, so I enter into a contract with them. When they have good attendance and get good grades, I pay. They get bonuses for graduation and college admission, like the kids at Stony High. The difference is we pay cash instead of the new cars and international vacations awarded by Stony High parents to their privileged offspring."

Vicki backed away, half turning toward my car. She took my hand. "Let's go, Zee. That was a terrible job of surveillance." She hugged me. "I'm surprised you underestimated these kids. That's not like you."

Then she turned back to Ms. Miller. "My apologies. I remember reading about this on *Stony Estancia Surfs*. They even had your picture."

"No apologies needed. Just get out of here so I can finish my work. These kids already don't trust the system."

As we walked back to the car, hand in hand, I said, "It's a heartwarming story. I'm glad someone is doing it. Let's go home and watch our movie."

Vicki bumped me with her hip. "I'll make popcorn and hot chocolate. After the movie, we can send money to SE-cubed."

'You're old softies,' Fitch teased me, but I could see his eyes were no drier than mine.

I wondered about the long-term results of Ms. Miller's social engineering, but from the looks of Louisa's grades, I expected nothing but good news.

Mr. Shelley was the one suspect still standing.

'I don't suppose you want my prediction, do you?' said Fitch.

"No way. Keep your trap shut."

36

PEER EDITING - WEDNESDAY

Wherein Zarand doesn't have a clue.

A flash flood roared in my ears. The weight of the water made it hard to breathe. I was paralyzed until my screams woke me.

Back in the real world, the Santa Ana winds rustled through the palm trees and Dahl kneaded my chest—time for first breakfast.

I reached for my glasses and staggered into the kitchen with that darn cat weaving between my legs. "Stop that. You won't get breakfast any faster if I trip over you."

Meow. She jumped onto the counter and waited by her jar of cat treats.

Our food was interrupted when Mr. Sendak, the Stony High substitute coordinator, called.

I answered, "Whassup, Jared?"

"Ms. Miller requested you again."

Fitch scratched his head. *'That's a surprise after you accused her of dealing drugs. Is she up to something?'*

After Vicki and I upset her routine at San Amano High, I figured that I owed her. "I'll be there."

Now that I had an assignment, I was late. For a quick breakfast, I toasted two thick slices of sourdough and scrambled four eggs to share with Dahl. I buttered the bread and put both plates on the table. Dahl enjoyed her eggs and licked the butter from her toast. Before I sat down to eat, my phone sounded a *ka-ching* notification for a new Cajon Treasure clue.

Fitch teased me, *'You're quite busy for a retired guy.'*

Stony Estancia Surfs reported that clue number six came from the New York Public Library lions. Patience, the south lion, said, THE FANS AT LOW LEVEL, and Fortitude, the north lion, added, STEAMERS ARE TURNINGS.

On Mount Olympus, *Apollo turned to Artemis, "New York Public Library? Really? It's over 2,000 miles from Stony Estancia."*

Artemis laughed, "This book is called The Library Club, isn't it?"

Apollo couldn't argue with his clever sister. "Good point. I always loved those lions."

While eating, Dahl and I perused the updated list of clues.

THE FANS AT LOW LEVEL. STEAMERS ARE TURNINGS.

NANOSECONDS DISAPPEAR BEFORE WOMEN EAT SILVER TRENCH PEARS.

SKYWATCHING CHIPMUNKS REJECT EVERY ECO KANYON AROUND CAMPS.

BIG CLUE AS JAR OPENS NIRVANAS AND ECSTASYS.

THE WAYS NO ONE READS TREASURE HOW UNCOVERS.

STAR-CROSSED TRIANGLES ORIGIN NEXUS YOU TRAVEL TWELVE MILES.

I scratched Dahl's ears. "What do you think?"

She finished her eggs and retreated to the sofa to enjoy the morning sun, not interested in treasure or crime.

'A canyon is a trench. Turnings? You should search everything turning around a twelve-mile radius,' Fitch said.

I studied his face, recognizing his sarcastic smirk. "450 square miles? You haven't a clue—pardon the pun—do you?"

He went over to sit on the sofa with Dahl. *'Nothing. Nada.'*

Dahl and my imaginary friend high-fived.

As I drove to the scene of Tiff the Tutor's murder, I willed the Cajon Treasure to fade from my thoughts. I only wanted clues pointing to Ms. Shelley's killer.

Ms. Miller's lesson plan called for peer editing of the 19th-century author reports followed by a movie if they finished early. She noted that she'd refilled the carbon dioxide canisters for soda water and replenished the popcorn supply. She left her computer on, so I could use the slides she prepared for the lesson. I projected the first slide. PEER

EDITING: THE 3 STEPS, and asked, "Who can tell me the three steps?"

January made little claps, turned her palms up and pushed them forward in an offering gesture, and traced an X. She had signed COMPLIMENT, SUGGEST, and CORRECT.

I gave her a thumbs-up before clicking on the next slide. "Who can give me an example of compliments?"

Jorge offered, "Lizzy's selection of Rabindranath Tagore is a welcome departure from all those European and North American authors."

Lizzy returned his compliment with, "Jorge's photos of Henry David Thoreau are an excellent addition to his report."

This was Stony High, and they were good at compliments, so I clicked the next slide. "How about some examples of positive suggestions?"

January smiled as she said, "Jorge, for such a serious author, you might want a different font. I don't see Thoreau using Comic Sans."

Everyone laughed at this.

"I already changed it to boring Bookman, but I doubt he would have cared. Thoreau said: *Our life is wasted on details. Simplify, simplify.*"

I put up the last slide. "Finally, the most important and sensitive step—corrections."

Lizzy jumped in. "The Thoreau quote is: *Our life is frittered away **by** detail*. Look it up."

I cut the discussion short. They needed to work on their reports, and I needed to track down a killer. "Find a partner and get to work."

While they did their peer editing, I considered Ms. Miller's social experiment—paying students for attendance and grades. *What had Vicki called the scheme? Heartwarming.* The story was too perfect. She was covering something up, but what?

My thoughts were interrupted by a chat popup on Ms. Miller's computer.

SAMMY: FAITH [HEART EYES] WHASSUP?

I may have been wrong about the drug dealing, but Zola and Alyce were right about the boyfriend.

Fitch jumped on the name. *'Sammy? Is this the same Sammy that met with Ms. Shelley—blue eyes—in the annex?'*

This was the clue I was waiting for. I wanted to keep Sammy chatting. **BROWN EYES**: HEY SAMMY. I'M TEACHING. WHASSUP WITH YOU?

Fitch jumped up and down. *'You're brown eyes. Sammy was two-timing you with blue eyes.'*

SAMMY: YOU'RE NOT FAITH [UNAMUSED FACE]

BROWN EYES: MS. MILLER IS OUT TODAY. I AM THE SUB.

The popup went away, but who was Sammy? I knew how to find out. I sent a text to my buddy, Vinnie Purcell, the one the three-letter agencies back in Washington, DC called, "the smartest guy in the room."

SZILARD: VINNIE. I'M ON MS. MILLER'S COMPUTER. CAN YOU FIND OUT WHO JUST CHATTED WITH ME?

VINNIE: GIVE ME A MINUTE.

I walked around the room to make sure everyone was on task. January's report was on Mark Twain. Following Jorge's example, she was adding photographs, as were several others.

When I returned to the teacher's desk, Vinnie had replied.

VINNIE: SORRY. NO CAN DO. STRONG ENCRYPTION [SAD FACE]

SZILARD: THANKS FOR TRYING [FOLDED HANDS]

Even though Vinnie couldn't track down Sammy, I was sure he was Mr. Shelley aka Gun Shell and this affair with Faith Miller added to his motive for murdering his wife.

I went to the Library Club meeting during lunch.

The treasure clues dominated the discussion.

They weren't any closer to an answer than Dahl and Fitch. When the buzzer sounded for end-of-lunch, January jumped up. She waved her hands in the air with her thumbs tucked in. "Eight. Eight. Eight," she said.

"Give that girl a prize. Every clue has eight words," Ranch shouted.

'What is the significance of eight?' Fitch pondered.

37

FOURTH ARREST - THURSDAY

Wherein Zarand gets a clue.

I started my day with the Library Club and a new clue. This latest clue included an affidavit signed by both Tish and César, "We affirm that we were told this by the ancient birch tree in our front yard."

THE MAPS TO THE CLUES ANNOYING VEX EVERYONE.

THE FANS AT LOW LEVEL. STEAMERS ARE TURNINGS.

NANOSECONDS DISAPPEAR BEFORE WOMEN EAT SILVER TRENCH PEARS.

SKYWATCHING CHIPMUNKS REJECT EVERY ECO KANYON AROUND CAMPS.

BIG CLUE AS JAR OPENS NIRVANAS AND ECSTASYS.

THE WAYS NO ONE READS TREASURE HOW UNCOVERS.

STAR-CROSSED TRIANGLES ORIGIN NEXUS YOU TRAVEL TWELVE MILES.

On Mount Olympus, *Apollo turned to Artemis, "Does this list of clues ever end?"*

Artemis ran her fingers through her brother's curly hair. "Just one more."

Lizzy laughed. "Finally a clue I understand. *Annoying vex everyone.* The clue is in bad English, but it sums up the situation."

"You make a good point Lizzy. Maybe we're going about this all wrong. The clues are gibberish. Nothing makes any sense," Ranch said.

January held up her hands showing all her fingers, but not her thumbs. "Eight."

Alyce agreed with January. "You're right. You found a pattern. Forget the meaning of the words. Find something else."

Jorge squinted his eyes. "Here's something. Three of the clues are longer and four are shorter. I bet tomorrow's clue is going to be longer."

Zola did a backflip. "Sharp, sharp, now we're getting somewhere."

Fitch disputed their enthusiasm. *'I don't call eight and longer or shorter real progress.'*

I didn't care. I was here to solve a murder, not find a treasure.

After school, I sat in the passenger seat as Vicki drove up Van Vleck Avenue to Stony Estancia Haciendas. After we passed through the gates, she squeezed my hand and said, "This is it. I have the arrest warrant."

I gave her a thumbs up. Our investigation had made some missteps, but we were going to close the case with the arrest of Mr. Shelley. We made a good team.

In the back seat, Tsui sat beside Vicki's black satchel and laptop.

When she parked in the circular driveway, I noticed that plywood still covered the front window.

Tsui rang the bell and Mr. Shelley welcomed us at the front door. "Are you here to arrange a police escort for my wife's funeral?"

Vicki had those excellent people skills that would get her promoted to Chief of Detectives. Without missing a beat, she replied, "Yes, where is the funeral route?"

Mr. Shelley invited us in.

Tsui looked at the long hallway lined with bookshelves. "You have a lot of books. Have you read them all?"

Mr. Shelley's shoulders drooped, and he frowned. "Not my books. Those are Tiffany's, and, yes, I'm sure she read them all."

Nothing more was said until we were in the front room, and he'd served tea with those biscuits from his London publisher.

He murmured, "The funeral route—"

We all leaned forward to hear him better.

"The funeral home will bring her here for the memorial service and then we'll need the escort for the procession down Van Vleck Avenue to the Bragg Vineyard Cemetery."

Vicki asked in a gentle voice, "When will this be?"

"Saturday. This Saturday. But I'm not sure of the exact time the cortège will leave. The list of people who want to be represented at the memorial service keeps growing."

Vicki turned to Tsui. "Can you make sure the traffic unit is briefed?"

We needed to move on from funeral plans to interrogating Mr. Shelley about his wife's murder. I left this delicate transition to Vicki.

She refilled his tea to give him time to recover from the funeral arrangements before she said, "We'd like to talk to you about something else."

She looked at me. "Zee, can you start?"

"Do you own a motorcycle?"

He looked baffled. "Yes. I own several, as does Tiff."

'Why do they own so many motorcycles?' pondered Fitch. *'I'm sure that's an important clue.'*

I nodded. "Has anyone ever called you Sammy?"

Now he was shocked. "How did you find out about that? When we go to karaoke—" He stopped himself and choked up. He wiped a few tears from his eyes. "I'm never going to sing again."

I gave him a minute to collect himself and repeated my question. "Has anyone ever called you Sammy?"

In a voice we could hardly hear, he said, "I always sang *Mr. Bojangles* and *The Candy Man*. It was all in fun. I didn't mean to be disrespectful to Sammy Davis, Jr. I liked it when they cheered, 'Sammy. Sammy,' while I performed."

Vicki sipped her tea. "I'm sure it's fine. Do you have a good voice?"

He relaxed. "No, but as I said, it's just a way to blow off some steam."

I jumped in. "Did you ever get into a fist fight when you were blowing off steam?"

He answered with a big smile like it was some kind of joke. "Fights? All the time. Like I said, just blowing off steam. My friends and I love to fight."

'That's some kind of a sick joke,' said Fitch, always quick to judge.

"The County Coroner found a lot of broken bones. Your wife has had a rough life," Vicki said.

Gun Shell smiled at that memory. "You can say that again."

I agreed with Fitch. Gun Shell was detached from reality—laughing at fist fights and his wife's fractured bones.

"Have you ever been referred to anger management?" I asked.

That erased his smile. "What? No."

"Do you have an alibi for the night your wife was murdered?"

"Of course not. You know that. I was home and Pax was out with friends or wherever they go at night."

I went in for the kill. "Did you murder her because she was having an affair?"

Mr. Shelley crossed his arms. "I'm not saying another word without my lawyer."

Vicki was all cop. "No problem. We're arresting you for the murder of your wife."

He jumped up. "You can't be serious. This is crazy. I loved her."

He'd already requested a lawyer and refused to answer any more questions, but Tsui still read him his rights.

Fitch celebrated. *'You have the correct person. He admitted to being Sammy. That was the final clue, but I knew it was him all along.'*

Vicki and I went to the Firehouse Barbecue to celebrate closing the case with ribs and hushpuppies. I ordered a large family feast to replenish the supply of leftovers in my freezer.

'Is Gun Shell's arrest the final chapter?' Fitch asked.

Not quite, we still have the funeral, I thought.

He reminded me, *'And we have to find the Cajon Treasure.'*

I didn't expect the funeral to require so many chapters and take up so many pages.

On Mount Olympus, *Artemis said, "Don't blame me for too many clues. When the book gets more chapters, I get more clues."*

Wherein Zarand is a cool cat.

My electric car stopped in front of the community center adjacent to the Pacific Electric Trail. I placed my phone on the ground and set it to read the Cajon Treasure clues aloud. I used the back of a bench to stretch my legs while I waited for Vicki to arrive. We had a jogging date in celebration of solving Tiffany Shelley's murder.

The robotic computer lady converted *Stony Estancia Surfs* into an almost human voice. "*Complete list of Cajon Treasure clues. Regulations procedure openly occur let crooks always steal. The maps to the clues annoying vex everyone. The fans at low level. Steamers are turnings. Nanoseconds disappear before women eat silver trench pears—*"

I stopped there. Those trench pears reminded me that the clues were complete nonsense. I didn't need to hear the rest.

"Mornin' Zee." We hugged before she took off shouting, "Let's go," and left me behind.

I went up on my toes for a burst of speed and soon was running beside her. "Vee, do you think we have the right person?" I asked with my last breath.

She didn't slow down. "Zee, you worry too much. When he confessed to being Sammy, I knew it was him."

By this point, I couldn't speak. I stopped, bent over with my hands on my knees, and took deep breaths.

She turned around. Seeing me panting, she waited. "Sorry, my love. Am I going too fast for you?"

I gasped. "Just a little," and walked to close the distance between us.

"I'll go slower. Ready to start again?"

"Give me a head start." She watched me jog ahead before she resumed running. We settled into a comfortable pace, and I recovered enough breath to continue our conversation. "Where's Gun Shell?"

"He's a guest of Stony Estancia at a meeting with his attorneys—in a secure conference room in the Civic Center."

I took a long breath before responding. "I don't think he's a flight risk."

"Not with Officer Tsui guarding him."

The trail ran through a neighborhood where the houses backed tight against the abandoned railroad right-of-way. Friendly dogs cheered us along—amid the aromas of frying bacon and warm maple syrup.

"What is going to happen at his wife's funeral? He can't attend if he is incarcerated."

"That will be decided by a judge at his arraignment this afternoon, but I will recommend that he be released on his own recognizance."

That was my Vicki. She always knew what to do.

When we reached Bohr Boulevard, I said, "This is the two-mile mark, far enough for me."

"Are you sure you don't want to run up the hill to Pauli Open Space?"

I kissed her nose. "Not today, Vee, but thank you for the offer."

"Good run, Zee. Let's have a water break and head back."

As we returned to Heisenberg Park, I saw the Stony Stoners hanging out with the Frank twins. "Let's go talk to them. Maybe they know something about the treasure."

She gave me a sweet smile. "Since we've solved the murder, you're welcome to indulge your treasure-hunting fantasy. Lock your knee and you can pretend you're a pirate with a wooden leg."

I repeated, "*Arr, arr*," in a deep voice, and limped over to the Stoners, much to Fitch's amusement.

"Allen, Joan, Kurt, this is Detective Yukawa."

"Far out. Cool to meet your old lady," Allen said.

Vicki bristled. "I'm not an old lady."

"Not old, like too many birthdays. It's our jive, our lingo."

Joan pushed Allen. "I told you. Stop that male chauvinist pig stuff."

Kurt bowed to Vicki and kissed her hand. "Pardon my uncouth acquaintance, dear lady."

"It's no problem," she said with a smile for these strange folks.

I continued with the introductions.

"Vee, you know the Frank twins. The others are Allen Ginsburg, Joan Didion, and Kurt Vonnegut."

She picked up the vibe and said, "Groovy," before turning to me and saying *sotto voce*. "You do know those aren't their real names, don't you?"

'It's cute that she explained that to you,' Fitch laughed.

I dove right into the treasure hunt. "Have you been following the treasure clues?"

"We're hip. We grok it," Kurt said.

'They sound just like the clues. More gibberish.'

"Do you want to make the scene and get it together?" Joan asked.

Vicki was into this. She said, "Send me."

"Frank, hit me with that big stick of chalk. Frankie, read the spaced-out clues," Allen said.

'Go man. That's the word everyone has been searching for—spaced-out,' Fitch said.

Frankie read, "**S**tar-crossed **t**riangles **o**rigin **n**exus **y**ou travel **t**welve **m**iles."

Allen said, "We just use the first letters," and wrote on the ground. "S T O N Y T T M."

"Do you dig it?" Kurt said.

"I dig it—Stony," Joan replied.

Vicki paused for a moment before she saw it. "Gosh. Stony. What about—?"

Frank interrupted her. "The rest is dullsville. Ignore the extra letters. Flaked out. A rip-off."

That satisfied Vickie. "Cool."

Frankie read again. "**T**he **w**ays **n**o **o**ne **r**eads **t**reasure **h**ow **u**ncovers."

Allen wrote. "T W N O R T H U."

I got into it. "North."

After a while, we had—Stony, North, Cajon, Creek, West, Falls, Cave, and Pool.

"Far out. Are you going after the treasure?"

"No way."

If the Stoners didn't want the treasure, I knew who did.

"Vicki, let's split. The Library Club is meeting. To the high school."

Lizzy announced, "Mr. S. has solved the clues."

Fitch corrected, *'The Stoners figured it out.'*

I took them through writing down the first letters and extracting the words. Everyone did it for themselves and soon they were all chanting. "Stony, North, Cajon, Creek, West, Falls, Cave, Pool."

"I've been searching those mountains for years. I know what those clues mean," Ranch said confidently.

Everyone looked at him expectantly.

"Starting in *Stony* Estancia, go *north* to Cajon *Creek*, then *west* along the creek to the *falls*. Through the falls, there is a *cave*. The treasure is in the *pool* at the end of the cave."

Lizzy looked at Ranch with admiration. "Do you know where that is?"

His chest puffed out. "Oh yes. I've been there. I didn't see any treasure." He added, "But I didn't look that hard."

"Walkabout. Let's go," Alyce said.

"Minimum day. School is out," Jorge declared.

Before the end-of-lunch buzzer sounded, they were gone.

'I can't believe they're all cutting class. That's not like Stony Estancia High School,' Fitch said.

ARRAIGNMENT – FRIDAY PM

Wherein Zarand eats a brownie.

I arrived early at Judge Díaz's courtroom on the second floor of the Stony Estancia Civic Center. I waited with Vicki. For her court appearance, she wore her uniform.

"You're looking good," I offered with a brief hug.

"Thanks," she said. "So do those two." She pointed to Ms. Brautigan and Mr. Yeats, a couple of local lawyers—good ones—representing Mr. Shelley. They waved to Vicki, and she waved back. They wore coordinated suits.

The city attorney, Mr. Blake, showed up last, followed by his assistant carrying a black document case. When he saw Vicki, he came over. "I hope you have your ducks in order. I hate courtrooms. They're so public and easy to misinterpret. Each time I'm here, César and Tish post something on *Stony Estancia Surfs* that costs me votes."

"I'm sorry you find your job challenging," replied Vicki, not disguising her frustration with his constant electioneering.

Fitch observed, *'It's strange how she has a better relationship with the opposition than with her own team.'*

I defended Vicki. *That's not surprising. The prosecution-shy Mr. Blake and the police department are natural enemies.*

When the bailiff opened the courtroom door, Mr. Blake rushed in to claim a position for his assistant behind the prosecution table.

Vicki and the defense counselors walked in together until the end when Mr. Blake motioned for Vicki to sit with his assistant. The assistant handed Mr. Blake one thin folder.

The defense table was strewn with papers, laptops—three of them, and books with sticky notes.

The bailiff brought in Mr. Shelley and sat him beside the defense lawyers. He wore an orange jumpsuit but no handcuffs.

Vicki leaned over and whispered, "Our star witness, Coroner Persey, is in the witness room."

The next two to enter were Mr. Blake's nemeses, Leticia and César of *Stony Estancia Surfs* fame. They sat next to Vicki and me. SE-cubed was well represented by Mr. Declan Beckett, Ms. Miller, and Dr. Chandrasekhar's wife, whose name I forgot. They also had someone who looked like a lawyer.

'*Nilanjana Rajagopalan,*' Fitch reminded me.

I leaned over to Vicki. "Who's that lady with them?"

"She's Declan's personal lawyer. He must be worried he'll get sued."

"Why do you say that?" I asked.

Tish overheard my question and answered, "The murder happened in his building and his bookcases collapsed on the victim."

Principal Golding represented Stony High wearing a dress with a bold floral pattern. I had no idea why the Stony Stoners chose to attend, but they were all dressed in black, so maybe they were Persey's fan club or showing support for their friend Tiff the Tutor.

Joan Didion passed out brownies. César pointed to a sign that read, NO PHONES, CAMERAS, OR RECORDING DEVICES. NO FOOD OR BEVERAGES. Regardless, he and Tish accepted one that they split between them. I took a whole one.

"Be careful with those," Allen Ginsberg said.

Kurt Vonnegut just smiled.

The bailiff said, "All rise for the Honorable Ms. Díaz," and the judge entered wearing a long black robe as required by California law.

Ms. Díaz addressed the defendant, "Mr. Shelley, how do you plead?"

Ms. Brautigan stood and replied, "My client pleads not guilty."

The judge looked surprised. She stared at City Attorney Blake.

I whispered, "She looks upset. What's going on?"

César laughed, "She expected a last-minute plea deal. Blake always has one. He campaigned on a platform not to waste the taxpayer's money on jury trials."

Tish added, "We've never seen him in a trial. That would be lots of clicks."

Judge Díaz banged her gavel. "If spectators cannot remain silent, you will be removed."

The Stoners pursed their lips to suppress their laughter.

"Mr. Blake, please call your first witness?"

"County Coroner Paterson."

After she was sworn in, Persey established that Tiffany Shelley showed evidence of long-standing abuse. "The person best positioned to inflict abuse over a long period is the partner. The Shelleys have been married for over twenty years. Her spouse had means, motive, and opportunity."

Mr. Blake sat down with a smug smile.

Her testimony matched my intuition. If this went to trial, it would be a short one.

The judge spoke to the defense. "Any cross-examination of County Coroner Paterson?"

Mr. Yeats stood. "Thank you, County Coroner, for your always clear and complete testimony. Perhaps I missed something. Did you state the cause of death?"

"No, Mr. Yeats."

"Do you often fail to identify the cause of death?"

"No."

Fitch was a member of Persey's fan club. *I love to listen to her. She's an experienced witness. No rambling. No extra information. She makes the lawyers earn their testimony.*

Mr. Yeats continued, "Is this what is called an unremarkable autopsy?"

"Yes."

"Have you ever failed to determine the cause of death?"

"No."

"So, is it possible Ms. Tiffany Shelley died of natural causes?"

"No."

"How can you say that?"

"Natural causes or old age is no longer used on death certificates. We always list a cause like cancer, heart disease, or diabetes."

"I see. So, this case is, indeed, strange."

Before Persey could respond, Mr. Blake stood up and said, "Objection. Counsel has not asked a question."

Judge Díaz agreed. "Sustained. The witness is instructed not to respond."

Fitch laughed. *'Persey didn't need all that. She knows her job.'*

Mr. Yeats sat down.

"Does the defense have further cross-examination?" Judge Díaz asked.

Ms. Brautigan stood and replied, "I have a few more—" She turned to look directly at Mr. Blake. "—questions."

Ms. Brautigan approached Persey. "I don't want to tell you how to do your job, but I understand there is something that causes death and results in an unremarkable autopsy."

She paused.

City Attorney Blake didn't object to the non-question.

Ms. Brautigan raised her voice and addressed the whole court. "Could this have been a case of sudden cardiac death? I've read that SCD produces death and unremarkable autopsies. Could Ms. Shelley have died of SCD instead of murder?"

"No," Persey replied.

Ms. Brautigan continued, "Can you please explain your answer? Is my research wrong?"

"Yes. Yes. Unexplained SCD is like old age, we don't list it as a cause of death anymore." She turned to the judge. "This is a technical issue. Would you like me to give a short tutorial?"

"Please do. Go ahead."

"We know SCD is caused by structural cardiac abnormalities. If Ms. Shelley survived a sudden cardiac incident, her doctor would order an MRI or CT scan to determine the underlying etiology." She paused. "I didn't need a scan. I was performing an autopsy and had the heart, in hand, as it were."

The Stony Stoners squirmed in their seats. Mrs. Golding closed her eyes and raised her shoulders. Mr. Blake looked sick.

Coroner Paterson waited for the room to calm down after her grisly image. "I examined her heart and sent it to the chief cardiologist at Stony Estancia Regional Hospital. Ms. Shelley didn't have any structural abnormalities. She was fit and healthy." Persey raised her voice. "No SCD."

Ms. Brautigan sat down. "I have no further questions. Thank you."

The judge asked City Attorney Blake. "Do you wish to call another witness?"

"Not at this time."

Judge Díaz leaned forward. "I am surprised and disappointed. In the 21st century, I've grown to expect more definite scientific evidence. Everything about this case is ambiguous, but that is why the jury system was created. I will set a trial date. Thank you all."

Ms. Brautigan stood. "Your honor. Ms. Shelley's funeral is tomorrow—."

"I was getting to that. Mr. Shelley is a long-time resident of Stony Estancia with many ties to the community. On the police department's recommendation, I am releasing him on his own recognizance."

Mr. Blake turned around and scowled at Vicki.

She squeezed my hand and smiled.

The judge gave a hard look to Mr. Blake. "Unless you have an objection."

"No, your honor," the city attorney said.

The bailiff cleared the spectators from the courtroom.

While I waited for Vicki, I asked a rhetorical question, "Do you think he did it?" not expecting any reply beyond a sarcastic thought by Fitch.

"I doubt it was him. This indictment is an example of sexist prejudice," Joan Didion said.

"Right on. We knew Tiff the Tutor. There was no way her sitting-all-day-at-his-computer husband was going to get the better of her," Kurt Vonnegut concurred.

"You're hip. I'd have expected her to do him in, not vice versa," Allen Ginsberg agreed.

Before I could reply, Leticia jumped in. "Thanks for the groovy brownies. Let me give you some hard data. *Stony*

Estancia Surfs crowd-sourced information on every death in Mr. Shelley's books—256 of them. They were all violent—guns, swords, bombs, clubs, and maces—caveman style."

César continued, "When it comes to death, he has no imagination. This murder is beyond him."

"I'm going to blow this scene. I'm off to Cocina de Cetto for tacos and chips, chips and tacos," Joan said.

The Stoners all thought this was a good idea and left. I agreed, but I waited for Vee. *Stony Estancia Surfs* also delayed their munchies, preparing to ambush Mr. Blake.

César stopped the city attorney outside the courtroom.

Leticia accosted him with her blue microphone. "Congratulations. You're going to have a jury trial. *Stony Estancia Surfs* doesn't remember your last one. The voters will be watching to see how well you do your job when you're not brokering a plea deal behind closed doors."

'Wow. She put it to him good.'

City Attorney Blake presented his best smile. "Senior Detective Yukawa has a strong case and I look forward to seeing Mr. Shelley in court."

After a brief pause, he added, "I'm always alert for ways to avoid taxpayer expenses and jury trials. I'm available to discuss a deal with Ms. Brautigan and Mr. Yeats."

Tish turned to Vicki. "Do you have a comment?"

"No."

Tish looked at me, but I preempted her. "No comment here, either."

40

ARTEMIS AND APOLLO AGAIN

Wherein Apollo and Artemis have one last dance.

Artemis asked, "May I offer you some tea?

Apollo held up his cup.

Artemis filled it, put down the teapot, and collapsed into her favorite throne with a sigh.

He looked at his sister. "You've made a right awful mess with those treasure clues, haven't you?"

"I don't see why you say that. They needed my help."

He sat on the arm of her throne, smoothed out some fine gray hair, and kissed her forehead. She reached out and held his other hand. They sat like this while the rosebuds opened into glorious blooms.

"Yes, they needed your help. Even the rosebuds need your help." He kissed her again like the bumblebee kisses the rose. "Did you need to make your help that complicated?"

She laughed like a bubbling brook in the spring. "Surely, you would allow me a little fun."

"Yes, but they were happy when they solved the puzzle, think how they'll feel when they discover they have the decoy solution."

"That disappointment won't last. That clever child living in the mountains, second cousin to the nymphs and satyrs, will find the treasure. That one with the rainbow hair is my favorite."

He could feel how his sister's joy rejuvenated her. She was like a young girl again.

She stood up and danced around the room. "Let's not be late for the final chapters."

Wherein Zarand has black desserts.

Stony Estancia Haciendas held the gate open and black signs directed traffic to TIFF THE TUTOR'S CELEBRATION OF LIFE. When I saw the cars parked on both sides of the tree-lined streets, I pulled into the first space I found. County Coroner Persephone Paterson parked behind me.

I greeted Persey, "Mornin' to you. I had to dig out my black suit today, but you were all set. You always dress in black, don't you?"

She gave me a look that said have you grown up under a rock? Don't you know anything about fashion? "Not so. This is my Victorian mourning dress of Parramatta silk. Along with my black gloves and veil, all this is reserved for funerals."

"I didn't realize that. You must attend a lot of them."

"That I do. Occupational perquisite, some say. Notice also that Cerberus has his black silk collar." At the mention of his name, he moved forward to receive scratches.

"Good boy," Persey said.

We walked side-by-side while Cerberus ran circles around us, checking out all the fancy landscaping—so many new smells.

We knew we were near when we saw a hearse in the driveway. When we got closer, a sign for valet parking stood beside Jorge collecting key fobs from double-parked cars waiting for him to move them to some distant location.

Persey said, "I'm glad I didn't try to use the valet parking."

Cerberus barked in agreement.

Ms. Blume, the Stony High librarian, approached us from the opposite direction. She carried a package wrapped in plain paper. Cerberus rushed over to her. She presented the package to him. He sniffed it, sat down, and gave two quick barks. Persey said, "Very nice."

Fitch gave me a smug smile. *'I recall that signal. Two barks for old books.'*

We walked to the door which was draped in black crepe. I was pleased that someone had removed the plywood and repaired the front window.

Fitch was impressed by the preparations. *'Look how they've organized the traffic flow.'*

Burgundy velvet ropes and black runners marked the way through the house. The ceremony was in the backyard.

"After you," I said to Persey, as she and Cerberus took up the full width of the narrow hallway lined with Tiff the Tutor's rare book collection.

"Mornin' Zarand." Vicki arrived with Tsui.

'What a strange procession,' remarked Fitch. *'Persey and her dog. You with the librarian. Vicki and Tsui.'*

I would have preferred to be paired with Vee.

The music that filled the house was familiar. I tapped Persey on the shoulder. "You've been to a lot of funerals. Why are they playing wedding music?"

"You need to get out more," she replied with a condescending grin. "That's Pachelbel's Canon in D. Its steady, unchanging nature provides a sense of calm, perfect for weddings *and funerals.*"

When we stepped outside, we turned right to pay our respects to Tiffany, approaching the open casket in silence. Even Fitch had the sense to refrain from sarcastic comments. I was surprised by how life-like she appeared. She looked better than when I uncovered her in the library annex.

I said to no one in particular. "It's sad that Pax isn't able to be here."

Leticia stepped between Ms. Blume and me. "Pax is attending online. César is livestreaming the ceremony for anyone who can't be here in person. Jorge is watching on his phone when he's not parking cars. César tells me that quite a few people from San Fernando Valley are in the audience. We have no idea who they are. Gunnar approved the logins."

Fitch noted, *'The major industries in the Valley are film studios and aerospace.'*

We sat in the chairs set up for the occasion. Beyond the seating was a catering table with coffee and pastries from that wonderful pâtisserie around the corner from Purcell and Associates. For the occasion, all the pastries were black. Beside the table was a large garden shed draped in black crepe. A matching one was on the other side of the yard behind the casket and similarly draped. After I'd collected my espresso, a blackout cupcake, a dark chocolate tart, and two black macarons, I discovered that servers were circulating through the crowd. I'd remember them when I was ready for seconds.

Mr. Shelley stood at a microphone beside the casket. "Our first speaker will be Lizzy Chandrasekhar representing the students at Stony Estancia High School.

"We knew Tiffany Shelley as Tiff the Tutor. When I was having difficulty with calculus, Tiff said to me, 'You are a visual learner.' She explained differentiation, integration, and the mean-value theorem with these pictures." Lizzy held up colored-pencil drawings on stiff cardboard. "After that, I had no trouble getting As."

After she placed the drawings in the casket, she pointed to Alyce. "Would you like to tell your experience in American Lit?"

Alyce stood. "*Vale* Tiff the Tutor. Mark Twain's use of dialect was driving me crazy. She told me I was an aural learner and found me an audiobook. That didn't help, but she didn't quit. She determined the American dialect in an American accent was still too much for me."

Alyce wiped a tear from her cheek. "Can you believe that she found an Australian narrator reading Mark Twain? It was *bonzer*. I enjoy Twain's humor along with everyone else after that."

"I'd like one more speaker. Zola?" Lizzy said.

Zola glided to the podium. "Tiff the Tutor was *lekker*. Each week she choreographed my physics lesson into a gymnastics routine. Turns for moment of inertia and angular velocity. Balance beam for center of mass. She said I was a kinesthetic learner." Zola choked up while telling her story. "I got an A in physics, and my floor routines improved."

Lizzy closed with, "Stony High won't be the same. We'll all miss Tiff the Tutor."

The students sat together and hugged each other while Lizzy eulogized their friend. I hugged Vicki and whispered, "I hope that I leave behind as many good memories."

"You will. Of course, you will," she said.

Principal Golding, wearing a plain black dress and shawl, sat with the students. When Mr. Shelley introduced her, she said, "The students have said it all, but the faculty has something to present."

Ms. Blume unwrapped her package. "This is a signed, first edition of *The Giver of Stars* by Jojo Moyes. Tiff the Tutor loved this book and thought of herself as a packhorse librarian, spreading wisdom." She placed the book inside the casket.

Before Mr. Shelley introduced the next mourner, he said, "In Tiffany's name, I thank you for the book. She loved books and requested that each of you borrow one from her library on your way out today. She wants you to keep it until you meet again. She said, 'There are no overdue fines in my library of love.'"

Mr. Beckett praised her community spirit and support of SE-cubed fundraising. "SE-cubed has commissioned a statue of Tiff the Tutor to be placed outside the California History Annex."

The next speaker was Rapper Amar, but he was interrupted by a helicopter that appeared over the Shelleys' backyard.

Zola shouted, "*Eish*. Terrorists!"

Fitch laughed, *'Doesn't she know this is a cozy mystery? There are no terrorists in a cozy.'*

Three men outfitted in combat gear stood outside the chopper on the landing skids firing their automatic weapons in the air.

I'd never seen anything like this during my years in the big city. What were terrorists doing in Stony Estancia?

Fitch was not impressed. *'This can't be real.'*

"Attention. We are here to honor Ms. Shelley. Gun Shell was not her murderer. If her real killer doesn't confess, there will be more bodies to bury."

'You can't be serious,' scoffed Fitch.

With that, the copter fired a missile. Everyone screamed. Cerberus howled. The rocket whistled over our heads and hit the garden shed behind the casket.

It penetrated the structure. I heard a faint ticking. The crowd's silence was broken when Gun Shell shouted, "Everyone down! Cover your heads."

Like the others, I fell to the ground and ducked under my chair.

'Really?' said Fitch, *'Do you think that chair is going to protect you?'*

The garden shed exploded like something out of a Chuck Jones Road Runner cartoon. Tiff the Tutor was forgotten, and personal survival reigned supreme for everyone except Fitch. He observed, *'Strange how no one was injured, isn't it?'*

Mr. Shelley was the first to his feet. "Stay calm. I'll take care of them." He ran to the other garden shed and returned with a missile launcher on his shoulder. "Cover your ears." He pointed at the chopper and fired.

'Rocket launcher?' asked Fitch.

The helicopter motor whined as the pilot did his best to evade the missile. The copter rose, zigging and zagging across the sky, but the missile found its target and exploded with a loud boom and a cloud of black smoke.

I jumped to my feet. "Puppets!" I shouted, "Take that! We showed you."

Everyone cheered—reliving the final scenes of *Independence Day*. We gathered around Mr. Shelley and showered him with congratulations.

When the smoke cleared, the chopper disappeared behind the surrounding homes, crashing to the ground in an enormous flash.

More celebrations, until January pantomimed a parachute and pointed up.

The terrorists had bailed out. They were hanging below their chutes, swinging back and forth. To our shock, they landed on the roof of the Shelleys' home.

Not everyone was scared. Fitch, unencumbered by a body, was entertained. *'This is better than a movie. Or is it a movie?'*

Tish turned to César. "Are you getting all of this?"

He gave her a thumbs up and said, "Viral. National, no, international."

The terrorists were also unfazed. They fired their weapons, strafing the catering table. Splattering black icing everywhere. "You cannot stop us. We're waiting for that confession."

'Strange and fortunate how no one was injured, isn't it?' observed Fitch with a smug smile.

We all looked at each other. The students looked at the teachers. *Stony Estancia Surfs* looked at the SE-cubed people.

Fitch wondered, *'Why did Gun Shell have a missile launcher in his garden shed?'*

I remembered the weapons on display in his front room and that he had a gun safe in the house and Ms. Shelley had one in her car.

I replied to Fitch, *He writes thrillers. It's natural for him to have those for research.*

Fitch was not convinced and asked, *'Then why wasn't a surface-to-air missile enough to scare the terrorists away? They hadn't come here expecting to enter a war zone, or did they?'*

Officer Tsui turned to his boss. "Don't those terrorists look like the Stony Stoners?"

Fitch used his posh British accent to quote Professor Higgins, *'By Jove! I think he's got it.'*

On Mount Olympus, Artemis said, "Who invited Jove? He's a Roman god."

Apollo agreed, "And where did these bad actors come from distracting everyone from your clues?"

Wherein Zarand can't figure it out.

The terrorists held the crowd's attention like a good movie, stomping back and forth across the roof. They chanted, "Confess. Confess." Their heavy boots cracked the terra cotta clay tiles which clattered to the ground, making piles of debris under the eaves.

My intuition told me nothing important was happening on the roof. I kept a watch on the people collected on the ground. My vigilance paid off when I saw Tsui unsnap his holster and reach for his gun. I rushed over to him, "The violence is over. This is not the time for escalation."

Vicki agreed. She touched his arm. "Not now."

'Not now or ever,' chuckled Fitch.

The Library Club also felt that the crisis had passed. They clapped in time to the terrorists' march and sang, "Confess. Confess," while dancing in a circle, and having a great time.

The noise on the roof stopped. The shortest terrorist opened a duffle and took out a rocket-propelled grenade.

Fitch exclaimed, *'Another rocket launcher? Who would have expected that in a cozy mystery set in Stony Estancia?'*

The explosion blasted a hole in the cement-block fence that surrounded the Shelleys' yard and knocked over a palm tree. Mr. Beckett and the other SE-cubed folks escaped through the hole to the neighbor's yard.

'Go call for help!' Fitch shouted, but no one heard him.

Everyone else scattered to avoid the long trunk that took out several rows of folding chairs. The only casualty was Principal Golding who was caught by the crown of fronds.

When the dust settled, Vicki and I ran to Mrs. Golding's rescue. Aside from minor lacerations covering her face and arms, she was okay.

Fitch was rolling on the ground, laughing uncontrollably. *'Clearly, the violence isn't over.'* He added sarcastically, *'You should have let Tsui shoot them.'*

While we'd been distracted, the terrorists had put on gas masks, making them look like insectoid aliens. The tallest one held up a pair of canisters and declared, "The poison gas is next." He twisted his pretend mustache and taunted the crowd, '*Muwhahaha*. No one will survive, not here, not even the neighbors."

"Stop. Stop," demanded Mr. Amar. He fell to his knees and crossed his arms in front of his wide-open eyes. I could barely understand his trembling voice. "Tiff met me at my store. Together we rode my motorcycle to the annex. I broke the window and we entered together."

Leticia held her blue mic over Rapper's head. César pointed his camera at Mr. Amar, then the terrorists, back and forth. The crowd was torn between watching the terrorists—would they be satisfied by Rapper's confession? And listening to Rapper—a murderer.

The terrorists sat on the roof, crisscross applesauce, sukhasana-comfortable pose, with their guns in their laps. The middle terrorist rubbed his hands together and chortled before speaking in the syrupy voice of an evil mastermind. "Please continue and don't leave out any details if you want to stay alive."

The panicked Rapper had trouble speaking. When he caught his breath, the words poured out with a staccato rhythm like bullets from the terrorists' guns. "Tiff and I planned to run away to Mexico. She wanted to take Pax with us. That required money—Pax wasn't going to sleep rough in the Sonoran Desert." He hiccupped. "When Nilanjana Rajagopalan donated the Cajon Treasure journals, she answered our prayers. We planned our escape. Journals. Treasure. New life." Rapper fell to the ground.

I prompted him. "What went wrong?"

He spoke as if in a trance. "The journals weren't there. Our plan was a quick smash-and-grab. When we couldn't find the journals, we fought. I said that her plan was stupid. She replied that we shouldn't have waited until Monday night. Sunday would have been better. Saturday, right after the dedication, would have been the best. We pushed and shoved until Tiffany fell over and hit her head on those shelves. They gave her a nasty gash. There was a lot of bleeding. I tried to save her, but she died." He cried, "I killed her. The love of my life and I killed her. It was an accident and I regret it every day."

He held out his wrists and Vicki cuffed him.

Gun Shell froze, his mouth agape, his arms reaching out for Rapper, his fingers wide open. Rapper was talking about Mr. Shelley's wife, his dead wife, Rapper's lover. Gun Shell made a sound like a siren, one that was far away and fading.

Vicki motioned to Tsui. "Make sure Mr. Shelley doesn't attack Rapper." She asked me, "Zee, do you believe him?"

'I think not. Persey would have known if this was the cause of death.' Fitch said as if he was a medical examiner.

I didn't respond, but Ranch did. "I know my dad. He would never kill someone, not even by accident." He turned to his father. "Dad, you're wrong." Ranch jumped up onto one of the folding chairs. "My father is a good person. He's the kind of a person who confesses to a murder he didn't commit."

He turned to Ms. Blume. "This is all your fault. You should never have let Ms. Miller check out those journals. They were too valuable."

Ms. Blume spoke. "I'm sorry about your father, but I thought the Cajon Treasure was a myth. I worried more about the first editions than those old journals."

Tsui again reached for his gun and Vicki again restrained him.

'That's the end of the show. Vicki has Rapper in custody. Someone better take care of Ranch.'

I put my arm around Ranch, and we entered the house, stopping at Tiffany's bookcases.

"Why don't you choose your book?" I said.

He calmed down as he scanned the shelves. He chose a signed edition of *Women, Race, and Class* by Angela Davis and took it to the front room, where he was surrounded by antique weapons, some of which had defended the privilege to enslave in the U.S. Civil War.

While he read, I said, "I'm going to brew you a chamomile tea and give you some of the best English cookies you've ever tasted."

After his tea, served with Gun Shell's imported biscuits, he dried his mustache, hugged me, and said, "I believe in you. My dad is innocent. Find the person who murdered Tiff the Tutor."

I left Ranch in the sitting room with another cup of tea and more of Mr. Shelley's special biscuits.

The stand-off between the three terrorists on the roof and the crowd on the ground was still underway. Before I could formulate an action plan, the situation completely changed.

Principal Golding yelled, "Roll camera!"

"Rolling," César replied.

She then said, "Roll sound."

"Rolling," Tish answered.

After the white-hair principal shouted, "Action," I watched in dismay as she ripped off her dress revealing a leotard underneath. Next, she extracted a small knife with a long thin blade from her plait, and tied it with her shawl, thus improvising a grappling hook that she used to scale the house and get on the roof.

Zola leaped high enough to grab the eaves and lifted herself to be at the principal's side. Gun Shell slammed the casket closed. With two strong jumps, he sprang onto the casket and from there to the roof.

All three of them now above us, they charged the terrorists who were caught unprepared—still sitting crisscross applesauce.

Mrs. Golding threw her shawl around one terrorist, but he ducked out of the way and hit her with a roundhouse kick. We all gasped as she rolled to the edge of the roof, grabbing the eaves just in time.

Zola had better luck with a handspring and trapping her target with a scissor lock around the neck. He wasn't fazed. He spun around while grabbing her legs. Once he freed himself, he tossed her against the chimney.

Mr. Shelley bowled over his target and soon had him in cuffs.

'What was he doing with handcuffs?'

Zola and Gunnar took one terrorist while Mrs. Golding with her long white plait and dressed only in a leotard took care of the other.

Tsui ran around collecting weapons, gas masks, and hand grenades as they clattered off the roof.

After seeing the weapons up close, Tsui told Vicki. "These guns were shooting blanks."

When the terrorists were all cuffed, our heroes presented them at the edge of the roof and the audience cheered.

Gun Shell announced, "This has been a production of the Stony Stunt Store, Stony Estancia's premier association of special effects actors."

The terrorists popped off their cuffs and removed their combat gear. Sure enough, there was Allen Ginsberg, Joan Didion, and Kurt Vonnegut.

Allen called down. "Officer Tsui, those are movie props, and we'll need them back."

"*Blimey*. What about the copter? Did it crash?" asked Alyce.

"No. Movie magic. It's fine," Joan Didion laughed.

The only person still in cuffs was Rapper.

That should have been the end of the show, but the crowd turned on Mr. Amar. The people who accepted his leadership of the search and rescue operation now saw him as Tiff the Tutor's killer. The fans who sang. "*Rapper, the phone wizard,*" from his ads on *Stony Estancia Surfs,* now moved in closer with clenched fists. The women who Vinnie Purcell had seen walking between his sammich shoppe and the swimwear store were calling him awful names.

Vicki and Tsui shoved him behind the casket. The Stoners, Mrs. Golding, and Zola moved in to reinforce the PD. We had a classic scene of a prisoner and an angry crowd separated by a few citizens.

Fitch was aghast, *'Is this a lynch mob in Stony Estancia?'*

Wherein Zarand becomes a kindergarten teacher.

It had gone too far, and I stepped up to the podium to restore peace to the suburbs. "One, two, three, eyes on me." All they really needed to know they'd learned in kindergarten. They all froze in place. I was the teacher, and they were my students. With this reenactment, I'd turned the angry mob into small children.

Like the opening of a fairy tale, I chanted in a deep voice, "The night of the murder began with a note."

Some of the children found folding chairs and relaxed into them to listen. Others dropped to the ground and sat crisscross applesauce. Vicki read the crowd and signaled her posse to stand down. Tsui got a seat for Mr. Amar.

I moved out from behind the podium and walked among the class. "The note was from Sammy to Blue Eyes. As Rinchen Amar has confessed, he and Tiffany had a perfect plan to steal the Cajon Treasure journals. He was Sammy, after Sammy Davis, Junior. Blue Eyes was a reference to Frank Sinatra and his pet name for Tiff."

I turned to the handcuffed Mr. Amar. "How am I doing so far?"

"Not very good. I don't know any Sammy Davis, Junior or Senior, or Frank Sinatra. Who are they? Never heard of them."

'You're off to a bumpy start,' chortled Fitch, always happy to see me fumble.

My students were getting fidgety. I didn't want the bubble of childhood innocence to burst. In a happy voice, I asked, "Excuse me. How confused do I have it? Are you Sammy and did you call Tiffany, Blue Eyes?"

"Of course, I called her Blue Eyes. Her eyes were blue, weren't they?"

That was perfect. They giggled when Rapper got the best of the teacher.

"So why were you going by Sammy?"

"I own a sammich shoppe, don't I?"

Puppets. Several of them laughed aloud and repeated, "Sammich shoppe," as if it was the funniest thing they'd ever heard.

"Right. My apologies."

The crisis had passed.

With everyone settled, I continued, "The bug in the program, the flaw in Rapper alias Sammy's character, was as old as Jason and Medea—wandering eyes. In addition to arranging a rendezvous with Blue Eyes, Sammy also had his eye on Brown Eyes. She discovered his duplicity."

Mr. Amar protested, "What character flaw? I couldn't help if the ladies love me, could I?"

This brought another round of giggles from the audience.

"*Mea culpa*, Rapper. It was Sammy's attractiveness that set off the events that brought us here."

Mr. Amar smiled at this portrayal.

"Brown Eyes had discovered that Sammy was two-timing her."

Rapper, Sammy, Mr. Amar, defended himself. "What did she expect? I'm too much for just one woman."

'*What century are you from?*' mocked Fitch.

The Library Club giggled and scorned him saying, "As if."

Persey and Mrs. Golding shook their heads. "Only in your dreams."

The Stony Stoner said, "You're nowhere, dullsville."

With that ridicule and contempt, the mob's anger dissipated.

"What did Brown Eyes do when she discovered she had competition?" Gun Shell asked.

Fitch puffed up to twice his normal size. '*Tell them Szilard. You figured it out, didn't you? I knew you could.*'

Like any good teacher, I paused until I had everyone's attention. "First, Brown Eyes removed the Cajon Treasure journals from the California History Annex. That solved the immediate threat. Sammy and Blue Eyes wouldn't be running away together."

"Did Brown Eyes kill Blue Eyes?" Tsui asked.

Lizzy flipped her long green hair back and snapped, "Sammy confessed to the murder. Weren't you listening?"

I was in teacher nirvana. The class looked to me for an answer.

Using my old trick, I walked around the yard until all eyes were following me. "Patience. I'm getting there, but I will continue this lesson later. Right now, we have a funeral. Let's not be distracted by murder. We're all here to pay our respects to Tiff the Tutor, Tiffany Shelley."

That reminder brought everyone back to Tiffany, wife, mother, teacher, and friend.

People straightened out the chairs and Gun Shell stood beside the now closed casket and resumed the ceremony. "For our final speaker, I want to introduce Mrs. Agatha Golding, also known as Action Aggie, to represent the Stony Stunt Store."

Principal Golding did a front flip on her way to the casket whipping her long plait in a dramatic arc. "One of the first people I met when I came to Stony Estancia to be the new principal, was Tiff the Tutor. We both embraced an educational philosophy centered around developing the individual talents of each student. When she learned of my interest in weight training and yoga, she invited me to join the Stony Stunt Store."

'That's how Tiffany acquired all those broken bones. She was a stunt actor,' said Fitch.

Gun Shell spoke to me *sotto voce*. "I lied. It wasn't a bookcase that smashed my front window. It was Tiff and I rehearsing for a fight scene."

"I see that. Why didn't you tell Pax about your side hustle?"

"Oh, Pax. They can't focus, flitting from one thing to another. Tiff and I didn't want to distract them from college."

"Did that work?"

"Absolutely. Pax has applied to colleges in the northeast, even farther from the fantasy world of Tinsel Town than Stony Estancia. Serious subjects like Anthropology and Archaeology."

Fitch observed, *'Serious parenting.'*

Action Aggie spun around—a perfect fouetté turn—showing off her middle-aged physique, obvious in her leotard. "Look at me. I protested to Tough Tiff, I'm too old for something like that. She replied, 'Many might be, but not you.' That was Tiffany in a nutshell saying, I see the glory in you, and I'll help you reach it."

Like the previous speakers, the principal had to dab her eyes as she remembered Tough Tiff. January and Lizzy ran up to hug her.

Mr. Shelley closed the ceremony. "Thank you, Action Aggie. Now the Stony Stunt Store will carry the casket out and you are all invited to join the cortège to the Bragg Vineyard Cemetery."

As the pallbearers took their positions around the casket, Mr. Shelley called Jorge to bring the cars around, and Vicki called for the black-and-white units to position themselves at the major intersections.

We all followed the casket through the house where Pachelbel's Canon in D was still playing, and everyone selected a book. Ranch, having finished his tea and biscuits, joined us. We all followed the hearse down the hill to the cemetery.

After everybody had an opportunity to throw a handful of dirt on the casket, I told them. "Meet me at the Stony High gym—midnight tonight. We will reenact the crime. All will be revealed."

REENACTORS – SATURDAY NIGHT

Wherein Zarand reveals all.

I was impressed by the size of the midnight crowd, a tribute to Tiff the tutor. "Follow me. We're headed to the top of the football bleachers."

Everyone climbed the hill and the stadium stairs under the ever-present eye of *Stony Estancia Surfs*. "César, does the orange glow of these lights give you a decent image?"

"No problem." He gave me a big smile and patted his camera. "True color night vision."

Leticia began her on-camera commentary, "*Stony Estancia Surfs* is live at the high school where substitute teacher Mr. S.—"

The camera panned over to me, and I waved.

"—has promised us an exciting and informative lesson."

Ahead was the football field, but behind us, we had a bird's eye view of the campus.

Jorge delivered welcome treats from Only Donuts. He juggled a large container of hot coffee, a smaller one of hot chocolate, milk, sugar, cups, and an assortment of donuts.

He pointed back down the hill to a long room lit with emergency lights. "Isn't that the California History Annex?"

Lizzy answered. "*D'oh.* What else would it be? If you look, you can see the bookcases."

Jorge wasn't offended. "So, is this where Brown Eyes waited for Blue Eyes and Sammy?"

"Correct."

Lizzy wasn't convinced. "How do you know someone was here?"

"Thanks to you and George." The two teens gave me a puzzled look. "Remember when you organized that search for evidence?"

"Yes, but we didn't find anything but a box of nuts and washers."

"Do you remember those washers standing on edge?"

"My group found those," Jorge said.

"An important clue," I said. "But some physics was needed to understand it."

They all looked puzzled as if I'd served eggplant and zucchini for dessert.

Ranch figured it out first. "It involves energy, like that experiment we did."

"Right." I smiled. This was something all teachers lived for—a teachable moment. "Where did the energy come from to bury those washers?"

"I get it. Someone created potential energy by carrying them to the top of the bleachers and then threw them off," shouted Alyce.

"The resulting kinetic energy buried them in the ground," added Ranch.

"Exactly, and that someone was Brown Eyes," Jorge said.

"Correct again. Thanks to physics, we know she sat up here tossing washers to the ground. Like us, she was waiting for something to happen."

After the cocoa and coffee got cold, the group got restless. January rubbed her hands together and blew on them. Ranch found a pair of gloves in his pockets and offered them to Lizzy. She accepted them, clapped her gloved hands together, and said, "Thanks."

"It's cold and windy up here. Why didn't you warn us to wear our winter clothes?" Mrs. Golding said.

"I checked the weather," said Ms. Miller wearing a puffy jacket and gloves.

"It's warmer on the ground and we can start a fire," Zola suggested.

"We're reenacting the night of the killing. No fire. Brown Eyes didn't want to be seen when Sammy and Blue Eyes arrived," I explained.

Right on schedule, a motorcycle sped into the courtyard.

"Everyone get down," I whispered with urgency.

The bike turned between the library and the gym and parked beside the annex.

"*Crikey*, there they are," Alyce said.

"Can you identify them?" I asked.

"No. They're wearing helmets."

Everyone forgot about the cold as we watched the Sammy and Blue Eyes reenactors pry open the plywood patch to enter through the broken window and walk along the wall of glass to the fireplace.

"How about now? Their helmets are off. Can you recognize them?"

"Still no, we're too far away, but if I was Brown Eyes, it wouldn't matter. Who else can it be but Sammy and Blue Eyes, Rapper and Tiff the Tutor?"

"Astute observation, Alyce. Let's see what happened next."

Ranch shouted, "They're fighting. Look at that. Blue Eyes ran away, but he was faster. Did you see that? He pushed her. She fell over and banged her head."

We watched the Sammy reenactor check the Blue Eyes reenactor lying on the floor.

Alyce said, "*Blimey*. There he goes. He took her helmet and one of the green boxes." She thought for a moment. "That's the missing treaty."

When Sammy sped away on the motorcycle, the green box fell to the ground.

Zola laughed. "*Eish*. And that's where the Frank twins found the treaty."

"Forget the treaty. She's not dead. My dad didn't kill her," Ranch said.

Lizzy answered, "Right. Look, she's staggering. She put her phone in one of those green boxes and her wallet in another before passing out again. I wonder why she did that?"

Tish jumped in, "Here's Pax on speaker."

"I'm not surprised. She was concerned about identity theft and would have hidden her phone and wallet if she felt she was going to pass out."

I knew Pax was on the other side of the mountains, but he sounded like he was standing with us.

Lizzy stepped in front of the camera and waved. "Good to hear from you. We found her wallet. What happened to her phone?"

Pax replied, "I tracked mom's phone, turned it off, and took it away."

Sammy and Blue Eyes stepped out of the annex and stood under a light to take their bows. I said, "Please give a round of applause for our reenactors, Senior Detective Yukawa and Officer Tsui."

As the clapping died down, Zola said, "Sharp. We've seen the show. Now can we go someplace warm?"

"I'll open the library. Don't leave a mess here. Please take your trash with you," Mrs. Golding said.

We all took seats in the library.

"They gave a great performance," Lizzy said.

Fitch objected. *'Nothing compared to the Stony Stunt Store spectacular at the Shelleys' house.'*

Ranch leaned back and folded his arms. "But it all seems like conjecture to me."

"Totally," said Jorge.

To my surprise, Vicki came to my defense. "Agatha Christie wrote that unless you are good at guessing, it is not much use being a detective." She winked at me.

I went into teacher-mode. "In cases like this, we need means, motive, and opportunity."

Lizzy raised her hand.

"Yes, Lizzy, what do you think?"

"Wasn't that fight about the missing journals a motive?"

"Excellent," I said. "What about opportunity?"

Now there were a lot of hands. I called on Zola.

"I'd call, 'I couldn't help if the ladies love me,' opportunity."

"Exactly."

I continued my lecture. "Much of that evidence is circumstantial. We'd have to convince a jury."

'Much harder than it sounds. City Attorney Blake won't let a risky case go to a jury,' Fitch reminded me.

"But, our real challenge is means. How did Tough Tiff die." I turned to Persey. "Coroner Paterson, do you have any more on the cause of death?"

"I have run every forensic test and the cause of death eludes science. Without a cause, means is impossible to establish."

Ranch jumped up. "You're all wrong. My dad isn't the murderer."

This was another teachable moment. "Ranch is correct. Where did we go wrong?"

January held her hands up to her face like she had imaginary binoculars, and then she moved them both quickly to the right.

I held my palms up and shrugged my shoulders. WHAT?

January smiled at me and said, "Distracted. We were distracted by the show in the annex, the fight, the motorcycle. All misleading."

"If, as Ranch says, his father isn't the murder, who is?"

"*Ojos cafés.* Brown eyes," said Jorge.

Fitch was enjoying himself. *'You're going to need a confession.'*

Working on it, I replied to Fitch.

"Okay. What happens if you are not misdirected by the fight scene and think about brown eyes watching from the football bleachers and tossing washers to the ground to pass the time?"

"Brown Eyes is cold and tired watching everything from those cheap seats. Blue Eyes has made too much trouble, but now Sammy has left her lying on the floor, passed out, comatose. Brown Eyes takes her opportunity and does in her rival," Zola said.

"That's a good start."

Persey interrupted. "It's all well and good to follow Agatha Christie's advice and guess. But how did Brown Eyes kill without leaving a trace? Everything hinges on the cause of death."

Lizzy agreed. "Right. How did she do it?"

"You can't find the cause of death, can you?" Ms. Miller challenged.

Everyone shook their heads no.

I looked around the library to see if Brown Eyes was going to make a run for it. She didn't. She appeared to be as puzzled as the rest of us. I was ready to nominate her for an acting award. She sat there calm and complacent. This wasn't going to work unless she cracked.

"Brown Eyes left Blue Eyes on the floor. She needed to get something. Killing with her bare hands or a convenient object—"

Tsui interrupted. "A weapon of opportunity."

I resumed. "Hands and other weapons of opportunity leave signs that Coroner Paterson would discover."

"*Blimey*, if she left her without calling nine-one-one, Tiff the Tutor could have died," Alyce said.

"Maybe that was her plan," said Ranch with a sneer.

"That wasn't the plan. Brown Eyes went home and returned with her CPAP machine, even though all she needed was the face mask and the air tube."

As I approached the cause of death, everyone got quiet, and Brown Eyes squirmed in her seat. I could see her checking out escape paths.

'*Run, Brown Eyes, run,*' urged Fitch.

"She needed one more thing, from the soda machine in her classroom."

Persey jumped up. I've got it. "Apollo 13. Ms. Shelley was murdered with carbon dioxide. Fast. Leaves no trace when used on an unconscious victim. Perfect."

Fitch gave a smug smile, '*That explains why you ran out of sodas on movie day.*'

Ms. Miller jumped up, knocked over her table, and ran out of the library.

'*Got you,*' cheered Fitch.

Faith sprinted away shouting. "You'll never catch me. She shouldn't have gone after my man."

Lizzy took a deep breath. "Wow, that lady is fast."

"*Eish*, you know, she ran track in the Olympics," Zola said.

"Go get her, Cerberus," Persey whispered.

Cerberus leaped down the library stairs, took off across the courtyard, and caught Ms. Miller just as she was opening her car door. He held her wrist until Tsui drove up with Vicki on his motorcycle, and they made the arrest. Faith Miller was in custody.

Persey said to no one in particular. "It looks like Peggy won the motive-for-murder pool. It was a love triangle."

'*I guess this book was a bit of a romance,*' Fitch said.

Tish whispered to César. "That video of the dog making an arrest? Pure internet gold."

'I knew it all the time,' bragged Fitch.

Whatever, Fitch. Whatever.

I was glad we'd finally closed the case of Ms. Shelley's murder. Only the mystery of the Cajon Treasure remained.

Wherein Zarand makes barbecue sauce.

With Ms. Miller's confession complete, my tummy reminded me that I'd missed second dinner. I took out my phone. "I'm ordering pizza. How many for Hawaiian Pizza with extra pineapple?"

Vicki put her arm around me and whispered into my ear so closely that I felt her lips, "I don't see any raised hands, Zee. It's just the two of us."

I switched to the high school favorite. "Pepperoni?"

Many hands went up, but before I could count them, they dropped. The library was filled with a cacophony of notification bells and beeps. Everyone reached for their cell. I had mine out, so I saw the message first.

PAX (THEY, THEM): CONGRATS ON CATCHING MY MOM'S KILLER. ATTACHED ARE THE GPS COORDINATES FOR MY CABIN. POTLUCK BBQ ON SUNDAY AT NOON. FOLLOWED BY A TREASURE HUNT.

That was the end of the impromptu pizza party. Everyone left to prepare for Pax's potluck.

Vicki and I stayed to help Mrs. Golding straighten up the library.

As Mrs. Golding locked up, she said, "I'm bringing baklava from Epicurean Eats, the 24-hour Greek restaurant."

"What are you bringing?" asked Vicki.

I gave her a squeeze. "It will be a surprise, but you know it will be good."

'And there will be plenty of it,' laughed Fitch.

"I'm sure." She bumped me with her hip. "See you tomorrow."

"Cajon Treasure, here we come."

I prepared to visit Pax's cabin, looking forward to driving myself without a bag over my head. The first thing I did was plug in my tiny electric car. I'd need a full charge to drive over Cajon Pass. Next, I checked the deep freeze for ribs. I found a rack of beef ribs, a rack of spare ribs, and a couple of racks of baby back ribs. I took them all upstairs to thaw.

I climbed the steps to the tune of Dahl's yowls. She sniffed my shoe before deciding to let me in. "Do you smell your friend Cerberus? He was the hero tonight, catching the bad guy. Outrunning an Olympic sprinter."

She purred until a can of food appeared in her dish. When second dinner should have been served, I was reenacting Ms. Shelley's murder to lure Faith Miller into admitting her method of killing Tiffany Shelley. I rectified this oversight, by ordering from Epicurean Eats—Greek salad, hummus, pita, and a side of grilled chicken for Dahl.

Then I set to work making barbecue sauces. I liked to give the sauces time to blend, so I had to start them before I went to sleep.

The St. Louis Style went first. My recipe used tomato puree, coffee, molasses, vinegar, and brown sugar—seasoned with fresh onions and garlic cloves, some salt, pepper, and cumin. I added a hint of chili powder. I preferred to taste the sauce, not the heat. I left it on the stove to simmer.

Next was Carolina Mustard. For that one, I started with a large jar of yellow mustard, plus cider vinegar, beer, and brown sugar. Again, I added some salt, pepper, cumin, and a hint of chili powder. Second dinner arrived just after the Carolina Mustard was put on the stove.

After Dahl and I ate, we bottled the barbecue sauces and went to sleep.

Pax had a row of charcoal grills lined up behind the cabin. In addition to my ribs, there were burgers, hot dogs, corn on the cob, russet potatoes, peppers, Brussel sprouts on skewers, mushrooms, baked beans, cole slaw, and sliced onions.

A group of people gathered around Ranch. He stood up, "I followed the clues. Stony, North, Cajon, Creek, West, Falls, Cave, Pool. I've been searching for this treasure since middle school. I had no problem finding that cave, but there was no treasure."

"Are you sure you went to the right cave?" Lizzy asked.

"Absolutely."

Pax laughed.

Everyone looked at them.

Ranch asked in a harsh voice. "What's so funny?"

"While you've been vacationing up here, we caught your mother's killer. Give us respect," Lizzy said.

Pax said, "Sorry. I solved the clues after the first two. I didn't see the interpretation you found—all that creek and cave nonsense—until George explained it to me." Pax ate a row of their corn on the cob. "Someone went to a lot of work to set up the decoy clues."

'That sounds like my favorite gods, Artemis and Apollo,' Fitch remarked.

Are you friends with Greek gods? I pondered.

He gave me a smug smile.

The Greek gods are real?

His smile got bigger, *'How do you think I know things before they happen?'*

"*Blimey.* First Mr. S. made us sit on the cold bleachers before he'd tell us who killed Tiff the Tutor. Now, what are you going to require before you tell us where the treasure is?" questioned Alyce.

Pax was enjoying the company and attention after many days alone at the cabin. "First, change all the letters in the clues to x's. For example, change THE to XXX."

"No problem. I'll write a quick script," Ranch responded.

Everyone went back to eating. I took a potato, split it open, and filled it with butter, chives, bacon, sour cream, and my secret ingredient, grilled mushrooms.

In a short while, Ranch shouted, "OMG. Unbelievable. After I ran my script, there were only two different clues, the shorter one and the longer one. After the first two, all the others are identical. I've messaged you with those two clues."

January showed her phone to everyone. "This is the shorter one." XXX XXXX XX XXX XXXXX XXXXXXXX XXX XXXX. She gave two thumbs up.

"Okay Pax, that's a good trick. We still don't know where the treasure is," Alyce said.

Pax addressed Ranch. "That was fast script writing. Can you replace each word with the number of letters in it? Like, replace XXX with 3?"

Ranch tapped his phone a couple of times. "Done. I'll text the numbers to everyone."

"Good job, Ranch," Lizzy said.

Zola read them aloud. "11, 9, 6, 5, 3, 6, 6, 5, and 3, 4, 2, 3, 5, 8, 3, 8."

"I'm going to visit every Spanish-language country in the Western Hemisphere. I use GPS coordinates to plan my itinerary. I recognize those numbers. 34.235838 north, 119.653665 west," Jorge said.

"I entered those coordinates into my dad's map app and the Cajon Treasure is just a few miles away," Ranch said.

"Congratulations. Do you want to know my big surprise?" Pax queried.

Everyone shouted, "Yes!"

"My lawyers have purchased the tract containing the treasure."

"Good move," said Jorge.

"I like to be prepared. Inside my cabin, you'll find shovels, axes, mattocks, and picks. Choose your weapon."

'Look at them. Dressed for a party but carrying shovels and picks. I hope they don't hurt themselves,' guffawed Fitch.

They piled into cars and headed for the elusive blue dot. I entered the GPS coordinates on my phone even though I didn't need them. I simply followed the line of cars ahead of me.

'Don't celebrate yet,' said Fitch.

Wherein Zarand hikes in the woods.

When I parked, the GPS on my little EV said, "Your destination is on the left."

Our map apps sent us down a dirt track. New-growth pine trees crowded the road on both sides. The unbroken undergrowth of ferns and poison oak testified that no one had recently hiked this area. In places where the road let in sunlight, wild California blackberries proliferated.

'If this is where the Cajon Treasure is buried, I can understand why it hasn't been found.'

"My blue dot is four-tenths of a mile away," Ranch said.

Pax, who was parked farther down the road, called, "I'm closer. Only three-tenths of a mile."

Lizzy was parked in the other direction—atop an open space covered with ferns. She called out. "I win. Less than a thousand feet."

Ranch advised, "We don't know which path will be the best. Everyone, head for the dot and we'll see who arrives first."

"Hey, Gun Shell," I called to one of the few adults. "Let's be buddies again." I shook my backpack. "I have snacks."

Gunnar and I joined Lizzy's expedition. Our first obstacle was a fallen tree, which we climbed over, followed by a shallow creek, which I jumped with the help of my trekking poles.

Lizzy was in the lead. She called, "We lose. There's a pretty waterfall here, but the drop is too much. Head toward Ranch."

In the distance, we heard Pax. "I've reached a clearing, but it is thick with berry bushes, we can't get through."

Ranch shouted, "I win. We'll wait until everyone gets here."

Ranch kept up a running commentary as we navigated around the massive trees. "This is a sacred land, an old-growth forest. These white firs and Jeffrey pines may be huge, but when Brother Humphries and Sister Rowley passed through here, they were seedlings."

Lizzy concluded, "So the treasure couldn't be buried here."

Jorge laughed. "No way."

We scrambled down a steep incline and across another creek, or maybe the same one.

Ranch whooped. "What is this section of sagebrush doing in the middle of an old-growth forest?"

"I wrote about this in one of my books. Big trees need deep soil. If something—in *Twelfth Knight,* it was suits of armor—is buried, big trees can't grow, so just bushes are found. In *Twelfth Knight,* the bushes marked a spot for the hero to recover the armor, equip his rag-tag group of volunteers, and win the day," Gun Shell said.

"Thanks, Mr. Shelley. After we recover the treasure, we'll get everyone to read your book. Sounds exciting," Ranch said.

Gunnar said, "That wasn't the most exciting—"

Ranch cut him off. "Everyone, check your blue dot."

"My dot is a little farther," Lizzy said.

"Just behind us," Pax said.

"Perfect. Spread out. Let's clear away the sagebrush. The treasure shouldn't be very deep," Ranch said.

Zola's shovel clinked on something. "*Lekker.* Got it. I hit something hard. I bet it's a jar of gold coins, too heavy to carry over the pass." She got down on her hands and knees to excavate the first part of the treasure.

January was digging next to her. "Another one."

Jorge was on the other side. "This is a big treasure. I found another one and it's too heavy to lift."

Pretty soon we'd located seven heavy ceramic crocks. After Zola cleared around the first crock, Pax forced their pick underneath and pried it from the ancient burial's grip.

Pax, Lizzy, and Gunnar raised it to ground level.

Lizzy shouted, "Tip it over. I'll shovel the dirt out and reveal the treasure."

She shoveled and shoveled. When all the dirt was cleared, the crock was empty.

'*Not much of a treasure,*' Fitch said.

"I know what those are—ceramic crocks. They were used to store pickles, flour, or even hardboiled eggs. By this point, they would have been empty. No reason to lug them over the pass," Alyce said.

"Sister Rowley used the word *treasure*. Empty containers are not treasures. Let's keep digging," Ranch said.

Mrs. Golding's pick sounded a loud clang. Everyone stopped to look in her direction. She reached into the dirt and retrieved a cast iron skillet. "Still in good condition. This is a treasure. Can I keep it?"

Ranch threw his mattock down. "Sure, keep it. You might call it a treasure, but I doubt Sister Rowley would have." He walked around the site.

"Mrs. Golding, please stand where you found the frying pan."

Principal Golding laughed. "This is a treasure trove. I can see more skillets, all different sizes, lids, and stew pots. Like Alyce said, treasures that were too heavy to haul over the pass."

Ranch called, "Lizzy, can you stand in the middle of your crock graveyard?"

Lizzy smiled at him and did as he requested.

Ranch stood halfway between Mrs. Golding and Lizzy. He buried his axe in the sagebrush. "This is where the real treasure is."

"Smart thinking. They buried the real treasure in the middle," Lizzy said.

January's pick struck something soft. She screamed. She crossed her arm in front of her and pantomimed clawing her shoulders. BEAR. She signed BEAR. She reached down and picked up a bear claw. Attached to the claw was a leg. And attached to the legs was an entire bear, even the head with ferocious teeth still in place.

Everyone ran over to see what was under the bearskin.

Mrs. Golding took advantage of her teachable moment. "Notice how it is still in good condition. Does anyone know why?"

The students were more interested in uncovering the treasure.

She explained, "This is because of our dry climate and alkaline soils."

Jorge was the first to find something. "Look at this. A native drum. We'll turn this over to our assemblywoman. It belongs to the Serrano band."

Next, Mr. Shelley found a violin case. He opened it. "Wow. A violin. I'm sure Sister Rowley would have called this a treasure. I'm surprised no one came back for it."

January discovered a wolf skin and Pax found three deer skins. Everyone was pulling on the pelts.

"This is the real Cajon Treasure," Gunnar said. Under all those protective layers, sitting on more pelts was a piano.

Fitch was not impressed. *'Is this the Cajon Treasure?'*

I reminded everyone, "Sister Rowley was the choir mistress."

Pax put on a brave face. "Let's go back to the cabin for barbecue and to sing songs around the campfire in Sister Rowley's memory."

'Pax can donate this all to the county museum for a tax write-off,' said Fitch.

EPILOGUE – SENIOR TRIP

Wherein Zarand has a sleepover at Vicki's house.

The next day Vicki and I joined the others at the Firehouse Barbecue. I congratulated Lieutenant Peggy, "Thank you for lunch. You won the motive pool. It was a love triangle."

'I knew that.' laughed Fitch.

"I'm happy to treat everyone. You paid last time."

While we feasted, I implored Vicki. "Please join me on the senior trip. We lost two chaperones—Faith Miller and Tiffany Shelley."

"With the murder solved, I'm sure I can get time off, but I insist we fly business class, so we're not trapped with all those teenagers for the long flight from Los Angeles to Dulles International Airport."

Fitch offered a cynical, *'Good luck.'*

Coroner Persey interrupted the festivities, "We're going to miss these two ladies. They were more than chaperones. Much more. Who is going to fill their shoes?"

We lined up for priority boarding with the infants in strollers, seniors in wheelchairs, elite frequent fliers, and others seated in the front of the plane.

Vee pursed her lips and shook her head, "Did you know all these students would be in business class?"

I gave her a peck on the cheek. "This is Stony Estancia. I'm sure some are avoiding the crowd at LAX and taking Mommy's private jet."

I hoped the trip would warm her to the idea of moving in together.

Fitch ribbed me, *'What part of traveling with a bunch of teenagers do you expect will help your case?'*

Vicki took the window seat and I sat beside her on the aisle. When the flight attendant gave us sparkling wine, we clinked plastic glasses and I said, "Good flight." Tamira Angelou, Ranch's mom, reached across the aisle to toast us, "The cutest couple in Stony Estancia."

Seated in the window seat beside her was Ranch. He had orange juice.

I responded, "Thank you for standing in for the missing chaperone."

"No problem. I wanted to let Rapper spend some time on his own. When Ranch and I return, we'll see whether he wants to be part of this family or not," she said.

As she expected, a week on his own taught Rinchen Amar how good he had it. Rapper still ran Rinchen Amar Phone Repair, but Tamira now operated the Sammich Shoppe. He had no chance to flirt with those customers, and she introduced several new sandwiches not sourced at the pâtisserie, using pita, tortillas, paratha, bagels, naan, and crumpets.

She also started a group called—**WH**EN? **N**OW! or **WE HELP** OUR **N**EIGHBORS—to continue Ms. Miller's work in San Amano and extend it to other cities, including Stony Estancia.

On the first day in the capital, Vee and I attended Jorge Nazario's presentation, *Henry David Thoreau's Advice for the 21st Century Latino*, at the National Museum of the American Latino. We sat proudly in the audience when they awarded him a fellowship to visit all the Spanish-speaking countries in the Western Hemisphere.

During his travels he produced a podcast, and, on his return, his agent got him a contract for a coffee table book combining his photographs and podcast episodes.

The next day, we went to Helen Keller University to see January Shaw perform her report, *Adapting American Dialect (as Written by Mark Twain) to ASL*. When we went to congratulate her, we overheard the chancellor. "That was excellent work. I want to offer you admission and a full scholarship."

"I would be honored to attend your fine school," she replied.

She added something else in sign language.

"What did she sign?" asked Vicki.

"You have to love the students of Stony Estancia. She thanked him but turned down the scholarship," I replied.

She graduated college in three years with a double major in molecular biology and disability rights.

That night we had a group dinner at a seafood restaurant overlooking the Chesapeake Bay. Vicki and I sat with Lizzy Chandrasekhar and Ranch Amar.

Lizzy invited Ranch, "There's a stable at Rock Creek Park. Would you like to go riding with me?"

He was so flustered that he dropped a raw oyster down his shirt. When he recovered, he said, "Name the time."

We saw them together at the National Museums of African Art. Then, at the Asian Art Museum, we overheard him brag, "I'm going to an engineering school in Massachusetts to major in Computer Science."

"What a coincidence. I applied to three women's schools, also in Massachusetts," she replied.

'There are no coincidences,' said Fitch.

Ranch seemed nervous when he asked, "Did you get accepted at any of them?"

She punched him. "O ye of little faith. They all accepted me. I'm majoring in political science and pre-law."

"Matthew 8:26. Goodbye California. Hello Massachusetts," he replied.

Vicki gave me a knowing smile, "They must have had a good time on the bridle trail. Pun intended."

It seemed like every day my honorary grandkids were performing or presenting. At The National Museum of African American History and Culture, Zola Butler dressed up as

Fredrick Douglass—they were both six feet tall. She chose his 1852 speech *"What, To The Slave, Is The Fourth Of July?"*

On the flight home, she told us that her performance and a glowing recommendation from the Stony Stunt Store got her an audition with a studio back home in Los Angeles.

Later I received an email that she was cast in a leading role in an Afrofuturist film.

Not everyone was happy with the visit to Washington DC. Alyce Fox confided, "I came to the United States to get away from the oppression of indigenous Australians. I was encouraged to see museums dedicated to African Americans, American Latinos, and American Indians. However, those visits showed me that America's treatment of its indigenous populations was no better."

"I'm sorry you were disappointed. Wherever you go, you'll find something similar. 40,000 years ago, Homo Sapiens encountered indigenous Neanderthals and out bred them into extinction," said Vicki.

Alyce disagreed. "I'm going to Iceland. The island had no indigenous population when the European settlers arrived. I'm enrolled in a program of civil and environmental engineering with an emphasis on geothermal energy."

On the other hand, Pax found the nation's capital exhilarating. Pax loved the Peace Corps. Alyce accused them of being imperialist. "This is colonialism wrapped up in a pretty package. Besides, aren't you going to college?"

"This is the 21st century. Forget college. Look what the Peace Corps says about differences," Pax said. They pointed their phone at us. INTERCULTURAL COMPETENCE, DIVERSITY, EQUITY, INCLUSION, AND ACCESSIBILITY ARE CORE PRINCIPLES THAT HELP THE AGENCY ACHIEVE ITS MISSION.

"Won't your father be disappointed?" Vicki said.

"I know Dad wants me to go to college, but I'm not returning to Stony Estancia. By next month, I'll be sleeping on the ground, miles from any high-thread-count sheets or electric blankets, to help build active communities and dig latrines," Pax replied.

Sure enough, Pax didn't board the return flight. Back in Stony Estancia, there were more events for Vicki and me to attend. Declan Beckett hosted the Frank Twins when they donated their extensive collection of Cajon Treasure documents.

After the ceremony, they approached Vicki. "You can cross us off your suspect list," Frankie said.

Vicki shook her hand. "Congratulations. Have you decided to go straight?"

"Better than that. With the tax write-off from this donation, we're going to purchase a yacht, which we'll christen *Reparations*," Frank replied.

"We're leaving Stony Estancia to cruise the Caribbean exploring for lost ships from the transatlantic slave trade. Even if we don't find anything, we still have a contract for a video series," Frankie added.

Vicki, being a good sport, said, "I'll look for your show."

Dr. Chad Wilde from Purcell and Associates and Jared Sendak, Stony High sub coordinator, also went on a cruise. They sailed the Aegean Sea from a base in Mykonos. Their two favorite spots were the Temple of Artemis in Ephesus and the Temple of Apollo at Delphi where they felt a connection to the Greek gods.

Declan Beckett and SE-cubed met with the families that protested against the California History Annex, installed their leaders on the board of directors, and established the CAFÉ Fund—College Ain't For Everyone—to address the needs of those in the Stony Estancia community that weren't destined for graduate school.

He also established the Tiff the Tutor Memorial Fund to raise money for the Stony Estancia Family Shelter.

Vicki and I have sleepovers together on most Saturday nights. Sometimes at Higgs Haven and other times at her house. We are at her house often enough, that Dahl has a litter box, food bowls, puzzle feeders, and a pantry shelf dedicated to her food. Dahl climbs into her carrier for the ride to Vicki's house purring the whole time.

To the Reader

Please accept my gratitude for finding and reading this book.

I am an independent author and appreciate how difficult it is to select my books from the flood of offerings. I am dependent on reader-to-reader recommendations.

If you enjoyed my novel and wish to support independent writers, I would appreciate any posts on social media, especially an all-important Amazon rating. A review on Goodreads also helps.

Even better would be a recommendation to a couple of your friends. Thank you.

If you would like to correspond with the author or receive infrequent updates about Zarand Szilard, substitute teacher, you can send an email to Zarand.Szilard at gmail.

You might also be interested in the first book in this series (previewed below) Mr. Szilard, Substitute Teacher Mystery #1, *The Ecology Club: A Cozy Mystery (and How to Save the Planet)*. Available from most online booksellers.

Omega Cat Press books can be found at:
https://amzn.to/2SpaDMN

Thank you.

Dr. O. (the name I wrote on the whiteboard when I subbed.)

P. S. Following this, you can uncover the treasures hidden in the story, see the authors who inspired the names in this book, and read a preview of *The Ecology Club*.

CHEERS, CREDITS, AND HIDDEN TREASURES

Many people and organizations (knowingly and not) contributed to this work of fiction. Acknowledgment here does not imply an endorsement, review, or even knowledge, of this book.

Special thanks to my many early readers on https://www.critiquecircle.com/, and my partner in crime, Joy, who was with me through the many rewrites. Thanks to my brother Leonard, another early reader and author of *The Pied Pipers of Autism: How Television, Video, and Toys in Infancy cause ASD* (https://amzn.to/3qopeys). Any remaining problems belong to me.

Also, thanks to Jason, Joy, Samantha, and Jennie for consulting on the cover design.

When Zarand checked for a corpse up the chimney in chapter 1, *Not a Typical Day*, he was paying homage to *The Murders in the Rue Morgue* by Edgar Allan Poe, published in 1841 and considered by some to be the first modern detective story.

The story of the Cajon Treasure, first mentioned in chapter 2, *Where It All Started*, is fictional but inspired by the actual struggles of families traveling west in the 19th century.

César, introduced in chapter 2, is named in honor of César Chavez, one of the leaders of the United Farm Workers in the 1960s and 1970s. "*Sí, se puede*," which he quotes in chapter 12, *Unexpected Visitors*, was the rallying cry of the United Farm Workers. Co-founders Dolores Huerta and César Chavez adopted the slogan during a 25-day fast in 1972. This was the beginning of the Chicano Movement.

The idea that the parents of Stony Estancia could fund a building through Stony Estancia for Educational Excellence, fondly called SE-cubed, is a bit of hyperbole based on the actual funding of California public schools. Since the passage of Proposition 13 in 1978, public school funding idiosyncrasies have led to similar, albeit less ambitious, organizations throughout the state.

In chapter 6, *Cajon Treasure*, the hashtag #BODYINTHELIBRARY used by *Stony Estancia Surfs* is the title of Agatha Christie's Miss Marple mystery: *The Body in the Library*.

The murder of the biology teacher mentioned in chapter 6, is from Mr. Szilard, Substitute Teacher Mystery #1, *The Ecology Club: A Cozy Mystery (and How to Save the Planet)*.

The computer game, Oregon Trail, also mentioned in chapter 6, was coded in 1971 in Minnesota. In the 1980s it was running on Apple II computers, and in the 1990s, it appeared on Macintosh and Windows computers. One of the most memorable events in this wagon train simulation from Independence, Missouri to the Willamette Valley in Oregon was: "You have died of dysentery."

Here is an example of a 19th-century Spencerian script mentioned in this chapter. [Retrieved from Wikimedia.org (public domain)]

The full quote Zarand remembers in chapter 8, *Pax Shelley*, is "Happy families are all alike; every unhappy family is unhappy in its own way." This famous first line is from Leo Tolstoy's novel *Anna Karenina*.

Holi, the Hindu festival of colors, mentioned in chapter 9, *Crime Scene Revisited*, is celebrated in India and around the world. Participants throw *gulal*, colored powder, at each other to celebrate the end of winter and the coming of spring.

Also in chapter 9, Fitch referred to the dog that didn't bark. This was the decisive clue in Sherlock Holmes, *"The*

Adventure of the Silver Blaze," published in *The Strand Magazine* in December 1892.

Chapter 9 also includes second breakfast. This was not original with the *Hobbit* by J. R. R. Tolkien, but that is where I learned of it. Second dinner, Zarand's and Dahl's mid-night snack, extends this idea.

The biscuit factory mentioned in chapter 10, *Gunnar Shelley*, is in Harlesden, north-west London, and traces its origins back to a Scottish biscuit maker established in 1839 on Rose Street in Edinburgh, Scotland. This factory, founded in 1902, is the largest in Europe.

The name of the Four Rivers Szechuan Chinese restaurant, first mentioned in the same chapter, is a bilingual tautological expression. The informal translation of Szechuan is four rivers, and the Chinese characters are four and river.

In chapter 13, *Meeting Halfway*, Zarand treats Zola and Alyce to lunch in the fancy faculty dining room adjacent to the Bruin Bistro. This dining experience is part of the Stony Estancia fiction. Students eat free in the Bruin Bistro. "Commencing in [school year] 2022–23, California requires [all] schools ... [TK–12] to provide two meals free of charge (breakfast and lunch) during each school day to students requesting a meal, regardless of their [Federal] free or reduced-price meal eligibility." Go California.

The story of Giles Corey recounted by Persey in chapter 14, *Dinner Guests*, is true. He was *pressed* to death in Salem, Massachusetts, on September 19, 1692.

In Chapter 15, *Finger Spelling*, Lizzy wears a T-shirt with a picture of Helen Reddy, whose signature song "I Am Woman" was a feminist anthem.

In chapter 22, *Stony Stoners*, Joan Didion (fictional character) mentions Route Sixty-Six. Route 66 was established in 1925 and connected Chicago, Illinois to Santa Monica, California. It appeared in John Steinbeck's *The Grapes of Wrath*, a 1946 hit song by the King Cole Trio, *(Get Your Kicks on) Route 66*, and in the Disney/Pixar animated film, *Cars*. It runs right through Stony Estancia but is no longer called Route 66.

In the same chapter, Kurt Vonnegut (fictional character) referenced *The Road Not Taken*, a 1915 poem by Robert Frost, that has been widely anthologized.

In chapter 24, *Apollo and Artemis*, Apollo refers to his temple at Delphi and Artemis to hers at Ephesus. Apollo's temple is a UNESCO World Heritage site in Greece. Across the Aegean Sea, the city of Ephesus in Turkey is also a UNESCO World Heritage site.

In chapter 29, *San Amano*, Zarand reads *The Ecology Club*, the first book in the series featuring himself and previewed at the end of this book. No wonder he falls asleep.

In chapter 33, *Kerouac Kanyon*, Zarand improvises on the 1980s and 1990s *Revenge of the Nerds* movies. *Revenge of the Dyslexics* is a made-up film name.

Cutthroat Island, the movie mentioned in chapter 35, *Third Arrest*, stars Geena Davis—founder of the *Geena Davis Institute on Gender in Media*. "Our research examines intersectional onscreen representation of six identities: gender, race, LGBTQIA+, disability, age 50+, and body type."

The social engineering experiment mentioned in the same chapter has been implemented numerous times with public and private funding. The results have been positive. A good overview article was published by The Decision Lab. "Should We Pay Students to Go to School?" by Tony Jiang, February 24, 2021.

The full Thoreau quote mentioned in chapter 36, *Peer Editing*, is "Our life is frittered away by detail. Simplify, simplify, simplify! I say, let your affairs be as two or three, and not a hundred or a thousand; instead of a million, count half a dozen, and keep your accounts on your thumbnail."

For a more contemporary reference in the same chapter, Zarand calls Dahl, "that darn cat." *That Darn Cat* was a movie about a cat called D. C. that solves mysteries. The movie was so good that it was made twice—in 1965 and 1997.

The book placed in Tiff the Tutor's casket in chapter 41, *Remembrances*, is *The Giver of Stars* by Jojo Moyes. It is about the packhorse librarians who, during the Depression, rode the back woods of Kentucky bringing books to the people isolated in those hills.

When Fitch questions the protective value of ducking under their chairs in the same chapter, he is referring to the "Duck and cover" drills widely conducted during the 1950s. Regardless of Fitch's skepticism, "Duck and Cover" has proven to be effective.

Independence Day, also mentioned in the same chapter, is a 1996 movie about everyone on Earth, regardless of race or religion, working together to defeat invading aliens.

The opening of chapter 43, *Burial*, refers to the 1986 book by Robert Fulghum, *All I Really Need to Know I Learned in Kindergarten.*

In chapter 44, *Reenactors*, when Persey referred to Apollo 13, she was thinking of high levels of carbon dioxide in the Lunar Module that threatened the astronauts' lives before they were saved by ingenuity and duct tape.

The GPS coordinates used in chapter 45, *Cajon Treasure Part I*, are wrong. I didn't want anyone to visit the fictitious Cajon Treasure. Those GPS coordinates are in the Pacific Ocean off the coast of California. This type of clue is not original. Something similar was used in the Oscar-winning movie *Close Encounters of the Third Kind* (1977) by Steven Spielberg.

The piano that inspired the Cajon Treasure in chapter 46, *Cajon Treasure Part II*, belongs to Abraham Hunsaker and is now in the Daughters of the Utah Pioneers Museum. It was buried with buffalo robes for protection and retrieved a year later. The Deseret News (Salt Lake City) reports three such piano burials and retrievals.

The history of Iceland mentioned in chapter 47, *Epilogue*, is accurate. As late as the 9th century, Iceland was uninhabited. It is located on the Mid-Atlantic Ridge over a volcanic hot spot. Other hot spots are Hawaii and Yellowstone National Park. Iceland gets a quarter of its energy from geothermal sources.

Now that you've discovered all the hidden treasures, you are welcome to read *The Library Club* again.

Do you wonder why Melvil Dewey of Dewey Decimal fame does not appear in this book? Do you wonder why the American Library Association award named for this ALA founder no longer carries his name? Their resolution to remove his name cites his history of racism, anti-Semitism, and sexual harassment. Enough said.

I must acknowledge these editors who believe this book and all books are about cats.

Chapter graphics
    School by Mike Wirth, US from the Noun Project 54581.
Pupils by David Khai, US from the Noun Project 2023631.
Paid licenses.

Cover art
    The cover was designed with Photopea.com, an advanced
online photo editor. Ivan Kutskir is the creator of Photopea.
He was born in Ukraine but lives in the Czech Republic.

ABOUT THE AUTHOR

D. R. Oestreicher grew up on Long Island, NY, and attended MIT as an undergraduate. After graduate school in Salt Lake City (Computer Science), he worked at Silicon Valley startups. Like Mr. Szilard, when he retired, he went back to school to get a California teaching credential. As a substitute, he wrote DR. O. on the whiteboard at the start of each day. Today he lives in Southern California with his wife, and often co-author, and their cats. They enjoy their grandkids, international travel (Covid-19 willing), reading, and writing.

Every author must invent names. For The Library Club, I turned to other authors for inspiration. Acknowledgment here does not imply an endorsement, review, or even knowledge, of this book.

Anandyn Amar: Author of the *Short History of Mongolia*. His advocacy for Mongolian independence led to his execution in Moscow in 1941.

Maya Angelou: American poet and author of seven autobiographies. *I Know Why the Caged Bird Sings.*

Jane Austen: British novelist. Her most famous novel, *Pride and Prejudice*, has been made into more than seventeen movies.

David Baldacci: American writer of over 40 best-selling novels. Funds adult literacy programs.

Richard Brautigan: American novelist and poet. *Trout Fishing in America. In Watermelon Sugar.*

Samuel Beckett: Irish author and winner of the Nobel Prize in Literature in 1969.

William Blake: English romantic poet in the 18th and 19th centuries. Author of *Songs of Innocence and of Experience*.

Judy Blume: Children's author, many books banned. *Blubber. Deenie. Forever. Tiger Eyes. Superfudge.*

Charlotte Brontë: Eldest of the three Brontë sisters—all famous 19th-century novelists. *Jane Eyre.*

Octavia E. Butler: American science fiction writer. Winner of Hugo & Nebula awards. *Kindred* and *Parable of the Sower*.

Roald Dahl: Children's author with a couple of banned books—*James and the Giant Peach*; *The Witches*.

Junot Díaz: Dominican-American winner Pulitzer Prize for fiction in 2008. M.I.T. professor.

Charles Dickens: English 19th-century author and social critic. *A Christmas Carol, Oliver Twist, David Copperfield.*

Joan Didion: American writer of the 1960s counterculture and beyond. *The Year of Magical Thinking. Slouching Towards Bethlehem.*

Mem Fox: Adelaide, Australian author of children's books. *Possum Magic.* Look for these. They are delightful.

Anne Frank: Teen author whose World War II memoir of hiding from the Nazis, *The Diary of a Young Girl*, has been banned.

Thomas Hopkins Gallaudet: Founded American School for the Deaf in Hartford Connecticut (1817). His son founded Gallaudet University (1864).

Elizabeth Gaskell: 19th-century English author of the poor in Victorian society. The author to read after Dickens.

Allen Ginsberg: American poet of the Beat generation— *Howl.* Activist against the Vietnam War and for gay rights.

William Golding: British novelist of the banned book: *Lord of the Flies.* Nobel Prize for Literature 1983.

Le Guin: American novelist. *Earthsea* and *The Left Hand of Darkness.*

Sue Grafton: American author of detective novels. *"A" is for Alibi* through *"Y" is for Yesterday.*

Ariel Henley: American author of *A Face for Picasso: Coming of Age with Crouzon Syndrome.*

Herman Hesse: German-Swiss writer and winner of the Nobel Prize in Literature in 1946.

Chuck Jones: Creator of animated films from the 1930s to the 1990s, featuring Bugs Bunny, Porky Pig, Road Runner, and Wile E. Coyote, plus many others. He won a Lifetime Achievement Oscar in 1996.

Franz Kafka: Bohemian author of the short story *"The Metamorphosis"* and novels *The Trial* and *The Castle.*

Helen Keller: American author and disability rights advocate. Lost her sight and hearing at 19 months old.

Jack Kerouac: Beat Generation writer. Famous for *On the Road.*

Stephen King: American author of over 60 novels. *Carrie. The Dark Tower. The Shining. The Stand. On Writing.*

Dean Koontz: American author of suspense thrillers. *Odd Thomas. Demon Seed.*

Jack London: 19th-century American novelist famous for stories of the Klondike gold rush. *The Call of the Wild.*

Miller: Wikipedia lists at least twenty authors with this name. Take your pick.

Sonia Nazario: American journalist. Winner of the 2003 Pulitzer Prize and author of *Enrique's Journey.*

Katherine Paterson: American author. Newbery Medal author of *Bridge to Terabithia.*

Megha Rajagopalan: Indian American journalist. Winner of the 2021 Pulitzer Prize for International Reporting.

Kathy Reichs: American forensic anthropologist and author. Detective series featuring Temperance "Bones" Brennan.

Byambyn Rinchen: Author of Mongolia's first published novel. Known for wearing colorful deels. His son, Rinchen Barsbold, postulated that dinosaurs evolved into birds.

Nora Roberts: American author of over 225 romance novels. She also authors suspense novels as J.D. Robb.

William Saroyan: Armenian-American author. *My Name is Aram. Tracy's Tiger.* 1940 Pulitzer Prize for Drama.

Maurice Sendak: American author and illustrator of *Where the Wild Things Are.*

George Bernard Shaw: Irish playwright. 1925 Nobel Prize in Literature. *Man and Superman. Pygmalion. Saint Joan.*

Mary Shelley: 19th-century English author, known for *Frankenstein or The Modern Prometheus.*

John Steinbeck: American author. 1940 Pulitzer Prize for Fiction. 1962 Nobel Prize in Literature. *Grapes of Wrath.*

Rabindranath Tagore: Bengali polymath. 1913 Nobel Prize in Literature. National anthems of India and Bangladesh.

Amy Tan: Chinese American author. *The Joy Luck Club. Sagwa, the Chinese Siamese Cat.*

Henry David Thoreau: American essayist and transcendentalist. *Walden. Civil Disobedience.*

Mark Twain: 19th-century American author. *The Adventures of Tom Sawyer. The Adventures of Huckleberry Finn.*

Kurt Vonnegut Jr.: American writer – satirical and darkly humorous novels. *Slaughterhouse-Five.*

E. B. White: American children's author. Stuart Little. Charlotte's Web. 1978 Pulitzer Prize Special Citation.

Oscar Wilde: 19th-century Irish poet and playwright. *The Picture of Dorian Gray. The Importance of Being Earnest.*

William Butler Yeats: Irish author. 1923 Nobel Prize for Literature.

Zarand Szilard #1 (The Ecology Club) used scientists for names. These are some of the scientists from the first book in the series who reappear here.

Hiroshi Amano: Japanese physicist who won the Nobel Prize for Physics in 2014.

Edward Victor Appleton: English physicist who won the Nobel Prize for Physics in 1947.

Niels Bohr: Danish physicist who won the Nobel Prize for Physics in 1948.

Patrick Blackett: British physicist who won the Nobel Prize for Physics in 1922.

Lawrence Bragg: Australian-born physicist who won the Nobel Prize for Physics in 1915.

Percy Williams Bridgman: American physicist who won the Nobel Prize for Physics in 1946.

Ana Maria Cetto: Mexican Physicist and Deputy Director-General of the International Atomic Energy Agency (IAEA) when it won the Nobel Peace Prize in 2005.

Subrahmanyan Chandrasekhar: Indian-American astrophysicist who won the Nobel Prize for Physics in 1983.

Val Logsdon Fitch: American nuclear physicist who won the Nobel Prize for Physics in 1980.

Werner Heisenberg: German physicist who won the Nobel Prize for Physics in 1932.

Peter Higgs: British physicist who won the Nobel Prize for Physics in 2013.

Robert Andrew Millikan: American physicist who won the Nobel Prize for Physics in 2023.

Cheikh Mbacke: Senegalese statistician who was awarded the Rockefeller Foundation Outstanding Achievement Award in 2003.

Peggoty Mutai: Kenyan chemist who researched parasitic worms and neglected tropical diseases.

Wolfgang Pauli: Austrian physicist who won the Nobel Prize for Physics in 1945.

Edward Mills Purcell: American physicist who won the Nobel Prize for Physics in 1952.

Leo Szilard: Hungarian-American physicist who wrote the letter that resulted in the Manhattan Project.

Daniel C. Tsui: Chinese-born American physicist who won the Nobel Prize for Physics in 1998.

John Hasbrouck Van Vleck: American physicist who won the Nobel Prize for Physics in 1977.

Hideki Yukawa: Japanese physicist who won the Nobel Prize for Physics in 1949.

Pieter Zeeman: Dutch physicist who won the Nobel Prize for Physics in 1902.

1. NOT YOUR TYPICAL DAY: MONDAY AM

The rear door burst open. Everyone turned to see what had disturbed our classroom. Brooklynn staggered in and dropped her backpack with a thump. Something was wrong.

Earlier that morning, when the substitute call came late and I missed breakfast, my gut told me this wasn't going to be an ordinary assignment.

The day began in a typical way. I handed out donuts in homeroom. The tardy buzzer gently reminded Ms. Salas's first-period AP Biology students to finish greeting each other. I allowed them a few minutes to settle.

Following the school district's policy and my intuition, I locked the hallway door. At Stony Estancia High, safety came first, even though this privileged suburban campus only made the news to celebrate student awards and accomplishments, never for trouble.

This school was an example of Stony Estancia's understated opulence. While it appeared ordinary, the cafeteria had an on-site bakery and a chef who prepared organic specialties. The library had current best sellers and subscriptions to academic journals. They donated shelf-worn books to other schools. The PTA provided each teacher with a stipend for enrichment materials and field trips.

Not expecting Brooklyn, I raised Ms. Salas's bell to signal the start of class. When they saw my hand go up, the chatter died down and the few students remaining in the aisles headed for their seats. Classroom management was not an issue with these well-behaved kids. I could focus on teaching.

But before I rang the bell, that rear door burst open.

I stared over the lab bench that served as Ms. Salas's desk and watched the girl charging across the room. She jostled a boy who was standing in the aisle. She bumped into a table knocking a laptop to the floor with a crash. Nothing slowed her progress. Tears pooled in her green eyes. Her black ponytail whipped back and forth.

Something was very wrong.

I braced my hands against that cold black countertop and leaned forward willing her to deliver the unwelcome news that I was sure she had.

Instead of approaching me across that barrier, she dodged around it, stood on her toes, and placed a hand on my shoulder.

I tensed up. *Here it comes.*

She whispered, "Ms. Salas is dead."

Impossible. Just this morning, Ms. Salas called me to sub for her.

The class stared at Brooklynn. Their blank faces confirmed they hadn't heard the whispered message. They looked at us expectantly.

The room was silent. Brooklynn and I froze. I faced her and touched my finger to my lips. When I didn't make an announcement, the class lost interest. The buzz of teenage socialization resumed.

I moved closer to Brooklynn and asked, "Whassup?" Surely, I misheard.

"Murdered," she reiterated even softer than before.

I didn't believe her. What could a teenager from Stony Estancia know about murder? How could she be so calm? Was this some new adolescent slang? She was mistaken, confused.

I checked the class. Their chatter continued unabated. Heads looked down as fingers tapped on cell phones. The students were blissfully unaware. To maintain our secrecy, I turned my back to them before I silently mouthed, "Murdered? Where?"

She looked at her backpack sitting alone on the other side of the room, and in her regular voice, she said, "In the Ecology Club workroom."

All prospects of a normal day evaporated.

My eyes followed Brooklynn's gaze. Rachel Carson's penetrating sage-green eyes stared at me from that closed door. The larger-than-life photograph said, "In nature, nothing exists alone."

I thanked my lucky stars that the computer selected me for this sub assignment. I was uniquely qualified as a retired

LAPD detective to respond to whatever was on the other side of that picture of Rachel Carson.

'You're welcome,' replied Fitch.

Fitch is my spirit guide—protector, advisor, and critic. Unfortunately, my intuition often disagreed with Fitch. Sometimes he was a timeless Buddha, and other times a teenage Loki.

My gut told me that everything beyond that closed door had its genesis on the previous Friday. Detectives prayed at the altar of cause and effect—no coincidences. Everything had to have a reason.

Friday had been uneventful until I received a text from Ms. Salas. U TEACHING TODAY?

The rules prohibited cell phone use during school hours, but we were between periods. I texted back, PHYSICS [SMILEY FACE].

I NEED A FAVOR.

NO PROB. WHASSUP?

SCIENCE GARDEN DURING LUNCH. [FROWNY FACE] PLEASE.

I'M ON IT. EASY PEASY. [ANOTHER SMILEY FACE].

The science garden was an Ecology Club project, and she was the club sponsor. I'd stood in for Ms. Salas before. That Friday lunch break should have been routine, but it wasn't.

When the lunch buzzer sounded, I went into the courtyard. Waving a green-and-white Ecology flag, I recruited students to prepare the new science garden. I offered them extra credit, but the gratification of clearing the land would have been sufficient, harking back to those primeval farmers who abandoned their hunter-gatherer ways. They stampeded across the field, eager to flex their muscles and tame that wild environment. Those enthusiastic teens attacked that last stand of chaparral with shovels, saws, and raw adolescent energy.

The satisfaction of our lunchtime activity was interrupted when my nemesis, Principal Kapitsa, hiked across the football field. He glanced at me and shook his head with disdain before addressing the students in a stern voice. "What are you doing on the wrong side of the yellow line?" He tapped his pen on a pad of referral slips. "And why are you digging up the native vegetation? You're all getting detention. If you're written up again, you'll be banned from prom."

Fitch sneered, *'He never goes to prom, so he's going to ban everyone else.'*

Prom was in two weeks and the principal had recently been using it as his go-to threat. As we neared the end of the year, detention had lost its effectiveness. The Ecology Club looked to me with questioning faces. Why was Kapitsa threatening them—after I gave them permission to clear this strip of land—more like I bribed them with extra credit to give up their lunch break. They were my adopted grandchildren. The ones that brought me back day after day and made putting up with Mr. Kapitsa worthwhile.

The principal was the last person I wanted to see mixed up in our activities. I backed out of the future garden to lure him away from the group. Once he followed, I closed in—until my chin practically rested on his bald spot—poorly disguised by a brown combover. He stepped back but I kept close enough to see the tracks of sweat dripping across his pallid cheeks. The short man reminded me of a steamed pork bun.

I was decades his senior, but I could still be intimidating—even without a uniform. My hair might be gray, but my buzzcut covered the territory. My face might have creases, but regular exercise kept my shoulders strong and my abs firm. Growing old is not for the weak.

He retreated further. With one long stride, I reentered his personal space. In a voice only the two of us could hear, I asked, "Principal Kapitsa, why don't you leave them alone?" I resisted adding, 'You petty tyrant.'

He startled and dropped his pad, not expecting anyone to question him, particularly not me. I was a substitute teacher, the bottom of the pecking order. However, I was also a retired detective and not intimidated by self-important bureaucrats.

I reached down to retrieve his fallen referral slips before he could react, returning them to him with a flourish. He snatched the pad. When he began writing, I explained in a calm voice, but loud enough for my students to hear. "I told the Ecology Club that they could work here."

The kids turned to each other with approving expressions. I relished the role of defender, one of the things that drew me to law enforcement.

The principal fumed. "Blast, it's you again, Mr. Szilard. Whenever there's trouble, you're in the middle of it. Those plants are historic."

With the principal's ire directed at me, the students returned to hacking away at the stubborn foliage.

He didn't upset my balance. I continued in an even tone with just a tinge of sarcasm. "Did you forget the school board directed us to create a science garden here?"

He pursed his lips and stuck out his chin. His lack of any other response signaled that he recollected the board's decision. Showing him no mercy, I added, "The project needs to be accelerated. The school year is almost over. It will soon be too late to plant our seeds." He should have known this, and I was delighted to see that it disturbed him even further.

He thrust an accusing finger in my direction. "You-you-you're just a substitute teacher. Stop thinking and just do what you're told."

I didn't pass up another opportunity to tweak the arrogant administrator. Clasping my hands and bowing my head in mock contrition, I retorted, "Ms. Salas asked me to do this while she was in an IEP meeting."

The students acknowledged my poke at the principal with suppressed laughter.

"Blast," he responded. Unable to rebut me, he redirected his frustration to Annie, a shy girl wearing a loose embroidered top. "Straighten out your skirt, young lady." He scribbled a detention slip and handed it to her. "Remember the dress code. Cover up."

Annie crumpled the paper and shoved it into her pocket. She wore her natural hair in box braids, each finished with an ebony bead. Those beads complemented her bronze complexion. True to her unassuming nature, her face didn't show any emotion. However, when the principal turned away, she shook her head and the beads clacked angrily.

Kapitsa smacked the pad of unused referrals against his palm and retreated to the courtyard, in search of others to harass.

As soon as he was out of sight, the Ecology Club's animated chatter resumed. I grabbed a pitchfork and joined in, stacking the gray-green plants. Later the maintenance crew would grind them up and compost them.

That composting operation had been an Ecology Club initiative. They had raised funds for the woodchipper that never found its way into any budget.

Annie pulled up a stump attached to a web of roots, spraying sandy soil over her skirt and blouse. In a surprisingly brazen move, she exclaimed, "Look at this! Look what I found!" She picked up something entangled in a stray root. The other students turned in her direction as she placed a bracelet of earth-colored disks on her wrist.

That artifact transformed our routine gardening into a celebration. There were shouts of "You go, girl," and applause. Some of them dropped their tools and moved closer to appreciate her find. Unaccustomed to being the center of attention, Annie covered her face. Her nose and cheeks darkened with a barely perceptible blush.

Charlie clasped his freckled hands behind his back like a small child whose parents had warned him. "Don't touch." He leaned over for a closer look and stuttered, "Th-th-that's from the S-S-Serrano Indians."

When I studied for my teaching credential, I read everything I could find on local history and never missed an opportunity to share this knowledge. "A Serrano relic would be big news. They haven't lived here for a long time. This was their land, but the Spanish, and then the Mexicans, and ultimately the Californios, drove them from Stony Estancia to make way for rancheros, which grew into villages, vineyards, and cities."

Brooklynn, always ready to show off, countered with. "Yes, but I agree with Charlie. That looks like a Yuhaviatam bracelet to me. I've seen similar ones in the county museum and—"

Richie, who had been leaning against the fence with his hands shoved into his pockets, snarled, "Yuha what?"

She flipped her ponytail and faced his acne-covered forehead. "Yuha-*vi*-atam. That's their name in their language—people of the pines." She pointed. "Notice the colors from light tan to deep brown, some even brick red. These shell disks came from the Chumash on the coast and were used for trading long before any Europeans arrived."

Richie stepped toward Brooklynn and the bracelet. He scoffed, "Okay, nerd, how do you know this isn't a copy?"

Knowing Brooklynn as I did, I wasn't shocked when she held her ground. "It's not. It is just like one in the museum labeled as *discolored by cremation rites*." A few of the students voiced disgust with this grisly detail. However, she ignored them and continued to berate Richie. "Use your eyes. Look how each disk is different and how they all fit together. This is obviously—"

Richie sprung at Annie, snarling. "That's mine. I saw it first!" He grabbed the relic destroying the twine that held the bracelet together. The disks exploded into the air and fell to the ground.

Annie looked straight into his brown eyes. "Not yours!" She moved swiftly to collect the tiny disks buried in the dirt between them.

They transformed into a pair of toddlers fighting over blocks or toy cars. "Mine." "No mine." Ineffectual grabs and slaps.

That assertive response was out of character for Annie.

Fitch gasped. *"Um, when did that puppy become a rabid hyena?"* In his overly dramatic way, he went on to suggest that she stood up to Richie because she was itching for a fight—because she was suicidal. That seemed a bit much, but Fitch was often closer to the truth than it appeared.

I had a history with Richie. He was a frightened child. I recalled the first day back after winter break.

He limped into the classroom wearing sunglasses and a hat, both prohibited by the dress code.

I walked over to where he sat. "Remove the hat and sunglasses."

He ignored me, surprisingly without any attitude or backtalk. He silently opened his laptop.

His subdued affect had me concerned. I knelt beside him and whispered, "Are you okay?"

"Fine, thank you. Please let me wear my hat."

Richie never said please or thank you.

"Are you sure you're okay?"

"Just fine. New Year's Eve party at my house. I fell down the stairs."

And Richie never explained himself.

Now that I was close to him, I saw his black eye, not something from falling down the stairs. I let him wear his hat and sunglasses. My grandfatherly compassion outweighed Kapitsa's dress code.

As a mandated reporter, I was legally required to notify Children and Family Services. That felt like a solution, but Richie's behavior hadn't improved. CFS never told me the results of their investigation. I suspected that they just ignored any report from a substitute. I kept a watch on him waiting for the next opportunity to help. Regardless of his behavior, he was still one of my surrogate grandchildren. I would support him.

"Richard Fowler," I warned. "Back off."

He continued to collect the shell disks.

Charlie looked up from sawing a sagebrush trunk. "Richie, you h-h-heard Mr. S. G-g-give those back to Annie. You know you c-c-can't keep them. They belong to the Serrano community."

That should have ended it. But instead of relinquishing the disks, Richie ranted, "Stay out of this. You can't stop me. I have a collection of old stuff that I sell at swap meets. Finders, keepers."

Then, he stomped on Charlie's saw blade making a loud twang. Richie's foot just missed Charlie's fingers. I pulled him away. "Drop those. They aren't yours."

The moment my fingers reached his shoulder, he howled as if shocked by a Taser and collapsed to the ground. "You can't touch me," he taunted, adding. "I don't *pose a clear and present danger of serious physical harm.*"

The reaction was so fake that I couldn't help smiling. That was privilege for you. He lay there with a smirk on his face and his arms crossed while quoting California's Education Code. Despite his defiant façade, he was still just a kid with acne and an abusive parent.

When he rose and advanced in the direction of the other students, I blocked him. We had a standoff, and his mini reign of terror was over.

I didn't need to arrest him. I was no longer a cop. I left that life in Los Angeles. In Stony Estancia, I was an honorary grandpa. The situation called for understanding. I let him strut around kicking piles of soil and crowing. "Everyone dig. Let's see if there is any more hidden treasure."

The others ignored him. They continued cutting down sagebrush and clearing the stumps. I took a cleansing breath giving him a respite to cool down. In my peripheral vision, Brooklynn approached.

Richie also noticed her. He kicked the bush Charlie was sawing. Charlie moved out of the way when the gray-green leaves sprang back. Richie taunted, "Oh Ch-ch-charlie. Look who's here, a girl to fight your battles."

Brooklynn approached Richie with fists clenched weaving around the students and chaparral in her path. Teenagers are a volatile lot, but usually good-hearted and harmless. There was no *clear and present danger*. I positioned myself between Richie and everyone else, isolating him for a timeout.

Then Brooklynn caught me off guard. She feinted to the left and cut to the right sidestepping my position like a pro running back. She invaded Richie's personal space. Her green eyes locked onto his brown ones. "Drop the disks. Apologize to Annie and Charlie." She paused and added in a threatening voice. "Then I might forget this."

With a disgusted look, he hissed, "Leave me alone." Like someone in a badly acted video, he stormed away. He tripped over a stump, regained his balance, and kept going. I imagined his exit surrounded by laughing emojis. He still had a few shell disks, but the audience had logged off from his viral moment.

Charlie resumed sawing. Annie returned to sifting through the soil to recover her spilled disks. A couple of girls joined her, and someone found a paper bag to hold the treasures.

Unfortunately for Richie, Brooklynn didn't subscribe to a forgive-and-forget philosophy.

Fitch chuckled, *'This is going to be good.'*

She took her phone out and called to his back. "Richard Fowler. Let's see what this says." She tapped a few times and then grinned. "Look at this. You have an arrest record."

He stopped and gave her a puzzled look.

"Oh no. My bad. That's your father. The apple doesn't fall far from the tree."

She tapped her phone a few more times.

"Here you are. Amen, Richie, you're old. An adult."

He turned around. His anger diminished to wariness.

Poor Richie. I didn't feel sorry for him. He'd started this and Brooklynn was the wrong person to cross.

She berated him in a sing-song voice. "Selling artifacts is a federal crime. The Native American Graves Protection and

Repatriation Act—NAGPRA—is older than you." She wagged her finger at him. "But you're old enough to go to jail."

He took a couple of steps in her direction and shook his fist. "Yeah? So what? No one will do anything about it."

He was right. The Stony Police Department didn't enter the campus unless invited and Mr. Kapitsa would never do that.

All activity ceased. The Ecology Club watched the players on our garden stage. Brooklynn stayed focused on Richie, but his eyes flitted back and forth checking out the crowd. Someone had their phone raised and was making a video.

"Well look at this. The FBI has an online tips form." She held her phone pointed at his face. "Smile for your mug shot." Her phone clicked.

Richie looked like a trapped animal, backing away, but the audience's attention held him like a leash.

Now I felt sorry for him, but not enough to interfere.

Her fingers danced over her screen. "F O W L E R. Amen, look at that. The FBI autofilled your contact info. Shall I tap send?"

Richie wilted. The other students smiled at each other. When he looked at me, I just raised my shoulders and palms to show that I wasn't getting involved. He threw the shell disks in front of Annie and mumbled, "Sorry."

It didn't end there. Brooklynn said, "Another thing. Our state assemblywoman is a member of the Serrano band. I'll be checking with her next week. You better have turned in your stash."

"That old stuff isn't worth anything. It's random bits and pieces I found in the hills. I doubt any of it is even Serrano."

"Just turn it in."

"I heard you." He walked away. "I didn't want to be here anyway. I'm just going to community college, so I don't need any extra credit."

After Richie disappeared across the football field, everyone resumed work.

What about the bracelet? Why were we finding artifacts in an area settled so long ago?

'The evidence doesn't add up. You missed something. You're not seeing the whole picture, how everything fits together,' Fitch said.

I filed away Fitch's enigmatic comments for later. His anxiety was no reason to upset my day.

Charlie paused from cutting a tough sage bush trunk. "Mr. Szilard, why are we clearing away the chaparral? Doesn't it sequester carbon and prevent erosion?"

I took off my slouch hat and ran my hand over my gray buzzcut, doing my best imitation of a dashing archeology professor. "True, but this little patch between the fence and the path is just a fire hazard and can be put to better use as a garden for biology classes." I pointed north. "There are the San Gabriel Mountains, as much wild space as Yosemite National Park. Plenty of chaparral there, a vibrant ecosystem, including deer, cougars, bobcats, coyotes, and even bears— our school mascot."

Another student struggling with a tenacious stump wondered, "How old do you think these bushes are?"

I grabbed the stump and together we pulled it out with a shower of dirt. "These plants can live longer than people. This strip of chaparral grew here before the school was built and long before that."

"What about this basket?" Annie asked shaking the ebony beads woven into her dark braids.

We all watched her hands scoop dirt from the indentation where she'd found the bracelet.

"What basket?" several voices asked.

She continued to scatter the dry dirt until we all could make out an arc of coils nestled between the sage plants. Her fingertips danced around the tightly woven grasses until she'd uncovered a full circle.

Basket! Fitch was right. Here was the missing piece. The shell disks were unexpected. But this basket was larger and more ephemeral. What had Annie uncovered? Even though I was no longer a detective, I still loved a mystery.

I formulated a plan—solving puzzles was in my DNA. First, we'd notify the county museum and then we'd post pictures on social media.

'What about the principal?' Fitch reminded me.

I had no intention of involving Kapitsa.

Everyone knelt around the basket, as Annie carefully scooped out the contents. The hole grew as we all watched.

"Eww. Bones!" Annie squealed and jumped up so quickly that she lost her balance.

Had we uncovered a Serrano burial site? But how old could it be if the basket hadn't decayed?

Everyone retreated from the bones, except Brooklynn. I admired her curiosity and fearlessness. She picked up what looked like a femur.

"My, my, a ch-ch-chicken bone," Charlie said.

Someone suggested, "Or a rabbit."

I'd been a homicide detective. I knew something about skeletons. "Brooklynn, it would be best if you didn't touch that."

She replaced the bone where she'd found it. "Do you think these might be human remains?"

Annie exclaimed, "No. No. Don't tell me that's a baby!"

I leaned forward and took a closer look. The bone was a femur, not much bigger than my hand. If it was from a human skeleton, the size meant we'd discovered a newborn. I buried my face in my palms and said a little prayer. I'd seen plenty of death with the LAPD, but I never hardened to it. And I didn't expect it here at the high school.

The reactions of the students ranged from laughter to fear. Everyone moved away, especially Annie who pressed against the fence—the ebony beads adorning her natural braids ringing against the chain links.

Charlie put his freckled arm around her shoulders. "Look how it was placed in that basket. This was a sacred burial for a loved family member."

That calmed Annie, but I hoped that he just had an overactive imagination. I'd be happy for this to be the remains of a picnic.

Fitch nudged me, *'Don't count on it.'*

No one moved. We could hear the crowd in the distant courtyard. A few small brown birds landed on our pile of debris feasting on the bugs we'd stirred up. They discussed their providential bounty with high-pitched chirps.

Slowly and silently, the students moved forward for a closer look. Each child viewed the still-buried skeleton and retreated. Death was foreign to Stony Estancia High School. Charlie collected a few students in a prayer circle. I saw sad faces and closed eyes as we all instinctively honored the dead.

As suddenly as it started, the memorial finished. The ever-practical Brooklynn ended our solemn interlude. "What should we do?"

That was adolescents for you. Shock, anger, mourning, and acceptance, all in a few minutes.

This wasn't a police matter. "We need a Native American archeologist. I'll call the county museum. They'll know who to contact on the reservation. In the interim, let's get something to protect our excavation."

This grisly discovery cut short our project to clear the science garden. The Ecology Club headed back to the courtyard to reclaim what remained of their lunch recess.

Charlie found a piece of plywood to cover our find. It would be safe over the weekend inside the locked perimeter of the school.

I tromped across the gridiron to join the others. While I enjoyed my lunch of leftover barbecue ribs—supplemented with oatmeal cookies and milk from the cafeteria, I considered these new mysteries—Annie's assertiveness, Richie's senseless aggression, and an archeology site that appeared from nowhere. All puzzles worthy of my detective skills.

I was most concerned about Annie and her sudden fierceness. What triggered this personality change? Fitch was convinced she was suicidal.

Stony Estancia might not be the bucolic small town I'd imagined, but it still wasn't Los Angeles. It was impossible to keep a secret here and I knew exactly where to go to learn the truth about Annie. Ms. Salas.

When the final buzzer sounded, I went to Ms. Salas's classroom, close by in the Science building where I was teaching physics for the absent Dr. Chandrasekhar.

She revealed so much more than I expected.

3. WARNINGS: FRIDAY AFTER SCHOOL

Stony Estancia was the epitome of a thriving suburb.
Wide boulevards lined with palm trees and maintained by city
gardeners. No graffiti or homeless people. Well-kept yards
(more gardeners) and late-model cars. It supported a
flourishing community of mobile pet groomers and auto
detailers. Upscale retail and a prosperous commercial district
of clean warehouses—no smokestacks or oil wells. Regardless,
this shiny suburban lifestyle didn't guarantee perfect lives for
the adolescents.

Annie wasn't in the red folder that warned substitutes of
health issues—asthma, diabetes, allergies, or seizure
disorders. Some things weren't documented. Even though it
should have been confidential, I knew Annie was at risk for
self-harm.

*On my first assignment of the school year, Annie was
sobbing, hiccupping, and blowing her nose. The class
whispered and busied themselves on their laptops. I offered
to let her wait in the teacher's workroom until she calmed
down. She refused. Charlie sat next to her, but he was unable
to console her. Ultimately Brooklynn escorted her to the
health office.*

*The next day I visited my mentor, Ms. Salas. I was pleased
when she told me that I'd done well. Then, she counseled me.
"Don't get emotionally involved. You never know the full
story."*

"You forget my years as a detective."

Ms. Salas said, "But—"

*I protested, "I'm good at reading people. I know Annie. She
may be quiet, but she's happy...except for today."*

*Lucy pursed her lips as if debating whether to say more.
Then, she took a deep breath. "On Prom night, last year, she
accelerated her car against traffic up the Van Vleck off-ramp*

of the Desert Freeway. The police report said quick thinking by the oncoming drivers prevented fatalities."

I'd seen my share of head-on collisions. Even with airbags, seatbelts, and crumple zones—the impacts were painful to recall.

My heart raced reliving Annie's brush with death. "I'd never have guessed. I'll keep my emotional distance."

"That's for the best," Ms. Salas said.

After a good dinner, I reconsidered that promise. I never shirked responsibility. I stayed up late researching teen suicide.

The warning that one of my students might hurt themselves never left me. That was the lesson I took from Ms. Salas's disclosure. I set up alerts for the latest studies on teen suicide and self-harm. Risk factors included previous attempts and unusual behavioral changes. Annie ticked both those boxes.

Annie was shy and reserved. I took her confrontation with Richie in the science garden seriously. I would not court catastrophe by ignoring the warning signs.

Fitch agreed, *'Either her parents are getting divorced, or her mother is dying of cancer.'*

I didn't know anything about Annie's home life. Ms. Salas had cautioned that I'd never know all the facts, but I didn't accept that as an excuse. Fitch jumped to the worst case. Either way, Annie remained on my suicide watch list.

'You should be watching Richie. He's itching for a fight,' Fitch said.

I discounted this. A bully picking on a weaker kid was nothing unusual.

'Do you call yourself a detective? Richie taunted Annie and Charlie just to incite someone stronger—Brooklynn.'

Fitch made a good point. Would Richie continue to escalate? The district had warned the teachers to be on the lookout for signs of violence. Would Annie harm herself? Would Richie bring a weapon to school? Regardless of Ms. Salas's sound guidance, I wouldn't let *'not getting emotionally involved'* invite disaster.

These considerations following the drama in the science garden dominated my afternoon. My classes passed in a blur. Had I monitored an exam or shown a video? I had no idea. I didn't even recall what I had for lunch.

I knew better than to take this anxiety home to my empty apartment. Unresolved student issues could spoil even the finest dinner.

Was Ms. Salas right? Did I care about them too much?

I cleared the science garden with the Ecology Club as a favor to her. These were her students. When the final buzzer sounded, I sought out her advice.

"Come in Zarand. I hear you had an unpleasant encounter with Kapitsa."

Ms. Lucinda Salas, a petite Latina with short black hair, wore a beige linen jacket over a red blouse. She had decorated her room with the AP Biology curriculum. To my left, she'd posted TIMELINE OF CELL BIOLOGY that started with Antonie van Leeuwenhoek and went to Emmanuelle Charpentier and Jennifer Doudna, recent Nobel Prize winners. On the opposite wall was EVOLUTION AND HEREDITY with Charles Darwin and Rosalind Franklin. She dedicated the back wall to CLASSIFICATION AND ANATOMY with Carl Linnaeus and Barbara McClintock. In the center of that wall was the door to the teachers' work area covered with a display for ECOLOGY— Rachel Carson.

I admired Ms. Salas's composure, energy, and ready smile. She was too old to have arrived at Stony Estancia High straight out of college. She always looked relaxed, like teaching was a simple matter compared to whatever she'd done previously. Beyond that hint, those missing years were a mystery—a cold case I hadn't solved but didn't abandon.

'Maybe she was a special forces medic,' Fitch helpfully offered.

Lab tables replaced student desks in the science classrooms. She was straightening out the round stools and picking up trash. I went to the back of the room and worked forward mirroring her activity.

"Don't worry about my run-in with the principal. Did you hear about Annie?" I said.

She greeted this with an enormous smile. "Oh yes. She found a shell bracelet from Santa Catalina."

"Yes, that and—" I paused not certain how to introduce the confrontation between Richie and Annie.

"Or are you thinking about that basket of bones? I heard about that too. There are no secrets here. Isn't it wonderful to have an archeological dig on our campus?"

Ms. Salas didn't have the same view of the events in the science garden as Fitch did. I blamed his paranoia on our time with the LAPD, but what history had Ms. Salas brought to the school? I looked around her workspace for clues. She displayed pictures on the wall behind her desk. Surely, she had pinned a key to her backstory among those snapshots.

None of them included her—no selfies. I narrowed in on one with a young woman holding a baby. I took a wild guess. "Is that your daughter and grandchild?"

Her face lit up with a big smile. I anticipated her revealing some of her story, but she went in a different direction. "Oh no. That's Megan Rainwater. She had that child while taking AP biology in my first year of teaching."

"That must have been awful."

"Not really," she responded to the judgment implied by my question. "I integrated her and her baby into several lessons on human sexuality and development. So much better than the textbook."

'Then what happened?' Fitch pondered in his morbid way.

"Did she marry the father?" I queried.

Ms. Salas beamed with pride. "Oh, no. That wasn't a promising idea. He'd already proven himself irresponsible."

"Was that hard on her?" I sighed thinking of all I'd heard about the plight of single mothers.

"You can decide for yourself. Do you want to know where she is today?" she asked rhetorically. "She's not married. She's in medical school, and I understand her little girl is excelling in pre-school, already reading the *Magic Tree House* books."

Lucy's eyes got big, and she stared into the distance. "Those lessons with Megan Rainwater's baby in the classroom remind me how well the students respond to learning without a textbook. This weekend I'm going to write a lesson about how archeologists use biology. I might even get some of those bones to have the classes examine them."

I doubted the County Museum would release them for a high school science class. I was more concerned about Annie than the bones. "Did you hear that Annie stood up to Richie?

"Oh yes. Isn't that great?"

"Is it? That's not like her. I've read that behavior changes are indications of deeper issues. Do you think she is considering another suicide attempt?"

"Once a cop, always a cop. You shouldn't jump to conclusions. I can tell you what's going on with her."

"Yes. Please." I was ready for something to balance Fitch's pessimism.

"Annie had found herself increasingly isolated as her middle school girlfriends became high school couples. That loneliness weighed heavily on her."

"Is that why she was so upset at the beginning of the year?" I asked remembering that day when Brooklynn escorted her to the health office.

"No. That was something else."

'She's not telling you everything,' warned Fitch.

I trusted Ms. Salas to fill in the details. I waited.

"Annie has a boyfriend. Someone she met at church. His name is Jackson."

"How do you know this? Do you attend her church?"

"No, but she introduced him to me."

"That was nice."

"Even better, his family is taking him out of private school, and he'll start here at Stony Estancia High School on Monday."

"Are you saying that all Annie required was a partner?"

"Oh no. There's much more to it, but that is the gist of it."

"So, the opposite of depression. I'll stop worrying about her." Silently, I stuck my tongue out at Fitch, 'You must stop being so suspicious.'

On each table, she stacked, aligned, and centered the biology books. I picked up papers scattered on the floor that had missed the recycling bins.

With the room prepared for class on Monday, she stopped smiling, checked the doors, and lowered her voice. "I could use your investigative skills."

Why did she require police assistance? "Sure. What do you need?"

"I've been doing a little detective work. It all started when the MIT admissions office called to follow up on my recommendation letter for Richie."

"Richie applied to MIT? He told the Ecology Club he was going to community college. Did you write him a good letter?"

"I might have if he'd asked, but he didn't. During my awkward conversation, I learned that in addition to the forged recommendation letter, someone had falsified Richie's transcript. I recalled him as an average student, usually earning a B, sometimes a B-, and rarely a B+. I checked my grade books—the backup copy I keep on my personal laptop— just to be sure. My memory was correct. However, on the transcript MIT received, each B had magically become an A."

"Did you report this to Kapitsa?"

"Oh, certainly, but he didn't believe me. 'Nobody can hack into the district's computers,' he said."

I agreed with the principal. Security was one of the annual training modules required by everyone, including substitute teachers, even though we never had access to anything. For example, the teachers entered attendance online, but substitutes took roll on paper. We weren't even trusted with attendance records. Still, I wasn't ready to blame this on a hacker. "Could his grades have just been entered wrong? Typos?"

"Don't you listen? She tapped her screen and spun her personal laptop around. Look at that. Check for yourself."

I countered with. "Hackers are less common than shown in the media, so they are an unlikely explanation."

"Whatever," she said shaking her head, treating me like a student who wasted class time debating evolution versus intelligent design. "You can believe whatever you want but that recommendation letter wasn't a typo. It came from my school email account." She paused.

I didn't expect what came next.

She slapped the table and raised her voice. "Whether you like it or not, it was hackers! You would have realized that had you stopped mansplaining and listened."

Whoops. She was more disturbed than I realized. No problem. I knew just what to do. "You're right. I don't doubt you. I just double-checked everything. An old detective's habit."

And that didn't help. Timeout. I noticed a few more papers that had missed the recycle bin and went across the room to collect them. I straightened out some biology books and admired Megan Rainwater's child.

Lucy's neck muscles were still twitching when I offered, "This is your investigation. I shouldn't have said anything until you'd finished."

"That's right," she said softly.

She was still frustrated. She shook her head. "You didn't give me a chance to show you the threatening notes I received."

She slid a sheet of paper across the table. It could have been from any of the printers scattered throughout the school. Everyone, even substitutes, had access to the printers.

She explained, "After I reported the forgeries to Mr. Kapitsa, I received this warning." The note read, MIND YOUR OWN BUSINESS OR YOU'LL REGRET IT.

'How did the hackers know she'd reported them?' Fitch queried.

"Did you notify Kapitsa about the forgeries with an email?" I asked seeking an answer to Fitch's question.

She slapped the table again. "Of course not. I'm not stupid!" She continued in a condescending voice. "We have hackers. They can see emails." She picked up another page and looked at it before pushing it in my direction.

That page said WE ARE NOT FOOLING AROUND. STOP OR WE WILL DOX YOU ON THE DARK WEB. After I read that, she handed me a printout of her personnel record including her Social Security number, banking details—everything. I no longer doubted that serious hackers were involved, but fortunately, hackers were rarely violent.

Then she passed me a final page. DON'T GO TO THE POLICE. WE KNOW ABOUT YOUR DAUGHTER.

"Daughter?" I blurted out. "Do you have a daughter? I didn't even know you were married."

"Oh, what does *married* have to do with *daughter*?" she spat back. Then, in a voice so soft that I felt like she was talking to herself, and I was eavesdropping. "I shouldn't have shown you that page. Don't worry about it."

She closed her eyes as if she were holding back tears. "You want to know the cruel irony? I don't know where my daughter lives or even her name."

I didn't follow up on this new mystery. There would be time to pursue her daughter when she'd calmed down. Experienced detectives knew the importance of asking the right question at the right time. "I'll find the hackers. I'll commence my investigation and see Vicki tomorrow morning. We'll make those hackers sorry."

"Vicki? She's your girlfriend in the Stony Police Department? Right?"

I nodded.

"Still not listening," she said shaking her head. "You can't go to the police."

"I won't get the Stony Estancia PD involved. It will just be Vicki."

"Can you trust her?"

"Yes," I assured her.

'*She's in over her head,*' Fitch warned in his not-helpful way.

I easily fell back into the role of detective. Familiar synapses fired in my brain. New energy flowed through me, and I felt years younger. I asked, "Is that the whole story?"

She leaned back in her chair, exhausted. "Yes. You can interrogate me now. Go ahead."

I dove in. "Do you think Richie could have done this? It was his application."

"No. he doesn't have the tech skills. Besides, he doesn't care about education. He just plans to slide into a local community college, not apply to a competitive out-of-state school."

"Do you have any suspects in mind?"

"His parents. His father. That's the place to start."

"Why his father?"

"Mr. Fowler travels overseas."

"Good point. We know that hackers could just as well be far away as around the corner."

After a shiver, she asked, "Am I safe?"

"Hackers never show up in person." I wondered about the daughter but didn't bring it up. "You're fine."

"Thank you," she said, appearing relieved.

"We'll run some background checks on Richie's parents for starters."

Fitch was concerned, *'You're retired and now you're also in over your head.'*

I didn't want to leave her alone. "I was planning a microwaved dinner-for-one tonight, but it can stay in the freezer. Would you like some company? This has been a difficult afternoon."

She nodded consent and headed for her car swaying like a sleepwalker.

We went to Cocina de Cetto, a popular hole-in-the-wall Mexican eatery. It had been a burger drive-up in the prosperous post-World War II years before corporate fast food took over. Here in So Cal, we supported our independent Mexican restaurants. No one cared that they hadn't updated the décor. We ate at a rustic picnic table covered with a thick layer of polyurethane.

After a couple of Carta Blancas and a pleasant debrief about Annie's new boyfriend and Richie's aspirations to leave home without leaving Stony Estancia, we went our separate ways.

I had so many questions, but I mistakenly believed there would be time for them next week.

Fitch woke me in the middle of the night to alert me that I should have taken Lucy's threatening letters more seriously. *'Did you consider that those notes were printed, not emails?'*

I ignored Fitch while constructing a midnight sundae—scoops of vanilla ice cream with fudge sauce heated in the microwave, whipped cream, and a maraschino cherry. The fudge wasn't hot enough and I ended up with brain freeze.

Fitch took advantage of my temporary incapacity. He harangued, '*Someone had to be on-site to deliver those threats—on paper, not email. The hackers are in Stony Estancia with access to the high school. Not just hackers. Domestic terrorists.*'

He made a good point in his paranoid way. Monday would be soon enough to warn Ms. Salas, but I didn't dare wait before involving the police. Fitch's conclusions demanded action. However, without a specific threat, I couldn't call nine-one-one or walk into the station and speak to a desk sergeant. Besides, Ms. Salas didn't want the police involved.

No problem. I'd go straight to the top.

Senior Detective Victoria Yukawa.

Unfortunately, Detective Yukawa had her own agenda, introducing another mystery before investigating mine.

4. MYSTERIES: SATURDAY AM

When I escaped Los Angeles, I required a car. I sentimentally chose a black-and-white one, but I didn't want it mistaken for a cop car. I selected an electric Mini—too small for any confusion. The Ecology Club loved it and it compensated for the lack of public transportation.

Saturday morning, I parked at Heisenberg Park, the recreation center of Stony Estancia. It housed the community center and adjoined the Pacific Electric Trail, named for the defunct Pacific Electric Railway—a missed public transit opportunity. I stretched while waiting for Vicki.

Victoria Yukawa, several years my junior, was the reason I retired to Stony. We'd met when she joined the LAPD. I remember that first encounter. Her uniform had military creases and her straight black hair had a white part across the center of her skull without a single hair crossing to the wrong side. Her black eyes sparkled with intelligence and if she was wearing makeup, I couldn't tell. I thought, this lady has strong attention to detail and will make an excellent detective.

I recruited her into my squad. She learned fast and eventually moved to the Stony Estancia Police Department for a nice promotion. We kept in touch.

When I retired, I asked her to turn in her badge and join me to cruise the world. But she had other ideas, like a promotion to Chief of Detectives. Our compromise was short cruises. We had tickets for an excursion to Baja California to embark in two weeks. Only if Stony Estancia wasn't hit by a crime spree.

'*Um, small chance of that,*' scoffed Fitch. He missed the action of the big city.

Vicki arrived at Heisenberg Park before I finished stretching. She took off shouting. "Let's go."

I went up on my toes for a burst of speed and soon was running beside her. But before I caught my breath to alert her about the terrorists, she said, "Are you going to tell me about your federal case?"

Still panting, I gasped. "Federal case? What federal case?"

"Tish and César are featuring a story about a Serrano burial at the high school."

César and Tish were our hyperlocal news team. If it happened in Stony, they covered it on their website—STONY ESTANCIA SURFS. Anything from school activities, youth sports, and library news to politics and business.

"They interviewed Brooklynn Curie. Isn't she your friend?"

We'd settled into a comfortable pace, and I recovered enough breath to respond. "Absolutely. She's an honor student and was there when the Ecology Club uncovered a skeleton interred in a coil basket."

"Gosh, she's calling for a federal investigation of NAGPRA violations. You should have heard her schooling everyone about the Native American Graves Protection and Repatriation Act."

I picked up my pace and smiled imagining Brooklynn giving that lecture.

"Can't you control your students?"

No one, not even Vicki, was going to disparage my grandkids. "My job is to encourage, not control. I'm proud that Brooklynn spoke out."

Vicki stopped. "We're not going to board that cruise if we have to host a NAGPRA investigation."

"S'cuse me, this is not a federal case yet. The Serrano band is sending an archeologist."

"Good. That bone posted on Brooklynn's social media looked like a chicken bone to me. I think you just can't stand being retired."

I resumed jogging while protesting. "I love retirement. My surrogate grandkids need me."

I must not have sounded convincing, because she beat her favorite drum. "Instead of stirring up trouble at the high school, you should join the Stony PD. I'm sure we can find a case to take advantage of your old-fashioned skills."

"Even though I love mysteries, I also like teaching. I can do both," I said.

"Do you crave a mystery? Instead of calling in the National Park Service, I can recommend a cold case involving your school."

I couldn't refuse. The baby-in-the-basket puzzle was good; another one would be even better. "Really? Tell me," I said. My legs warmed up as we coasted along shoulder-to-shoulder.

"We call him the graduation ghost. When they announced Alex Marconi's diploma, no one stood up."

That didn't seem as interesting as the basket. "So? Who cares?"

"The parents cared, and the case continued all summer with volunteers combing the mountain trails and reviewing CCTV videos from San Diego to San Francisco. They thought they spotted him on the UC campus in La Jolla, but that lead was a dead end like so many others. The Marconis had Alex late in life and both parents passed away without any resolution."

"S'cuse me, didn't you say the case was still open?"

"Yes. Mr. and Mrs. Marconi were long-time Stony Estancia residents and had burial plots at the Bragg Vineyard Memorial Cemetery. The county coroner, my friend Persey, raised money to buy the space next to the parents and erected a headstone for Alex. That empty grave kept the case open. The department assigns each new detective to the graduation ghost until they can add something to the file. Sort of an initiation."

"Seems gruesome, but I'm game. I'll look for him too. But that doesn't mean I'll join your police department."

The path narrowed where the sage grew to shoulder height, and the chaparral encroached on both sides. The jogging trail was recent, but the regrowth looked like those ancient shrubs at the school. The sagebrush in the science garden wasn't as old as I'd assumed. If the plants were recent, then the infant's grave could be also.

We jogged along with a silent camaraderie. As we loosened up, Vicki gradually picked up the pace.

I took deep breaths and stopped talking as I struggled to match her speed.

"I'm anticipating our cruise to the Mexican Riviera. I even bought a new bathing suit."

I took a long breath before responding. "A new bathing suit sounds—" I stopped myself before saying *sexy*. Vicki was in good shape, but not a sex object. She hadn't selected that suit to attract a male gaze. I started again. "What color is it?"

"Violet rose and periwinkle."

"Sounds lovely," I replied wondering what those colors were and what happened to purple and blue? I returned to my initial topic. "I don't want to be the one to delay our cruise, but there is a problem at the high school. Ms. Salas—"

"Isn't she the one that helps you with all the teenage angst?"

"That's her." I told Vicki about the hacked email, the tampered transcripts, Lucy's daughter, and the desire to not involve the police.

She slowed down. "No worries. Computer crime is outside of the PD. We refer those cases to a consultancy that the city has on retainer."

"Is that legal? Do you deputize them? Can you trust them to interrogate suspects? Will judges issue them search warrants?" My head was spinning. "Why would you do that?"

"Gosh, no. They don't have any contact with people," she lectured me like I was a confused child. "I don't think they are even in Stony. They have experts and do all their investigating over the internet. When they find the culprits, they email us, and we make the arrests."

"The internet," I scoffed. "So-called scientific crime-fighting never works, and certainly won't in this case." I explained how someone had delivered paper notes to Ms. Salas. "The people we're looking for have been to the high school. They're in Stony Estancia. Local terrorists. A case for real detectives. How can you contract policing to some distant office?"

"You've been retired too long to understand how much can be done over the internet. It is so much more efficient. You'll see."

"I doubt it. Is that your plan? Well, don't worry. I'll keep my eyes and ears open. That's the only way this case is going to be cracked."

Vicki shook her head. "Whatever. Remember that you said that Lucy wants a low-profile investigation. She's concerned about her daughter. Nothing is more low-profile than these computer nerds who never leave their cubicles. Don't mess it up."

"I'll be careful. I won't jeopardize her child." Lucy's daughter brought me back to the infant buried in the science garden. Charlie's description of the basket as a sacred burial resonated in my mind.

"I couldn't sleep last night, so I did a bit of research," I said.

"Don't tell me you're looking for another cruise. When I agreed to Mexico, I'd figured we were set."

"No, nothing to do with cruises."

"That's good. We're embarking in two weeks and I'm working to clear my caseload. A senior detective can't just disappear."

'Um, especially one who wants to be Chief,' Fitch interjected.

"Yes. I know. I've been there. No time off year after year." I stopped running. My glasses had slid down my nose. "Wait up." I pushed them back and turned to her. "Not another cruise. I was researching that grave at the high school." I winked at her. "See? I can use the internet too. You don't need that secret consultancy."

"Gosh, what did your internet wizardry reveal?"

I started with the background. "The California Environmental Quality Act requires a survey for cultural resources before any project is approved."

"What does that have to do with your basket of chicken bones?"

"Not chicken bones," I corrected her. "Those surveys locate tribal remains before construction starts. They use the latest technology—GPR—ground-penetrating radar. No one should discover anything afterward, especially not a basket so close to the surface. Don't you find that suspicious?"

She dismissed me. "I'm not convinced you haven't uncovered chicken bones."

The trail ran through a neighborhood where the houses backed tight against the abandoned railroad right-of-way. Friendly dogs cheered us along—amid the aromas of Saturday morning—frying bacon and warm maple syrup.

While we waited to cross Bohr Boulevard, the two-mile mark, she said, "Until Persey determines that you have uncovered human remains, I'll stay with the real crimes—especially if you want to embark on that cruise."

The light turned green, and she raced ahead.

When I caught up with her, puffing loudly, she joked, "You're getting old. Are you sure you have the energy to solve this chicken-in-a-basket mystery?"

I laughed. "Don't underestimate us. Fitch and I will solve the case of the unwanted infant."

"Unwanted infant? That's a bit dramatic but let me know when you need my help."

"Same to you. I'm also available to pitch in with any of those real crimes."

My phone vibrated. It wasn't a school day. Vicki was right there. "Who can be calling me on Saturday?"

"Let me see. Do you have another girlfriend?"

I passed Vicki my phone without looking at the notification screen.

"It's a text from your buddy Brooklynn. It says ARCHEOLOGIST HAS ARRIVED."

I stopped running. "That's going to be the answer to our chicken-bones-or-human-remains question. I'm going to the school."

We turned around and headed back to Heisenberg Park.

"For a retired guy, you're awfully busy."

"Sure am," I said proudly and sprinted ahead of her with a second wind.

As we jogged side by side, I reflected on my retirement. I had acclimated myself to the tranquil suburbs, exchanging my urban high-rise with its elevator for Higgs Haven where I carried my groceries up a single flight. Instead of urban sidewalks, the Higgs Haven grounds were landscaped like a resort with palm trees wrapped in fairy lights and serpentine pathways of decomposed granite.

Recently this idyllic environment had taken on a sinister turn with the graduation ghost, the unexplained burial at the high school, and hackers threatening Ms. Salas and her daughter.

D. R. Oestreicher

Fitch told me that there were more mysteries to come.

Before I parked my car at the high school, I spotted the signs of trouble. A crowd had collected. They were shouting and someone was beating on a drum. High school students and a group from the Serrano community had gathered in the parking lot. As I exited my car, I identified the difficulty. It wasn't hard and I wasn't surprised.